I0665204

LOVE MY CHILDREN FIRST

EVERNIGHT PUBLISHING ®

www.evernightpublishing.com

Copyright© 2019

Kory Steed

Editor: Melissa Hosack

Cover Art: Jay Aheer

ISBN: 978-0-3695-0020-5

LOVE MY CHILDREN FIRST

.

DEDICATION

For Mark, who believed in me first.

I also dedicate this book
To all gay fathers who have found the strength to love
again…
To their children … and
To the men who have dared to love them back.

LOVE MY CHILDREN FIRST

LOVE MY CHILDREN FIRST

Family Men, 1

Kory Steed

Copyright © 2018

Section One
It's Never Easy

Chapter One

April and Showers

Saturday, April 9, 2010
Under a clear, star-filled April sky, a crescent moon lent its thin, reflected beams to the silhouette of a well-appointed, three story Tudor mansion. 417 Spring Meadow Drive lay silent, its occupants left to their dreams.

****

"Toby! Toby, wake up! Wake up, Toby. It's time! It's time!"

"Huh? What? What?"

"Toby, my contractions … they've started."

"Huh? What did you say? Contractions! What time is it?"

"It's 2:44."

"2:44? In the morning?"

"Of course in the morning."

"Oh, Sydney! It's time? Time! Time! It can't be time. It's not due for another ten days. Are you sure?"

"Hell yes, I'm sure. They're regular now. We better hurry."

"How far apart?"

"Three minutes."

"Three minutes? Three minutes? But... But... But with the last one you said they were seven when we left."

"That was baby number four. This is number five and she's not waiting! Oh, God! Here comes another one!"

"Breathe, baby, breath like they told us!"

Sydney pursed her lips and began to blow, short, quick breaths.

"Pant, Sydney. Pant."

"I'm panting I'm fucking panting!"

"What can I do?"

"Nothing. Nothing! Get my bag."

"Oh, God," Sydney screamed as she leaned into the contraction.

"Sydney, stop pushing!"

"I can't help it!"

"Shit!" Toby ran to the closet. "I can't find it! I can't find it! Fuck! Fuck! Where the fuck is it?"

"Did you find it, Toby?"

"No! Where the fuck did you put it? Oh, here it is. Never mind." He returned just as the contraction ended.

"That was a big one. Hurry, Toby! Hurry!"

"Don't push, Sydney! Whatever you do, don't push!"

****

As Toby helped Sydney out of the bedroom and into the hallway, their oldest, August, came out of his room, rubbing his eyes. "Mommy, what's wrong?"

"Nothing's wrong, August. Mommy's just going to the hospital right now."

"But, Mommy, I heard you scream."

"That was just your new little sister. She's making herself known."

"You mean the baby's coming, Mommy?"

"Yes, August, your new little sister will be here soon. You'll get to meet her tomorrow." Sydney stopped and buckled over. "Toby, here comes another one!"

"Pant, Sydney, pant. Don't push! Don't push!"

Sydney screamed again.

"Mommy! Daddy, what's wrong with Mommy?"

"It's the baby coming, August."

"Is the baby hurting Mommy?"

"No, August… Well yes, it hurts Mommy, but this is what happens to a Mommy when the baby is ready to come out. The baby isn't doing it on purpose. All babies do this."

"You mean I hurt Mommy when I came out?"

"Yes, I mean no. No, you didn't hurt Mommy. It just hurts when the baby comes out."

"Mommy!" A cry sounded from the girls' bedroom.

"Mommy!" This time it came from the boys' bedroom. Then another voice yelled, "Mommy! Daddy!" From the girls' bedroom, again.

"Oh, God, Toby, they're all up. Go wake Aunt Vera."

"I'm up. I'm up." At five foot five and with curlers in her hair—a spry and wiry, sixty-seven-year-old—Aunt Vera came bouncing out of what would become the Nursery as she cinched the tie on her robe. "Now what's all this ruckus?"

"Aunt Vera, it's time."

"I can see that, my dear. How far apart?"

"Three minutes."

"Then what in world are you doing lollygagging around her. You better get a move on."

"We're trying, Aunt Vera," Toby said. "She's having a contraction. The kids..."

Two girls and another boy filed into the hall to join their brother. Together they surrounded their mother, all calling her name.

Vera nodded. "Now what's all this ruckus you kids are making? Huh? Mommy's fine. Mommy's just fine. Daddy's taking her to the hospital." Vera spread her arms like a goalie and began to herd the four children back to their rooms.

"I want to say goodbye to Mommy." August ducked under her arm and raced forward, followed by the other three.

"I love you, Mommy."

"I love you, Mommy."

"I wuv you, Mommy."

"Mom Mom Mommy!"

"August."

"Yes, Mommy."

"August, you're my big boy. You're my good boy. You watch out for your brother and sisters until I get home. Okay? You take care of them."

"You mean I'm in charge, Mommy?"

"Yes, August, you're in charge. You take care of your brother and sisters now."

"Yes, Mommy, I will, and I'll take care of my new baby sister when she comes home too."

"That's my good boy."

"Now, Sydney, love. Don't you worry about a thing," Vera said as she waited for the children. "I've got it all under control. Toby, bring an umbrella. They were calling for showers throughout the night."

"Thanks, Aunt Vera."

"Okay, August, July, May, and June, kiss Mommy goodbye. You'll see her in the morning."

Once the children had said their goodbyes, Vera announced, "Now who wants a cup of hot chocolate?"

"Me!"

"Me!"

"Me!"

"Me!"

****

3:17 AM, MST

Hinnen Valley Medical Center, Labor and Delivery, Room 7

"Boy oh boy, Sydney, this little girl means business." Dr. Fricker looked over the top edge of her glasses. "I can see the head. Ready now? Push!"

Sydney grunted. Toby wiped her brow.

"You're doing great, baby!" He blotted again.

"Toby, this isn't like the other ones. I need ice. Give me ice!"

"Here, baby, here's the ice."

"Mmm, it's so cool. More, more ice."

"I love you, Sydney."

"Fuck that, Toby! Oh! Sorry! I love you too. Now give me more fucking ice!"

"The head's almost out, Sydney," Dr. Fricker announced. "Oh, she's coming fast. Push again, Sydney. Now give me one big push!"

Toby lifted Sydney up from behind as she grunted. In a rush of amniotic fluid that splashed to the floor and all down the front of Dr. Fricker's gown, the baby made her entrance.

"Here she is!" Dr. Fricker laid the newborn on Sydney's chest. "Your new baby girl! And she's perfect."

"My little April. April? Right, Toby?"

"Yes, Sydney, our little April."

"Perfect," the delivery nurse said as the sound of drumming rain hit the delivery room window. "April and showers. It's sure pouring out there right now."

****

Monday, April 12, 2010, 12:55 PM, MST
417 Spring Meadow Drive

"I wanna see her!"

"No, me first!

"No, me first. I'm her biggest sister!"

"Me! Me!"

"Kids! Kids! Simmer down." Aunt Vera stepped between them and took baby April from Sydney's arms. "Now let me have a look at you, my little precious."

"Thanks, Aunt Vera. I don't know what we'd do without you."

"My pleasure, Toby, my pleasure. Now let's get this little girl into her bassinet."

"I wanna hold her!"

"No, I wanna hold her!"

"Me too!"

"Me! Me!"

"You'll all have your chance, but your little sister just came into this world. She needs her rest."

"Oh, Aunt Vera!" August planted his hands on his hips.

"Don't Aunt Vera me, young master August, and don't take that tone with me. Like I said, you'll have your chance, but not without supervision you won't. Now all of you, wipe those sour pusses off your faces.

There's chocolate chip cookies in the kitchen, right out of the oven."

"I want one!"

"No, I want one!"

"Me! Me!"

The three youngest raced down the hall toward the kitchen.

"Humf, I'll wait!" August folded his arms in front of himself.

"August, you go with your brother and sisters and see to it they don't break anything."

"Oh, Aunt Vera!" August planted himself where he stood.

"Go on now. Go watch your brother and sisters."

When Vera turned around, August stuck his tongue out at her, then he turned in a huff and stomped his feet as he marched toward the kitchen.

Sydney and Toby broke out laughing.

"I'll just put her down and then come right back and help get you settled.

"Thanks, Aunt Vera, but Toby can help me into a chair."

"If that's what you want, dear. I thought you'd want to go right upstairs and lie down."

"I'll be fine. I need to sit down here for a few minutes before I climb that staircase. You go ahead with April."

Chapter Two

A Loss Beyond Comprehension

Tuesday, May 4, 2010, 12:14 PM

"How are you feeling, dear?"

"It's just a little headache, Aunt Vera."

"How's your tummy?"

"I'm a little sore under my ribs on the right side."

"Oh, I meant nausea. Were you lifting something that you shouldn't have?"

"No, I promise I wasn't. I can't figure out what I did though."

"Your face has been looking a little puffy, and your ankles are swollen again. Have you been into the dill pickles?"

"Only one or two. It's funny how I'm still craving them."

"Only one or two? Since you came home?"

Sydney looked away.

"Sydney?"

"Okay, okay, one or two a day."

"Well, they're certainly not helping your ankles, and they'll sour your milk. You need to lay off them from now on. When's you next checkup?"

"My one-month checkup is this coming Friday, the seventh. Dr. Fricker said I was doing just fine on my two-week visit, but I think I've actually put on some weight since then. I'll ask her about it when I see her."

"It's probably fluid from those pickles. For the next three days, no more pickles, not until you see her again and she says yes. Agreed?"

"Yes, agreed."

"And don't you worry about the weight. With

some women it takes time and this is your fifth. Why don't you rest for a while? Take a nap. I'll thaw some of your milk and give little April a bottle if she starts to fuss."

"Thanks, Aunt Vera. I've been pumping up a storm. I think there's more than a months' worth in the freezer right now. Would you mind pulling the drapes? The light's been bothering my eyes. It's probably my allergies."

"Sure, dear. Now you have yourself a good nap."

"Thanks, Aunt Vera."

****

There was a crash.

"What in the world?" As Vera rushed up the stairs, she heard a thumping sound coming from the master bedroom. She opened the door...

****

1:06 PM

"Jaron Enterprises. Fiona speaking. How may I direct your call?"

"This is Vera Jacobson. I need to speak with Toby. I'm his aunt. It's an emergency."

"Yes, ma'am. I'll put you right through to the conference room."

****

"Aunt Vera?"

"Toby, you've got to come home. Right away!"

"What is it, Aunt Vera? What's happened?"

"It's Sydney. She's had a seizure! She was taking a nap. I heard a crash. I found her on your bedroom floor."

"What? She was fine when I left the house this morning."

"I know, Toby. I know. It just happened.

"I'm coming, Aunt Vera. Did you call 911?"

"Yes. They're on their way."

"Is she conscious?"

"She's delirious. The kids are in a panic. She keeps saying her head hurts."

"The kids? What are the kids doing home?"

"Remember, they had a half day at school today.

"Oh, right. I'll be there as soon as I can. I'll meet you at the hospital."

"Toby, remember, I don't drive. And what about the children?"

"Sorry, Aunt Vera, sorry. I'm not thinking straight. I'll call you from the hospital."

"Okay, Toby. Hurry!"

****

1:08 PM

Headquarters, Jaron Enterprises, L.L.C., Executive Office

"Jason, I have to leave right now!"

Jason Ackerman, the CEO of Jaron Enterprises and a former army medic, looked up from the blueprints he was studying with Aaron Jaeger, the former starting quarterback for the Nevada Bighorns football team, and now president of Jaron Rehabilitative Services. "What's wrong, Toby?"

"It's Sydney. She's had a seizure."

"Eugene!"

"Yes, Jason?"

"Find Royce. Tell him to get Gypsy warmed up."

"Right away, Jason."

Jason pressed the intercom. "Fiona, get me Simone Jones on the phone."

"Right away, Jason."

"It's gonna be all right, Toby. We'll get you down there as fast as we can."

"Thanks, Jason."

"We're coming with you. Aaron?"

Aaron stood up. "Absolutely!"

"Jason, I have Miss Jones on the phone."

"Thank you, Fiona." Jason picked up the handset. "Simone? Jason. I need a favor."

"Anything, Jason," Simone, the CEO of Hinnen Valley Medical Center and an Air Force Reserve, Registered Nurse said.

"You remember, Toby Jacobson."

"Yes. Why?"

"His wife's about a month postpartum. She's had a seizure. She'll probably be rolling through your doors in less than a half hour."

"Hmm. Does she have pitting edema? Any right costal margin tenderness? Photophobia?"

"I'm not with her, she's at her home. The ambulance is due to arrive any minute."

"If she does, it could be late postpartum eclampsia. I'll see that they're ready for her."

"Thanks, Simone. We'll be flying down in Gypsy. All right if we use the hospital's auxiliary helipad?"

"Yes, of course. I'll meet you there personally."

"Thanks, Simone. Bye."

Jason hung up and hurried around from behind his desk.

"Wow, Jason. Just like that?"

"Just like that, Toby."

"Thank you, Jason. Thank you."

****

1:47 PM

Hinnen Valley Medical Center, Emergency Department, Room 1

"I feel funny."

Dr. Sylvia Gladstone, Director of Emergency Medicine walked to the bedside. "What is it, Mrs. Jacobson?"

"I feel like I'm not all here, and my head. The pain is incredible."

"We're giving you something for that right now, Mrs. Jacobson." Dr. Gladstone turned the IV bag and checked the dosage of magnesium sulfate while Bryce, the ER nurse, pushed 4 mg of morphine sulfate into her second IV line.

"Thank you, doctor."

A clerk stepped behind the curtain. "Dr. Gladstone. Mr. Jacobson just arrived."

"Thanks, Rhonda, send him in." Dr. Gladstone walked around the curtain and waited at the doorway. Standing next to three men, two who she immediately recognized as Jason Ackerman and Aaron Jaeger, former patients of hers, was Simone Jones, CEO of Hinnen Valley Medical Center, a tall, statuesque, African-American woman, dressed in a navy-blue woman's business suit. Dr. Gladstone exchanged glances with her. *"Whatever they need,"* Simone mouthed. Dr. Gladstone nodded.

Dr. Gladstone addressed the third man. "Hello. You must be Mr. Jacobson. I'm Dr. Gladstone."

"Hello, doctor. I'm here to see my wife."

"Of course. She's right in here."

Toby rushed into the room. "Sydney! Baby! Are you okay?"

"I don't know what happened, Toby. I laid down for a nap and the next thing I knew I was on the floor and there were paramedics over me.

"How are you feeling?"

"My head is killing me."

"We've giving her medication for that, Mr.

Jacobson."

"Thank you, doctor. What's wrong with her?"

"Everything is pointing to late postpartum eclampsia."

"What's that?"

"No one knows the cause for sure, but her blood pressure is very high and she's been retaining fluid. She has protein in her urine and her urine output is down, which means her kidneys aren't functioning normally. Her liver is enlarged, and she has photophobia, or a sensitivity to light. She's had a severe headache since she arrived, and she's already had one seizure that we know of. We're treating her for all these things right now."

"Excuse me." Toby turned around and walked to the doorway. "Jason, I need you in here with me."

Dr. Gladstone smiled as he walked in. "Hello, Jason."

"Hey, Jason," Bryce said. "How you doing?"

"Hello, Dr. Gladstone, Bryce. I'm fine, but I'm here for Toby and Sydney right now."

Dr. Gladstone nodded. "Understood."

"Sure. Sure." Bryce patted him on the shoulder.

"Doctor," Toby said, "please tell Jason what you told me."

"Of course, Mr. Jacobson."

Jason stood at the foot of the stretcher and listened intently until Dr. Gladstone finished. "I see."

"What's it mean, Jason?"

"Let me talk to both of you." Jason walked to one side of the stretcher and took Sydney's hand and kissed it as Toby walked to the other. "Hello there, love. How are you feeling?"

"Not too good right now, Jason. My head is killing me and these lights are so bright."

Dr. Gladstone snapped her fingers. "Let's lower

the lights."

"Got it." Bryce hit one of the two light switches, effectively cutting the light by two-thirds.

"Sydney, you had a seizure because your blood pressure is very high and because of the changes in the chemistry of your body. Those things happen with something called postpartum eclampsia. It's rare for it to happen so long after delivery. They're treating you for all of those things right now."

Sydney looked at her husband. "I'm scared. Toby, I'm scared."

"I know, love. I'm scared too."

She looked back at Jason. "Jason, if anything happens to me, you take care of my Toby, you hear me? I know how close you two once were, and I'm so happy you've become friends again. Promise me, Jason. Promise me you'll look after my Toby. Promise me now."

"I promise, Sydney."

"Thank you, Jason."

After Jason answered, he glanced at Toby with a questioning look on his face.

"Yes, Jason. I told her about how close we grew that summer." Then he whispered, "I left out nothing. She knows everything." Then he began to cry.

Jason reached across the ER stretcher and rested his hand on Toby's shoulder. "They're doing everything they can for her, Toby."

Toby pulled away and leaned over the side rail. He kissed Sydney's forehead.

"Oh, baby," he said through his tears. "Nothing's going to happen to you. It can't. You can't let it. We need you, Sydney. The kids and I need you."

"Toby." Tears poured down Sydney's cheeks.

"Bryce, a milligram of Lorazepam for Mrs.

Jacobson. Right now, please."

"Right away, doctor."

"Mr. Jacobson, try to keep calm. I understand how difficult this is for you, but emotional upset isn't good for your wife right now."

Just as Bryce connected the syringe to the IV, Sydney cried out. "Oh, my God, my head! My head! It's exploding!" Her eyes rolled back. She began to convulse.

"Push that Lorazepam right now."

"Yes, doctor, pushing."

"Do you still have the other milligram?"

"Yes, doctor, it's right here."

"Give that too. *Stat!*"

Toby screamed. "What's happening?"

Jason moved around to Toby and pulled him back. "She's having another seizure, Toby. Step back and let them work."

"Doctor, her sat's dropped!"

"I see that, Bryce. Turn her oxygen up to eight liters."

Thirty seconds passed. "The seizure isn't breaking. Damn!" Dr. Gladstone slapped the wall.

"Set me up for a crash intubation. Two milligrams of Etomidate, now!"

Bryce punched the red button on the wall above Sydney's head. Ten seconds later the operator paged overhead. "Code Blue, Emergency Department, Room One. Code Blue, Emergency Department, Room One. Code Blue, Emergency Department, Room One."

"As soon as she's under give her forty milligrams of succinylcholine."

"Yes, doctor."

"Bryce, give me a number 7 ET tube with a 10 cc syringe!"

"Done and ready. They're right here, doctor."

"Call respiratory and tell them to set up a ventilator. Call CT and tell them we'll be heading over there in five minutes."

****

4:35 PM

Neuro Intensive Care Unit, Room N-644

With the ventilator quietly whooshing in the background, Dr. Ewé, the Intensivist, met with Toby.

"I'm sorry, Mr. Jacobson. Your wife has had a cerebral bleed. It means a blood vessel has ruptured in her brain. The bleeding has been extensive. It's compressed her brain almost completely to one side."

"What does that mean?"

"It means that the blood vessels that feed the part of her brain that allows her to function as a person have been pressed closed, and her brain tissue can't get the blood and oxygen it needs." Dr. Ewé rested her hand on Toby's shoulder. "When that happens, the brain tissue dies."

"Dies? You mean like it's dead? Part of her brain is dead? Like a stroke? Is that why she had another seizure?"

"We can't say for certain whether it has died, not yet, but yes, I believe she had the seizure because of the bleed. I'm sorry. Her brain has been without oxygen for an extended period of time."

"So what do we do about it?"

"We're doing everything we can for her, Mr. Jacobson."

A female nurse pulled back the curtain. "Excuse me, doctor. Is it okay if I give Mrs. Jacobson her meds?"

"Yes, Sonya. Absolutely. Mr. Jacobson, this is your wife's nurse, Sonya. She'll be taking care of her tonight."

"Hello, Sonya. Thank you for what you're doing

for her."

"Of course, Mr. Jacobson."

"What are those drugs, doctor?"

"Mr. Jacobson, we're providing her with supportive care. We're giving her drugs to try to reduce the swelling on her brain. That's what Sonya is giving her right now. We're breathing for her. We're giving her fluids and other medications to prevent further seizures."

"So when will she be able to come home?"

"Mr. Jacobson, sir … it doesn't look good."

"But what about the baby? What about my children?"

"I don't have an answer for you about them. I wish I did. I'm very sorry. If you think it's appropriate, you might want to consider bringing them in to see her. That is if you think they can handle it."

"They're all so young. My oldest is only eight."

"I can't say how the next few days are going to go, Mr. Jacobson. I can't even predict the next few hours, but they might want to see her. Time is of the essence. What about her parents? Brothers? Sisters?"

"Sydney was an only child, like me. Her parents died before we were married. I don't understand, doctor. Why isn't she awake? Why isn't the other half of her brain working?

"Mr. Jacobson, her entire brain has been compressed in half. It has been without oxygen for a very long time. The part that makes her her isn't functioning anymore."

"You mean she's brain dead!"

"I didn't say that, Mr. Jacobson."

"But that's what you're thinking, *isn't it*?"

"It's too early to tell, Mr. Jacobson, but as I said, it doesn't look good."

"Are you giving up on her? You can't give up on

her. She's only thirty-four."

"We're not giving up, Mr. Jacobson, not at all, but I have to be straight with you. It doesn't look good."

"No! No! This can't be happening! No!" Toby rushed to Sydney's side and took her hand. "Sydney! Sydney! Wake up, baby!" He kissed her hand.

"She's so cold, doctor. Why is she so cold? Why won't she wake up?"

"Mr. Jacobson."

"Sydney! Sydney! Wake up, baby! You have to wake up!" Toby began to wobble. "Help her, please! Do something! Anything!" As Toby's legs buckled, Sonya pushed a chair behind him just as he went down. He fell back into it. He began to sob.

****

4:50 PM

Aaron waited at the door as Jason entered Sydney's room. "Toby, buddy, I'm here."

"Where were you, Jason? I needed you."

"I'm sorry, Toby. I was making the calls you asked me to make."

"Oh, sorry. I'm sorry, Jason."

"Toby, it's okay."

"She's gone," Toby said as he stood up. "My Sydney is gone. Her brain. It's … it's squashed."

Jason wrapped his arms around Toby. "I've got you, buddy. I've got you, Toby."

Quaking sobs escaped from Toby. His body shook and shook as he held onto Jason for support. "My kids, Jason, my kids. They need to see her."

Tears began to fall from Jason's eyes.

Aaron walked in and placed his hand on Jason's back, rubbing it gently.

Jason turned his head toward Aaron.

"What can I do, Jason?" Aaron mouthed.

"Make the call," Jason whispered. "Make the call."

****

"Mrs. Jacobson? Mrs. Vera Jacobson?"

"Yes? It's Andrews, Vera Andrews. Who's this?"

"My name is Aaron Jaeger. I'm Jason Ackerman's partner. Jason is a friend of Toby's. He asked me to call."

"Yes, I've met Jason, and he's spoken of you."

"Toby has asked that his children be brought to the hospital."

"I understand. I'll have to call a cab. I don't drive anymore."

"No, ma'am, we're sending a car. It should be there in fifteen minutes, but it will wait as long as you need it to."

"How much time do I have, does she have?"

"I don't know, ma'am, but you should get here as quickly as you can."

"Thank you, Mr. Jaeger. We'll be there a soon as we can."

"Thank you, ma'am. Goodbye."

Chapter Three

An Impossible Decision

5:30 PM
SICU staff lounge

Jason sat at a table. "Braden, Penelope, thank you for coming."

"Of course," they said together.

"Whatever you need, Jason," Penelope Whitley, the Administrative Director of Nathan's Promise, the new LGBTQ rehabilitation center under construction by Jaron Rehabilitative Services, said. With her was Braden Darby, RN, the Managing Director of Physical Therapy for Nathan's Promise. Both were formerly employed by Hinnen Valley Medical Center and still had close ties with all the staff there.

Jason shook his head. "Where are the children?"

Penelope patted his back. "They're in the waiting room with their aunt."

"Thanks, Penelope." Jason's body shook with chills. "Sorry, but I had to collect myself for a minute. They let me come back here to their lounge, but this room isn't helping much."

"I know, Jason." Penelope rested her hand on his shoulder. "Sorry, this is where you learned the man who attacked you was still alive. Are you okay?"

Jason shook his head to clear away the images that returned of the man who had tried to take his life only four months earlier. "Yes, I'm fine. How's Toby doing?"

"As well as can be expected, I suppose, and don't worry about needing a few minutes. I'm sure all of this is very difficult for you."

"I'm not important right now. Is there someone you can recommend to help them?"

"Yes, there's a child psychiatrist and two child psychologists on staff. I've already spoken with Simone. She's setting it up."

"Good. Thanks. What about help for them at home?"

"I've contacted a nanny agency. They're putting a list of candidates together."

Jason nodded. "Thank you. Well, I guess we better get this done."

"Where's Aaron?" Braden asked.

"He's in with Toby right now."

"What do you need? What can I do for you?"

"Stay close, Braden. Just stay close."

****

5:32 PM
Room N-644

"Well, my dear," Sonya said as she applied rouge to Sydney's cheeks, "you have some important visitors coming, and I'm not going to let you look anything but your very best for them."

Toby burst into tears. "Thank you, Sonya," he choked out.

Aaron braced him from behind.

"It's my pleasure, Mr. Jacobson," Sonya said. "Now, Sydney, which color lipstick should we use. I think ... coral, yes coral looks just right for your skin tone."

****

5:36 PM
SICU waiting room

"Hi, Uncle Jason."

"Hey, little man. How's my August?"

"I don't know, Uncle Jason. Mommy's sick."

"I know, August."

"Where's Daddy?" June held a crayon drawing in front of her.

"He's in with Mommy. We're going to take you in to see her right now, if that's okay."

"Yes, it's okay."

"I want Mommy. I want Mommy."

"Mom. Mom. Mommy."

"Yes, July. Yes May," Aunt Vera, said, her eyes brimming with tears. "We're going to see Mommy now."

"Are you okay with the baby, Aunt Vera?"

"Yes, I'll be okay, Jason. Thank you."

"Okay, kids," Jason said as he squatted down in front of them. "Mommy was so tired that she fell into a deep, deep sleep," Jason said.

"Just like a fairy princess?" June asked.

"Yes, June, just like a fairy princess."

Jason could see the wheels turning in her head. "What is it, June?"

"Oh, nothing."

"Okay, kids, you're going to see some machines and hear some whooshing sounds in her room, and there's a tube in her mouth. That's part of the medicine the doctors are giving her. They also gave her some medicine that made her very sleepy so she won't wake up when you talk to her. Do you understand?"

After they all nodded, Jason and Aunt Vera, with April in her arms, walked them into the SICU, followed by Penelope and Braden.

****

Room N-644

"Daddy!"

"Hello there, Munchkin."

"Why is Mommy asleep?"

"Because she's tired, June."

"Can you wake her up, please? I want to talk to her."

"Not right now, Munchkin. She needs to rest."

"I drew her a picture, Daddy."

"Oh, how pretty."

"It's all of us, Daddy, even baby April."

"I see that. It's very pretty. How about I lift you up so you can put it next to Mommy so she can look at it later?"

"Okay, Daddy." As Toby lifted his daughter next to her mother, June reached out and stroked Sydney's face. "You look very pretty, Mommy. I brought you a picture. You can look at it later. I can't wait to talk to you, Mommy." Then she leaned forward, cupping her hand to Sydney's ear, and whispered, "August didn't eat his peas again. He hid them in his napkin."

Toby began to lower her back down. "No, Daddy. I want to give Mommy a kiss. Here, Mommy, this is my kiss to wake you up. That's what the prince did for the princess when she was in a deep, deep, deep, deep sleep."

Toby began to shake. "That's very nice, Munchkin," he choked out and then lowered her to the floor.

"Me next! Me next."

"Jason, I can't."

"It's okay, Toby. I've got this."

"Here you go, July. I've got you."

"Thank you, Uncle Jason."

"Toby, come sit down next to Aunt Vera." Aaron guided him to the chair.

July leaned down and kissed his mother. "I love you, Mommy."

"Me! Me!"

Jason lowered July to the floor. "Go sit with your

Daddy now, July."

"Okay."

"Your turn, May." As Jason lifted her up, May scrambled out of his grasp and laid across her mother's chest. "Mommy." She closed her eyes and began to suck her thumb. In a moment, she was fast asleep.

August began to cry, making soft, high pitched squeaks in-between each breath. "No... No ... Mommy, Mommy," he whispered. He ran to his father. "Daddy!"

"I've got you, August. I've got you." Toby shifted July to his right thigh and then lifted August onto his left. He pulled August close as he buried his head into his neck.

July looked at his brother, then to June.

Aunt Vera hurried from the room with April in her arms. Penelope followed her.

Seeing her brother, June began to cry, then July did too, but May slept soundly on her mother's chest.

****

11:30 PM

In the quiet of the SICU there was a particular stillness that had settled into room N-644. Only the soft, rhythmic whoosh of the ventilator disturbed the peace. Toby sat holding Sydney's hand while he spoke of their life together.

"I remember that summer, by the lake. Do you remember it, honey, before the children? We were so young then. When I told you I was going to build you a mansion, you told me you didn't need one, but I built it anyway, and you filled it up. You're in every room, honey. Your touch is on every piece of furniture and every painting.

"The children were here, Sydney. May even slept on your chest. I don't know how she managed to do it, but she did. June has drawn you another one of her masterpieces. It's of our family. There's a tree with red leaves and purple grass covers a hillside, but the sun shines yellow in a blue sky.

"The house is like ours with the Tudor half-timbering in brown and multiple paned windows. In front of the house is our family with you holding April. We're all holding hands with June next to you then May, then July, then August, and then me at the other end. There's a butterfly on a flower as tall as the house and a dog jumping in the air in front of all of us. Funny how she added the dog since we don't have one."

"I'm sorry to disturb you, Mr. Jacobson," Sonya said as she pulled the curtain aside. "I have Sydney's medications. I'll only be a minute."

"No, of course, please do what you need to do."

"I'll only be a minute."

"Take all the time you need."

"Thank you."

"How long have you been a nurse, Sonya?"

"Twenty years, fifteen in critical care."

"That's a long time. Have you taken care of a lot of patients like Sydney?"

"Yes, too many."

"Have they been as sick as Sydney?"

"Some."

"And how did they do? Did any of them wake up?"

Sonya closed her eyes for a moment. "Mr. Jacobson…"

"No, please call me Toby."

"Toby, every patient is different. We can never know how someone will respond to the medications or how they will heal."

"You're evading my question, Sonya."

"Yes, I'm afraid I am. Sorry."

"Please, Sonya, tell me the truth."

"No, Toby, I've never seen anyone as sick as your wife wake up. I've never known anyone as sick as your wife, with as much damage as she has, survive this long."

"So she's a fighter then. So if she's lasted this long, maybe she'll pull through."

"I didn't say that, Toby, and I didn't mean that. I've seen a lot and like I said, every patient is different. Some hold out longer than others. It might be because she's young, but with the damage she's suffered..."

"Go on."

"When people get old, their bodies don't have many reserves to call upon. For example, an older person can go into cardiac arrest immediately after some kind of incident, like trauma, because they're more fragile, but if we can get to them in time, we can often get them back.

"When a younger person suffers a trauma, their bodies call upon all their reserves to keep them going, sometimes for hours, but when their hearts finally give out it's because they've depleted every last ounce of those reserves. There's nothing left for them to come back with and they don't make it.

"Sydney is young. She's been using her reserves to keep her going, along with the supportive care we've been giving her."

"Do you believe in miracles, Sonya?"

"I've seen some things that defy scientific explanation. The only thing that's left is a miracle, so yes, I do believe in miracles."

"Thank you, Sonya. Thank you for being honest with me."

"Of course, Toby. Can I get you anything? A cup of tea, coffee, hot cocoa?"

"No, thanks. I'm just going to sit here with

Sydney and tell her how much I love her."

"Have you eaten today?"

"I can't remember."

"When did you last sleep?"

"I don't remember that either. I'm sure I've fallen asleep in the chair at some time."

"Tell you what. I'm going to bring you a sandwich and a cup of hot cocoa, just in case you get hungry. I'm also going to bring in one of the fold-away beds we have so that if you feel like you want to lie down for a few minutes, you can."

"Thanks, Sonya, that would be great."

****

May 5, 2010, 2:45 AM

When Sonya pulled the curtain aside, Toby was asleep on the fold-away. There were a few crumbs on an otherwise empty plate and an empty mug sitting on a tray on the parson's table along the wall. She returned with another blanket and covered him. Then she began to document Sydney's neurological assessment.

****

3:00 PM

SICU Waiting Room

"Jason, I can't do it. I can't tell them to turn off the ventilator."

"What have the doctors told you?"

"They shake their heads and say they're sorry. They say, 'It doesn't look good.' They say that her brain was without oxygen for a long time. They say that her brain is half its size because it's been squeezed by the blood from the burst blood vessel."

"Have they talked to you about stopping life-support?"

"No, but I can tell that that's coming. They're doing an EEG on her right now. I think they should be done soon."

"What would Sydney want? Did the two of you ever discuss this?"

"Yes, and she's signed a donor card, but I can't do it."

"What did Sydney want, Toby?"

"She didn't want to be hooked up to any machines or receive any treatment that would keep her alive if she was brain dead. She said she wanted her organs to be donated. Oh, Sydney, Sydney, why did this happen to us?"

"Toby, you don't have to make this decision right now." Jason reached for Aaron's hand for support and squeezed it. Aaron squeezed back. Jason went on. "I've never had to do this, Toby, so I don't know what it's like to go through what you're going through, but my parents had to, back when my brother and sister were in a car wreck. They agonized for days, but in the end, they realized Kail and Zoie weren't coming back and they made the decision to donate their organs."

"But that's it, Jason. What if she's not dead? What if I say yes and they take them and give them to other people? Where would she be then?"

"They would never take her organs unless they knew without a doubt that she was gone, and only with your consent."

"Jason, she's starting to smell. Not just like she hasn't bathed. There's another smell in the room. I've never smelled it before, but it makes me afraid. It's like death."

Jason looked up as the door to the waiting room opened. "I'm sorry to interrupt, Mr. Jacobson, but we need you to come in right now."

"What is it, Sonya?"

"It's your wife, Mr. Jacobson. Her pulse is

dropping."

****

3:12 PM
Room N-644

"Mr. Jacobson?" Dr. Ewé said. "Your wife's heart is failing. We need to know whether you want us to treat her."

"What's happened? What's that cart?"

"Sir, that's the crash cart. It's used to resuscitate patients when his or her heart stops beating. The swelling on her brain hasn't improved. In fact, it's gotten worse and it's pushing on the lower part of the brain that controls her heart, just like it did on the part of her brain that made her her."

Sonya focused on the cardiac monitor. "Doctor, her rate is down forty."

"One amp of Atropine, Sonya."

"Yes, doctor. Right away."

"Mr. Jacobson, I need to know right now. Do you want us to start CPR on your wife?"

"Oh, God!" Toby's body stiffened. His face and neck turned beet red as he reached toward the ceiling and then folded his arms over his head. "God, help me! Oh, God!" Then he turned to Jason. "Jason, what do I do? What should I do?"

"Trust your heart, Toby."

Aaron moved in from behind Toby and placed his hands on each side of his arms to steady him.

"Mr. Jacobson?" Dr. Ewé said. "We're out of time. I need an answer right now."

"Jason, what do I do?"

"Sonya," Dr. Ewé ordered, "prepare for CPR."

Sonya climbed onto the bed and placed her palms over Sydney's breastbone.

A high-pitched tone filled Toby's ears as a

stillness fell over the room. Everyone else faded away. The high-intensity spotlight over Sydney's bed turned blindingly bright, and her ethereal image appeared to him, as it hovered over the bed. *"Toby, my love. Let me go. Let me go. It's time. Let me go, my love."*

Toby reached out to her. "Sydney, don't leave me."

"I'm okay, Toby. I'm with Mom and Dad and Granny and Pops. Take care of our children and be happy, Toby. Be happy for me, my love, and let me go."

"No, Sydney. No!"

"You'll find someone to love again, someone who will love our children and you as much as I do. Trust your heart, Toby. It will tell you when you find the right person if you open yourself up to their gift, I promise."

"I can't, Sydney!"

"You must let me go."

"I can't!"

"Yes, Toby, you can. Please, my love. I can't go until you let me."

Sydney's image faded. The sound that filled his ears grew softer and then disappeared. The light over the bed suddenly snuffed out. Dr. Ewé was talking. "Mr. Jacobson. I need your answer. Please!"

"No! Stop!" Toby shouted. "Stop! Stop! Let her go. She's made her decision. I have to let her go." Toby fell against Jason's chest. "Sydney," he sobbed, "how will I go on without you?"

Chapter Four

A Rocky Road

Saturday, May 8, 2010, 11:00 AM
Graveside, Sleeping Pines Cemetery
  The minister cleared her throat. "This concludes the service. After the family pays their last respects to our sister, Sydney Jacobson, they invite you to do the same, with a flower from these baskets." She waving her arm toward the two shallow, ornate wooden baskets, brimming with white roses that sat near each end of the casket.
  "For those of you who are unfamiliar with the area, the ushers are standing by to hand out maps with directions to Founders Lakeside Restaurant for a memorial luncheon as you make your way from the gravesite."
  Toby led the children to Sydney's coffin with baby April in his arms. Aunt Vera brought up the rear, followed by Toby's parents. He handed a white rose to each of the four oldest children and then placed one in April's hand, closing his fingers around it. After he lowered the baby to the casket, he opened his hand, allowing the rose to lie on top of it. Each of the children followed his example and then walked to Aunt Vera's extended hand. As they walked to the waiting limousine, the mourners laid roses on top of the coffin as they passed it.

****

Sunday, May 9, 2010, 10:00 AM
417 Spring Meadow Drive
  "Toby, dear…" As Vera knocked on the master bedroom doorframe, she found Toby sitting on the edge

of the bed. "The director from the nanny agency is here with the resumes of the candidates."

"How am I going to do this, Aunt Vera?" Toby began to cry. "How can I pick a stranger" —his voice broke— "to replace Sydney?"

"Nobody's going to replace Sydney, Toby, not ever." Vera walked to him and pulled his head to her breast. "No one ever could. They're going to manage the practical things the children will need done for them like meals, laundry, dressing, and bathing the little ones."

"How am I going to manage without her, Aunt Vera? How?"

"You're going to manage because these are your children, and you love them. You're going to find a strength in yourself you never knew existed, that's how. Now come on. You've got to be the one to make this decision. No one else can do it for you. I've put Mrs. Shelty in the den. Go splash some cold water on your face. I'll wait for you downstairs."

****

10:15 AM

Toby's face and eyes were still red and puffy. "What kind of assurances do I have about the integrity of your staff, Mrs. Shelty? I mean no disrespect, but these are my children who will be taken care of." His eyes welled up. He reached for a tissue. "I apologize."

"Of course, Mr. Jacobson. None taken. You've been through a terrible ordeal. It's completely understandable. All our staff have gone through vigorous background checks. They've each been run through the NCIC database, and we use a private criminal investigation firm that works closely with the police. All of our hires have clean records. None have ever been convicted of a crime, and we investigate thoroughly to ensure none have ever been accused or arrested for a crime."

"Very well, then I think this woman looks like the best candidate for my children, this Lola Tinker."

"A fine choice, Mr. Jacobson. She's been with us for several years, and she's received glowing reviews from all the families she's been with."

"When can she start?"

"Tomorrow morning. She'll be here at 7 AM."

"We'll get the guest room ready for her."

"I'm afraid Mrs. Tinker's not available to stay overnight, Mr. Jacobson. She's a married woman, but she will stay until seven in the evening for the first few weeks."

"Oh, I see. Are any of these other candidates available to do that, to move in?"

"I'm afraid not. I'm sorry. You see, with school letting out for the summer soon, all our live-in staff have been scooped up by other families to care for their children over the summer."

"Do you have anyone who could move in to be with the children around the clock? Anyone at all? We need someone right away. Aunt Vera can't stay here indefinitely."

"No, not at this time."

"What do you think, Aunt Vera?"

"Toby, it's the best you can do right now. Mrs. Shelty will keep looking. Won't you, Mrs. Shelty?"

"Yes, of course. The moment someone becomes available, we'll notify you."

"Very well, Mrs. Shelty. Please have Mrs. Tinker come tomorrow morning, but keep in mind I'm really looking for a live-in nanny.

"We'll keep looking for you, Mr. Jacobson. I promise."

"Thank you, Mrs. Shelty and thank you for

coming on a Sunday morning. I'm sure this has been a terrible inconvenience for you."

"Not at all, Mr. Jacobson." *With what you'll be paying*, she thought to herself, *it's no trouble at all.*

****

11:30 AM

As his call rang through, and with the phone's handset gripped in his shaking right hand, Toby propped his head in his left.

"Jaron Enterprises. Fiona speaking."

"It's Toby, Fiona. Is Jason there?"

"Yes, Toby. He's right here. One moment please."

"Hello?"

"Hi, Jason."

"Hey, Toby. How are you doing? How are the children?"

"Terrible and terrible, but I guess that's to be expected."

"I'm sorry, Toby. All right if I put this on speaker? Aaron's here too."

"Sure. Sure."

"Hi, Toby. How are you?"

"Hi, Aaron. Lousy."

"I'm sorry, Toby. Is there anything we can do?"

"No, Aaron. Thanks. You've both done so much already."

"Are you sure, Toby?"

"Yes, Jason. Thanks. I do have some good news, if you can call it that."

"Tell us about it."

"I've hired a nanny for the kids. She's not what I want, but she's the best they have right now. Aunt Vera and I just finished meeting with the agency director."

"Why's that, that she's not what you want?"

"She can only stay 'til seven at night. They don't have anyone who can move in."

"Is this the Nannies and More agency Penelope set you up with?

"Yes, Aaron. They're supposed to be the best in the area."

"You said they told you they don't have anyone who can move in?"

"Yeah. That's what Mrs. Shelty said. She's the director."

"Toby, if there was someone who could take care of your kids, and cook, and move in right away, would you be interested?"

Toby sat up straight. "Yes! Absolutely! What are you getting at, Aaron?"

"Toby, I know someone, highly qualified, great with kids, but they don't fit the traditional mold of a nanny."

"Hell, Aaron, I wouldn't care who or what they were as long as they were good to my kids."

"It's funny that the agency didn't mention them, but I have my suspicions as to why."

"What are you getting at, Aaron?"

"I happen to know someone, someone I went to high-school with who's looking for this kind of work."

"Why didn't you tell me about her before, Aaron?"

"Because I was hoping you'd choose them on their own. You see, my friend recently applied to that agency."

"Damn, Aaron! I guess she already took another position. Mrs. Shelty said all their live-ins had already been taken because school is finishing soon. I guess the timing just wasn't right."

"I don't think that's the case."

"What do you mean?"

"Toby, I spoke with my friend just a few days ago. They said they've only been given fill-in assignments. Nothing permanent, so I was sure to mention you, because I knew that was the nanny agency you were going to use."

"I don't understand, Aaron. Why wouldn't she tell me about her, Mrs. Shelty, I mean?"

"Okay, Toby, I'm just going to say this, straight out. My friend, the nanny, is a manny. A male nanny. He's a guy, Toby. He tracked me down over a month ago after he realized I was living here, you know, after he saw the news stories about me and then saw my name in the paper about Nathan's Promise.

"He told me he'd moved here to be close to his family and about what he's been up to these past six years. I hadn't seen him since high-school, but we'd stayed in touch off and on through email. Anyway, he told me he took a job as a male nanny while he continued to look for something in child development. It figures after all he's been through. He's traveled a rocky road, but he's come out on the other side a stronger man for it."

"What do you mean, Aaron?"

"He had to raise his brother and sister after his mom died. We were on the football team together in our senior year. He had to quit because of his mom. Went through the courts to get custody and then focused on raising them. It was amazing what he accomplished in school, considering how hard he worked to keep his family together."

"Tell me more, Aaron."

****

12:04 PM
Headquarters, Jaron Enterprises, L.L.C.,

Executive Office

After Toby had ended the call, Aaron looked at Jason. "You know, Jason, Cliff and I talked on the phone for a long time last month. Then we caught up for an hour in a coffee shop down in the valley when I was down there seeing Rod and Jack about a supply delivery. He wanted to meet you too, face to face. I thought we could do it sometime when we were down in the city again, but we've been so busy with Nathan's Promise, I haven't found the time to set something up. Now this is what I wanted you to know, while we were talking, he told me he's still a virgin."

"What do you mean, 'he's still a virgin?'"

"I mean, when I asked him if he was seeing anyone, he told me no. I told him he'd find someone again. That's when he said he'd never dated, ever, that he'd never been with anyone."

"You mean you don't see him in six years and he just divulges that kind of personal information, the first time you sit down together?"

"He was very matter of fact about it, almost as if he was proud of it. It just never came up over the years. I just assumed, but I guess I never got around to asking. Our communication was haphazard at best. I don't ever remember him dating when we were in school and then after his mom died, I rarely saw him other than in passing in the hallway. He went to school, worked three part-time jobs, right after school, in the evenings, and on the weekends. That was his life.

"He even had a job at school in the cafeteria, cleaning up during lunch. They were really sympathetic to his plight. They let him rearrange his class schedule so that all his free periods were before, during, and after the three lunch breaks so he could earn some money that way."

"So what's this about him being a virgin?"

"He told me he had to dedicate all his time and energies to keeping his family together. His Dad's military pension helped, but even when his mom was alive, it wasn't enough. That's why she had to take on waitressing."

"Where was his Dad?"

"His dad died when he was in the service. Something about an explosion. That's why his mother was getting his pension."

"Oh, so he was really alone then. I guess he sort of had to act like a father for his brother and sister then."

"Sort of, but we were in grade school when that happened."

"So if his mom was a waitress, her take home wasn't that great."

"No. They took up a collection at the diner after she died, but it only came to a couple hundred dollars. He got around ten-thousand from her life insurance policy, but it wasn't enough to pay off the mortgage, clothe and feed the three of them, pay the bills, and keep up of the house. He had to commute to a local college because he couldn't leave his brother and sister, but even so, it wasn't cheap. He still had to pay for the expenses that weren't covered by his scholarship.

"How'd he get a sports scholarship if he wasn't on the team?"

"It wasn't, it was an academic scholarship. He was smart as a whip."

"Impressive."

"I don't know how he managed once his brother started college. Cliff was in his senior year then, too. Two of them in college at the same time. Oh, now I get why he wears his being a virgin like a badge. His commitment to his family is absolute."

"Wow, Aaron, that's almost impossible to believe."

"I believe him, Jason. If he's anything, he's honest, always been that way."

"Do you think he's gay?"

"Jason, I have no idea, really. I didn't ask, and he didn't offer."

"It's almost unimaginable to think someone's not had sex at what, what is he, about twenty-five now?"

"Twenty-four, like me or twenty-five. I don't know when his birthday is, but I will say one thing, he sure cut a nice profile on the field and an even better one in the showers." Aaron bared his teeth and wiggled his eyebrows. "If you know what I mean. When I saw him last month, he'd filled out and let me tell you, he's strapping, handsome, and has a smile that goes on for miles."

"Always the joker, Aaron. Always the joker."

"I'd've done him, Jason. I'd've definitely done him."

"Really? Aaron?" Jason slapped his hands down on his desk and shook his head.

"Jason, I'm kidding. I'm kidding. That would have been before, before even Nathan. You have nothing to worry about."

"Sometimes, Aaron! Sometimes!"

"I know," Aaron said, placing his hands over Jason's. "I go too far."

Chapter Five

Hook, Line, and Sinker

3:45 PM
417 Spring Meadow Drive
Toby drummed his fingers while the phone rang.
"Nannies and More. How may I direct your call?"

"Mrs. Shelty, please."

"May I say who's calling?"

"Tobias Jacobson."

"One moment please."

"Mr. Jacobson, a lovely surprise. How can I help you?"

"Mrs. Shelty, I've changed my mind about Mrs. Tinker. I've just learned that you have a new employee by the name of Clifford Turnbull. Is that correct?"

"Ah..." There was a long pause.

"Mrs. Shelty? Are you there?"

"Yes. I'm sorry, Mr. Jacobson. I'm here. How did you hear about him?"

"That's not important, Mrs. Shelty. I'm sorry to ask this of you, but can you come over and bring his resume? I'd like to take a look at it."

"Certainly Mr. Jacobson, but I'm not sure he'd be the best candidate for your children."

"Why's that, Mrs. Shelty?"

"I really can't say over the phone, Mr. Jacobson, but I believe it will be made clear when we meet."

"Be that as it may, Mrs. Shelty. I'd like to make that decision for myself."

"If that's what you want, Mr. Jacobson. Say six-thirty?"

"That will be fine, Mrs. Shelty. Thank you. We'll see you at six-thirty. Bye."

As Toby hung up the phone, he turned to the group assembled in the den. "Hook, line, and sinker. If I wasn't so happy right now, I'd be mad as hell, and I'd have told her straight out."

****

6:28 PM

No sooner had the bell chimed, then Toby opened the front door. "Mrs. Shelty, right on time."

"Hello, Mr. Jacobson. I have the resume you asked for right here."

"Why don't we sit at the kitchen table while I can look it over? The children have finished eating, and Aunt Vera is giving them their baths upstairs. That will give us enough privacy."

"Certainly, Mr. Jacobson."

After seating Mrs. Shelty, Toby asked, "May I offer you a piece of bundt cake? It was just baked today."

"That would be lovely. Thank you."

"Coffee? Tea?"

"Yes please. Coffee, black."

As Toby poured, he continued. "I'm just curious why you didn't present this candidate to me this morning."

"I can tell you, Mr. Jacobson, that this individual is new to us. After reviewing his qualifications and interviewing him, we could find nothing on paper to disqualify him, so we accepted him."

"Here's your coffee, Mrs. Shelty, and your cake. I believe it's lemon custard."

"Marvelous. Looks delicious." She took a sip of her coffee and then continued. "We've never had a male work for us in this capacity before, but he is extremely qualified, on paper. He's a double-major bachelor's degree, one in child psychology and the other in child development, but we haven't been able to place him permanently. Only temporary fill-ins."

"Why's that? I'd think with his qualifications, families would be knocking down your door to get a chance at him."

"Oh, this cake is divine," she said after her first bite. "Because he's a man, Mr. Jacobson. A very nice young man, mind you, but a man nonetheless and no one has wanted to trust their children with a man unless it's an emergency. In view of these facts and in consideration for what you and your children have been through, I didn't feel it appropriate to present his file to you."

"I don't understand. Is there something wrong with him?"

"I can't say that there is, but I have to be honest with you, Mr. Jacobson, he's big, like a football player big. And, as far as our investigation was able to determine, he's single."

"So, he's single. What's wrong with that?"

"Mr. Jacobson, we have a non-discrimination policy, but we've been unable to identify any attachment to any young lady as far back as we've been able to check. We do have to bend to the wishes of the clients. We have our reputation to think of."

"Oh." Toby now understood without a doubt. "So you're suggesting…"

"Mr. Jacobson," she whispered, "it's very likely he's gay."

Toby laughed out loud, startling her. "I don't have a problem with that, Mrs. Shelty. One of my dearest friends is gay. I wonder though, were you as forthright with all the other clients you've contracted with regard to this individual, about your suspicions I mean?"

"What do you mean?"

"It's none of my business, really, Mrs. Shelty, how you run your company, but this is two-thousand and ten. Things are changing. People are much more open to alternative lifestyles today."

Mrs. Shelty's tone was measured. "Not where their children are concerned."

"I do appreciate your openness with me, Mrs. Shelty. Is it because of my wealth and my social status?"

"Mr. Jacobson, we care about all the children who are cared for by the staff from our agency. We have to be certain their children are safe."

"Well, it's a relief to know you've been as open with other families as you have been with me."

"Absolutely, Mr. Jacobson, absolutely, but with a lot of them, I didn't even have to go that far. Once they knew he was single, good-looking, and wasn't involved with a woman, they were able to come to their own conclusions."

"And you didn't feel it necessary to try to dissuade them."

Mrs. Shelty shook her head and answered softly. "No, sir."

"Well, that's none of my concern, but again, I have no problem with it. Now, back to this young man. You say he passed your background check, correct?"

"Yes, of course. Otherwise there would be no file to present to you."

"Then may I please see his bio and references?"

"Yes, I have his folder right here."

"Thank you."

Toby took the offered folder and began reading out loud from the pages. "Worked at both boys and girls summer camp organizations for four years in-between his college years."

"Actually during college classes. He attended

classes over the summer."

"Amazing." Toby continued reading. "Suggests high motivation, I suppose, and there's more. Hmm … certified in CPR and is a swimming instructor. A 4.0 GPA, and as you've already noted, was a double-major with two bachelor's degrees, one in child psychology and the other in child development. Oh, that's how he was able to complete a double major in four years, those classes over the summer."

"Yes. I believe that is correct, Mr. Jacobson."

"It also says here that he completed three triathlons … hmm … yes. Graduated Summa Cum laude and was the Valedictorian for his graduating class not only in college, but also in high-school. And he can cook. He's taken cooking courses?"

"Yes, Mr. Jacobson."

"What's this about raising a brother and sister?"

"He was orphaned … *they* were orphaned when he was eighteen. He petitioned the courts for legal custody of his younger brother and sister. There's three years between him and his brother and two years between the brother and sister."

"So he's raised his brother and sister, he can cook, and he has a clean criminal record and all these other qualifications, and you still haven't been able to place him in someone's home to care for their children?"

"No, we haven't. When you present it that way, Mr. Jacobson, everything else seems superfluous, I know, but we have to look out for our clients."

"You're right about that, Mrs. Shelty. May I keep this?" Toby held up Clifford Turnbull's folder.

"Yes, that's for you, Mr. Jacobson."

"Thank you. When can he start?"

"I'm not sure, Mr. Jacobson. He hasn't worked for us that often. As I said, we've only been able to place him as a temporary fill-in. I believe he has another job, as a bouncer of all things, if I recall."

"Well, I guess the poor guy's gotta eat. Can you reach him? If he's willing to move in here and can start immediately, I'd like to meet him as soon as possible, this evening even, if you could arrange it."

"I'll see what I can do."

Mrs. Shelty excused herself and walked outside to the back patio, just off the kitchen. She dialed the contact number at the top of the candidate's file. After speaking on the phone, she came back inside, smiling.

"Mr. Jacobson, this is quite unexpected, but I have good news. He said he's just happens to be the area and he'll be right here."

"Really? That's wonderful!"

"Yes, isn't it?"

With that, the sliding French doors that led from the den opened. "Hello, Mrs. Shelty."

"Mr. Turnbull? How ... how are you here already?" Clifford Turnbull closed the doors behind him and approached the table, but he remained standing.

"That's my fault, Mrs. Shelty," Toby said with a smirk. "You see, I invited Mr. Turnbull here earlier today. After meeting the children, Mr. Turnbull prepared dinner for us. The children cleaned their plates. Aunt Vera and I haven't been able to get them to eat since my wife…"

Toby took a deep breath and then went on. "I've already hired him to care for my children. Today was the first time I've seen any of them smile in the past week. Even though they were just hints of smiles, they happened after they met Cliff."

"I'm sorry, Mr. Jacobson." Mrs. Shelty's face flushed. "And I'm sympathetic to your loss, but you can't hire him directly. He's under contract with us. You must hire him through our agency."

"Mrs. Shelty..." Toby paused for effect. "I think you'll not only not want to enforce that, I think you're going to want to release him from his contract with you, immediately."

"I'll do no such thing, Mr. Jacobson! We've paid for his background check! We've vetted him! We've got a contract! We've..."

"If I may, Mrs. Shelty." Toby got up from the table and slid open the French doors. Several more people entered from the den. "Please allow me to introduce Mr. Joshua Bergmann, Mr. Turnbull's attorney, and this is Jason Ackerman, the CEO of Jaron Enterprises, and Mr. Aaron Jaeger, Mr. Ackerman's life-partner. Mr. Jaeger is the president of Jaron Rehabilitative Services. They're building Nathan's Promise, the new LGBTQ rehabilitation facility that's been all over the news. And this is their attorney, Miss Claudia Duncan.

"You may recall seeing Mr. Bergmann in the news as well, Mrs. Shelty. He's representing the plaintiffs, of which, Mr. Jaeger is one, in a discrimination lawsuit against the former coach and general manager of the Nevada Bighorns football team. He was wrongfully terminated as their quarterback. The story's been covered heavily. You must have seen something about it."

"Oh, hello, Mrs. Shelty," Vera said as she walked in from the center hall. May I offer anyone coffee, or perhaps tea? Cliff just baked the most wonderful bundt cake. It's lemon custard. How about a piece? Anyone? No?

"He also baked lemon custard cupcakes for the children. Wasn't that just wonderful of him? He's a wonderful, wonderful cook. Made hamburgers, macaroni salad, coleslaw, and even french fries, all from scratch.

The children ate it right up."

Mrs. Shelty answered through clenched teeth. "Nothing for me, Mrs. Andrews." Mrs. Shelty answered through clenched teeth.

Vera cut a piece of cake and poured a cup of coffee and then disappeared out the door to the patio, unnoticed.

"Mrs. Shelty," Joshua began, "we've collected enough evidence and secured witnesses to the fact, all here presently, to proceed with a discrimination lawsuit against *Nannies and More*, and yourself, on behalf of my client, Mr. Clifford Studwick Turnbull. You have discriminated against my client because you believe he is gay." Joshua held up a miniature digital voice recorder and pressed play.

"Mr. Jacobson, it's very likely he's gay."

"That's your voice, Mrs. Shelty, as is this." Joshua pressed another button on the recorder and then pressed play again. "When you present it that way, Mr. Jacobson, everything else seems superfluous, I know, but we have to look out for our clients."

"Shall I play more, Mrs. Shelty?"

"No!" Mrs. Shelty became even redder in the face. "We have the right to protect our clients."

"Protect?" Claudia said. "Mrs. Shelty, a little free legal advice. You may want to remain silent and not dig yourself in any deeper. Mr. Bergmann is a top-notch attorney. He's never lost a case and let me tell you, Mr. Turnbull's case is rock solid. He's wonderful with the children. I've witnessed it for myself."

Mrs. Shelty stammered. "Those … those recordings will never stand up in court."

"You wanna bet, Mrs. Shelty?" Joshua said. "Mr. Jacobson has had a surveillance system installed in his home for years. It records everything. It will be admissible in court. That I can guarantee you. Perhaps you noticed the sign to that effect, posted just outside the front foyer when you came in?"

Vera slipped back in and then walked over and stood next to Claudia.

"What do you want, Mr. Bergmann?" asked Mrs. Shelty.

"You are the director of *Nannies and More*, correct?"

"Yes, I am."

"Then all you need to do is sign this and this all goes away." Joshua placed a document and pen on the table in front of her. "It releases Mr. Turnbull from his contract with your agency in exchange for an agreement to not sue your agency or you for discrimination regarding this incident or any other time you discriminated against him since his employment with you.

"I'll subpoena all your records, Mrs. Shelty. Based on what I've just heard, I'm certain I'll uncover plenty of corroborating evidence for prior incidents. In addition, should you, in any way, at any time, make such claims again, or make any derogatory statements with regard to Mr. Turnbull in the future, our options will remain open."

"Where do I sign?"

****

Toby escorted Mrs. Shelty out of the kitchen, followed by Cliff.

As Vera watched him walk away, she couldn't help but notice the twin lobes of his buttocks that filled out the rear of his pants. "Oh, if I was a younger woman. The things I could do with that boy."

"Me too, Vera, me too," Claudia whispered.

Vera blushed. "Oh my, God. Did I say that out

loud?"

"Just loud enough, Vera," Aaron said.

"I know what you mean, Vera," Jason added. "It's one of those, 'I hate to see you go, but I love to watch you leave,' moments." Then the four of them started to giggle.

Joshua turned red, shook his head, and said, "You three are so incorrigible."

"What do you mean, three, Joshua?" Vera poked him in the belly. "I'm the one who started it."

"I have no comment on that, madam."

Vera's eyes twinkled. "Really? Well what if I told you about the things I could do with you?"

Claudia guffawed. Jason bent over, covered his mouth, and snorted. Aaron gave a high five to Vera. Then Joshua started giggling too.

****

As she reached the front door, Mrs. Shelty turned to the two of them. "Good night, Mr. Jacobson."

"Good night, Mrs. Shelty.

"Mr. Turnbull." She said this with a curt nod of her head.

"Thank you, Mrs. Shelty," Cliff said. "Thank you for doing this."

"Right." She paused, as if she was going to say more, but all that came out was, "I'll be going then."

Toby opened the door, and then she was gone. He turned toward Cliff. "I'm going to go up and read a bedtime story to the kids."

"Would you like me to come with you, Mr. Jacobson, so I can see how you do it?"

"Sure, Cliff. That would be great. I'm sure at some point…" Toby got a faraway look on his face. "I'm sorry, I'm sure at some point you'll be reading … you'll be reading to them before they go to bed. Yeah, that would really be great of you. Thanks."

"Sure thing, sir."

Chapter Six

Shedding Tears

7:15 PM

"And don't let the door hit you in the ass on the way out."

"Aaron, that wasn't very nice!" Claudia covered a smile.

Aaron stood next to the front door and pulled the sidelight's curtains to one side as he watched Mrs. Shelty's car roll down the hill. It curved around the long, treelined driveway until the taillights disappeared. "No, it wasn't, Claudia, but that's how I feel. Cliff's a great guy, and I'll not see him treated like that. I'll not see anyone treated like that."

"Well, she's gone now, Aaron," Jason said. "It's all over."

"No, Jason," Vera said, "it's just beginning. I'm glad Toby found a cause to fight for. It's helped to distract him from Sydney's death, but how long will it last? This battle's over, but there's dozens more, hundreds more on the horizon."

"Mrs. Andrews is right," Joshua said. "There are going to be many battles. Many, many more battles."

"Please, call me Vera."

"How about Auntie Vera, if you don't mind?"

"That would be fine, Joshua."

"Well, I better get going, Vera." Claudia stepped forward and gave her a hug.

"Thank you for coming, Claudia." Vera returned the hug. "It was wonderful to meet you. You've been a big help to Toby."

"I really didn't do anything, Vera."

"Oh, yes you did. You came. You spoke on Toby's behalf. You supported his family. What more is there?"

Claudia nodded in response.

"I'll be going too," Joshua said. "Please tell Mr. Jacobson I wish him all the best. If there's anything I can do, tell him to please not hesitate to call."

"Thank you, Joshua. Thank you for making this all possible."

"My pleasure, Auntie Vera."

"We're going to go too," Jason said. "We all came together. Aaron and I will be staying in town tonight. Then we'll fly back up home in the morning."

"You'll do no such thing, Jason. I've already prepared a guest room for the two of you."

"Vera, you didn't have to do that. We'll be fine at a hotel for the night."

"I'll not hear of it, Aaron. The two of you are good for Toby. He needs his friends around him right now. I'm sure he'd appreciate it if you were here in the morning, friendly faces and all."

"If you insist, Vera."

"I do, Aaron. I do. Do you have bags? If not, I'll wash and dry your clothes after you go to bed so they'll be fresh in the morning."

"You wouldn't have to do that, Vera," Jason said, "but yes, our bags are in the limo. I had the driver park around the side of the garage so Mrs. Shelty wouldn't see it."

"I know where he is. I brought him a piece of cake and coffee while Mrs. Shelty was getting schooled in the kitchen."

"I'll run out and get the bags," Jason said, "and then I'll tell the driver he can run Claudia and Joshua home and then take off."

"I'll take care of your bags, Jason, and I'll take care of the driver. It's been a long day for everyone. Now why don't you both go take a shower and then go for a soak in the hot tub in the solarium? Your room is up the stairs. When you get to the top, turn left toward the guest rooms. Yours is the first door on the left. I've put out fresh towels and robes for you both."

"Thanks, Vera. You're a peach. I could use a shower."

"My pleasure, Jason. Once the children are tucked in for the night, I'll bring out some wine and cheese for you, maybe a few grapes and apple slices too."

****

As Vera, with Claudia and Joshua in tow, approached the car, the driver got out. "Thanks for the cake and coffee, ma'am," he said, handing her the plate, fork, linen napkin, and mug. "They were delicious."

"You're welcome, Dwayne. I'm just going to get their bags. They're spending the night. They said you could take off for the evening after you drop Claudia and Joshua off at their homes. They'll call you tomorrow when they're ready to be picked up."

"Very good, ma'am, but please, let me get those bags for you."

"You don't have to do that. I'm stronger than I look."

"If you will allow me. It would be my pleasure, ma'am."

****

Tilting back and forth in the rocking chair, Cliff cradled April in his massive arms as he listened to Toby read to his children. April looked like the single remaining corn kernel left on the cob of his forearm. Snuggled tight against their father, the older children took up only a fraction of his king size bed.

When April let go of the nipple and started to fuss, Cliff placed the bottle on the small table beside him and lifted her with the receiving blanket to his shoulder. While he gently tapped her back, Toby finished the story.

"And then Wilfred, the little hedgehog, finally climbed into bed and fell asleep, dreaming of beetles and earwigs and walnuts. The end."

"Eww! Daddy! Earwigs!"

"Eww, beetles!"

"Yum, walnuts!"

The three oldest children yelled out their opinions on the book's ending.

"Eww! Yum!" May added.

"Burp!"

They all turned their heads toward Cliff.

"Eww, April. Eww." The children moaned at their baby sister, then they started to giggle.

Cliff smiled and then wiped April's mouth with a soft, baby washcloth. "Good one, baby girl," he said, as he returned her to his arms, chuckling. "I'll go put her down, if that's all right?"

"I wanna say goodnight!"

"Me too!"

"Me! Me!"

"And me!"

"Okay, kids, everyone say goodnight" —Toby lifted May and July off his lap— "and then we'll let Cliff put her to bed. Then it's your turn for bed."

"We know, Daddy," June said. "We know. One story only. That's what Mommy…"

"Mommy. Mommy!" June began to cry. "My mommy… My mommy!"

"Mommy."

"Mom, Mom, Mommy."

"Oh, Mommy!"

July, May, and August began to cry too. Tears welled up in Toby's eyes as he pulled them to him, then he also began to cry. April began to wail. "I miss her too, babies. I miss her too."

Overcome by their grief, Cliff stood up and hurried out of the room with April in his arms as he tried to suppress his own tears. *Those poor kids. Those poor, poor kids. That poor man. All of them grieving so. I don't know if I can do this.*

****

"Just put the bags down there, Dwayne," Vera said, pointing to the bottom of the staircase.

Shrill crying exploded from the second floor, startling the driver.

"Oh, no! Vera looked up the staircase, then she turned to the chauffeur. They just lost their mother, Dwayne. I better get up there. Thanks, so much. You can show yourself out."

"Yes, ma'am. I'm sorry. Goodnight."

****

7:35 PM

When Vera reached the top of the staircase, she found Jason and Aaron standing quietly, just outside the master bedroom door.

"We had another piece of cake and were coming up the stairs," Jason whispered. "We had just gotten to the top and turned toward our room when we heard laughing, so we turned around and headed the other way to see the kids before they went to bed. We waited while we heard Toby tell them to say goodnight to April, and then June mentioned Sydney. That's when all hell broke loose. Cliff came racing out of the room carrying April and went into the room next door. I don't think he saw us."

"That's the nursery," Vera said as her eyes welled up. "I better go and see if I can help." She pulled a hankie from her pocket, wiped her eyes and blew her nose, and then walked in to Toby and the children, closing the door behind her.

"I'm going to go check on Cliff," Aaron said, softly.

Jason nodded.

****

"Hey, Cliff." Aaron knocked on the nursery door as he and Jason entered. They found Cliff, bent over the basinet, softly crying with his huge hand cradled over April's chest. "Just wanted to check to see how you're making out. You okay, buddy?"

Cliff didn't answer right away.

Aaron and Jason waited.

"Sorry, Aaron. Life is so fragile, isn't it?" Cliff sniffled. "Look at this little baby, lying here, breathing. She's so fragile, Aaron."

"Yes, Cliff, life is fragile, very fragile. Are you okay?"

"Yeah, sorry, it just got to me for a minute. All those little kids. They just lost their mom, and Mr. Jacobson lost his wife. This poor family."

"You know what they're going through, Cliff."

"It wasn't like that for me, Aaron. We were older. They're so little. How am I going to make it better for them?"

"You're not, Cliff," Jason said. "That's not your job right now. No one can make it better for them, not for a while. Not for a long time. I lost my parents when I was twenty-five, and I lost my brother and sister when I was seventeen. Yes, you and me were older, and yes we know what loss is, but not like them. Their loss will be harder to get past, but they will get past it. I promise you that.

What they need right now, more than anything, is stability and routine, something they can rely on to always be there, to never let them down. That, you *can* give them."

Aaron put his hand on Cliff's shoulder. "Cliff, you're about the best person for those kids right now because you've been through it too. Though it might be tough, use that. Use those memories to help them. You'll know when the time is right to share your loss with them. I think they'll believe you and trust you even more because of it."

"Thanks, Aaron. Thanks, Jason. You're both right. It's just that I've never taken care of kids like them, kids that have suffered their kind of loss."

"Cliff, you did those summer camps for four years. There must have been kids there who had recently lost someone. How did you deal with them?"

"Yeah, Aaron, but not four of them at the same time, not the same Mom. There wasn't a Dad there who was grieving too."

"I know this is going to be tough, Cliff, but I know you've got it in you. You've never been one to turn your back on someone in need. I remember back when we were in school. You were only eighteen then. You were remarkable."

"Thanks, Aaron. Thanks for saying that. I'll be okay now."

"You want us to stay with you for a bit?"

"No. Thanks, Jason. I'll just sit here with April for a little while longer."

"Okay. We're going to go take a shower. Vera invited us to go soak in the hot tub. She's going to put out some wine and cheese. Maybe you could join us, if you're feeling up to it. Maybe it would help to take the edge off."

"Thanks, but I really don't know what's expected of me. Mr. Jacobson and I haven't gone over all my responsibilities yet. I should probably stay up here in my room. There's a baby monitor in there so I can listen for April. Right now, I have to go put the children to bed."

"Excuse me, boys." Everyone looked toward the door. Vera stood there, wiping her nose with her hanky. "I'll take first watch. Why don't you three go take showers and then go on down to the solarium for a couple hours. Let some steam off. Talk. Let the wine do its work."

"Thanks, Mrs. Andrews."

"Call me Vera or Aunt Vera, Cliff. Mrs. Andrews is only for formal occasions or people I don't know. You'll make me feel old if you keep calling me Missus."

"Sure, Aunt Vera."

"Just give me about a half hour. You and I will put the kids to bed, and then I'll go down and put together a cheese platter. Then I'll put it all in the icebox. Just take it out when you're ready. And while you're at it, see if you can get my nephew to join you on your way down. He needs it more than all of you put together."

Chapter Seven

Animal Lust

8:10 PM

"Oh, baby. I love you," Jason said as he soaped Aaron's chest. "You were so good with Cliff just now."

Aaron leaned down and kissed him, then pulled him into a hug, grinding his manhood against Jason's. "Cliff's not who I'm thinking about right now." He took the soap from Jason's hand and rotated it in his palm. Reaching down, he began lathering their swelling cocks, together.

"Oh, baby," Jason moaned. "Baby. Baby, you're going to make me hard! We can't. Not now. Not here."

"The hell," Aaron quietly growled. "I want you, Jason. I need to be inside of you."

"Then we'll have to be quick about it. Let me go get the kit. I'll only be a moment."

"You brought it with you?"

"Yeah. I thought, while we were at the hotel, we might…"

"Don't waste time talking. I can't wait much longer."

After Jason finished cleaning himself out, he returned to the shower with a bottle of lube. "Clean as a whistle."

"Good, now come here." Aaron pulled him in and covered his face with tender kisses, then his chest, then his abdomen. When Jason's body began to writhe, Aaron intensified his ministrations, sucking and nibbling at Jason's nipples while he massaged his glans between his fingers.

"You're so wicked, Aaron, so good. So damn

good."

Aaron squirted shampoo into his hand and returned it to their swelling manhoods. He held them together and began to massage their shafts and around and under their balls, forming a thick lather. Once they were covered in suds, he slowly pumped until they were as stiff as two by fours.

"Oh, baby! Aaron! Yes. Yes! Do me. Do me!"

Aaron increased the pace, forcing Jason to rise up on his toes and thrust his hips into the air, literally fucking Aaron's clenched fist.

Jason wrapped his arms around Aaron's neck and pulled himself up to straddle Aaron's hips, locking his ankles behind him.

Aaron turned with Jason clinging to him until the stream of water flowed between their bodies, rinsing the lather away. When he stepped back, he reached for the bottle of lube. He squirted a generous amount into his hand and then applied it to his and Jason's shafts. He reached beneath Jason and began to slowly open him up, first one finger, then a second, then a third.

Soon, Jason was bouncing against his abdomen in rhythm with the pace of his advancing fingers, grinding his frenum against the hair and ridges of Aaron's six-pack abdomen.

The moment Aaron withdrew his fingers, Jason lifted himself up. As Aaron steadied his shaft, Jason lowered his hips until he felt the familiar, swollen helmet of Aaron's manhood press against his gaping hole. He thrust himself downward, instantly taking all of Aaron's ten inches into himself. Then he began to moan.

"Oh, God! Oh, God, Aaron! I need you. Fuck me, baby. Fuck me!"

"Not so loud Jason," Aaron cautioned.

"Sorry. Fuck me, Aaron," Jason growled. His lip

curled up, bearing his teeth. "Fuck me like you mean it!"
****

"You guys ready?" Cliff called from the hallway. There was no answer. "Guys?" he called again as he opened the door and entered their guest room. *Maybe they've already gone downstairs*, he thought.

As he began to turn around, he heard a commotion coming from the bathroom. Innocently, he went in to investigate.
****

Neither Jason nor Aaron heard Cliff's calls or saw him through the steam-covered shower glass when he entered the bathroom.

"Jason, my Jason." Aaron moaned. "I love you, Jason. I love you."

"Your cock, Aaron. Drive it deeper, deeper inside me. Yes! Yes! Oh, my prostate! You're hitting it just right. Keep going, Aaron. Keep going. Yes, just like that, now harder. Oh, God yes! Oh Aaron! Make me cum, baby. Make me cum."
****

Cliff froze like a deer in headlights. He knew he should leave, but he couldn't make his legs move. He felt a stirring in his loins. Instinctively he reached down, spreading open his robe in the process. Then his bathing trunks were down to his knees. Then his penis was in his hand. Then it started growing. Then his hand began to move along its length and there was nothing he could do to stop it.
****

With his hands firmly grasping and spreading Jason's hairy, muscular butt cheeks, Aaron lurched upward, causing Jason to nearly bounce off him, then he lowered him back down, driving his shaft back in to its full length. It finally stopped when Jason's ass landed against his pelvic bone. "When do you want to come, Jason? When? Now, baby?"

"Oh, Aaron! Oh, my God! Don't do that again or you'll make me come."

"That's what you wanted. That's what you asked for."

"No, baby, please. I don't want to shoot yet, not yet. Keep me right here. Right here is wonderful. Your glans, it's pounding my prostate, just right."

Aaron began to gently bounce Jason up and down as he drove his shaft in and out.

"Yes! Yes! Just like that. Just like that, Aaron!"

****

Cliff looked down. He was stroking his massive, thick as a soda can, vein-riddled, ten inch penis. Thick, clear fluid slicked the purpled head as it swelled with each pounding heartbeat while his plumb size testicles swung to and fro, striking back and forth between this thighs and clenched fist.

He had no control over what his hand was doing. It was as if he was an unwilling participant to his body's desires, what the animal inside him needed, but he was aware of the beautiful sensations that coursed from his loins. They were overwhelming.

****

"I'm close, baby." Aaron moaned. "I don't know how long I can hold out."

"Then come, baby. Come inside me. Fill me with your seed." Jason began to moan. "Aaron." Jason moaned his name. "Aaron. Oh, Aaron! Oh… Oh… Oh…Aaron!"

"Oh, baby, when you moan… Jason, when you moan… It makes me… It makes me…"

"I'm going to come, Aaron." Jason moaned again. "I'm going to come!"

"Oh, baby, I can't hold out any longer. I can't. I can't stop it."

"Then do it, Aaron. Do it! Do it! Fill me, baby. Fill me up!"

"Here it come, baby!" Aaron cried. "Here it comes!"

****

When his knees began to buckle, Cliff was violently pulled back into the present. He was dizzy. He felt sensations like he'd never felt before. Waves of pleasure built and built until suddenly, he realized what was happening. He'd read about it in books.

Then he remembered it had happened to him once before, but only once, when he was looking at those pictures of naked men he found in a magazine stashed in the boy's bathroom at school. He'd hidden the magazine down his jeans and took it home. Just like now, when he was looking at the pictures that night, of the men doing those things to each other, mouths on penises, penises inside butts, his hand had found its way to his penis then too. He'd felt the same thing he was feeling now.

He knew what was coming, what was going to happen. He looked around, grabbed a hand towel and shoved it against his hard penis. Then he pulled up his trunks and rushed out of the bathroom.

When he reached the bedroom door, he looked out into the hallway. It was clear. He hurried to his room and closed the door. Then he went into the bathroom and closed its door too.

Now safe, Cliff looked down at himself. His penis was sticking out of the waist band of his trunks. Mostly clear fluid was oozing from his piss slit. When he pulled his trunks down, his penis was so hard it almost hugged his belly, and it began to bounce against it, all on its own. It was red, no, dark red. The swollen cap was an

69

even deeper purple than before. Even more of the fluid started coming out, and it dripped down the shaft, but now it had white stuff in it too. He knew what the white stuff was.

He touched it. It was slippery. He smelled it. It was intoxicating. He brought it to his lips and licked it. It tasted like nothing he'd ever tasted before. It was sweet and savory at the same time. It was wonderful.

Shit. No. I've got to clean this off. I can't let anyone see what's happened. If they came in, I'd get in trouble.

Cliff stepped into the shower. He rotated the faucet to hot and turned it on full blast. As steam began to rise, he couldn't help himself. *One more taste.* He wiped up more of the thick liquid and brought it to his lips. He swirled it around his mouth. His mind began to reel. *It's like ambrosia on my tongue.*

He became delirious as he savored the new, subtle, musky and fruity flavors. He wanted more, so he tasted it again. Then he tasted it again. He surrendered to the animal. He wouldn't fight it, not again. He let the animal guide him.

His hand reached down and encircled his shaft as he spread his legs apart, bracing his feet against the shower walls. His right hand began to pump the length of his hard penis. He leaned forward, spreading his meaty left hand against the tiles.

Cliff felt an overwhelming sense of pleasure rise from his depths. It was so new, so beautiful. The sensations washed over him, urged him on and on until he floated in a haze of delirious ecstasy.

He looked down and watched his hand—disconnected from his mind—move faster and faster up and down his hard penis. More of the fluid was coming out of the opening. Then his knees buckled as the most intense feelings of pleasure he had ever known raced from his groin, down his thighs, and up into his abdomen.

His chest tightened as the sensations spread out around to his back and over his shoulders. He watched as a thick stream of white fluid shot out of the tip of his penis and struck the shower wall. He recognized what it was. Semen. He'd read that word in books. He'd read man seed, cum, jizz, and spunk on bathroom walls. He knew those were wrong words, but oh, how it felt good to think them.

A muffled cry escaped his mouth. Another stream was propelled outward and another cry, then again, and again, and again.

When the streams slowed, Cliff regained control of his body. He captured the last three pumps of the thick liquid in his cupped palm as it surged outward. He milked the shaft to get the last few drops. He brought the puddle to his mouth and sucked it in, savoring the flavors all over again, but this liquid felt and tasted different. It was thicker, muskier, more masculine, more animal.

He licked the last traces from his palm and swallowed. As its odor traveled up the back of his nasal passages, his senses were flooded with new sensations. The taste and smell together made him dizzy. It smelled good—no, better than good—and the smell made it taste even better. It smelled right, like something that he should, no needed, to experience again and again, and now he knew how to get it. He could have it any time he wanted it.

Chapter Eight

First Good Cry

8:50 PM

As Cliff walked out of his bathroom, he froze. Aaron stood in the doorway, staring at him. He hadn't heard his bedroom door open, and he certainly hadn't expected to find his former classmate gawking at his 'naked as the day he was born' body, but then he thought, *I'm not like the day I was born.*

He jumped, covering his still thickened penis with his hands as he quickly turned around and finished pulling on the robe. He'd completely forgotten to put his bathing suit back on. *Darn. Damn. Darn. Did he see it? Was it still hard enough for him to tell?*

"Good God, Cliff, you're hung like a horse, and when'd you get so ripped and so hairy? Your clothes didn't do much to conceal that you were big underneath, but I never expected this."

"Aaron!" Jason exclaimed as he pushed him into the room and closed the door behind them. "You don't say things like that!"

"Oh, come on, Jason. I've known Cliff since we were kids. He doesn't mind."

When Cliff turned back around, he was beet red.

"I think you're wrong about that, Aaron. I think you've embarrassed him."

"No, it's okay, Jason," Cliff choked out. *God that was close*, He thought. Quickly, he cleared his throat. "I was just startled, that's all. After all, we used to shower together after practices. I'm not embarrassed or ashamed of my body." *Well at least that last part's the truth,* he thought again.

"And you shouldn't be, buddy," Aaron continued. "You've really filled out nice. I know a couple of guys who'd just love…"

"Oh, for God's sake, Aaron," Jason said as he hit him on the arm with the back of his hand. "Enough already."

"Sorry, Jason. I was just trying to make you jealous."

"Should I be, Aaron?" Jason asked with a slightly hurt expression on his face.

"Oh, Jason! No! No! Sorry, baby, I was just kidding. Just kidding."

"I see you still kid too much, Aaron," Cliff said with his arms folded across his chest. *God love him, but he can still be a jerk.* "Don't worry, Jason. I'm not into that. At least I don't think I am."

"Sorry, Cliff," Aaron said, "I thought… Well I thought you might…"

"It's okay, Aaron, no offense taken, really. I just wanted you to be clear about me."

"But you just said you didn't think so."

"That's right Aaron. I don't know anything for certain. You know I'm a virgin. But should that matter? Really? Yeah, I've never been with anyone. I've never had sex of any kind with anyone. So what?"

"And if you're good with that, Cliff," Jason said, "then good for you. That's your right."

"Thanks, Jason, but please, don't repeat it. I don't want Mr. Jacobson to know, not right now anyway. Like I said, I'm not ashamed of it, but he's got enough to think about. He doesn't need to add wondering about my sexuality to all the balls he's got in the air right now."

"Can I tell you something, Cliff?"

"What's that, Jason?"

"Toby wouldn't care, not one iota. Didn't he just

73

prove that to you by hiring you?"

"Yes, he did, but still, it was a non-issue if you will, not a non-entity. He doesn't care if I'm gay. He can accept that because he knows you're gay, and you're friends. Being gay isn't the issue, but if it was a known fact that I'm a virgin, it could leave questions. It could be one more thing to occupy his mind and anyway, if anyone's going to tell him, it should be me."

"You're right. End of discussion. Right, Aaron?"

"Yeah, Jason's right, Cliff, sorry I pushed it."

"No worries, Aaron. I'd have been surprised if you hadn't said something like that. I've known you for far too long. Now Aunt Vera said something about wine and cheese. Just let me put my bathing trunks on and we'll go check it out."

"Don't bother, Cliff," Aaron said. "We don't have anything on under out robes, and you know we'd all be taking them off once we got in the hot tub."

"I want to check on Toby before I head down, Aaron, to see if I can convince him to join us. Why don't you and Cliff go ahead and then I'll meet you there?"

"Okay, Jason. Shall we?" Aaron motioned with a wave of his arm to Cliff.

As they walked out of the room together, with Jason in the lead, Aaron hung his arm across Cliff's shoulder, then Cliff did the same.

"I'll see you guys in a few minutes."

"Okay, Jason," Aaron said.

****

9:00 PM

Jason knocked on the door and then opened it. "Hey, Toby?"

The sound of sobbing came from inside the room.

As Jason entered, both Cliff and Aaron dropped their arms and waited by the door.

"Toby?" Jason called. "Toby, buddy? You okay?"

"Sydney! Sydney!" Toby cried from somewhere in the room. "My Sydney."

Jason hurried in the direction of the cries. They were coming from the bathroom.

Aaron and Cliff walked just inside the door.

"Do you think I should go with him, Aaron?"

"No, Cliff, let Jason handle this, but we'll stay close, just in case. Close the door so he doesn't wake the kids."

****

"Sydney! My Sydney!"

When Jason entered the bathroom, he found Toby down on the floor of the walk-in shower leaning against the glass next to the door, mumbling Sydney's name. His feet were pulled tight up against his butt, and his face was in his hands. The water was on full blast, striking his feet and legs. The bathroom air felt cool, not hot and steamy like it should be when someone was taking a shower. Overhead, Diana Ross's song, "Missing You," was playing.

"Toby, buddy, it's me, Jason. I'm coming in."

As Jason opened the door, he immediately felt the air was even cooler inside. He put his hand under the stream of water. It was cold to the touch and Toby was shivering, violently. "Shit! Aaron!"

Like a flash, Aaron was in the bathroom with Cliff right behind him.

"Help me." Jason struggled to lift the sobbing, naked Toby into his arms. "Turn the water on hot, not too hot, but hot and help me get him under it."

As Aaron stepped in and adjusted the temperature, Cliff threw off his robe and helped Jason to steady Toby. Together, they guided him into the stream of very warm water.

"Turn them all on, Aaron."

Aaron fiddled with the controls and in a few seconds, more hot water was shooting out of nozzles from all directions and levels.

"What in the world?"

Cliff, Aaron, and Jason all turned their heads to find Vera standing in the bathroom doorway with her hand over her mouth. There were three men in various stages of undress surrounding her nephew.

"What's going on? What's happened? I heard Toby crying, then it disappeared."

"That's because I closed the door, Mrs. Jacobson," Cliff said, "so as not to wake the children."

"Sydney!" Toby cried.

"I found him in the shower, Vera," Jason said. "I came in to invite him down to the whirlpool when I heard him crying. I came in to check on him. The water was running cold and he was shivering on the shower floor. I have no idea how long he was under it."

"Oh, no!"

"Sydney. Sydney," Toby moaned.

Vera lifted her hand to her mouth. "Oh, my poor, poor Toby."

"We're trying to warm him up right now, Vera. We just got him under the hot water. It's going to take a few minutes 'til he stops shivering."

"I'll get more towels, Jason."

"Sydney. Sydney," Toby moaned again.

"Jason's and my robes are soaked, Vera," Aaron said. "Are there any more?

"I'll see what I can find. I'll be right back."

"And somebody turn off that blasted song!" Jason yelled.

Vera hit the power switch to the music console.

"I'm going to close the door again. I don't want the children woken up, if they haven't been already. They don't need to see their father like this." Then she was gone.

"Sydney. Sydney," Toby said in a hushed voice, as he crumbled in on himself. The three of them held him up while the warm water cascaded down his chilled body.

****

Vera returned to a steam-filled bathroom in less than five minutes. She could just make out four male forms on the other side of the shower glass. "I've brought more towels," she called out, "and I've found more robes." The pile in her arms went up to her nose. "Where do you want them, Jason?"

"Great, Vera. Throw a couple towels on the floor just outside the shower door. We're going to give him a few more minutes."

After the minutes had passed, Jason called out, "Okay, Vera, we're ready. Pass me two towels and Toby's robe. I saw it on the hook out there. Once we get him dry, Aaron and Cliff are going to carry him right downstairs and put him straight into the hot tub. Once he's really warmed up, we'll decide what we're going to do with him."

"Okay, Jason. I threw the towels down, and I've got towels for him and his robe right here."

"Okay, guys, just like I told you."

Jason's robe lay with Aaron's in a sopping pile in the corner of the shower. As he opened the shower door, Vera averted her gaze. "Thanks, Vera. Cliff's robe is right there on the floor. We're all going to need towels too, and Aaron and I will need two of the other robes you brought. Ours are soaked."

"I didn't bring enough towels," Vera said. "I'll

have to go get some more from the other bathroom. I'll be right back."

****

When Aaron turned the water off, Cliff held Toby from the front to steady him. As Jason began to dry him off, Toby wrapped his arms around Cliff's neck, causing him to lose his balance. As Cliff adjusted his stance, and grip on Toby, his penis grazed Toby's.

At the contact, Toby rocked forward, pressing his body against the larger man. Buried deep below his grief, there was a momentary recognition of that sensation— the grinding of two men's pelvises against one another, of his time with Jason.

After Aaron slipped the heavy terry robe onto Toby, he reached between him and Cliff and cinched it tightly closed from the front. Toby's head hung down. He had stopped crying, and he had stopped shivering.

****

"I'm back," Vera called into the bathroom. I hope I've brought enough because there aren't any more towels."

"We should be okay with what you brought, Vera," Jason said. "I'll take a couple of those towels now and two robes. After Aaron and I dry off and get them on, you can hand Cliff a couple towels and his robe."

Again, Vera averted her eyes as she held out the towels and then the two robes up to the shower door. Once Aaron and Jason had their robes on, they held onto Toby while Vera handed towels and then the robe to Cliff. Again, she averted her eyes.

Aaron and Cliff guided Toby out of the bathroom with Jason in front of them.

"Okay, guys, I've got Toby," Jason said as he wrapped his arms around him. "Now just like I said, lock your arms and stoop down. Don't forget to duck at the doorway."

Jason guided Toby back into the seat created by Aaron and Cliff's interlocked arms. Then he swung Toby's arms around their shoulders. "Okay, guys, up and over to the door."

When they reached the door, they turned and stooped down, lowering Toby enough to clear the doorframe, and then quickly walked to the top the staircase and began to descend.

"What's Uncle Aaron and Mr. Cliff doing with Daddy?"

Jason and Vera turned around to find August right behind them, watching through half opened eyes. He yawned.

"They're giving him a ride, August," Jason said. "They're giving him a ride down to the hot tub."

At the sound of his son's voice, Toby lifted his head.

"A ride? Daddy?"

Jason placed his hand on August's head. "Yeah, sure, grown-ups like to go for rides too. Just like I gave you a horsey ride when you visited my cabin."

"Oh, okay."

Toby forced himself to speak. "All right, Aaron and Cliff, giddy-up."

"Okay, young mister," Vera said, at Jason's quick thinking, "back to bed now. Let's get you tucked back in right now."

As she led August back to his room, Vera mouthed, *"Thank you,"* over her shoulder to Jason.

Chapter Nine

Letting Go of Guilt

9:15 PM

When Vera entered the solarium, she was carrying a tray with a carved wooden plank arranged with an assortment of cheeses, a platter with grapes and apple slices, two cheese knives, crackers arranged on a tray designed for them, and a stack of small plates. She set the tray down on the ledge of the hot tub, designed for just such a thing, that projected into the water from the edge. "Careful with the sliced apple. They might be a touch sour. I rubbed them with lemon. Now, I'll be right back with the wine."

When she returned, Cliff was portioning out servings of cheese, crackers, and fruit onto the small plates. Vera brought two bottles each of red and white Merlot, a bottle of whiskey, a bottle of Amoretto, five wine glasses, and a tumbler filled with ice on another tray. She set it down on a low table next to the hot tub and then took a baby monitor out of her pocket and placed it next to the tray.

"I'm going to fix Toby a Godfather. He needs it. Red or white boys?"

Toby looked at her sheepishly. "I'm so sorry, Aunt Vera, that you had to see me like that."

"Nonsense, boy." Vera began to mix Toby's drink. "You've been through hell. It's quite understandable. After what you've been through, I'd think there was something wrong with you if you didn't have a good cry, and let me tell you, it was only your first. There'll be more, plenty more. When I lost your Uncle Randolph, I cried for days. Weeks later, I started all over again. Now drink this. Drink it right down. Then I'll fix you another."

"Thanks, Aunt Vera."

"Red or white, boys?" Vera asked again.

"Red."

"Red."

"Red."

"Then I'll have a little white," she said. "Just enough to say I did. Then I'll head back in. I've got the robes from the shower floor and all the towels in the washer. As soon as they're done, I'll throw them in the dryer and then I'll go up for the night."

"Sure you don't want to sit for a while? Join us maybe?" Jason asked.

"Not on your life, young man! I've got four virile, naked, male specimens in front of me. I wouldn't trust myself with all of you if I got tipsy. Who knows where the night might end or who or how many I'd find in my bed come morning."

Aaron guffawed, Cliff spewed his drink right across the hot tub, spraying Toby, and Jason snorted wine out of his nose, but Toby just shook his head as he lifted his hand from the water and wiped Cliff's spray from his face.

"I'm so sorry, Mr. Jacobson."

"Don't worry about it, Cliff, and better get used to it, guys. If you're around her too long, she'll get comfortable with you. Before you know it, she'll start talking like a sailor on shore leave."

Vera kept the wine flowing. As second and third glasses were consumed, the conversation remained light and general as everyone made sure to avoid any talk about Sydney or her death.

When Toby finished his second Godfather, Vera took his glass.

"Thanks, Aunt Vera. That's enough for me."

"I'll just mix you another, in case you change your mind. Sip it if you like, or not, and you boys just leave everything. I'll clean it all up in the morning."

After she mixed his drink, Vera handed the tumbler back to Toby. "I'll say goodnight then and thank you all for being here and for looking after my Toby."

As she kissed Toby's forehead, and probably because of the effects of the wine or the long day, or perhaps just good manners, the other three were already standing up, not thinking about their state of undress.

"Don't you boys dare!" Vera sucked in her breath. "You're still naked!"

Though it happened quickly, and they sat right back down, it was too late. Even though Jason was the shorter of the three, the water level stopped just at the base of the V between his hips, allowing his penis to bounce like a log on the swirling water's surface.

Aaron and Cliff didn't fare as well. For an instant, their well apportioned male appendages hung above the water while the tips jostled in the turbulent waves. Driven by mammalian, male instinct, the eyes of all four men instantly shot to groins, quick appraisals were made, and then it was over as they disappeared beneath the water's surface.

"I shouldn't have seen that!" Vera exclaimed with a twinkle in her eyes. "I'm glad I did, but I shouldn't have. And now I'll take my leave. Goodnight all."

****

After she'd gone, Toby exhaled and let out a sigh.

Aaron looked at the other three. "Whoops."

Cliff blushed. "Mr. Jacobson. I'm sorry. I don't know how that happened. I was up before I realized…"

"It's fine, Cliff. Don't worry about it. It's been one hell of a day."

"That's one grand dame you've got there, Toby."

"Thanks, Jason. I wouldn't trade her for anything. Now, I've decided, I'm going to finish this drink and then I'm going to have some wine. Who's with me?"

****

Monday, May 10, 2010, 12:45 AM

Toby could barely keep his eyes open. His speech was slurred and his head kept dropping forward. "Time for beddy-bye ... boys. Nighty ... nighty ... night."

When he tried to rise, Toby staggered and fell forward, but Cliff and Jason caught him just in time. "Okay there, big guy," Jason said. "Let's get you up to bed."

Aaron climbed out and put on his robe, then he picked up Toby's. Together, Cliff and Jason helped Toby out of the hot tub and onto the tile floor. The more Toby tried to help Aaron with his robe the more tangled he became.

"Toby, just stand still," Aaron said, "Let me do this."

"'kay, Aaron."

With the robe finally on him and secured. Cliff and Jason sat him in a chair and then put on their own robes.

"If you two can get him upstairs, "Cliff said, "I'll get this all cleaned up. I'm not leaving it for Mrs. Jacobson in the morning."

"Sure thing, Cliff," Aaron said. "Thanks."

"I'll see you in the morning."

"In the morning then," Aaron said.

"Goodnight," Jason added.

"Nighty ... nighty ... night," Toby slurred.

"Good night, Mr. Jacobson."

****

While Cliff tossed and turned in the unfamiliar

bed, he recounted the evening. He'd had his first sexual experience in years, and he didn't feel guilty about it. Not in the least. As a matter of fact, he felt great because it was wonderful.

Then he remembered that night, that deeply buried secret memory, the night the police had come to the door to tell him his mother was dead. He'd blamed himself, but he'd never told that to anyone.

She'd slipped on the greasy floor at the diner and struck her head on the corner of the counter at almost at the same moment he'd had his first orgasm. While he drooled over the pictures in that magazine, experiencing the most incredible pleasures he had ever known, his mother had died, instantly.

The guilt had grown in the days and weeks that followed until he came to the belief it was his fault. He believed God had punished him for looking at those pictures of the naked men who were doing those things with each other. He had no one to talk to about it. He didn't have time. He had to take care of his brother and sister. He became driven to do everything he could to ensure they'd stay together.

But now, with the return of that buried memory, he knew enough about psychology to understand how a sheltered, innocent, eighteen-year-old could have thought those things on his own and how that eighteen-year-old could have closed himself off from the world and, as a result, any kind of relationship.

Cliff felt his cheeks. They were wet. He was weeping, weeping for that boy, weeping for his mother, weeping for the lost relationships and lost opportunities that had passed him by. Finally, when it stopped, he forgave himself for hurting himself by blaming himself. *It has to stop here. I've got to move forward. I have to let it go.*

Then he drifted off to sleep.

****

"I just remembered something, Jason," Aaron said as he cradled Jason in his arms.

"What's that?"

"What you told me, after you rescued me."

"I have no idea what you're talking about, Aaron."

"We had sex tonight, right here in a house that's filled with people morning the loss of a mother and a wife, the wife of your friend."

"What are you getting at?"

"Don't you remember?"

"I don't think so. No."

"You told me that after a loss or some great tragedy people often have sex because they need to reaffirm life and that it's often mindless. It's how they cope."

"I do remember that now."

"You were serious, weren't you?"

"Yes, Aaron, about something like that, of course I was serious."

"Now I get it. What we did, the sex we had in the shower, I was so down about Sydney and all that Toby and the kids were going through, all of a sudden I was driven to make love to you. I couldn't think of anything else. It was like I was possessed."

"Yes, Aaron. We both needed it. It was wonderful." Jason yawned. "Now go to sleep."

"I love you, Jason."

"I love you too, Aaron."

****

Toby's dreams were fragmented, painful, and wonderful. Images of Sydney filled his mind, images of her with the children, images of the two of them, alone.

He dreamed about becoming aroused just from holding her hand, about her mouth on his cock, about her sitting on top of him as he shot his load into her, when they made their first baby.

He dreamed of walking hand in hand along the beach in San Diego with Sydney with their sandals in their hands and the sound of the waves gently lapping at the shore. He dreamed of sitting on a giant boulder in Yellowstone with their legs dangling in the air high atop the edge of a cliff. He dreamed of blushing when older women whispered to one another as he held her purse while she shopped for baby clothes when she was pregnant with August.

He dreamed of the times when they made love, just to make love. He felt the intensity of his orgasms and the love he felt for her. He heard her moans and screams as she shuddered while he drove himself into her; and he felt her tender caresses after they'd finished, and her kisses, and he heard her loving whispers.

He dreamed of their best sex, he dreamed of his best orgasms, and then there was a dream about Jason. It was about the first summer he'd ever had sex, the week they'd camped above the construction site that became Jason's home, when Jason had given him the best orgasms of his life, fucking him and sucking him at the same time.

He dreamed of Jason teaching him how to make love to a man. How Jason had moaned and encouraged him as he opened himself up and asked Toby to drive himself into his pleading hole. During that week, Jason helped him to refine his technique, showing him how subtle differences in the angle, depth, and rate of penetration could make a man lose his mind, and just as important, he taught him how to receive pleasure from a man.

Toby had carried those finer points of lovemaking with him into his marriage. He knew they worked, because Sydney had told him that he pleased her better than she had ever been pleased before.

He dreamed of the time he told Sydney about his summer with Jason. She had hugged him and told him how wonderful it must have been for him, because she knew the pleasures that having a cock deep inside her could bring. She told him how much she loved him and that she wanted him to be happy in every way. She said it would be all right if he sought out men for that kind of pleasure again, but he said no. He was married to her now, and he was committed to their marriage, and besides, it would be too risky for the business, and it would hurt them and their marriage in the long run.

He dreamed of Sydney offering to do that for him, that there was a way. That was when she started pegging him with the strap-on. She loved to put the harness on and it made her so happy to be able to give him that kind of pleasure.

Then he dreamed about Jason, naked in the shower, holding him up. Jason looked even better than he did when they were younger. The smell of Jason brought back memories of his cock and what he could do with it.

Then his dream recalled that there were two other men in there with them. They were naked too. They surrounded him and held him up. Their hairy bodies brushed against him. Their strong hands were on him. Their comforting words coaxed him and supported him.

One of those men was Aaron, but Aaron was Jason's and Jason was now Aaron's. Jason could never be his again and for that reason, neither could Aaron, but, there was another. Cliff was the biggest of all of them, the strongest of all of them, the one with the biggest cock, the cock that brushed up against his own.

He dreamed of Sydney in the ICU, of the tube in her nose, of the words he spoke to her through the night. He dreamed of the smell of her body as she lay dying. Then he dreamed of her coming to him to say goodbye.

Then Cliff's thick, meaty hands were supporting him, holding him close while Jason rubbed towels against his body. Cliff's cock dangled above the swirling water in the hot tub.

He heard Sydney's words again, but now they seemed clearer, more real, and he now believed that he would find someone to love again, because she promised. She promised that someone would love their children and that his heart would know who it was. She told him to trust his heart.

The smell of Cliff, his animal musk, haunted him. Cliff didn't belong to anyone. Cliff was single. He envisioned Cliff's cock inside him. Cliff could be...

"Trust your heart, Toby. It will tell you when you find the right person—if you open yourself up to their gift, I promise."

****

7:30 AM

"Daddy!"

"Daddy. Daddy."

"Da ... Daddy."

"Daddy!"

Suddenly there were hands all over him, tiny hands, pulling and pushing at him.

Toby opened his eyes.

"Daddy, are you coming down for breakfast?

"Daddy, Mr. Cliff made French toast! You want some?"

"Daddy, we told Mr. Cliff you love French toast!"

"Yeah, Daddy, hurry up before Uncle Jason and

Uncle Aaron eat it all."

"Daddy, you should see how much French toast Uncle Aaron can eat! He ate a thousand pieces!"

"Oh, God!" Toby moaned. His head was pounding. "Kids, kids, stop. Please!" He moaned again.

"Come on, Daddy."

"Kids!" Cliff shouted, "Daddy has a headache!"

The room fell silent. August stood at foot of the bed and made a face at his siblings. "June, May, July, hush! You're making Daddy mad."

Toby rubbed his hands up and down his face and lifted his head. "No, babies, no. I'm sorry. I'm so, so sorry. Daddy's not mad." *Oh, God. My head*, he thought. "My head just hurts. Tell you what… Let Daddy take a shower and then I'll be right down. Okay?"

"Okay!"

"Okay!"

"You promise, Daddy?"

"Yes, June, I promise."

"Yeah!" they all squealed.

God, make it stop.

After they left, Toby tried to sit up. His head pounded even more. Finally, in one quick motion, he swung his legs over the side and he was up.

Immediately, he felt something pulling on his dick and something yanked at the hair on his thigh. He whipped off the covers and looked down. He was naked. His dick was stuck to his thigh. The hair on his thigh was crusted together. There was hair stuck to the sheet.

Then he remembered his dreams of Sydney, and then he remembered who he was dreaming of when he woke, and his massive cock.

Riddled with guilt, he started to cry.

Chapter Ten

Responsibilities

11:50 AM

"I don't even know how to begin to thank you both for all that you've done."

"That's what friends are for, Toby." Jason hugged him goodbye and then kissed his cheek before he pulled away. "You're my friend, and I love you. Don't ever forget that."

Toby nodded quickly as tears welled in his eyes. He suppressed a sob as he turned to Aaron.

"You call us if you need anything, anything at all." Aaron hugged him, too. "We'll be back for the weekend."

"That would be great. Maybe we can take the kids to a movie or even the zoo if the weather's nice."

"If you're up to it." Aaron leaned away. "Otherwise, we'll rent some movies, maybe let the kids pick a few." He turned to the children. "What do you guys think? We can make popcorn, watch movies, eat lots and lots of candy 'til our stomachs hurt…"

Jason made an exaggerated motion of wagging his finger at Aaron. "Not *that* much candy, Uncle Aaron. Just look at them. With all that syrup in them, they're full of sugar right now. What do you think a box of candy would do?"

Toby patting them both on the shoulders. "Whatever you guys want to do is fine with us."

"No, Toby, whatever you want to do."

"Thanks, Jason."

August tugged on Aaron's pant leg. "Can we go for a helicopter ride?"

"If that's what you want, August." Aaron picked him up and threw him into the air. "You're gonna have us for the whole weekend! We could fly right over your house. Wouldn't that be neat?"

August squealed. "Yeah! Could we really?"

"Sure thing!"

"I want to go to the zoo!"

"I want to go to the zoo and have candy!"

"Candy! Candy!"

"See what I mean, Aaron." Jason frowned. "Sugar."

"Okay, kids." Vera interrupted. "Say your goodbyes so Uncle Jason and Uncle Aaron can get going. They have a helicopter waiting."

"Helicopter!"

"Helicopter! Zoo! Candy!"

"Helicopter! Popcorn!"

May threw her hands into the air, jumped up and down, and squealed. "Cop ... ter! Pop!"

"See what you started." Toby smiled and hugged them both again.

Jason hugged him back. "We'll stay in touch."

"Thanks, Jason. Thanks, Aaron."

****

After Jason and Aaron had gone, and while Cliff and Vera were trying to herd the children out of the foyer, Toby motioned for Cliff to come to him.

"Yes, Mr. Jacobson?"

"Cliff, I wanted to talk to you about last night."

"Yes, Mr. Jacobson."

"After the kids have settled down, come see me in my study."

"Sure thing, Mr. Jacobson, and if you have time, I have some questions about my responsibilities and how you like things done."

"I wanted to talk to you about that too. We're on the same page. That's a good thing."

****

1:15 PM

Cliff knocked on the door to the study.

"Come in."

"Yes, sir, you wanted to talk to me?"

"Yes, Cliff. Have a seat. Last night was a one time thing. Though I'm grateful for the kindness, I don't expect you to be looking out for me."

"Mr. Jacobson, you've been through so much. Your family has been through so much. I know my job is to be a nanny for the children, but you come as a unit. If you're hurting, if you're in need of something, your children are going to sense it. They're going to feel it. You're going to need some looking after too, if you don't mind my saying, sir, and I don't mind doing it. Even if it's just someone to lend an ear."

For a fleeting moment, Toby remembered his dreams. He remembered Sydney, their talks, her good advice. He remembered his summer with Jason, again, but Jason had Aaron now. He remembered Sydney wearing the harness and what she did to him with it, and he remembered Cliff, his body, naked in the shower, his hands, holding him, and his manhood, his massive manhood, brushing up against his own.

He felt a pressure begin to build. His testicles contracted as blood surged into his loins. His dick began to stir. His chest began to tighten. His pulse quickened.

Then he thought of his children, and his mind drifted off. Cliff waited.

****

"Are you okay, Mr. Jacobson?" Cliff was holding out a tissue.

"Yes. Sorry," Toby said as he reached for it and

wiped his eyes.

"That's very kind of you, Cliff, I mean the tissue. I'm sorry for the tears. I'm afraid there's going to be a lot of bad days around here. I've got to learn to handle them better. It's just that it's all so raw right now."

"I understand."

"Please know that I appreciate the sentiment, Cliff, I mean about you offering to look out for me, really I do, but your job is to take care of my children."

"Yes, sir. Understood."

"You'll be in charge when I'm not here, and when I am here, there's things that I'll want to do for them, like reading to them at night, you know, Daddy things. Your job is to dress and feed them, clean up after them, change April's diapers. You do know how to change a diaper, right?"

"Yes, sir, I'm an ace at it."

"Good, good. You'll be responsible for their laundry, making sure fresh linens are put out in their bathrooms, things like that. Oh, and don't worry about my clothes or my laundry. I'll figure out how to work the washer. It's been a few years, but I'm sure it will come back to me."

"Mr. Jacobson, it's no trouble, really. I'll be doing laundry every day. Your children are small. Combined, their clothes won't even make a full load. You've got a large capacity washer. If it's going to be running, we might as well fill it, and April's things shouldn't be left go too long before being washed. You don't want to give bacteria colonies time to get a foothold in a newborn's things. So, as I was saying, what's another set of your clothes every day?"

"Okay, Cliff, I'll tell you what. We'll play it by ear, but remember this, you're here to do the things a mother would do, not a wife. Does that make sense?"

"Yes, sir. Very good, sir. Oh, and speaking of little April, would you be receptive to changing her over to cloth diapers? I've been thinking about how much of our landfills are filled with disposables. Of course, I'd wash them separately, and your washer has the high temperature setting for just such things."

"If you think it's safe, I'll go along with it, but if you see she begins to develop a problem, we'll go back to disposables. Sydney ... sorry..." Toby's breath caught. He paused for a moment and grabbed another tissue. "Sorry. Sydney did that with our first two. When July came along, her hands were too full with three. She switched to disposables for convenience sake only."

"I don't think it will, but absolutely. I believe that done right, you can keep a baby's tushy plenty clean and dry with cloth. I'm a big believer in topical skin ointments with Vitamins A, D, and E in them and good ole' petroleum jelly takes care of a multitude of maladies. That's what my mother used. 'It's good for what ails you.' she used to say. I'll promise you this, she'll never be left to lie in a wet or soiled diaper."

"Very good, now where was I? Oh yeah. We have a housekeeping company that comes in twice a week to clean, so you're not responsible for that, but making their beds, putting their laundry away, that will fall on you. Are you good with all of that?"

"Yes, sir. Absolutely, but if I may..."

"Sorry, Cliff. Sorry to interrupt, but let's drop the *sir*. I'm not comfortable with it. My wife called me Toby, Aunt Vera calls me Toby, Jason and Aaron call me Toby. My children are accustomed to hearing adults call me by my name. If you start calling me *sir*, it's going to change the dynamic around here, and I don't want that. I want things to stay as normal as possible."

"Certainly, sir."

"Not even in private, Cliff. From now on, it's Toby."

"Yes ... Toby."

"And please try to not be so formal when you speak to me. The children pick up on that as well."

"Yes, sir, I mean Toby, sir, I mean Toby. Sorry, it's going to take some getting used to."

"I understand."

"In regard to what we were talking about, about my responsibilities, I mean, I have a few thoughts."

"Go on."

"I think it's important for children to learn how to do things for themselves, age appropriate things of course, like putting their clothes away, making their beds, wiping up after themselves when they've spilled something, things like that. I also think it's important for them to understand how their meals are made, not just having a plate put down in front of them, ready to eat."

"Go on."

"I think they also need to know where their food comes from and what it looks like before it's put into the packages you buy in the store."

"All of this sounds interesting, but what did you have in mind about the food?"

"I'd like to teach them how to cook, once they're old enough, of course. They can start by washing fruits and vegetables, stirring bowls, pouring ingredients, making sandwiches, nothing on the stove or anything dangerous though. Knives and cutlery would come much later, but they should know that there's work involved in getting food on a plate and what that work is."

"That sounds fine."

"How is your grocery shopping done, sir, I mean, Toby?

"You know, I really don't know, my wife ...

sorry, Cliff." Toby held up his hand while he collected himself.

"It's okay, sir. We don't have to do this now."

"No, it's important. Sydney took care of that. I guess the easiest thing would be to have the groceries delivered."

"Is there a car I could use, Toby?"

"Yes, you could use ... Sydney's."

"That would be great. My car isn't big enough for five children. I'd like to take them grocery shopping as a starter, but I'd really like to take them to a local farm so they can see where their food comes from. I can't tell you how many children don't know what a carrot looks like coming out of the ground, or a head of romaine lettuce on the stalk, or peas in a pod. I think it would not only be good for them to learn about those things, I think it would be fun for them as well. It could be beneficial for them to have something new to focus on."

"Cliff, that's a great idea. Did you know that Jason and Aaron are starting a farm, called Gypsy's Grove, for Nathan's Promise just outside of Craggy Bend? It's going in right next to the rehab center. I'm sure they'd be delighted to have you take the children there, once it's up and running. I know the guy who's going to be running it for them. He has his own small farm right now, but he's going to be moving everything to Gypsy's Grove. If you'd like, I can ask if the children can visit that in the meantime."

"Sure. I'll go check it out first to see his setup, but if you have an in with the owner, I think they'd have a much better experience with it."

"Do whatever you think is best."

"One more thing, Toby."

"Yes?"

"Do the children know how to swim? I'm an

instructor."

"Yes, I saw that on your résumé. The two oldest do. July and May still use water wings."

"If it would be all right with you, once the weather warms up, I'd like to take them to a pool. I'll evaluate their abilities and teach them proper swimming skills."

"Sorry, Cliff. I never showed you the pool room. We have an indoor pool. It's next to the solarium and it connects into there through glass French doors. It's always locked and only opens with a fingerprint scan and then a keyed in passcode. I'll scan you today, if you like."

"That would be great, sir. Sorry, I mean, Toby. Would I be allowed to use it?"

"Of course."

"Thanks. I usually try to get at least a mile or two in, three times a week, sometimes more. I wasn't sure about days off. We never discussed that."

"No we didn't." *And God what you must look like in one of those skimpy, barely there, clinging to the hips lycra bathing suits. Jesus Christ, what's wrong with me?*

"I also do a cardio work out every day for at least an hour, followed-up with weights on the days I don't swim. I have my own set of free-weights that I'd like to bring, that is if there's a place I could set them up."

"I have my own exercise room. It's off the master bedroom, next to the bathroom. You're free to use it any time. Sydney and I ... sorry." Toby paused. *Sydney, I'm sorry. I can't help it, He's just so ... so... God, Sydney, he's a ... he's a ... just look at him, Sydney.*

Toby closed his eyes and remembered Cliff as he stood in the foyer, the afternoon before. Six foot plus if he was an inch; short brown hair, with the ears cut out and parted on the left; clean shaven with short sideburns; a dazzling smile with perfectly aligned white teeth; hazel eyes, with blue highlights; a cream polo shirt with short sleeves that strained against a pair of muscular, tanned and veined arms, thick as logs, thighs even thicker; a chiseled chest that projected outward, stretching the shirt even more and highlighting his nipples; an obvious defined six-pack abdomen to which the shirt miraculously clung, tightly; all ending at a thirty-four inch waist, if that. His khakis were snug at the crotch too, with a bulge that couldn't be concealed.

"It's okay, Toby. Take your time."

"Sorry, Cliff, Sydney and I worked out in the mornings together. There's also two treadmills in there. Once she hit five months in her pregnancy with April, she started to cut back and just did a half mile on the treadmill. By six months she'd stopped all together. She said taking care of the children was enough exercise. Then I stopped."

"If it's okay with you, I'll have a look at it."

"Sure, Cliff, and if you're not comfortable working out in my bedroom, I could have the equipment moved down to the pool room. There's a room off it, designed just for that reason. It's nearly empty, just a few toys and floating chairs are in there right now."

"Well, I do have my own equipment. There's about six-hundred pounds of free weights. I don't think you'd want me throwing that kind of weight around in your bedroom anyway. What kind of floor does the room off the pool have?"

"It's concrete. Like I said it was designed as an exercise room. The sample we looked at had an array of free weights and machines in it so I think it would be fine for your equipment. There's even a rolled-up, thick, heavy-duty, foam kind of liner for the floor. It's still in the packaging. We never had it installed. It's supposed to protect the floor from dropped weights."

"Thanks, Toby. That would work out great for me."

"There's also a small, private shower room just off it."

Cliff smiled, excitedly. "That's even better."

"It's been a good four months since I've hit the treadmill, and I've put on more than a few pounds. Maybe you'll motivate me to get back into it. Maybe we could work out together sometime." *All six foot of you, your muscles rippling, your veins bulging, your hair, no, your fur, plastered to your skin. Sweat dripping from your head, dripping from your chest, down the inside of your thighs, your jock drenched in your musky, salty sweat. God, its smell. I remember that smell ... Jason. Maybe you don't even wear a jock.*

"Toby? Toby?"

"Oh, sorry, sorry, Cliff. Yes?"

"I was saying sure. Sure, Toby, I'd be happy to do that for you. I figured I'd be working out in the evening, to start, after you got home from work. I wouldn't be able to do it while I was taking care of the children. We definitely wouldn't be doing it in the morning, not unless we got up at like 4 AM, which I wouldn't mind at all, if it would help you to get back into shape."

"That's a little early for me, Cliff, let's just play it by ear. We'll see how this whole thing works out. Regardless, I'll be sure to see that you get your workout time."

"Thanks, Toby. There's one more thing, and I'm sorry to bring it up, but I need to know."

Oh, God. What does he need to know? Does he think ... does he know... that I, that Jason and I...?

"Toby, I'm so grateful for this opportunity you're

giving me. This work, helping children, is very important to me."

"Of course, Cliff. Aaron vouched for you and if Jason trusts Aaron then I trust him, too. Jason is a dear friend, maybe my best friend."

"Thanks. I was only getting a day here and a day there or half days when one of the other nannies needed time off."

"I know. Aaron told me."

"The thing is, Toby, in order to make ends meet, I had another job at night. I was a bouncer at a night club. In order to work for you as a live-in nanny, I had to quit that job. I didn't even think twice about it. You offered me a great position doing something I love, working with children."

"I can see that. You're wonderful with my children."

"Toby, I'm sorry, but I have to ask. I need to know how long this position will last. The pay is good, but my brother is in his senior year in college and my sister is in her sophomore year. They're both on scholarships, but there are other expenses that I have to cover. I know this may sound stupid, seeing as I couldn't get anything full-time with the agency, but with them you're guaranteed a six-month contract, once you take a position. I'm sorry, but I need to know how long you'll want to keep me on."

"Cliff, I have a real good feeling about you. You're kind, you're great with the kids, and you're willing to do just about anything."

"I will, Toby. I am. I'll do anything to help you and your family."

"Then there's nothing left to discuss. I want you for as long as you want to stay. How's that sound?"

"That sounds great."

"Now about that contract you mentioned. We agreed on five-hundred a week, right?"

"Yes."

"You're here seven days a week. I just realized that doesn't even come to a hundred a day. I'm going to fix that right now. Let's make it fifteen-hundred a week. It'll be up to you to decide for how long."

"Sir! Sorry, Toby. I can't accept that!"

"Cliff, I'm trusting you with my children, and they're worth a hell of lot more to me than that. I'm getting you at a bargain. Shake."

Toby held out his hand.

Cliff began to shake in his seat.

Toby got up from his desk and walked around behind him. He placed his hands on Cliff's shoulders and patted them. They were rock solid to the touch.

"Toby, I don't know what to say. I've never seen that kind of money."

"You've got sixty-seconds to make up your mind … fifty-nine … fifty-eight … fifty-seven…"

"You're serious, aren't you?"

"Yes, I am … fifty-six … fifty-five."

"Yes! Yes! I accept!" Cliff jumped up and rushed around to lift Toby off the floor in a bear hug. "You have no idea what this will do for my family. Thank you, Toby. Thank you!"

"You're welcome Cliff. Now shake."

Chapter Eleven

Like Whiplash

Thursday, May 13, 2010, 8:02 AM
Cliff's body shook as the phone rang on the other end.

"Jaron Enterprises, Fiona speaking. How may I direct your call?"

"Hello, this is Cliff Turnbull. I'm the nanny for Mr. Jacobson's children, Mr. Toby Jacobson. He's a close friend of Jason Ackerman. Are Jason or Aaron there?"

"Yes, sir, I know Toby. I'll put you right through to the cabin."

"Hey, Cliff, what's up?"

"Aaron?"

"Yeah, Cliff."

"Aaron, it's Toby. He isn't doing well. He hasn't eaten…"

"Hold on, Cliff. I'm putting this on speaker. Jason's right here."

"Hello, Cliff. What's going on? What the hell happened?"

"It's Toby, Jason. He isn't doing well. He hasn't eaten or drank anything, except for a few sips here and there, or gotten out of bed in nearly two days. I've tried, but he just rolls over, away from me. Jason, he peed the bed. I had to change the sheets with him in it and clean him up. Thank God there wasn't much and there was a rubber sheet underneath. I don't know what that was about, but it saved the mattress.

"The children are acting out. They're scared. They want their father. Even April is fussing. She barely takes her bottle now. She's only had two wet diapers since last evening. Toby won't even look at the children when they go in to him."

"Did something happen? Does April have a fever?"

"No. No fever. She just fusses and cries. I can't settle her. She spits the nipple out after a minute every time I give her the bottle."

"And Toby?"

"That's just it, it doesn't make any sense. We sat and talked for almost an hour Monday afternoon after you left. He was very upbeat, very positive. Heck, he even gave me a raise, tripled my salary."

"Yes, but what happened?"

"Again, Jason, I don't know. Tuesday morning, he wasn't acting like himself. He went right back to bed after he sat for breakfast with the children. He only had a few sips of coffee. Since then, he hasn't left his room."

"Shit! Was his urine concentrated?"

"Yes. What is it, Jason?"

"He's dehydrated and last Tuesday was when Sydney was admitted to the hospital. It was the last time he saw her conscious. That's the day she had the cerebral bleed. She died the following day. It's been a week and a day."

"What should I do? I don't have this kind of training. Should I call 911?"

"Is he conscious?"

"Yes, but he just stares."

"Don't call 911 unless his condition changes. Stay with the kids. Where's Aunt Vera?"

"She's with the children. She begged me not to call 911. She said the children would freak out if they saw their father being taken away in an ambulance. That's how they saw their mother leave. I'm sorry, but you were the only person I knew to call."

"Vera's right, Cliff, and you were right to call. We'll be right there, and we're bringing reinforcements."

"Okay, Jason. Thanks."

****

8:08 AM
Jason and Aaron's home

"What is it, Jason?" Aaron asked. "What does it all mean?"

"Toby's in trouble. He's withdrawing from life. He's been without any significant fluid intake for almost two days. If he doesn't turn around, he'll likely die.

"We've got to get down there. If Braden was here, I'd ask him to come along, but he and Shane won't be back from their vacation until next week. I'll start assembling the troops, starting with Miss Charity. You get Royce." Jason disappeared into the kitchen.

Aaron picked up the phone in the living room. "Fiona, please have Royce get Gypsy fired up. We're heading back down to the valley. We're leaving in twenty minutes. Then call Dwayne. Tell him to meet us with the car at our hanger at the airport."

"Right away, Aaron."

"Eugene," he called toward the bedroom, "please pack our bags. Enough for a week."

"I heard what Jason said, Aaron. I've already started."

"And, Eugene, pack one for yourself as well. You're coming with us."

"Yes, Aaron. Right away."

****

Jason walked into the kitchen. The color had drained from his face. "Miss Charity, I need a favor, a big favor."

"What is it, Mr. Jason?" Charity took his hands as she looked into his eyes. "What's wrong?"

"I need your help. It's Toby and his baby, and his kids."

"Oh, that poor man. What's wrong with the baby?"

"She's not taking a bottle, not really, only sporadically since last night. Only two wet diapers since then. She's fussing and spitting the nipple out."

"I'll bet she's missing her mama. That bottle doesn't taste like her and nothing smells like her. That's probably what it is. When I was a wet nurse, I'd have to lay a piece of a mama's clothing over my chest for the first week or so, so the baby would smell her. After that they didn't need it anymore 'cause they got used to me."

"Would you come down with us, please?"

"Of course. I'll go and pack a bag. How long?"

"Better pack for a week."

"I'll be ready."

"Thank you, Miss Charity. Thank you."

"Evelyn!"

"Yes, Mama."

"Evelyn, you're in charge of the kitchen until I get back. Mr. Jason needs me down in the valley. You pack me a cooler of meats and vegetables right away. Make sure I'll have everything I'll need for a pot of chicken soup. I have no idea what their food situation is, and pack a box full of dry goods while you're at it. Now I have to go pack my bag."

****

Jason knocked on the cottage door. "Conrad?" He walked right in.

"Jason, my boy! Jason, what's wrong? Your face."

"Conrad, it's Toby and the baby."

105

"Give me a rundown."

****

Jason walked into the bedroom. "Has everyone been notified, Aaron?"

"Yes. Poor Toby, he's been bounced back and forth so much. First a new baby, then Sydney has a brain bleed, then she dies, then he seems to be coming out of it after hiring Cliff, then he breaks down, then he seems to bounce back, then he withdraws so far from life that he could die."

"Exactly, like whiplash."

****

9:45 AM
417 Spring Meadow Drive

As the limousine came to a stop by the front entrance, Vera ran out the door from the vestibule.

"Thank you, Jason. Thank you all for coming. My Toby, Jason, I think he's given up."

"We're going to do everything we can to pull him through this, Vera." He leaned down and gave her a hug and a kiss on the cheek.

"Thank you. Thank you all for coming." Vera took in the group. A tall, heavyset African-American woman with kind eyes between fifty and fifty-five, a stocky white man with a neatly trimmed mustache around fifty, and a tall, young, energetic African-American man, in his mid-twenties if that.

"Hello, Vera." Aaron stooped down to hug her.

Jason turned around. "Vera, this is Dr. Conrad Tolbert, he's the medical director for Nathan's Promise. Miss Charity Hopewell is our Chief of Household Operations and cook, and this is Eugene Hopewell, her son. Eugene is Aaron's and my personal assistant. They're all here to help."

"Thank you, all of you." Vera vigorously shook

their hands.

Conrad stooped down and picked up his medical bag from the pile Dwayne was unloading from the limo's trunk. "So where is the lad? Take me right to him."

"Right this way, doctor." Vera waved her arm toward the front door.

"Thank you. Madam, as soon as we get inside, give the baby to Miss Charity. She knows what to do. Aaron, if you will, grab my other medical bag. Now let's all get moving."

Charity waved her hand behind her as she hurried toward the front door. "Eugene, bring the cooler and the box of staples, and don't forget Mr. Jason's large stock pot. Find the kitchen and set everything out wherever you can find space. I'll start cooking just as soon as I take care of the little one."

"Yes, Mama."

****

Toby's bedroom

"Yes, he's definitely dehydrated, Jason. Look at his skin turgor. It sucks. He's tenting for nearly seven seconds. Let's give him two liters of saline. Get it into him as fast as you can, but draw a set of rainbow tubes for analysis first. Call Miss Jones. See if she'll take care of getting the blood analyzed for us, A-SAP."

"Yes, Conrad. Aaron, would you make the call?"

"Doing it right now, Jason."

"Thanks. We can have Dwayne run it over to the hospital as soon as I draw it."

"While you're doing that," Conrad said, "I'm going to do a finger stick. I want to see what his blood sugar is. I'm sure it's rock bottom. Madam?"

Vera stepped forward. "Yes, doctor?"

"Brew him a good quart of bouillon. I don't care what kind. He'll be ready for it in about two hours."

"Yes, doctor, right away." Vera disappeared out the door.

"Jason, what can I do?"

"Just stand by, Cliff, in case we need something. Once we get him stabilized, I think he's going to want a shower. Aaron can help me with that."

Cliff nodded. "Sure, Jason, sure, I'll get everything ready, but I can take care of that."

"No, Cliff, you take care of the children. See if you can find a plastic chair we can sit him in while he's in there."

"Right away."

Conrad looked up from the glucometer. "Yup, I was right, his blood sugar is thirty-two. As soon as you have those fluids running, push an amp of D-50, slowly. I'll recheck him after a few minutes. If need be, we'll add another one to his first bag."

****

"Miss Charity?"

"Yes, Miss Vera?"

"The doctor wants bouillon, I'll need to get to the stove."

"You can have it from the stock I'm making for the chicken soup I've started. How much did doctor say?"

"A quart."

"Consider it done. I'll use salt substitute in it. It's regular salt but with potassium too. Dr. Tolbert taught me that. Good for all kinds of dehydration.

"That stock smells wonderful."

"It's Mr. Jason's recipe. Best I've ever come across, better than my own even. When did doctor say?"

"Two hours."

"I'll have it ready. Now why don't you have a sit down? There's a fresh pot of tea on the table, and I found some cake in the refrigerator. It's all cut up now. I'll get you a slice."

"Thank you, Miss Charity."

"Where are the children, Miss Vera?"

"I've told August to keep them playing in his room."

"Have they had their baths?"

"I don't think so. Cliff and I have just been trying to keep everything together, I don't remember."

"That's all right. Once you've caught your breath, why don't you go check on them? See what they need. I'll have their lunch ready, lickety-split.

While Charity was serving Vera, Cliff came rushing through the kitchen as he headed for the solarium.

"Young man!" Charity's voice stopped him in his tracks. "You're the nanny, right?"

"Yes, I'm Cliff."

"I'm Miss Charity," she said as she returned to the stove. "Soon as you're done doin' what you're doin' why don't you come in here and make the children some sandwiches. In fact, make a whole heaping pile of sandwiches. People are gonna need to eat, and there isn't going to be any kind of schedule around here for at least a day. Folks can grab a bowl of soup and a sandwich as they come and go."

"Jason said Toby's going to need to spend some time in the shower once he's gotten the fluids into him, and I'm supposed to find a plastic chair to sit him in."

"You're the nanny. You're to take care of the children. Leave Mr. Toby to the doctor and Mr. Jason and Mr. Aaron. They'll manage him just fine. Anyway, he's not going to be ready for that for quite a bit yet. The children need to eat first, but go on, get the chair. Then come right back here."

"Yes, ma'am."

"Once you've finished with the sandwiches, come and sit with me for a spell." Charity rocked the combination car seat/baby carriage that was tied to her hip through the apron string while she stirred the pot. I'll teach you how to get this baby to nurse. She's sleeping, now that her tummy's full, bless her little heart."

"You mean ... she's taking a bottle?"

"Sure thing, already finished one."

"How'd you do it?"

"Come sit with me, and I'll show you how."

"Yes, ma'am. I'll be right back."

"Good boy." Charity smiled as he disappeared around the corner. "Young people today." She looked over her shoulder at Vera. "Don't know what they don't know."

Vera smiled to herself and let out a sigh. *Everything's going to be all right now. Jason's brought reinforcements, and they know what they're doing.*

****

Vera sat quietly and watched while Charity spoke to Cliff.

"Now this little angel has been missing her Mama." Charity rocked the carriage again with her hip. "She knows her smell and nothing smells like her anymore, especially you. You're going to have to get her accustomed to your smell if you want her to thrive. The best way to do that is to use something that smells like Mama whenever you hold her. Before you know it, she'll take to you just as well."

"So how did you do it?" Cliff asked.

"I went into the front closet and found a lady's scarf. I put it against me and then settled her down into it. She took to here bottle right off."

"That makes sense then. I started using one of the

receiving blankets that was in the nursery. It probably smelled like Mrs. Jacobson."

"Exactly, but I bet you had to go and wash it, probably a few more too."

"Yes, I did, and when I washed it" —Cliff's eyes became wide— "I washed away her smell."

"That's exactly what happened." Charity draped a receiving blanket and then a knitted scarf she had just taken from the coat closet over Cliff's chest and left shoulder. Then she lifted April and placed her in his arms. "Now, you try. This is a new scarf that doesn't smell like her mama *and* me, together."

Immediately, April began to nurse.

Charity smiled. "See that? She ate just over an hour ago, and she's hungry again. Even though she's way behind, let's not give her more than a third of a bottle for now, just to be safe. We don't want her spitting up. Eventually we'll get her caught up."

Cliff's body shook with excitement. "You're a genius, Miss Charity, a genius."

"Not so much a genius as having learned from my own Mama. She was a wet nurse, too. Now, another thing, that breast milk is going to run out before too long. You're going to have to start introducing formula along with it before what the missus put aside is used up. Otherwise you're gonna have a whole 'nother hurdle to jump."

Vera remembered Sydney's words. *"Thanks, Aunt Vera. I've been pumping up a storm. I think there's more than a months' worth in the freezer right now."*

"How should I do that?"

"Start to add a little formula into Mama's milk. Every day add a little more and cut back on the breast milk until she's on all formula by the time the breast milk is gone."

With tears in her eyes, Vera spoke up. "Yes, there's about two and a half more weeks left."

"That's about what I figured," Charity said.

"You're a genius, Miss Charity. I know, I know, you say you're not, but you are. You really are. Thanks so much."

"My pleasure, Mr. Cliff, now I have to get back to getting lunch ready."

"Thank God for these people," Vera thought as she wiped her eyes dry. *"Thank God."*

Chapter Twelve

Chicken Soup

11:15 AM

"His skin turgor is improving," Conrad said, "but he's nowhere near out of the woods yet. He still has five-hundred to go from bag number two. I'll decide whether he needs a third liter once I have those blood results back. It would be better for him in the long run if he can replace everything orally, but he might be hypokalemic. If he is, I'll add some potassium to another bag. His chemistry will tell me for sure."

"Jason?" All three men turned their heads.

Jason hurried to the bedside. "Hey, Toby, welcome back."

"Dr. Tolbert?"

"Yes, Toby."

"What are you both doing here?"

"Cliff called me, Toby. You've been out of it for two days."

"What?"

"Yes, my boy," Conrad said. "You're quite dehydrated right now and your blood sugar was hovering at the unconscious level. We've given you about three pints and some sugar, but I'm certain you're going to need more of both."

"I feel like shit. Where are my children?"

"Vera, Cliff, and Miss Charity have everything under control," Aaron said.

"Aaron, you're here too? Shit, Jason, you brought the cavalry with you."

"I had to, Toby."

"I need to see them. I need to see my kids." Toby

sat up. "Whoa, my head's spinning." He started to fall back.

Jason caught him. "You need to stay lying down, Toby. You're not strong enough yet. You haven't eaten in more than two days and you're dehydrated, so you're going to be very weak for a while yet. Don't expect to try to get out of bed for…"

"For a few hours," Conrad interjected, "if that."

"No, I have to see my children. Fix me up now so I can go to them."

"Toby," Conrad said sternly, "I've a good mind to put you in the hospital. That's where you really ought to be. If you don't listen to us, that's where you're going to wind up."

"They're right, Toby," Aaron added. "Better listen to them."

"How bad am I?"

Conrad patted his shoulder. "You're better, Toby, but you were hanging over the edge when we got here."

"Please let them help you," Aaron said. "Your children just lost their mother. They can't lose their father too."

Toby looked between the three men, then he began to cry, and they let him, but there were few tears. He was still terribly dehydrated.

****

The kitchen

"I've finished unpacking everyone's bags, Mama. What do you need me to do?"

"Good boy, Eugene.

"Mr. Cliff, meet my son, Eugene."

"Nice to meet you. Your mother is quite a cook, and it's Cliff, both of you. Please just call me Cliff."

"Pleasure. Yes, she is."

"Eugene, you can start by peeling me half a

dozen carrots and eight large potatoes. Then cut them up with two stalks of celery into bite sized pieces and cut up that pound of fresh green beans for the soup the same. I've just taken both chickens out and split them to cool. I'll break them up in a few minutes and then bone them. When you've finished, add the carrots and potatoes to the stock.

"I've already taken out and seasoned and salted what I need for Mr. Toby, but I'll still need to season the pot. By the time the carrots and potatoes are cooked enough, I should be finished dicing up the chicken. Once I've added it back to the pot I'll season it. Then we'll bring it back to a simmer. Lastly, I'll add the green beans and bag of fine egg noodles Evelyn packed."

"Sure thing, Mama."

"When you've finish with those vegetables, set the table for the children."

"I'll get started right away, Mama.

"Cliff, have the children had their baths yet? Miss Vera didn't know."

"They could probably use it, Miss, Charity," Cliff said. "They didn't get them last night. There was too much going on with Toby and trying to get little April to take a bottle. I'll go take care of that right now. The sandwiches are done."

"Good. You did a nice job with that platter, Cliff, but we're going to need a heap more. And while you're at it, cut them into quarters on the bias. When people are stressed, they eat better if you offer them finger sandwiches and triangles are more attractive. A whole sandwich can look overwhelming, but a finger sandwich is just a couple bites. No one thinks twice about taking one or three. Before you know it, they've eaten an entire sandwich or more."

"There isn't any more lunchmeat, Miss Charity."

"Then we'll boil a dozen eggs and open a couple cans of tuna. Who doesn't like egg or tuna salad sandwiches? When the children come in, show them what you made and let them choose."

"I did make some peanut butter and jelly too."

"That was a good idea. If they can't make up their minds, cut the quarters in half again and give them an assortment. Let them eat what they want. Once they're settled, we can make a tray to take upstairs. You can make more sandwiches after you're finished with the children's baths."

"I'll take care of the baths," Vera said. "Cliff, you stay and help miss Charity."

"Thank you, Miss Vera. Lunch will be ready by then."

"It smells like home, Miss Charity," Vera said.

"I just add the ingredients. The soup takes care of itself."

Vera's breath caught as she stifled a sob.

"It'll be okay, Miss Vera. Don't you worry now."

"Thank you. Thank you for coming. I think it will now, I really do. I'll head right up there now, Miss Charity. I'll bring the children down about noon."

"That will be perfect, Miss Vera."

"I made a grocery list on Monday," Cliff said, holding it up, "but I'm adding more lunchmeat and cheese to it right now. I wasn't counting on the extra people. Do you know how long everyone plans on staying?"

"Mr. Jason said to plan for a week, so you better count on at least that."

"Do you really think it will take that long for Toby to recover?"

"I have no idea, Cliff, but there's more to coming back from what's ailing Mr. Toby than physical. If Mr.

Jason said a week, whatever's involved, it'll likely take a week."

"I understand. I was going to go to the supermarket on Tuesday, but that's when things started to go downhill. I'll go pick some stuff up, but before I do, what will you need?"

"Give me your list and I'll add to it, but the family and I need you here."

"Okay, I'll have the groceries delivered."

"I'll send Eugene to do the marketing. I don't trust just anyone to make decisions about the food I'll be serving. With Eugene taking care of it, I can be sure about what we'll prepare. I hear you make a mean coleslaw. I'd like to see how you do it."

"You mean you want to cook with me?"

"Most definitely! I always like to work with another cook."

"I'm afraid I'll disappoint you. I've taken some courses, but I've only prepared simple meals for the family so far. I'm better than I was when I was taking care of my brother and sister, but there's no way I'll ever hold a candle to you."

"Nonsense, you never know what you'll pick up from someone else's ways. I started out self-taught. Then I was fortunate enough to apprentice under a restaurant chef, but that was years ago. You've learned some new ways, so I'm looking forward to picking up a few of your tricks."

"That would be great, Miss Charity. Thanks."

****

12:15 PM

"Some soup and sandwiches for you all," Charity said as she set the tray down on the dresser, "and a thermos of chicken bouillon for Mr. Toby. There's a mug and straw here too."

"And here's some tray tables," Eugene said as he walked in behind her. "Miss Vera knew where they were."

"Great, Miss Charity. Thanks, Eugene."

"You're welcome, Mr. Aaron. How's the poor man doing?"

"He's given us all a scare, Eugene, that's for sure."

"He still looks peaked," Charity said.

"I think he's coming around, Miss Charity," Jason said, "but Conrad had to give him a mild sedative a little while ago. It didn't take much though. He's very weak. He's out cold right now. I just hope he stays down until he's stronger."

"I know you and the doctor will take good care of him, Mr. Jason. We'll go now, but you let me know if you need anything."

"Sure thing, Miss Charity. We're just waiting to hear back from the hospital about his blood work."

"I heard Dr. Tolbert inquire about that on the phone to Miss Jones on my way up. Oh, and I added potassium salt to the bouillon."

"You're a quick study, Miss Charity."

"I only have to be told something once, Mr. Jason, just once."

****

2:00 PM

Cliff knocked gently on the door and then walked in. He found Aaron sitting next to the bed and Jason asleep in a recliner in the corner. "The children are napping. They almost passed out after lunch. Vera's napping too. She was wiped out. How's Toby doing?"

"He's sleeping. Conrad sedated him about two hours ago after he tried to get up. He broke down when I reminded him that his children just lost their mother and they couldn't lose their father as well."

"How is he going to cope, Aaron? How does someone come back from something like that?"

"I don't know, Cliff. I really don't know."

"Can I do anything? Do you guys need anything?"

"No, we're fine," Jason answered.

"Oh, Jason, sorry, I didn't mean to wake you."

"You didn't. I was just resting my eyes. I'm hoping to get him in the shower later on, once he's stronger. Hopefully, he'll come around in a little while."

"Cliff? Is that you?" They all turned their heads toward the bed.

"Yes, sir."

Jason sat up. "Well look who's awake."

"Jason, what the hell did you give me?"

"Conrad gave you a touch of lorazepam, Toby. He felt you needed it."

"I'm sorry about that, guys. I'm sorry I broke down in front of you … again."

"Don't be silly. You've been through so much. Give yourself a break."

"I'm trying, Aaron. I really am trying. Can you guys give me a moment with Cliff? Alone?"

"Sure, Toby. Let us know when you're finished, Cliff."

"I will, Jason."

****

2:10 PM

When Jason and Aaron entered the kitchen, they found Conrad at the table talking with Charity and Eugene.

"Well, if you two are down here, he must be awake. Who's with him?" Conrad said.

"He wanted a few moments with Cliff."

Charity smiled. "He's a good one, that boy. He may be green and young, but that Cliff's a good one."

Aaron smiled. "That he is, Miss Charity."

"Coffee's fresh," she said. "Can I pour you both a cup?"

"Yes, I'm bushed, and a piece of that cake, if there's any left."

"Coming right up, Mr. Jason."

"Me too. I definitely need coffee."

"Well, take a seat, Mr. Aaron. You both have had a hard day, and it's only half over."

Chapter Thirteen

Coming out of the Dark

2:10 PM

"Come here, Cliff." Toby patted the bed. "Sit down next to me."

After Cliff sat, Toby took his hand like two arm wrestlers would grasp their palms. His hand seemed to disappear within Cliff's, but he held on.

Cliff's grip was firm, but not overwhelming, as if he knew he had to be gentle with smaller folks. "I wanted to thank you, Cliff, for what you did for me."

"I didn't know what else to do, Toby. I had to call them."

"That's not what I mean, Cliff. Thank you for cleaning me up. I'm sorry you had to do that. I'm so embarrassed. I'm so ashamed of myself."

"You shouldn't be. And anyway, it had to be done, but of course, I was worried. Aunt Vera was worried. I couldn't let her do it. We didn't know what to do for you, and she was afraid that if we called 911 the children would think…"

"Would think I was dying. Right?"

"Yes, sorry."

"No, I'm sorry. It's like I was in a fog, Cliff. It was a very dark place. I could hear you and Aunt Vera and the children, but I couldn't get to you. It's like there was a weight on me, holding me down."

"That's sort of what happened to me, after my mother died. I had a real low spell, but we were alone. I had to take care of my brother and sister, Marshall and Whitney. I cried every night after they went to bed, but I had to push through it. There wasn't anyone else to help."

"Then you're a stronger man than I am."

"It's not a contest, Toby. We each suffer loss in our own way."

"What I wanted to say to you" —Toby rocked their hands back and forth— "is that I'm not going to hold you to our agreement. You don't have to stay. You didn't sign up for any of this. I'll give you a good severance, and I'll write you a glowing reference. Then you can be on your way and start fresh with another family."

"If you'll allow me to say this, Toby…"

"Yes… Please."

"No sir, I'm not planning on going anywhere. I care about *all* off you, not just the children. You've got a great family, Aunt Vera included, and you've given me a rare opportunity to make a difference. Because of your generosity, you've taken a tremendous weight off my shoulders.

"I now know that I can get my brother and sister through college, and please believe me when I say that this not about the money, not at all. Yes, you're paying me an exorbitant salary, and that's going to make a substantial difference, but I'd be just as happy to go back to our original agreement. What I'm grateful for is that you were willing to stand up for me, because of what you thought I was, or maybe that wasn't even it at all. Maybe it's that you don't like to see people discriminated against, but whatever the reason, you did stand up for me, and you don't even know me, not really. I can never repay that kind of kindness, sir. I will forever be in your debt. No, I'm not going anywhere, not unless you tell me to leave."

Toby began to cry, softly. He kissed the back of Cliff's hand. Eventually, he was able to speak. "Thank you, Cliff. Thank you. I can't tell you how much it means to me to hear you say that."

Oh, my God. What was that? What's he saying? What did he just do? Cliff's mind raced. He searched his memory. *Grief. What did the books say about grief? Suffering loss creates grief and the degree of grief associated with the loss of a child, parent, or spouse is heightened exponentially.*

Grief makes people vulnerable and hypersensitive. Their minds can become stuck in a loop of grief/loss/grief. Their thoughts can be fragmented. Their grip on reality can be sporadic.

They can suddenly begin to weep. They can become overjoyed by the simplest things. They can become extremely grateful for the most basic of courtesies, and their emotions can be supercharged. That's what this is, nothing more.

Cliff smiled and patted Toby's hand. "It's okay, Toby."

"I have to be honest with you, Cliff. It was because of Aaron that I became involved. Aaron shared your story with me. He vouched for you and of course I believed him because he's Jason's partner, and Jason has been my friend for a very long time.

"We were extremely close once, but that was a long time ago. We've both grown up, but I still carry those memories and the lessons I learned from him with me to this day. I'm so grateful that he's come back into my life."

"Whatever the reason, Toby, I'm still grateful, and I always will be."

"So then you'll really stay?"

"Yes, I'm staying."

"That makes me very happy. Thank you."

"I'll leave you to rest now. Do you need

anything?"

"To tell you the truth, I'm starving, and I want to get out of this bed."

"Not…"

"I know, I promised I won't get up without Dr. Tolbert's blessing, but I really need to take a shower, and I remember hearing someone say something about bouillon. I'd love some if you can rustle it up for me."

"Miss Charity put the bouillon in a thermos." Cliff looked around. "There it is."

Cliff returned with a mug and the straw. "Here you go. It should be just hot enough."

"Thank you. I won't need the straw." Toby took a sip. "Oh, God, it's like ambrosia on my tongue."

It's like ambrosia on my tongue. Did he just say that? Cliff's loins stirred. *I've got to get out of here.* "I'll go let know the doctor know that you want to get up."

****

2:35 PM

As Cliff approached the kitchen, he could hear several voices in conversation. He tried to adjust the bulge that wouldn't stop forming in his pants.

"I just gave him a mug of bouillon," he said as he walked in. "He loved it. He said it was like ambrosia on his tongue, Miss Charity."

"Well, now isn't that just the sweetest compliment."

"He also said he wants to get out of bed, that he's hungry, and he wants to take a shower."

"I guess that's our cue," Jason said.

Conrad pushed his chair away from the table. "I'll check him over first, but he's not getting up unless he passes orthostatics first, and he better eat before he even tries that. He's got no calories left in his liver, his glycogen levels have got to have bottomed out by now."

"What does that mean, doctor?" Eugene asked. "Glycogen and orthostatics?"

"Orthostatic or postural hypotension occurs when a person is volume depleted, like with dehydration or blood loss. When that happens, they can pass out if they stand up. I want to be sure we've replaced enough of his fluids so that doesn't happen. If his blood pressure drops more than twenty points from lying to sitting, or sitting to standing, he's still in danger.

"Glycogen is the sugar compound that's manufactured by the liver and stored there. It's the primary source of calories for the body but our cells can also use any sugar that's absorbed from food in the gut, as soon as it finds its way into the bloodstream. The critical thing is that glycogen keeps us alive while we sleep. If the liver didn't perform that function, we'd have to eat all the time. Without the liver making it, we'd have no source of energy reserves, and we would die after we fell asleep.

"He needs to eat to build that level back up, and he needs to start taking fluids by mouth. The sooner the better. Let's go up and give him the once over, boys. We'll check his orthostatics. If he passes muster, we'll feed him something and then get him up. If he fails, we'll recheck him after he eats. If he passes then, you can help him to the shower, but he's not getting out of that bed until he passes. Sound good?"

"Fine with us," Jason said.

"Let me know if you need any help, Jason."

"Will do, Cliff."

Charity stood up from the table. "Cliff and I will make him a tray and then one of us will bring it up."

"If you like, Miss Charity, I'll wait and carry it up. Jason and Conrad can head up first."

That would be fine, Mr. Aaron. Then Cliff and I

have a date with little Miss April. She has a bottle waiting."

****

2:47 PM

Conrad sat on the edge of be bed while he felt Toby's pulse and looked at the color of his conjunctiva as he pulled down his lower left eyelid.

"You had a close call, Toby. Your blood work showed you were significantly dehydrated. Your electrolytes were completely out of whack. I had to add 20 milliequivalents of potassium to your third IV. Your kidney function was down, and your liver enzymes were a little elevated, probably because you remained in one position for an extended period of time. That can cause muscle tissue to start breaking down, which is what those levels suggested. The only good thing was that your blood sugar had come up to low normal, the last time I checked it. How do you feel?"

"Better. Not normal, but better, and I'm starving. I'd love another mug of bouillon."

"Coming right up," Jason said as he reached for the thermos.

"Oh, sorry, Jason, I've emptied it."

"Well, that's good," Conrad said. "Hunger is a good sign. Aaron will be up in a minute or two with a tray that Miss Charity and Cliff are preparing for you."

"Thank you both for what you've done. You probably saved my life."

"Normally, I'd poo poo what you said," Jason answered, "but in this case, you're right."

"Do you feel lightheaded at all?"

"No, doctor."

"Then let's let Jason check your blood pressure. Then we'll sit you up and check it again. You need to tell us if you feel dizzy or weak when you sit up, okay?"

"Yes, doctor. I will."

After Jason checked Toby's blood pressure and pulse, lying down and sitting up, he reported his findings. "His blood pressure was 110/60 supine, pulse 88. Sitting, he dropped to 92/50 and his pulse went up to 110."

"You're not ready to get up yet, Toby. I'm afraid you're right on the edge of orthostatic hypotension. You're still dehydrated."

"Okay, I won't push it, but I really want to take a shower. I need it and I want to see my kids tonight. They need to know I'm okay. I can't have them seeing and smelling me like this. Please, is there any way we can make that happen?"

"Jason, hang another liter of saline. That will make four. Hopefully between that and him eating and drinking more, we can get him stable enough for a quick trip to the shower."

"Right away, Conrad."

"Now, Toby, you're not to stand in the shower other than to get into the chair and out of it. The combination of the hot water and your unstable condition could make you pass out. Do you understand me?"

"Yes. Absolutely."

"Jason, I want at least one of you in there with him at all times, and I mean in the shower, not outside the door. Don't turn your back on him, not for one second."

"I was planning on that anyway. Aaron and I already discussed it."

"Good. Now, Toby, you're to tell them if you start feeling strange in even the smallest way. Understand?"

"Yes, doctor, thank you so much."

"Knock, knock," Aaron said as he opened the door. "I've got a tray with your name on it, Toby."

"Great! I'm starved. Wow! Daffodils and Tulips! That was so sweet of Miss Charity."

"They were Cliff's idea. He said an attractive presentation increases the appetite."

"I want you to take this pill sometime after your shower, Toby, not before."

"What is it, doctor?"

"It's a half milligram of lorazepam. It'll help you sleep."

"Whatever you say, doctor."

Chapter Fourteen

Unsteady

3:45 PM

"Now you just sit here, Toby. I'll get your hair washed while Aaron scrubs you down."

"Thanks, Jason. It seems like all I say to you guys anymore is thank you."

"What are friends for anyway?"

"Not this, Aaron, that's for sure."

"We're happy to help, Toby."

"Thanks, Jason. Thank you, both of you. See there I go again."

Aaron began to lather up Toby's chest. "Then just stop saying it. We know. You'd do the same thing for us."

"I doubt it. I wouldn't know how to do most of the things you guys have done for me and my family."

"That might be," Jason said, "but you'd help. I know that for a fact."

Toby leaned back for Aaron. "You know something, guys."

Aaron used the hand sprayer to rinse off his chest. "What's that?"

"This is twice in a week that I've had an intimate shower with other naked men. You might just turn me back, Jason, if you keep it up."

Other than the sound of the shower spray, the bathroom fell silent.

"Uh oh! Oops, Jason, I'm sorry."

"It's okay, Toby." Jason patted his shoulder. "Aaron knows about our past. I just didn't think it would ever come it up in front of him."

"I must be more out of it than I thought, but I'm feeling so relaxed, so open, like I don't have a care in the world."

Jason used the handheld shower head to rinse Toby's hair. "It could be from the lorazepam I gave you in your IV. It can last for a while. Between that and the hot water, I'm not surprised."

"Tranquilizer or not," Aaron said, "it's true that Jason told me—not everything, I'm sure—but he told me about that summer and anyway, worse things could happen. And by the way, we're not naked. We've got our swim trunks on."

"Well I can dream, can't I? I'll just have to hold on to my memories from the other night to carry me through." Toby giggled. "Sorry, guys. I can't help it." He snorted. Then he started to laugh. Then Jason and Aaron laughed.

When the laughter died down, Toby closed his eyes and focused on the hands that caressed his body. "Feels good, guys. I'm just going to zone out for a little while. And no, I'm not feeling weak or dizzy. Just relaxed is all."

"But you'll tell us if you feel that way, right?"

"Yes, Jason, I'm not going to jeopardize anything. Oh, one more thing..." Toby opened his eyes. "If you see me getting aroused, it's your fault." He giggled again. Then his eyes closed.

Aaron smiled. "Sweet dreams."

Toby started to drift, and feel. He felt every caress of their hands across his back, his arms, and his legs. He felt the slickness of the bar of soap and the warmth of the water, and he felt his muscles as they relaxed under the streams of warm water that flowed down his chest and between his legs.

They lifted him up and helped him to stand. One

held him in front while the other ran a soapy washcloth across his pelvic bone. He felt his balls lift up, and his dick begin to tingle when the cloth was pulled over and around it in circles. Then fingers grabbed the head of his dick through the cloth and squeezed and pulled at the shaft. He could hear the squishing of the soap as it was worked into a thick lather through his pubic hair and into his groin. The more the cloth passed over his skin, the more intense the sensations grew.

Then he felt the washcloth move around to his butt cheeks and between them. He felt fingers on the other side of the cloth as it was worked around his hole. He opened his mouth and sucked in a breath, about to moan, but his legs buckled when his asshole puckered as the touch probed and wiggled against the outer sphincter.

They caught him as he dropped and then lifted him back up, but the jostling only silenced him. It did nothing to stem the memories that that touching represented. Memories, long buried, reawakened and came flooding back in.

****

Toby dropped his head and licked his lips. *Jason, the way you touch me down there.* Then his vision of Jason began to blur.

Cliff sent me flowers.
Cliff, you're so strong.
Hold me, Cliff. Hold me and never let me go.
"Cliff."

When Toby opened his eyes, his arms were around Aaron's neck. He let go and backed away. He opened his mouth to speak. "It's okay, Toby," Aaron said. "It's all good."

"Aaron, I'm sorry. I was dreaming."

"No harm done, buddy."

****

4:30 PM

While Jason and Aaron returned Toby from the shower, Cliff had his back to them. He was just finishing changing his bedsheets.

Toby looked out the window. "Sun's already low in the sky. Where's the day gone?"

Jason patted his shoulder. "You've slept a lot today."

Cliff looked behind him as he ran his hand over the top sheet to straighten it. "All clean and ready for you, Toby."

"Thanks, Cliff." He thought to himself as he turned towards the bed, *Cliff, I'm sorry for having those thoughts.* Toby averted his eyes. "You didn't have to do that."

"Why not?" Cliff turned around to face them. "Didn't we just have this conversation?"

"Yes, sorry, but I still think this is all a lot more than you signed on for. I'm sorry."

"I'm happy to do it."

After they lowered Toby to the bed, Jason handed him the lorazepam pill and a glass of water. "Remember, Conrad wanted you to take this after your shower."

"Thanks, Jason, I will, but I want to wait until after I see my kids."

"The last I checked on them, they were still asleep," Cliff said. "I'll go see if they're up. If they're still sleeping, do you want me to wake them?"

"Normally I'd say no." Toby briefly glanced at Cliff, then dropped his eyes. "But right now, I think it's important for them to know I'm okay."

"I'll be back with them in a few minutes."

****

4:50 PM

Cliff opened the door to the master bedroom. "Daddy!"

"Daddy, I missed you!"

May squealed. "Da … Da … Daddy, Daddy!"

"Hey, July. Hello, Munchkin," Toby said as they ran to him. "There's my little May." The three children climbed onto the bed and laid against and on top of their father.

August hung back at the door, his eyes brimming with tears. "It's okay, August. I'm okay, my little man."

Cliff reached for August, but Toby waved him away. "Come here, little man. Daddy needs a hug."

"Daddy!" August ran to the bed and leapt onto it. As he landed, he scurried into Toby's arms and began to sob. "Daddy," he said again and again, "Daddy, my Daddy."

May, June, and July began to cry too.

"I'm okay, little man, I'm here now. Oh, my babies, Daddy's here now." Toby wrapped his arms around his children.

"What …" August choked. "Daddy…"

After the crying stopped and August's sobbing turned to whimpers and then to sniffles, he spoke. "Daddy, what did I do?"

"You didn't do anything, August. What do you mean?"

"You wouldn't talk to me, Daddy. You wouldn't look at me? What did I do?"

"Oh, August, my August, you didn't do anything wrong. Daddy was sick, but I'm better now."

"Daddy, I was afraid."

"I know, August. I was afraid too, but I'm better now."

"Daddy, I was afraid you were going to be with Mommy."

"I miss Mommy," June whimpered.

"I miss Mommy," July mumbled with his thumb in his mouth.

"Mommy. Mommy." May began to cry again.

"No, August. I'm not going anywhere. All of you, listen to me. I'm never going away. I'm never going anywhere. I missed Mommy too. I missed her so much I got sick from missing her, but I'm here now."

"You promise, Daddy?"

"Yes, June, I promise."

The five of them clung to each other while Cliff, Aaron, and Jason stood silently by.

****

After Cliff and Aaron took the children down to the kitchen for dinner, Jason gave Toby the lorazepam. As he lay back in the bed and closed his eyes, Jason sat down in the chair next to it.

"I miss her so much, Jason."

"I know, Toby, I know."

"Jason, you're my friend. I think I can trust you with anything.'

"Yes, Toby, you can trust me."

"Jason, can I ask you something, but you have to promise not to repeat it?"

"You can ask me anything. I give you my word I won't repeat it."

"I miss my wife, Jason. I miss Sydney more than I can say, but something's happening to me, Jason, and I don't know why."

"What's that, Toby?"

"Jason, do you think I'm really gay?"

"I don't know, Toby."

"Jason, you're my friend, and I love you, though not like I used to love you, back during that summer. I really did love you, Jason. You know?"

"I know, Toby. I loved you too."

"After I met Sydney, I fell head over heels in love with her. The feelings I had for you just faded away, but after a few years, I remembered the sex we had, and I realized I missed that, the sex I mean. I couldn't have that with Sydney. One night I just unloaded. I told her everything about us, what we had."

"Yes, she told me, in the ER."

"Oh, that's right. Jason, that beautiful woman, that beautiful soul, my Sydney, she was happy for me. She was happy I had found you and loved you. She said she understood, even gave me permission to go out to have sex with men when I needed it, but I refused. So do you know what she did?"

"No, Toby."

"Jason, she took care of me like that. She'd put on this harness and took care of me like that. Jason, it wasn't the same, but still, it was incredible."

"Then you're a very lucky man, Toby."

"Jason, what do I do? I know this sounds crazy, that I can even talk about this now, after I've just lost her, but those memories of us keep coming back, flooding back."

"Toby, you're my friend and yes, I love you, but no, I could never…"

"No, Jason, that's not what I meant. I'm sorry if you thought…"

"It's okay, Toby."

"After I start to remember about us, all of a sudden the memory changes. There's someone else there with me."

Jason remained silent. After a moment, Toby continued.

"Jason… Oh, God, I can't."

"Toby, whatever it is, you don't have to tell me. I

can see that this is difficult for you."

"Jason, it's so wrong."

"Toby, you're a good man. I don't believe doing wrong is in you. Why don't we let this drop for the time being?"

"No, I have to tell someone. I have to know I'm not going crazy."

"Toby, I've given you my word. You can tell me anything."

"Jason." There were tears in Toby's eyes. "Jason, in my dreams, it's Cliff. Cliff becomes you."

"I know, Toby."

"What do you mean?"

"You called out his name in the shower. You put your arms around Aaron and called Cliff's name."

"Oh, my God! I did? I called Aaron Cliff—when I had my arms around his neck?"

"Yes."

"Am I a freak, Jason? Am I sick?"

"No, Toby, you're not a freak."

"Then what's wrong with me. How can I go from loving a man to falling in love with a woman, marrying her, making a life and a family with her, and then suddenly start thinking about a man again?"

"That's above my pay grade."

"Jason, when he told me his story, about his mother and how he had to raise his brother and sister, I felt so sorry for him. Jason, he's so kind. He's so good with the children. He's been so kind to me. Before I knew it, I started having these confusing feelings for him and the next thing I knew, I was lusting after the man, and it is lust, Jason. Oh, God, the things I've dreamed."

Jason took Toby's hands. "Toby, there's nothing wrong with you. You're a good person. I think you look at people and see them, not what is or isn't between their legs. I knew a few soldiers, men, when I was in the army. They had had relationships with both men and women. I also knew a couple nurses, women, when I worked in the ER They did the same."

"Then I'm not crazy?"

"No, Toby, you're not crazy. Does Cliff know, how you feel about him, I mean?"

"No! No way! I haven't said a thing. I've been afraid to. I don't even know if it's real. I'm just so damned confused, but he's so damned handsome, Jason. Have you seen him?"

Jason chuckled. "Yes, Toby, I've seen him, and I have to agree, he is quite a specimen, but he's more than that, and you know it."

"I know, Jason, I know, and I need him to take care of the children. I can't take the chance of scaring him off. Besides, for all I know, this isn't real. Maybe it's just a phase. For all I know it could be that I'm just missing Sydney … and sex. But when you, Aaron, and Cliff were in the shower with me last week and then you and Aaron again today, I remembered the feeling of a man's hands on my body, your hands on my body, Jason. I remembered everything. I remembered how you made me feel."

"Toby, give yourself some time to grieve. Give yourself some time to think about everything, but I would caution you to wait. Decide whether your feelings for Cliff are real before you act on them.

"He's awful young, not only in years, but also emotionally. Don't ask me how I know that, but it's true, and he's carrying a lot on his shoulders right now. Not only is he responsible for your children, he's also responsible for his brother and sister. I know I couldn't do it.

"If you come on to him, he may not know how to

handle it. You've only known him for a few days, and he's your employee. It wouldn't be fair to him."

"You're right, Jason. I feel so unsure about everything right now, like I don't have control over anything anymore, but thanks. Thanks for listening."

"Of course, I'm here for you."

"God, I'm feeling so sleepy. Sorry, I think I need to go to bed."

"Okay, you nod off. I'll sit with you. Aaron and I are going to take turns through the night."

"Thanks, Jason. I don't know how I'll ever repay you for all that you've done."

"There's no debt here, Toby. We're friends."

Chapter Fifteen

An Affair to Remember

Almost immediately, Toby fell asleep. His dreams were filled with that long week from years ago. That week in the mountains with Jason, when Jason made a man out of him.

****

Jason hovered above him. His shoulders were broad, and his bulging biceps were as heavily veined as his own. His thickly muscled, labor-honed forearms ended in ample, calloused hands. A gorgeous and perfectly proportioned landscape of thick, curly blond hair, bleached by the sun, canvased a deeply-tanned and brawny chest. His rigid six-pack quivered and heaved with each panting breath, and his treasure trail led to the base of his engorged, vein-snaked, eight inch cock. It glistened with the essence of pre-cum as it oozed over the swollen, crimson head. All of it was nestled within an impeccably trimmed and shaped mound of dark blond pubic hair.

Toby, at twenty-two was only four years Jason's junior. The pearly white skin of his groin, ass cheeks, and legs was unaccustomed to the sun. Stretched high in the air by Jason's clasping hands, it was turning pink with the first hints of sunburn. As he lay on his back, Jason lunged forward and pounded away at his tight, hungry hole under the bright, sunny sky on the hottest day it had reached, early that summer.

"Yes! Yes!" Toby yelled. "Pound my ass!"

"With pleasure." Jason leaned down and lifted Toby with his hands cupped behind his neck and kissed him, drawing Toby's tongue into his mouth. Jason released him and spit into his hand. He reached down and palmed the slit of Toby's thick, leaking, seven inch cock. Then he rolled his hand across the dancing nerve endings beneath the surface of the swollen helmet.

Toby jumped. "You bastard! You'll fucking kill me if you keep that up."

"No, I'm not gonna kill you, but I am going to fuck your brains out!" Jason grasped the shaft with his meaty hand and began to stroke it, coating it with Toby's musky essence and his own saliva.

He drew his hand to his face and inhaled the scent, then sucked his mouth around his fingers. He shuddered at the hint of what was to come while he licked it clean. He spit back into his palm and grasped the quivering cock again, stroking the shaft and rolling his palm over and around the head and across the oozing slit.

Toby screamed. "Oh, my God! Fuck me, you bastard!"

Jason's pupils dilated. He bore his teeth in a rabid smile and began to pounded harder and harder as his balls slapped loudly beneath Toby's ravenous hole.

"Oh my God! Oh, my God!" Toby yelled as he thrust his hips into the air and fucked Jason's clenched fist. "You're gonna make me come!"

Jason slowed his pace, but continued his ministrations as Toby writhed beneath his grasp until he began to beg for mercy.

"Please, Jason! Please let me come!"

"Not yet, baby. Not yet." Jason sneered. He released Toby's cock and gripped him behind his back, lifting him up into his lap until they were chest to chest.

Toby wrapped his arms around Jason's neck and squeezed his knees tightly against his sides. He pulled himself in until their sweat-slicked torsos were pressed tightly together while Jason thrust violently with his hips.

Toby bounced in the air as Jason drove all eight inches of himself deep into his depths, creating sucking and slurping sounds as his cock withdrew and advanced. Jason's balls swung forcefully back and forth between his thighs.

Toby covered Jason's mouth with his own and drove his tongue in to its hilt. He clenched his ass tight and released it, clenched it and released it, over and over again, forcing pre-cum to spew from his cock slit and leak down between the two of them, coating and lubricating Jason's turgid shaft each time he pulled it out, slicking its path even more.

"Oh, baby," Toby moaned, "make me come. Please make me come!"

"Soon, baby, soon."

Jason leaned forward and gently placed Toby back onto the sleeping bag he'd laid over a massive boulder that projected nearly three feet from the ground on the hillside above their campsite and adjusted his tempo to Larghissimo.

Toby reached out with his muscular arms and grasped the boulder, then slid his ass to the edge. With each thrust of Jason's hips, he grimaced and smiled at the pleasure/pain assault on his swollen, battered balls, now concussed by Jason's pelvic bone as he drove his shaft in and out of his pleading hole. The metronome of Jason's striking sack never lost a beat as his balls continued to slapped to and fro.

Toby tightened his muscular thighs around Jason's hips and locked his ankles behind his back. He lifted his hips into the air each time Jason thrust forward to position his prostate directly into the path of Jason's swollen, advancing cock head.

As Jason lunged, his glans hammered against

Toby's knotted, spasming orb, only to be deflected downward as it continued to travel farther along its course. When Jason withdrew, his cock's helmeted ridge would catch again, striking the orb from the other side, creating double, buffeting blows until Toby lost his mind.

For minutes on end Jason continued his assault, slowing at times and then picking up the pace, like a rapid maestro, as they each took turns sliding a hand along the length of Toby's shaft until he couldn't take any more. By the time he was driven to the point of no return, Toby had become a blubbering fool.

Toby bit his bottom lip, drawing blood. "Oh my God!" he cried out. "I'm coming!"

As Toby exploded in rapture, Jason grabbed at his cock and pulled it tight against his abdomen, directing the first, thick, white ribbon of cum toward his mouth as it shot from Toby's quaking shaft. Jason caught the crest of the eruption between his lips and rolled Toby's thick, creamy man-spunk across his tongue as the remainder of the ejection clung to the fur on his chest and belly.

Toby's cries of ecstasy echoed between the canyon walls into the valley, far below. Startled birds took to flight while fauna took to their burrows or growled and raised up as they snarled toward the disturbance that came from the mountain above.

The taste and smell of Toby's fresh cum combined with his cries of ecstasy seemed to push Jason over the edge. With one final thrust, he drove in deep and pressed his entire weight against Toby's burgeoning hole, impaling himself there as he released his load. His own howls were added to Toby's cries.

As their prostates spasmed and their vas deferens contracted in unified bliss, their man-seed was driven from their cores. Together, they thrilled in the forbidden pleasure that only two men could create when they came together.

Jason leaned down and placed his mouth over Toby's purpled cock head, sucking and swallowing until he'd withdrawn the last drop of Toby's musky nectar.

As the end of their passion neared, Jason collapsed on top of him.

Toby clasped his arms around Jason's back, squeezed his legs tight, and pulled him in fast while Jason's cock expelled his seed.

They lay like that for minutes, Jason, still hard and swollen and deep within Toby while Toby clenched his sphincter tightly around Jason's thrumming shaft. He moved his hips to and fro, milking the shaft, until the last drop of Jason's essence had been pulled free.

When Jason's cock slid, limp and sated, from Toby's gaping hole, cum oozed out and dripped down the boulder until it found its resting place in the soil below, soon to become fertilizer for the growing wildflowers, where once again, it would blossom into something beautiful and sacred.

"I never knew it could be like this," Toby whispered in panting breaths, when it was over.

Jason began to lift himself from Toby.

"I never dreamed … I never dreamed anything like it. Thank you, Jason. Thank you for giving me this. I'll never forget it as long as I live."

He pulled Jason back down and kissed him deeply with all the passion he could muster, tasting the remnants of his own man-seed on Jason's tongue, while his legs continued to cling around Jason's torso.

Jason returned the passion as he lifted Toby, belly to belly, from the boulder into his arms. "Oh, it can be much better, baby," Jason whispered. "Much better." He hugged Toby tightly and then lowered his legs to the ground.

"Can we do it again?" Toby asked, before his mouth sought out Jason's once more.

"Absolutely, baby," Jason said as he pulled away. "Absolutely. Just give me a few minutes to recharge. Drink plenty of fluids. You'll need them. Then I'll fuck you again even better and after that, you can repay me the favor. I want you to fuck my ass and make me moan. Make me beg for it. Make me plead. Remember, we have all week."

"Oh, Jason, you're on! You're on, baby!"

****

Friday, May 14, 2010

When Jason came out of the bathroom just after sunrise, he noticed a smile spreading across Toby's face, so big that it exposed his perfect teeth. "Good morning to you too," he whispered so as to not wake Aaron, but Toby didn't answer. When he walked to the bed to check on him, Jason realized Toby was still fast asleep. *There's something familiar about that smile*, he thought.

****

8:45 AM

Cliff opened the bedroom door carrying a large tray filled with steaming breakfast food and a small vase holding two daffodils and one tulip. "How was his night?" he whispered.

"Uneventful for the most part," Jason whispered back, "but he did call out a few times. There was also some tossing and turning."

"But he slept?"

"Yes, through the night."

"Good, I'm glad."

"Are you two talking about me?" Toby said as he ran a hand across his face and then propped himself up on his elbows. He threw off the covers and swung his legs over the side of the bed.

Jason hurried over. "Whoa there, buddy. You might want to take it a bit slower."

Anxiously, Cliff followed him.

"I'm fine, Jason, really, I feel great."

"Then do it for me. Just sit a minute before you try to get up."

"Fine, but what am I going to do about him?" Toby looked down and then pointed at the tent that had formed in his pajama bottoms. "I really gotta pee, Jason."

When he wiggled his butt, the head of his penis and part of shaft slipped through the open fly of his PJs. Toby looked back up at them in time to see Cliff's eyes lock on his erection.

When he saw Cliff blush, he quickly averted his eyes and covered himself with his hands, but not before he felt a surge in his loins. *Oh my God, he's staring at it.* "Sorry, guys," he said aloud.

Jason put his hand on Toby's shoulder. "Just give it a minute, Toby."

I need to make this erection go away. "Jason, I'm not dizzy. I'm not weak, and I don't feel like I'm gonna pass out."

As he began to stand, Jason moved to steady him, but Toby waved him away. "I appreciate the concern, Jason, really I do, but I need to see if I can do this. By myself." *Now get the fuck out of my way. I've embarrassed myself enough.*

"Fine, but I'm right here if you need help."

"See, I'm fine," Toby said after he stood up.

"I see that, but let me come in with you."

"No, Jason. I'm not having you stand over me while I take a dump. I'll be fine. And I'm closing the door."

"Then I'll stand on the other side in case you

need help."

"If it makes you happy, but you don't need to baby me, Jason. I'm a grown man." He closed the door behind him with a bang.

A moment later a loud moan came from behind the bathroom door. "I'm fine! I'm fine!" he called out. "It's just me taking a piss. God, that feels good!"

****

As Toby came out of the bathroom, he had a sheepish expression on his face. "Sorry about biting your head off there, Jason. I didn't mean it."

"I know."

"I'm gonna take a shower, Cliff. Thanks for bringing up breakfast. I really appreciate it, flowers and all, but I think it's important for me to eat at the table with my kids. They need to see that I'm okay."

"Sure, Toby, if that's what you want, but they've already eaten."

"It doesn't matter. I still think it's important for them to see me up and moving around. Please don't be offended."

"Not at all, Toby. You're absolutely right. I'll just put everything in the oven to keep warm."

"That would be great. Thank you."

"Now, Jason, if you wouldn't mind, I'd like you to stay while I'm in the shower. I'm not stupid enough to push my luck."

"I'd be happy to, Toby."

"I think I'll be okay in there by myself. You can come in, but I'll shower by myself. Just stand by on the other side of the shower door in case something happens. I don't think it will, but just to be on the safe side."

"Absolutely."

"You can go back downstairs, Cliff."

"Sure, Toby. I'll see you down there."

Chapter Sixteen

A Bump in the Road

10:45 AM

When Toby and Jason entered the kitchen, Charity was at the stove and Aaron was sitting at the table.

"Where are they?"

"I sent Cliff and Eugene with them into the playroom, Mr. Toby. I forgot how energetic young ones can be, and I need to move around when I cook. I've starting to get lunch together."

"Is it that late already?"

"It's a quarter to eleven. They didn't want any more soup, so I'm making a pot of macaroni with ground beef and a can of tomato soup. I've never met a child who doesn't love it. Cliff put your breakfast in the oven to keep warm, but it's probably dried out by now. Shall I fix something for you?"

"Thank you, Miss Charity. I don't want to be a bother, and I need to go see them."

"It's no bother. I have eggs scrambled and batter mixed and ready to go. Besides, Mr. Jason hasn't eaten yet. I'll have something ready for you when you come back."

"Jason, why don't you sit down? I'll be fine going in to them by myself."

"Sure, Toby. I'll get started on my breakfast. Holler if you need me."

"Will do."

"How are you feeling, Toby?"

"Better. So much better, Aaron. Thanks. Now I need to see my kids."

****

Toby peeked around the doorframe. "So … this is where my family has been hiding!"

"Daddy!"

"Daddy!"

"Daddy!"

"Da … Daddy!"

August was the first to reach him, almost knocking him over as he wrapped his arms around his waist. Then June ran to him and hugged him around his hips. July wrapped his arms around his right thigh, and May bounced up and down in front of him with her arms held up, still gripping her teddy bear in her left hand.

When June let go and ran back to the table, Toby leaned down and picked up May. She held him so tight around his neck, she nearly choked him. When June returned, she held out a crayon drawing. "Here, Daddy. I drew this for you!"

"It's very pretty, June. I love yellow and red flowers."

"Cliff said flowers help people feel better. That's what he put on your breakfast tray, so I made you more so you can feel better all the time. I helped Cliff pick your flowers, Daddy."

"And they were beautiful, Munchkin. Thank you."

Are you better now, Daddy?"

"Yes, July. I'm much better."

"Good, 'cause I want you better."

"I want to be better for you too."

"Come on, Daddy," June said, pulling on his pants pocket. "I want to show you my other pictures."

Beads of sweat began to form on Toby's forehead.

"Are you okay?" Cliff mouthed.

"A little weak," Toby mouthed back.

"Hey, kids," Cliff said. "Why don't you let your daddy sit down in the recliner? You can all snuggle better there anyway. Then he needs to go and eat his breakfast. You want him to keep his strength up, right?"

"Right! I'm going with him."

"I wanna come."

"No, I wanna come."

"Me too! Me too!"

"Looks like we're going to skip the recliner and head straight to breakfast. You can all come," Toby said, "but you're going to have to let go of me first. I can't carry all of you."

"We missed you, Daddy."

"I know, August. I missed you too." Toby tussled his son's hair and then leaned down and kissed the top of his head.

"Okay," Cliff said. "Let's all let go of Daddy for a minute."

When Cliff held his arms out to May, August gave her a dirty look and shook his head, *"No,"* but she immediately reached for him and then laid her head on his shoulder once he had ahold of her. Then he leaned down and picked up July in his other arm. "Now, who wants to lead the way?"

"I'm the oldest," August said, as he puffed up his chest. "I will."

"Then lead the way, master August," Cliff said with a smile. "Lead the way."

****

No sooner had the family sat down at the kitchen table and Toby began to eat his pancakes and bacon, then Vera entered, carrying baby April. Cliff poured a bag of Sydney's breast milk that he was thawing in a pot of warm water into a bottle that held some warm formula and then checked the temperature with a digital thermometer.

"Ninety-seven degrees on the nose," he said as he screwed a nipple on and shook it up to mix it.

When he sat down at the table, Vera laid a receiving blanket over his left shoulder, then one of Sydney's knitted winter scarves on top of it. Then she laid April in his arms.

Toby swallowed visibly when he saw the scarf. With misty eyes, he rested his fork down on his plate.

"Are you done, Daddy?"

"Yes, June, I'm stuffed," he said, clearing his throat.

"Can I have some?"

Toby's voice wavered. "Sure, Munchkin." He cleared his throat again.

"There's macaroni surprise for lunch, little Miss," Charity said. "Don't want to ruin your appetite, do you?"

"Just a taste, Daddy. Please?"

"Sure, Munchkin, just a taste."

Toby passed his plate to June and then sat quietly as he watched April while she took the bottle. Between the four children, they cleaned Toby's plate of the remaining one and a half pancakes and two pieces of bacon. When the children finished, he said, "I'm pleased with how easily May and July went to you, Cliff."

"We've spent a lot to time together the past few days, Toby, while you were under the weather."

"I'm glad they had you during all of that."

"That's what I'm here for."

"I love, Cliff," July announced.

"I love, Cliff." May copied.

"I love him too," June said.

August's body started to shake. He pounded his fists on the table and then screamed, "He's not our

Mommy!"

Everyone in the kitchen fell silent. Tears began to spill from August's eyes as he clenched and opened his hands. "You're not my Mommy!" He shrieked as he pounded the table again.

"August!" Toby shouted.

August pressed his face into his hands and began to cry.

June, July, and May froze. Expressions of shock and fear covered their faces. Baby April began to wail. When Vera reached for her, Cliff handed her over. Then Vera carried her from the room up to the nursery.

"No, I'm not your Mommy, August," Cliff said softly.

Jason began to get up, but Charity placed her hand on his shoulder and shook her head. At the same time, Aaron placed his hand over Jason's forearm and shook his head as well, mouthing, "No."

"I know you miss her," Cliff said. "No one can ever be her. I'm sorry your Mommy isn't here, and I'm sorry you're sad, August. I'm so very sorry you're sad, but I also think you're a little mad, maybe even at me."

August lifted his head and stared at Cliff. There was hatred in his eyes.

"I missed my Mommy too when she died. I got mad a lot, all the time, and so did my brother and sister. I got sad, and I cried a lot too. We all cried a lot, me and my brother and my sister. We cried all the time, and you need to know that it's okay for you to cry whenever you want to. It's okay for you to be mad and to be sad, August, if that's how you feel."

August's face softened. "Why?" he choked out. "Why did Mommy have to go away?"

"I don't know, August. I just don't know."

Toby got up from the table and walked around to

August. "Thank you," he whispered to Cliff. He picked up his son and carried him out of the kitchen and up to his room.

****

"Mr. Cliff?" August said as he walked into the nursery.

Toby remained at the door.

Cliff looked up from the rocking chair while he rocked April, lying quietly, while she slept. He put his finger to his lips. "Hi, August, how are you feeling?" he said softly.

"Mr. Cliff, I'm sorry I yelled at you," August whispered back.

"That's okay, August. I know you were upset. Sometimes, when we're mad because we're sad, we don't know what to do so we yell and scream and throw things and say things, and after we've done all of that, some of the pain goes away. Do you feel better? Maybe even a little?"

"Yes, but I also feel sorry 'cause I know it isn't your fault that Mommy went away. I'm sorry I said those things to you."

"Thank you for telling me that, August, but you were right. I'm not your Mommy. I'm Cliff. I'm your nanny. I don't ever want you to think that I'm trying to be anything else."

August walked to the rocking chair and looked down at his new baby sister. He leaned down and kissed her forehead and then turned around and wrapped his arms around Cliff's neck. "I'm sorry," he whispered. He stood there, holding onto Cliff.

Cliff reached up with his free left arm and hugged August back. When August nuzzled his face into Cliff's neck, Cliff sighed and patted his back, then he lifted him into his lap. "It's okay, August. It's okay."

While Toby watched from the door, he looked up and closed his eyes. *He's so good for our kids, Sydney. Thank you for sending him to us.*

****

7:00 PM
Behind closed doors in the den

"I've been thinking, Toby, that after May's birthday I should go back home, that is, unless you think you'll need me to stay longer."

"No, Aunt Vera, I'll think we'll be all right. Not that I don't appreciate all that you've done, but I know you have to get back to your own life, eventually. I don't think you staying any longer would make it any easier for the kids or for me for that matter. It's going to be rough no matter who's here with us and how much help we have.

"I was going to ask Jason if he could give her that ride in the helicopter he'd promised before I had my breakdown. I don't think a whole lot of presents would be appropriate right now, and giving her a big party would be more difficult for her than helpful."

"I think you're right. Now, I wanted to tell you something that I think is important for you to hear."

"What's that, Aunt Vera?"

"That young man you've hired, Cliff, has been a godsend. He seemed nice enough at the start, but the proof is in the pudding. He's wonderful with the children. He always seems to know the right thing to say in those moments when Sydney's passing hits them hard."

"Yes, Aunt Vera, he does. I think it's because he can relate to them because he's been through it too, and he's had training for it in school and with the children he was a counselor for at those summer camps where he worked."

"Well, I just wanted you to know that I think you made the right choice in going with him, and I think Sydney would approve."

"I know she would, Aunt Vera."

"There's something else."

"What's that?"

"When are you planning on sending the children back to school?"

"I haven't even thought about it. I guess I should, huh?"

"Yes, I think you should. They need to get back to a normal routine as much as possible and as soon as possible. It's not good for them to stay in the house. Everywhere they look, they see their mother. Going back will provide a distraction for them and give them a little break from it each day."

"When do you think I should?"

"I would think before the end of next week, but you know what? You've got a child development specialist at your fingertips. Why don't you run it by him?"

"Good idea, Aunt Vera. Thanks."

****

While Cliff gave the children their baths, the remainder of the adults were sitting in the family room watching television. Toby turned to Jason. "I'd like to ask a favor of you."

"Sure, Toby. Anything."

"Doctor Tolbert said he's going to give me the once over tomorrow, and I plan on passing. If I do, I don't think you need to stay any longer. We're almost tripping over each other right now anyway. I appreciate everything you've done for my family and me, more than I can ever find the words to express, but we're going to have to start figuring this all out on our own at some point.

"Aunt Vera's going to stay until after May's birthday so we'll have an extra set of hands until then. In the interim, I think Cliff and I should start talking about how we're going to make all this work, and having Aunt Vera here will be a cushion for us. I just don't think you all need to stay and babysit me too."

"If that's what you want, Toby, sure, but what's the favor?"

"If you all leave tomorrow, would it be possible for you and Aaron to come back on Tuesday? It's May's birthday, and I wanted to ask if you could give her a ride in Gypsy. I think a big party with presents is out of the question this year, but a helicopter ride would be a great present without being a present. You know what I mean?"

"I think that's a great idea, Toby. We'd be happy to do that for her."

"Absolutely!" Aaron added, "A ride in Gypsy is a great idea, and if you realize you need some help with anything in the meantime, we're just a copter flight away."

"Thanks, Aaron, that means a lot."

Chapter Seventeen

Leave Him Be

Saturday, May 15, 2010, 10:00 AM

"I'm very pleased, Toby. You've turned around quite nicely," Conrad said as he put away his stethoscope and sphygmomanometer. Not that I don't appreciate these palatial accommodations, but you really don't need me here anymore."

"Yes, I'm feeling almost back to normal, doctor. I've surprised even myself. I would never have thought just three days ago that I'd be feeling this good, this soon."

"Well you're young, and you've got lots of help. Just don't push it too hard for the next few days."

"I won't, doctor, I promise, but I wanted to ask you, do you think I can return to work soon?"

"I don't see why not, as long as you feel up to it. When were you thinking?"

"After May's birthday. It's on the eighteenth. Maybe the nineteenth or twentieth?"

"If you feel strong enough, I'd say, go for it."

"Wonderful, doctor. Thank you."

"Any time, Toby. Any time."

"I'm thinking of sending the children back to school at the same time."

"I think it will be good for all of you."

There was a knock at the door. "Come in," Toby called.

"Hey, Toby. I was wondering if you would mind if Aaron and I went for a swim before we leave. Are we leaving today?"

"Absolutely, Jason, I might even join you. I'm

feeling pretty good right now." Toby gave Conrad a questioning look.

"Fine with me, Toby. There's no reason you shouldn't. Just don't try to swim a mile."

"I won't. I promise."

"Jason, I've given Toby a passing grade so we can all head back up whenever it's convenient for you."

"Sure, Conrad, sure. All right if we get that swim in first?"

"Yes, of course. I'm at your disposal."

"Great," Jason said. "We'll meet you there then, Toby?"

"I'll see you there."

****

10:40 AM

When Toby came into the playroom, Cliff was building an airplane out of snap-together, brightly colored plastic toy pieces with August.

"Cliff, I'm going to go for a swim with Jason and Aaron. Doctor Tolbert's given me the okay. When I'm finished, I'd like to sit down with you to go over a few things."

"Sure, Toby. I'll be sure to be available for you whenever you like."

"I wanna go swimming!"

"I wanna go swimming too!"

"Me too!"

"And me!"

The children spoke enthusiastically.

"Really? All of you want to go swimming?"

"Yes!" They all yelled.

"Then we're all going swimming."

"Can Cliff come?" July asked.

"Sure, if he wants to."

"Cliff, do you know how to swim? Will you go

157

swimming with me?"

"Yes I do, July. I teach children how to swim. I'd love to go swimming with you."

"Can you teach me so I don't have to use my water-wings anymore?"

"I'd like that, July. Sure, I'll teach you."

"Can you teach me too?" May asked. "I can't swim so good."

"Yes, May, I'll teach you too. I promise you, in a few weeks' time you won't ever need your water wings again."

"Yippie! No more wings! No more wings! Daddy, I'm going to be a big girl. Cliff's gonna teach me. Cliff's gonna teach me!"

"That's great, peanut."

Toby looked at Cliff. "I guess you have a pair of trunks? I don't think I have anything that would fit you."

"Sure do. I've brought everything I own with me. I have a couple pairs of nylon swim trunks and a couple pairs of lycra racing suits too. I think the nylon trunks would be more appropriate around the children."

More appropriate. I wonder what he looks like in…

July tugged on Toby's pant leg. "Let's go now, Daddy!"

"Huh? Oh, sure, kiddo, let's get going."

"I'll get the children ready, Toby. We'll meet you down there in a little while."

"Thanks, Cliff. I appreciate it."

****

11:15 AM

"I'm taking the children to the pool, Miss Charity," Cliff said as he followed them through the kitchen, carrying an armload of towels. "I promise we'll be finished in plenty of time for lunch. I'm sure they're going to work up some big appetites by then."

Charity nodded as she followed him with her eyes. They held on the spot where he disappeared around the corner. "Lord have mercy," she said under her breath. When she looked down at her hands, she'd spread peanut butter right off the piece bread she was holding, across the back of her thumb, and up her wrist.

She turned toward Vera. "Now that's a man!"

Vera smiled. "You're telling me!"

****

11:15 AM

Jason, Toby, and Aaron were talking at the far corner of the pool at the deep end while they hung in the water with their arms gripping the edge behind them. With Toby hanging between the two, he had a direct line of sight to the entrance from the hallway.

When Cliff walked in with the children, he waved to them and then immediately bent over some deck chairs to spread out the children's towels.

Toby fell silent. His jaw dropped. His eyes were fixed on Cliff.

Jason and Aaron turned their heads to see what he was focused on.

"Jesus Christ," Jason said under his breath, "would you look at that."

"And you were giving me a hard time about what I said last week after he came out of the shower," Aaron whispered. He reached in front of Toby and hit Jason in the arm with the back of his hand. "He is a looker. I'll give him that."

"He's more than that and in those trunks, my God! Not only do they highlight his torso, they also don't do much to conceal anything," Jason said. "Now do they?"

"I don't think anything could," Toby whispered.

"He's got a python in there."

Aaron pointed at Toby.

"Toby," Jason whispered as he pushed up beneath his chin. "Shut your mouth."

Toby quickly turned his head away. "Shit! Sorry," he hissed.

"Toby," Aaron said quietly, "you better get a hold of yourself." He looked Toby directly in the eyes. "Whatever's going on in your head, you need to get it under control. He's here to take care of your kids. Remember that."

"I know, Aaron. Thanks. It's just that he's so…"

"It doesn't matter, Toby. I know you're going through some shit right now, but you don't want to scare him away. You'll never find another one like him."

"What do you mean?"

"Toby, I was in the shower with you. I'm the one you wrapped your arms around and called Cliff. I know."

"Is it that obvious?"

"Yes, like a hard-on and whatever it is, whatever this turns out to be, you better be careful, damn careful about where you go from here. He's my friend, Toby, and I don't want to see him get hurt. He's not who you think he is, believe me on this. He's very vulnerable, so think about it, hard."

"What do you mean, Aaron?"

"I can't say. It's not my place. Besides, it would be wrong of me, but I'm telling you the truth. Treat him with kid gloves."

"I'm sorry, Aaron. Thanks. I never would want to do anything that would hurt him."

"Good, now pull yourself together. Here he comes."

"Hey, guys," Cliff said as he walked up. "I was thinking, Toby, it might be nice if you worked with me to teach July and May how to swim. We can have them swim back and forth between us, one at a time. That way they'll feel more secure. With you there, I think they'll do much better."

"Thanks, Cliff. I'd love to."

****

11:25 AM

While Cliff and Toby worked with May and July, August and June dove off the diving board and swam in the deep end with Aaron and Jason.

After spending fifteen minutes in the shallow end with Toby supporting July under his belly and Cliff doing the same with May, the two children became comfortable in the water. They learned to kick their feet, blow bubbles with their faces in the water, take breaths, and use their arms to make windmill strokes without the use of their water wings.

"Ladies first," Cliff said. Toby sat July on the pool's edge. "Now, May, just like I told you. I'm going to hold you around your waste while you swim to your daddy. Are you ready?"

"Yup, I'm ready!"

"Okay. Here we go."

As May kicked and pulled with her arms, Cliff walked beside her until she reached the short distance to her father.

"That was great, May!" Cliff exclaimed. "You did that almost all by yourself!"

"Really? I did? All by myself?"

"Almost! Now it's Daddy's turn to help you come back to me. Ready?"

"I'm ready!"

After repeating the process several times, Cliff and Toby doubled the distance between them. Cliff held May above the waste and as she approached her father, he gave her a slight push toward him and let go.

In two strokes, she reached him. "I did it! I did it, Daddy! I did it all by myself!"

Toby lifted her out of the water and hugged her to him. "Yes, you did, peanut. Yes, you did!"

For another ten minutes, Cliff and Toby moved farther and farther apart as they passed May back and forth between them until they each stood with their backs pressed against the walls at opposite sides of the shallow end.

"Why don't you rest now, May, and let July have a turn?"

"Okay, Cliff. I'm gettin' tired anyway."

"I thought you might be."

Cliff lifted May to the side of the pool. "Ready, July?"

July jumped right into Cliff's arms. "It's my turn. Let's go!"

Just like with May, everything went smoothly with July until Cliff and Toby were eight feet apart. As Toby pushed him toward Cliff, August lunged from the diving board and landed a cannonball just five feet away, creating a large wave. When July turned his head to take in a breath, the wave hit him square in the face. As the water entered his lungs, he began to flail and choke, and then he went under the water.

Cliff and Toby lunged for him, but Cliff got to him first and pulled him up in less than a second. Immediately, July began to cough and cry while he flailed about, but Cliff held on to him tightly.

A moment later, Toby was there with a look of fear on his face. He wrapped his arms around his son and lifted him from Cliff's grasp.

"Toby, we need to get him out of the water right away," Cliff said as Toby held onto his son. "He's got to clear his lungs of water or he's going to vomit. Then he could aspirate."

Seconds later, Jason surfaced beside them with Aaron right behind him.

August began to scream. "I almost killed him! I almost killed July!" Then he started crying.

Jason began to bark out orders. "Aaron, go take care of August. Get him out of the water. I'll check July."

"June, find doctor Tolbert and tell him to come right away."

"Toby, get him out of the pool. Now!"

"Help! Help!" June screamed as she ran from the pool into the house.

Toby didn't move. He looked petrified, and he was shaking. He held tightly to his son.

"Help me," Jason said to Cliff.

Together, they carried Toby with July in his arms to the steps and then helped him to climb out.

Charity and Eugene came running into the pool room. "Miss Vera's goin' for the doctor," Charity said. "He'll be right here. What do you need, Jason?"

"A bucket or trash can. He's about to vomit."

Eugene ran to the corner and returned with a plastic trash can just as July bent over and hurled up the remainder of his breakfast, catching Toby's leg along the way. Charity lifted the towel that was attached to her apron and wiped his mouth in between each wave. "Eugene, get me more towels."

"Right away, Mama."

"Someone tell me what's happened?" Conrad shouted as he worked his way between the group surrounding July.

Vera arrived a moment later.

Conrad put his medical bag on a chair and pulled

out his stethoscope. "Good thing I was packed. My bag was already in the center hall."

"I didn't see what happened," Jason said. "What did you see, Cliff?"

"As he turned his head to take a breath, a wave washed over his face. Then he went under. It wasn't more than a second before I had him out of the water, but I'm sure he's inhaled some."

"Okay, I doubt he's taken in much," Conrad said. "The epiglottis shuts immediately, but some might have gotten past it. We'll just have a listen once he's stopped vomiting, but because he's vomiting, he should get a chest X-ray to be sure there's no aspirate down there."

Eugene returned with June who carried a stack of dry kitchen towels. He handed his mother a wet one. "Here, Mama. You can wipe his face with this one. I ran it under the sink."

Vera and Aaron took a hysterical August away into the kitchen.

While Charity cleaned up July's face and Toby's leg, Toby continued to shake as he stared off into the distance.

"I think it's more likely that he's had one hell of a scare," Conrad said as he lifted his stethoscope from July's back. "Dad too, I think. I don't hear much of anything in his chest, but that doesn't mean he's completely in the clear. We should still get that X-ray to be safe."

July began to shake and then he began to cry. He reached up and wrapped his arms around his father's neck.

Toby looked down at him. He grasped him tightly and buried his face into July's neck while they cried in each other's arms.

"Toby," Jason said calmly. "Toby, July is going

to be fine. He's going to be just fine."

"I can't lose him," Toby cried. "I can't lose him too."

"Toby, he's going to be all right. He's just had a scare."

"Leave him be, Mr. Jason," Charity said. "Just leave him be for now. He's got to get it out of his system."

"You're probably right, Miss Charity."

"I know I'm right. Father got scared for his child and Father's been through a lot. Just leave him be."

"You're right, of course, but Miss Charity, Conrad, Eugene, we're staying a few more days."

Chapter Eighteen

I'm Doing the Best I Can

Sunday, May 16, 2010, 9:30 AM

A voice boomed as it entered the kitchen. "What the hell? Who are you people?"

Charity and Eugene jumped and turned around from the kitchen counter. Standing before them was a man who appeared to be an older, shorter version of Toby. At five foot seven, his voice belied his stature.

"You people?" Eugene hissed, his arm at his side with a butcher knife gripped in his fist.

"I beg your pardon, sir?" Charity answered sweetly as she pressed her hand against Eugene's arm.

"I said, who are you people? What are you doing in my son's house?"

The sound of his voice echoed up the staircase and down both wings of the second floor.

****

"Heaven save us," Vera cried out from the chair she was sitting in in her room. She jumped up and ran down the hall to the top of the stairs. "Tobias! Tobias, it's all right! They're friends, Tobias! They're friends!"

****

"What in the world?" Cliff exclaimed as he carried April to the door of the nursery and stuck his head out. The baby began to fuss.

****

"Oh, God! This is all I need!" Toby groaned loudly. He ran from his room and followed Vera down the staircase.

****

Jason quickly hung up the phone in Toby's office

and looked at Aaron. "Oh no, it's the old man. This is going to get interesting." He stood and walked toward the French doors that opened into the kitchen.

****

"Grandpa!" The children shouted together as they jumped up from the table in the playroom and ran toward the archway that opened into the family room.

****

"Wonderful water in that pool," Conrad said as he turned the corner and entered the kitchen, wearing a robe with a towel thrown over his shoulder.

"Jesus, Mary, and Joseph! What the hell is going on around here?" the Toby look-a-like exclaimed. "Somebody tell me what the hell is going on!"

"Tobias! Tobias, calm down," Vera yelled as she ran down the center hall toward the kitchen.

"Dad! Dad," Toby called out, right behind her. "It's okay! It's okay!"

****

The four children came barreling into the kitchen from the family room.

"Grandpa!"

"Miss Charity, it's Grandpa!"

"Pa! Pa!"

"Grandpa, I almost drowned yesterday!"

As the four of them surrounded him and hugged him, Vera, Toby, Jason, and Aaron came in, one after the other.

****

Cliff stood at the top of the staircase listening. When all the commotion quieted down, he made his way down the stairs. Then the shouting started again. He hurried down the center hall.

"Dad, would you quiet down! You're going to wake the baby!"

"Don't tell me to quiet down. I have a right to know what's been going on around here!"

Vera reached up in front of him, her hands on his shoulders. "Tobias, that's enough! This is Toby's house, not yours! Now get ahold of yourself!"

As Cliff entered the kitchen, carrying April, she began to fuss. "What in the world is going on?"

Vera, Toby, and Tobias turned to face him.

"God save us!" Tobias's eyes bugged out. "Who is this behemoth," he said, pointing, "and what's he doing with my granddaughter?"

"Well, I see you're still making up for your lack of stature with over exaggeration and that damned booming voice of yours!"

Everyone turned toward the voice that came from the kitchen doorway, right behind Cliff.

"Grand Mom!" the children cried.

"Mom!" Toby exclaimed.

"Patsy, thank God!" Vera said with relief on her face.

"On no!" Tobias senior's shoulders dropped.

****

9:47 AM

Toby sat in a leather chair in his study, while Tobias paced back and forth, looking down at him. "Toby, I appreciate what you've been though, really I do, but why the hell do I have to hear it through the grapevine that you nearly died? I almost had a heart attack! Why the hell am I just learning today that my grandson nearly drowned? And who is that Viking who was holding April?"

"Dad, what are you talking about? July did not almost drown. Who told you that?"

"Your mother!" He pointed towards his ex-wife.

Patsy sat on the leather sofa in her coral skirt with

matching, waist-length jacket with three-quarter length sleeves and cream-colored blouse, with a forced smile plastered across her face. "Vera told her that you almost died last week. That woman" —he pointed again— "took great pleasure in telling me that she felt it was her duty to inform me, but only because I am your father. Then, July tells me just now that he nearly drowned yesterday, and now you've gone and hired some Neanderthal as a babysitter? What's that all about?"

"Dad, I did not nearly die, I…"

The French doors flew open. "Tobias, stop your exaggerating!" Vera marched in. "Patsy is no grapevine."

"I never said any of that, Tobias," Patsy said calmly, "and you know it." She took out a cigarette from a silver case from her pocketbook.

"I tell you that's what she said me."

"That may be what you heard, Tobias" —she paused and ceremoniously put the cigarette back its case— "but it's not what I said. I told you that Toby had a breakdown and that there were friends here who were medical people, taking care of him. From the looks of him now, I'd say they did a damn fine job of it."

"That's right," Vera said. "Well, little brother, what do you have to say for yourself?"

"I'm telling you…"

"Oh, God help me." Toby moaned. He stood up and walked toward the French doors.

"Where do you think you're going?"

"Away from here, Dad. You've obviously already made your mind up about everything. What do you need me for?"

"Toby," Patsy said, "please come back. Your father is just upset. You know how he gets. We're all adults here. We can have a civil discussion about this."

Toby turned around.

"Am I right, Tobias?" Patsy glared at her ex. "Can we discuss this calmly?"

"Yes, yes of course. I'm sorry, Toby. I didn't mean to upset you. I just got so scared. Please come back and sit down."

"Fine, but only if you listen, Dad."

"Very well."

"I mean it, Dad. You listen. I'll talk. Agreed?"

"Yes. Agreed."

"Good." Toby walked to a leather chair opposite the sofa and motioned toward a place next to his mother. "Dad, please have a seat."

"If you insist," Tobias muttered.

Once his father was seated, Toby sat back down.

Vera found a place in a matching chair at the end of the coffee table between the sofa and Toby.

Toby cleared his throat. "Thank you. This is going to take a few minutes and it's not easy for me to talk about, so I'm going to need you to just listen. You can ask questions when I'm finished."

"Go on, Toby," Patsy said encouragingly. "We're listening."

"First, let's get one thing straight. His name is Cliff, Dad. You've insulted him all three times you referred to him. He is not a behemoth, nor is he a Viking or a Neanderthal. He has two degrees, one in child psychology and the other in child development, and with a 4.0 GPA no less. He is the children's nanny.

"He's raised his brother and sister from the time they were orphaned, and he's putting them both through college. He's a water safety instructor. He's certified in CPR, and he was a summer camp counselor for four years. He was also the Valedictorian in both high-school and college, and he graduated Summa Cum laude. On top of all of that, he can cook. He's a great cook, Dad."

"Then how did July almost drown if he's so damned qualified?"

"Dad, you promised!"

"Sorry."

"July inhaled a little water in the pool because August did a cannonball next to him when Cliff and I were teaching him to swim without his water wings."

"Oh."

"He's great with the children, all five of them, and they all love him. When August had a meltdown about Sydney's death…" Toby paused for a moment and took a deep breath. "Sorry, when August had a meltdown, it was Cliff who talked him through it. Because he'd experienced the loss of a mother, he knew exactly what August was going through. They're the best of friends now. Every day with Cliff is a new adventure for the children, and that's exactly what they need right now."

Tobias raised his hand.

"Yes, Dad?"

"Toby, what happened to you?"

"It all caught up with me. I went into such a deep funk that I couldn't even think. I was in bed for two days. Ask Aunt Vera. She'll tell you. Cliff and Aunt Vera were the ones who kept this house going while I sank deeper and deeper into despair.

"It was bad, Tibias," Vera said. "You have no idea how bad it was."

"Well, I would have if you had called me sooner!"

"How can you say such a thing? Just look how you've been acting for the past twenty minutes! I've known you since the day you were born. You're the last thing this house needed. The last thing!"

"It's okay, Aunt Vera."

"Sorry, Toby, I didn't mean to interrupt, but my baby brother…" Vera wrung her hands together as if they were around Tobias's neck.

"May I continue?"

"Yes. Sorry."

"Finally, Cliff called Aaron. They went to high-school together. Aaron is Jason's partner. You know about Jason, right?"

Tobias shook his head in disgust. "Yes, Toby, I've heard things."

"That's not what I meant, Dad. God no! It's not like that. They're a loving, committed couple.

"How can you even think that about him when Jaron Enterprises has given our company the biggest building contract in its history with Nathan's Promise? Since that contract, our company is now at the top of the heap, throughout the entire region. Besides, that rehab center is going to do a world of good for professional and amateur athletes, not to mention military and law enforcement personnel, whether they're gay or not, and they're not going to charge any of them a single penny. They're two of the kindest, most generous people I've ever known.

"I don't care whether you accept their lifestyle or not, but know this. It was because of them that I'm here and not in some mental hospital right now. Jason was a medic in the army. He knew exactly what to do and who I needed."

"Yes, I remember. Oh, that's what you meant."

"Exactly! Jason and Aaron put a team together to run Nathan's Promise. They brought part of that team with them to take care of me and my kids. Miss Charity and her son Eugene have been tremendous. They just stepped right in and ran this house while Cliff and Aunt Vera focused on the kids and me.

"Doctor Tolbert took care of my medical needs, and he even checked out July when he had that episode in the pool yesterday. Before I knew it, we were whisked into an Urgent Care center yesterday and had his chest X-ray done in less than ten minutes. I never signed a single piece of paper. All of that is because Jason, Aaron, Miss Charity, Eugene, Doctor Tolbert, Cliff, and Aunt Vera all worked together on behalf of me and my kids when I needed them the most.

"There's one more thing. If it wasn't for Miss Charity and Cliff, April would most likely have been admitted to a pediatric intensive care unit because she stopped taking her bottle around the time I had my breakdown. It was Miss Charity who immediately knew that the reason was because nothing smelled like Sydney.

"I'm not exaggerating when I tell you that after two days of barely nursing, in less than a minute, Miss Charity had her back on the bottle. Since then, she and Cliff have worked out a schedule for transitioning her over to formula because the extra milk that Sydney froze has almost run out."

"I have one question," Patsy said.

"What's that, Mom?"

"Why a man and not a woman, Cliff I mean?"

"Because of all the women the agency presented to Aunt Vera and me, none were available to live-in. The best they could do was someone from 7 AM to 5 PM."

"Well that would never work," Tobias said. "You need someone here around the clock."

"Exactly, and that's why I went with Cliff."

"Well, no one's got any business second guessing you, Toby."

"Thanks, Mom."

"You made the right choice, Toby," Tobias said. "Son, I'm sorry."

"I'm doing the best I can, Dad."

Toby lowered his head into his hands and began to cry.

****

A crack formed in Patsy's veneer. She raised a hand to her mouth. Her eyes began to mist when she slowly shook her head and turned to look at Vera. "*My son*," she mouthed.

A moment later, Tobias stood in front of his son. With tears in his eyes, he leaned down and hugged Toby.

Vera stood up and Patsy walked around the coffee table and rubbed her hand up and down his back.

Toby stood and hugged his father, pulling his mother and Vera in with them.

****

While Charity stood at the kitchen island, gently rocking April in her cradle, Toby, his parents, and Vera came through the French doors from the den, into the kitchen. "I've had Eugene set up for lunch in the dining room, Mr. Toby, since we're having two more dining with us."

Tobias continued on to the bar in the dining room.

A shocked expression spread across Toby's face. Standing behind his mother, he pressed his palms to his forehead.

"Oh, I wouldn't want to impose," Patsy said.

"Not at all, ma'am, I expect you'll want to visit with your grandchildren for a spell, seeing as you're here now. Would tropical infused, plank-grilled Salmon and roast chicken be acceptable for dinner?"

Toby's eyes opened wide as he drew his hands down the sides of his face.

Hearing the menu, Tobias stopped in his tracks momentarily on his return from the bar.

"That's an awful lot of work on but a moment's notice," Patsy said.

"Not at all, ma'am, it was Cliff's idea. He's out back right now, scrubbing up the grill. He said it would be a shame to let it sit idle when we've got company visiting. He told me he's wanted to do a nice big meal ever since he got here. Now you've given him an excuse. Why not let him?"

"Well, we can't disappoint the lad, now can we?" Tobias said. "Sounds wonderful. I accept your invitation."

"It was Cliff's invitation, and with the little one's birthday coming up in just two days," Charity continued, "it would sure be nice if you both could stay with us until then. I hear there's an exclusive, luxury helicopter tour of the entire valley planned."

Toby's eyes nearly popped out of his skull. He frantically waved his hands at Charity. "*No. No,*" he mouthed.

"If we're going to be eating like that," Tobias said, "a team of wild horses couldn't pull me away, but I'll be returning to my home in the evening."

Toby's look of shock was replaced with one of mild relief.

Patsy snorted when she saw Toby's face out of the corner of her eye. "Still thinking with your stomach I see, Tobias."

"Well…"

"That would be lovely, Miss Charity," Patsy said. "I accept your invitation. I'll call home and have my girl pack me a bag. I wasn't expecting to be here for but a few hours."

"Wonderful! Then it's all settled."

"My usual room, Toby?"

"Sure, Mom."

"Now where are my grandchildren?"

"They're in the play room, Miss Patsy, with my son, Eugene."

"Then that's where I'll be if anyone is looking for me."

"Mr. Toby," Charity said, "I've called in orders to the local fishmonger and meat market. They'll be delivering the chickens, salmon, and cedar planks in a few hours. Mr. Jason's taken care of everything."

"Thank you, Miss Charity."

"My pleasure, and Cliff and I will put our heads together and figure out menus for the next two days. You put your mind at ease. You won't have to worry about a thing."

Chapter Nineteen

I'm a Winner

2:30 PM
Toby's Study

"We never had time to talk yesterday, Cliff."

"With all that's happened, I completely forgot about it. I'm sorry."

"No, it's not your fault. That's not what I meant at all."

"Oh, good."

"To get to the point, I've been thinking about how things are going to work after everyone goes home and it's just the two of us here with the children. Seems I might be jumping the gun though with the dramatic turn of events that's overtaken my home in the past few hours."

"They are a lively couple. I'll say that for them."

"Oh, no, they're divorced. Have been since I was a teenager."

"Oh, I didn't realize."

"It doesn't matter, and they'll be gone in two days anyway. Now, getting back to what I wanted to talk with you about. I'm planning on going back to work the same time I send the oldest three back to school. You'll be alone here with May and April. Are you okay with that?"

"Sure. Of course. What time should I expect the children home from school?"

"You'll have to take them and pick them up. It's a private school."

"Sure, I can do that. And you? When do you get home from work?"

"It depends on what I'm working on and there will be days when I won't be home at all if I'm up at Jason and Aaron's headquarters late into the evening. Gypsy doesn't fly at night unless it's an emergency. Sometimes I'm gone for two days at a time. If I'm coming home the same day, I'm usually no later than seven."

"I see. Who's Gypsy?"

Toby laughed. "Sorry, Gypsy's their helicopter. Once the road is completed, I'll be able to drive up and back, but until then, if it gets dark, I'll be spending the night."

"Well, the children and I will figure out a schedule, but I think seven's a little late for them to eat dinner, don't you?"

"No, I mean yes, sorry. I didn't mean that. I just wanted you to know that I won't likely be home for dinner with the rest of you."

"Then I'll have your dinner waiting for you whenever you get here."

"You don't need to do that. I usually get takeout, unless I know I'll be home in time."

"Well, you can forget that! Oh, sorry, Toby, that was a little forceful. I didn't mean anything by it, but you did say you wanted to take off a few pounds. Takeout would certainly be one of the things that's adding to your difficulty. I'll have a healthy meal waiting for you, just like the children are going to be eating."

"I appreciate that, Cliff. Really, I do, but I..."

"No, I insist and regarding the children—"

"May I finish what I was going to say?"

"Oh, sorry. Yes. Please."

"I started working out on my treadmill and stationary bicycle this morning."

"That's great, and remember, if you want to start

working out with weights, I've got everything set up downstairs in what I've turned into my weight room, the room next to the pool you said I could use."

"I'll probably take you up on that."

"Good, now about the children, I'll need some kind of documentation for the school so they know I'm permitted to pick them up when they're finished for the day."

"I've already taken care of that through the agency. Mrs. Shelty was more than happy to forward a photo ID for you."

Cliff smirked. "I'll just bet."

"No really, she was quite amicable about the whole thing. Seems they deal with the schools all the time."

"Good, do you have any special instructions for the children? You know, bed times, do's and don'ts about food, snacks—healthy snacks that is—and activities, things like that?"

"I'll leave that to you, but I'm afraid you'll have your hands full. You've seen how they can be."

"We'll do just fine, I'm sure. Now as far as dinner when you're home and meals on the weekends… Any special requests?"

"Yes, no liver. Never liver."

Cliff laughed out loud. "You'll have no arguments from me on that!"

"I've prepared a list of phone numbers for you in case of an emergency as well as local merchants we have accounts with for various things. I've also had my lawyer draw up documents permitting you to consent for medical treatment, and in case of emergencies, or God forbid, surgery."

"Very good. You're very thorough."

"I try. Now do you have anything?"

"Yes, I wanted to talk to you about July. He needs to get back into the water as soon as possible. The longer it's delayed, the more likely it is he'll develop a phobia to it."

"I didn't think of that. When should we do it?"

"Today, now if possible. I've already mentioned it to him."

"How'd he take it?"

"He was on the fence about it. That's why I urge you to consider it sooner rather than later."

"Then I'll meet you in the pool in fifteen minutes."

"I'll have him ready."

"Thanks, Cliff. I'm really impressed."

"I'm just doing what I think is best for you and your family."

"I can see that."

****

Patsy was talking with Charity, Vera, and Eugene when Cliff walked through the kitchen holding July's hand. Tobias had Conrad cornered in the family room while he touted the benefits of dietary supplements.

"We're going out to the pool to finish July's swimming lesson," Cliff said to the room. "Toby's going to meet us there."

"He's already out there," Patsy said her eyes glued to Cliff's muscular physique.

Tobias must have overheard Cliff, because he broke away from Conrad and hurried into the kitchen. "We're all going to come and cheer him on."

"If I may, sir, I don't think that's a good idea. July has some trepidations about it, and I think an audience will put too much pressure on him."

"Nonsense, we'll just…"

Vera cleared her throat. "We'll just wait right

here."

"Cliff's the teacher," Patsy added, "and if that's what he says, that's what we'll do." She held out her arms. When July rushed to her, she picked him up and kissed him on the cheek. "Good luck, my little man. I know you'll do just fine."

"Thank you, Grand Mom. I hope so."

Vera got up from the table, went over to him, and kissed him on the head. "You'll do great! You always do."

July beamed. "Thank you, Aunt Vera."

After they walked away, Patsy turned to Vera. "Now that's one tall drink of water!"

Charity giggled and fanned herself. "That's an understatement, if I ever heard one."

Eugene cringed.

To egg her ex on, Patsy placed the back of her hand in front of her mouth and exaggerated a whisper to Vera. "Boy could he quench my thirst."

"Good grief woman!" Tobias scoffed at his ex. "You're old enough to be his mother!"

Patsy laughed. "Maybe so, old man, but it doesn't mean I can't take a sip."

****

"You can do this, July. Believe in yourself."

"Okay, Cliff, if you say so."

For a twenty minutes, Toby and Cliff passed July back and forth between them as he kicked and pulled with his arms while they slowly increased the distance between them. When they were all the way across the shallow end, Cliff called out, "This is the last one, July. If you can do this, you'll get a blue ribbon."

"What's that, Cliff?" July shouted from his father's arms.

"A blue ribbon is for winners," Toby said.

July didn't wait. He pushed off from Toby and swam across the pool, kicking and splashing until he crashed into Cliff's belly.

Cliff pulled him up and cheered, but July didn't stop there.

He climbed right up Cliff's chest to sit on his shoulder and began to shout. "I'm a winner! I'm a winner, Daddy! I'm a winner. You made me do it, Cliff. You made me! I didn't think I could, but you made me. You made me!"

Toby knew his face had to be one big smile as watched his son.

"You did it all by yourself, July." Cliff lifted him down and hugged him. "I just caught you. I'm so proud of you."

July pushed back and ran his hands across Cliff's chest. "Oh boy, Cliff," he said loudly. "You're so furry."

Cliff bared his teeth in a smile and shifted July to his left arm. With the other fist, he beat his chest like a gorilla as he lumbered in a circle while grunting animal noises.

July giggled and bounced up and down. When Cliff finished, July wrapped his arms around Cliff's neck. He hugged him and then kissed his cheek. "I love you, Cliff."

"I love you too, little man."

Toby felt a tug of longing. *Oh, God, to hold him like that. To touch him like that. To kiss…*

"Come on, Daddy. Come hug Cliff. Come hug Cliff, Daddy! Please? He teached me how to swim. He teached me. Hug him, Daddy! Hug him!"

Toby shook his head. His face felt hot. He cocked his neck and looked at Cliff with a questioning expression.

Cliff shrugged his shoulders and called out, "Why

not?"

As July continued to call to him, Toby sheepishly walked toward them while he paddled his arms through the water. When he reached them, he tentatively extended his arms.

July put his arms around both of their necks and pulled them together.

Their arms brushed against each other, then their chests touched, then their abdomens.

"No, Daddy, tighter," July said. "Like this." He pushed Toby away and wrapped his arms around Cliff's neck. Then he pulled his hips into Cliff's abdomen with his legs wrapped around him as far as he could reach. He squeezed tightly and kissed Cliff on the cheek.

"Just like that, Daddy," he said as he pulled away. "Just like that!"

****

Toby reached in and hugged Cliff tightly for just a moment, but it was enough.

Cliff felt his loins stir. Without knowing, he pulled Toby in closer. Instinctively, he nuzzled the other man's cheek. Then he began to grind his groin against Toby's.

Toby's groin responded.

****

Toby tried to pull away, but Cliff held firm and sighed, so softly it was barely audible, but Toby heard him just the same. For a moment Toby remained there, blushing, but then he pushed again and whispered, "Cliff, let me go. July. Think of July."

Immediately, Cliff released him. His face became red, then redder, and then redder still. "I'm sorry, Toby. I'm so sorry. I don't..."

Toby leaned his mouth to Cliff's ear. "Don't say anything. Not a word. This is all normal. As far as July is concerned, it's all normal."

"Now I want everyone to see!" July climbed out of the water and ran for the door.

When he was gone, Cliff said, "Toby, I'm so sorry."

"Later." Toby walked back through the water to the opposite side of the pool.

****

"Come on, everybody. Come on. I'm gonna get a blue ribbon!" July shouted as he ran into the kitchen. A puddle began to form on the floor beneath him. "Come on! Come on or you're gonna miss it!" Then he disappeared through the den into the play room. The same shouting could be heard emanating from it as well.

A moment later, August, June, and May were racing behind him, headed for the pool.

****

As the audience assembled on chairs and stood around the pool deck, July jumped up and down. "I'm a winner! Just watch this!"

He jumped into the water and pushed off from Toby, splashing, kicking, and pulling with his arms, all the way until he reached Cliff. Cliff pulled him up and cheered. Then he lifted him high into the air and shouted, "Win-ner! Win-ner! Win-ner!"

"I'm a winner! I'm a winner, everybody!"

The audience burst into applause and cheers and called out, "Win-ner! Win-ner! Win-ner!"

****

After the children had their evening baths and were tucked away into bed, Cliff went to the laundry room and began sorting the clothing he'd gathered from hampers into different loads, but his mind wasn't on the task. He remembered Toby's touch. *So that's what it feels like to hold a man.*

When he came to one of Toby's shirts, he stopped. *I shouldn't.* But before he knew it, he had the shirt against his face. He inhaled deeply and sighed. *It smells like him. It smells just like him, and it's wonderful.*

Quickly, he dug through the pile of cloths until he found Toby's workout jockstrap. He brought it to his nose and inhaled again. *That heavenly smell. The smell of a man. A smell like mine, but better. It's Toby's smell through and through. His musk. His essence.*

Cliff folded the jockstrap and shoved it down the front of his pants. After he closed the lid of the washer, he snuck up to his room and closed the door behind him. Once safe, he pulled the jockstrap out from his pants and breathed in again. Then he shoved it under the mattress of his bed. He hurried back downstairs to join the family.

****

"I have to compliment you both," Patsy said as she took a sip of hot tea with a splash of brandy. "That dinner was magnificent. The chicken was succulent and roasted to perfection, and the salmon, the salmon was to die for, just to die for."

Cliff beamed. "Why thank you, ma'am. I'm so glad you enjoyed it, but I have to give credit to Miss Charity and Eugene. Miss Charity showed me a few tricks I'd never seen, and it seemed like every time I needed something, Eugene was right there with it ready and waiting."

"I'm used to helping Mama in the kitchen," Eugene said. "You get to know how things work after a few years."

"Oh now hush, Cliff," Charity said. "You showed me a few tricks too. They were your recipes we followed. It's like I always say, you never know what you'll learn from someone else's ways, and I've learned plenty these past few days."

"That's very kind of you to say, Miss Charity. I've wanted to try that pineapple juice and papaya marinade on a large scale ever since I made it up. I read a few different recipes and took the best from each to come up with it, but I've only prepared single portions for myself in the past.

"After you marinade for three hours, you top the salmon with crushed, fresh pineapple and papaya and then add fresh, grated coconut. You have to be careful to slow grill it on the soaked cedar planks. Otherwise it dries out and the fruit burns. If you bring the leftover marinade to a boil and then simmer for thirty minutes, it makes the best reduction ever. It really makes all the difference."

"It seems like Cliff reveals new talents by the day," Toby said. "I knew you could cook, Cliff, but my mother's right. That meal was really something."

"I try, Toby. Sometimes it even comes as a surprise to me. I've discover a lot of new things about myself since I got here. I've learned over the past few years that when I put my mind to it, there isn't much I can't accomplish. I could have never pulled it off without Miss Charity and Eugene's help though. They worked as hard as me."

Aaron raised his glass of scotch. "A toast. Here's to Miss Charity, Eugene, and Cliff."

"Hear, hear," everyone exclaimed.

"Well, folks, I'm going to head out," Tobias announced. "What time is lunch tomorrow?"

Patsy covered her mouth as a smile began to form. She looked at Vera.

Vera winked back.

"Lunch is always served at twelve noon, sharp, Mr. Jacobson," Charity said.

"Then I'll be sure to be here by then. Thank you

and good night."

"Aren't you going to come along for May's helicopter ride, Dad?"

"Oh, yes, forgot all about it. What time?"

"Late morning I'd think, sometime before lunch."

"Very good, I'll be here by ten."

"Thanks, Dad. I'll walk you out, Dad."

"No need, son. I know my way. Thank you all again for a most pleasant day."

Chapter Twenty

Urges

11:10 PM
The Family Room

One by one, people excused themselves and headed for bed until only Cliff remained on the sofa and Toby sat in a chair next to the far end of it. Each was consumed by his own thoughts about what happened between them in the pool. Each tried to speak several times, but neither could bring himself to begin.

When they would work up the courage to steal a glance at each other, they would turn away when the other one met their eyes. The silence between them grew until it was deafening.

Finally, Cliff couldn't take it anymore. *Maybe if I start talking about something else, I can make it go away.*

"Toby, I…"

"No, Cliff." Toby's head was lowered. His eyes were misty when he looked up. "You don't have to say anything. It's as much my fault as yours."

"I was going to say how happy I am for July. What are you talking about?"

Oh, God, please don't let him say it. Don't let him.

"Um," Toby began. "When we … when July…"

"Oh… That."

"Yeah, that."

"I'm sorry, Toby. I don't know what came over me. Maybe I should call you, Mr. Jacobson for the sake of this conversation. I'm your employee, not your friend. I'm not your equal. Today was for the benefit of the children. This is much more serious."

"No, Cliff, I meant it when I told you to always use my first name, regardless of the setting."

"This thing that happened between us…" Cliff looked directly into Toby's eyes. "It's uncomfortable for me. I don't really know you, and I know you really don't know me. Heck, I've only been here a week. How did this even happen?"

"It's okay, Cliff. I'm uncomfortable too. To tell you the truth, I'm a little scared."

"Toby, it's not that I'm uncomfortable about it. I'm uncomfortable that *it* happened between us."

"I don't understand."

"I don't know where to begin, Toby … or even if I should. You know, TMI. Heck, I work for you. You have no reason to even care about me like that. To tell you the truth, I don't know if it's even safe to tell you or what to tell you, because I'm not clear about it myself."

"Cliff, I've entrusted you with the lives of my children and with my home. Yeah, I know we've only known each other for a week. It's so hard to believe my life is where it is right now. I would have never imagined this, never. Just know that I trust you, and you can trust me. You have my word."

God, what am I doing to this man? What am I doing to myself? I don't even know what this is. Who am I? What am I? He's just lost his wife. I didn't mean to.

God, forgive me. I really didn't mean to do that to him, but it felt so good, so damn good. Oh, God, this is wrong. It's so, so wrong. I don't belong here.

"Toby, I'm sorry, but I think it would be best if I resign. I know this will put you in a tough situation, but I'm afraid it could be devastating for you and your family if I stay. I've caused enough harm already. I'm sorry. I'm so, so sorry. You should start looking for a replacement right away."

Cliff stood up and brushed the front of his pants.

"No! Please, Cliff. Don't go." Toby jumped up from his chair and rushed to the sofa. He gripped Cliff's hands and folded them between his own. "I beg you, Cliff. Please don't leave. I don't know if I could take it."

"Toby, this whole situation is so confusing. We both know something could have happened and that scares me. I've begun to feel these emotions that I've never felt before, and I don't understand them. Almost since I got here there have been these urges that nearly consume me. This is not the place to try to figure them out. Your children just lost their mother. You just lost your wife."

"Cliff, I'm begging you. Please don't leave. I'll do anything to make this work. I know this sounds selfish, but I can't handle this right now."

"Toby, it's not the same."

"Don't you think I know that? Every time I think I'm holding it together, something else happens, and I lose it all over again. I can't go through another loss right now. I can't have to go looking for another nanny for my kids. Not now! I've put my trust in you, Cliff. Tell me what you want. What do I have to do to keep you here? Please, talk to me." Toby tilted his head forward until it rested against Cliff's chest. "Please, Cliff."

Oh, this poor man. Cliff pulled his hands from Toby's and gently wrapped his arms around him. "It's going to be okay, Toby. I won't leave. Not right now. I'm sorry. I didn't think through how this would impact you, but I need to talk to someone about it. I just don't know who."

"Thank you, Cliff. Thank you." Toby leaned back and began to reach his right hand to Cliff's face. It hovered in the air, but Cliff pulled him back against his chest.

Cliff's entire body shook. *No way. I can't let it happen.* "Please, Toby. Don't. If you want me to stay, don't."

Toby put his hand down. "Cliff, it happened before I realized what I was doing. I'm sorry. Maybe I need to talk to someone too."

Cliff slowly pressed Toby away until they were a few feet apart. "Maybe you do."

"Oh, no, my parents are going to be here for the next two days and there's May's birthday. Jason and Aaron are here and Miss Charity and Eugene and Dr. Tolbert too. What are we going to do?"

"I don't know, Toby. Maybe we should just focus on what we have to do, on what's expected of us."

"I think you're right. That's what we'll do, but can you promise me something?"

"If I can."

"Will you promise that we'll talk again so we can clear the air about whatever all this means?"

"Yes, I can promise that."

"Thank you, Cliff. Suddenly, I'm very tired. I think I better call it a night."

"You're right. It's nearly midnight. I'm going to head up too."

Cliff followed Toby up the staircase and down the hallway. When they reached Toby's room, Cliff murmured, "Night." Then he continued walking to the nursery to check on April.

****

No sooner had Toby's head hit the pillow, then he was fast asleep. Within minutes he was dreaming.

****

"That's going to be one hell of a home, Jason," Toby said as he looked down at the construction site far below in the valley. "Now that the piers have cured and the footers are in, the floors and walls are going up quickly. They should be ready for the roof in about a week and a half. You sure you want three acres inside the stockade?"

"Yeah, I want plenty of grazing for the animals. They'll be safe from predators inside the walls."

"I guess you're right."

Jason ran his hand up Toby's back. "Ready for round two?"

A shiver ran through Toby's body. "Definitely."

"Good, 'cause I could take you right here."

"You can take me anywhere you want to, Jason."

"I'm glad you said that." Jason swept his left leg behind Toby, catching him behind the knees as he threw his arm behind his back to break his fall. "Your ass is going to beg for mercy by the time I'm done with you."

Immediately, Jason was on top of him. He pinned Toby's shoulders to the ground with his hands and swept his legs apart with his knees.

Toby lifted his legs and rested them on Jason's shoulders while Jason spit into his left palm and used it to slick the fingers of his right. He reached down and began to probe Toby's hole. It puckered tightly shut.

Toby grimaced. "You're right, baby, it's screaming, "Mercy! Mercy!" but I need to feel you inside me again."

When Jason opened him up again, cum from his last assault leaked out. He held up his fingers. "Look here, Toby. You're already lubed up for me."

"No, wait. I want to taste you again." Toby reached down and took hold of Jason's growing shaft. "Please, baby, let me suck you first."

Jason moved up to straddle Toby's shoulders and slid his cock head into his waiting mouth.

Toby latched onto it and darted his tongue along the sensitive underside of the shaft, then swirled it around and around the thickening head.

"Oh, baby. Just like that." Jason closed his eyes and let his head fall back. "Just like that." Jason's body began to spasm while he hips twitched, involuntarily, and his ass bounced above Toby's chest.

"Fuck my mouth, Jason."

Jason let out a moan and dropped his torso forward, supporting himself on his hands. He began to slowly thrust his shaft deeper and deeper past Toby's lips until he felt his cock head hit the back of his throat. When Toby gagged, Jason looked down at him. Tears began to spill from his eyes, but Jason just kept pounding away. He increased the pace of his advances. Within seconds, Toby's salivary glands went into overdrive, making his saliva thicker and slicker.

"I need to feel your tight hole around me." Jason pulled back and moved back down to between Toby's legs. He lifted them into the air and pressed his cockhead against Toby's hole. Coated with Toby's thick saliva, and aided by his own cum, the head slid right in. With one powerful thrust, he shoved forward until his balls slapped against Toby's ass.

"Yes!" Toby cried. "Oh, God, yes!"

Toby closed his eyes against the bright sunlight as Jason grunted while he pounded his ass harder and harder. Immediately, he felt a mouth surround his cock. The sucking was intense.

The grunting turned deeper. Toby squinted against the sun and reached up to pull Jason's mouth to his own, but he wasn't there. He opened his eyes to look, but something was different. The hair on his head was shorter, and it was brown. His shoulders were like a linebacker's, and his cock, the cock that was inside him was painful. It was huge. *Oh, God, he's going to tear me apart.*

"I've wanted this for a long time, Toby. You have no idea how long I've wanted to fuck you."

Toby blinked. "Cliff?"

"Yeah, Toby. It should have been me. It should have been me all along."

"Oh, Cliff! But how?"

"Who cares? I'm here now. I'm yours, Toby. I'm all yours."

"Cliff! I've wanted you for so long. Oh, God, you're ripping me apart, but I don't care. Fuck me, Cliff. Fuck me!"

"You got it, Toby, like you've never been fucked before."

Cliff's thrusts grew quicker and more violent.

Toby felt his prostate tighten. "Oh, God, Cliff, I'm going to come. I'm going to come!"

"Come, baby, come for me."

Cliff lowered his mouth to Toby's cock and sucked with abandon. Then he slammed his shaft into Toby's hole to the hilt.

Toby began sliding along the ground, but Cliff dug his feet in and drove forward as if he was driving an offensive guard back from the line of scrimmage. Cliff lunged one final time, then he exploded.

Cum shot from Toby's cock the same moment Cliff released deep inside him. Warm cum, in huge waves, filled him to beyond his limit. It splashed from his hole with each of Cliff's thrusts.

Cliff swallowed against Toby's shaft so greedily that the head of Toby's cock was drawn down his throat.

When it was over, Cliff collapsed on top of him, nearly crushing him, but his hips continued to spasm and his cock, still buried inside him, continued to twitch.

Toby began to struggle. "Cliff, you're suffocating me. I can't breathe."

"Never, Toby," Cliff said as he pulled himself up and rolled onto his back, pulling Toby with him. "I'd never hurt you, Toby, never."

"Even with your cock shrinking inside me, I still feel so full." Toby sat up. He ground his hips downward and in circles. "Is there any life left in there?"

"What? You think that was it? No, baby, I'm just getting warmed up. Now let me pump another load into you." Cliff grabbed Toby's thighs and lifted him up and down, stroking the length of his shaft with Toby's stretched hole.

"I can feel you growing, Cliff. It's getting harder and harder. It feels wonderful."

In Toby's dreams, Cliff continued making love to him through most of the night.

****

Cliff stopped at the nursery and checked on baby April. She was dry and sleeping so he left her as he found her. He walked out of the nursery, then down the hall another fifteen feet farther and turned into his room. After changing into his pajamas and before getting into bed, he checked the volume on the baby monitor.

"What did you just do, Cliff?" he whispered to himself. "You should have told him. You owe him the truth."

No, Cliff. You were right to push him away. It could destroy him and his family.

"But you want him, Cliff, and he wants you. Couldn't you see that?"

No. He's vulnerable. He just lost his wife.

"Stop lying to yourself. He got a hard-on, damnit! He got a hard-on when you rubbed up against him."

That could have been anything, and besides, he

195

never said it.

"Neither did you. You didn't give him the chance to say it. You didn't give yourself the chance either."

Don't you think I know that? But I couldn't. I just couldn't.

"But you know what you want, Cliff. You want him. You want … him. You know you do. You're drawn to his musk. He's your ambrosia. Remember ambrosia? Why else would you have stolen his jockstrap?"

His jockstrap! Oh, God!

Before he could stop himself, Cliff had retrieved it from under his mattress. He brought it to his face and inhaled. His penis twitched. He reached down and wrapped his hand around it and squeezed. It twitched again.

He laid down and pulled his body pillow against him, hugging it to his chest and wrapping his legs around it while he pressed his face into the jock's pouch.

Toby, what are you doing? We can't. We can't.

Yes we can, Cliff. I want you. I want to taste you.

Kiss me, Toby. Kiss me.

Cliff opened his mouth and brought the fabric of the jock's crotch to his tongue. He hesitated, then licked it. There was a faint saltiness to it.

Toby, you taste so good.

So do you, Cliff. Now kiss me, harder.

Cliff pulled the material into his mouth and ran his tongue against it. His salivary glands began to secrete, moistening the fabric.

As more saliva flowed, it began to reawaken Toby's dried sweat and musk. "Mmm," Cliff moaned.

I didn't know it could be like this, Toby.

It can be so much more, Cliff. Let me show you.

Cliff's hand threw the covers off, yanked his pajama bottoms off, and began to pump his shaft.

Oh, God, Toby!

Now take my cock, Cliff. We'll suck each other together.

As the material grew wetter and wetter, Cliff began to suck against it. Toby's essence filled his mouth. Explosions began to go off against his tongue as subtle changes in intensity of muskiness and saltiness began to assault his taste buds. Toby's musk wafted up into his nasal passage. His toes began to curl and uncurl.

"Toby." He moaned.

Precum oozed from his slit. Cliff ran his palm over it, coating it with the slick fluid. He rubbed it across the head while he caressed the coronal ring with his fingertips, like a jellyfish propelling itself through the water.

Toby. Oh, the head. Yes. Yes, Toby, just like that.

More and more of the lubricant trickled out. When it began to flow, he coated his hand and began to pump his shaft while he thrust his hips into the air.

Toby, your cock, it's so sweet. I have to taste your cum. Give it to me. Give me your load. Cliff filled his mouth with the jockstrap's crotch. As he sucked harder, slurping sounds filled the room. He pulled away for a moment. *Please, Toby, give it to me.*

Seconds later, Cliff's balls pulled up tight.

Here it comes, Cliff. It's all yours.

Cliff threw himself upright and leaned forward, forcing the head of his cock past his lips and into the knitted fabric of the jock's crotch in his mouth. *I'm ready Toby. Shoot your load. Give it to me. Give it to me. Shoot it right down my throat.*

Cliff, I'm coming. I'm coming.

As wave after wave of his cum shot from his cock, Cliff wrapped his mouth around the fabric that covered the head and swallowed, pulling it through the knitted stitching.

Once he'd finished, he pulled the sheet up over himself and hugged the body pillow to him as he began to drift off. *Thank you, Toby. Thank you for giving that to me.*

You sicko, he answered himself. *You know that wasn't his cum.*

Don't ruin it for me. It was the closest I could come.

Yeah, you came all right.

Shut up and go away. I want him. How can I make him mine? How?

Chapter Twenty-One

A Fear of Flying

Monday, May 17, 2010, 5:40 AM

Toby's last dream was of Sydney. They were laughing and carrying on until she turned to him and said, "I'm sorry, my love, but you know this is a dream. I know you know this, Toby, and I know you know I'm gone. Here, in your dreams is where I can still come to you, but you have to move on. You're still here, Toby. You're still here.

"I know it will be difficult for you, but you must think of our children. They need a stable home, and they need love. You can give them that love, Toby, but you must take care of yourself if you're going to be able to take care of them. You're not going to be able to do that without someone to love you, too. Please do this for me and for our children.

"He's young, Toby, and inexperienced, like we were when we first met. Yes, he's been through a lot, and he's strong in his heart, but he doesn't know love. Not our kind of love. Love him, Toby. Love him. Love our children. Love yourself and take care of yourself, Toby. Please, let me go."

****

While Pachelbel's Cannon in D played in the background, Toby hummed to himself while he shaved in front of the bathroom mirror.

"Daddy! Daddy, look! My blue ribbon. Cliff gave me a blue ribbon!"

Toby jumped. He looked into the mirror at his son, standing behind him. "Good grief, July, you nearly made me nick myself."

"Sorry, Daddy, look at what I got! It's my blue ribbon!"

Toby turned around. "That's great, July, and it's so big."

"I know Daddy. I know. I found it on my night table when I woke up."

"Did you say thank you to Cliff?"

"I did, Daddy. Three times I said it. He said it's the same blue ribbon he gave to winners when he taught camp."

"That was very nice of Cliff. Where is he now?" Toby began humming again.

"Daddy, that's Mommy's song."

"Yes it is, July."

"I like that song, Daddy."

"I like it too, July. It makes me happy."

"Me too, Daddy."

"Where's Cliff now, little man?"

"He's in with April. He just changed her and now he's giving her a bottle. Pee-ew, does that stuff stink!"

"Your diapers smelled just as bad. Believe me. I used to change them."

"Oh. I'm just glad I don't have to do it, 'cause it's a-sgusting.

"You mean disgusting."

"Yeah, a-sgusting."

"Babies do that. Have you had your breakfast yet?"

"Yep. Toasted O's and no sugar. That's how Cliff eats them."

"You like Cliff, don't you, July?"

"Yes, Daddy, he's the best."

"What do your brother and sisters think of him?"

"They like him too, a lot."

"That's good, July. I'm glad you're all getting

along."

"Have you seen Cliff's weights, Daddy?"

"No, I haven't been in there since he set them up."

"He's so strong, Daddy. I watched him lift some of them. And he's got big muscles too. Giant! I couldn't even lift a small one. It was too heavy."

"Well they're for adults. Children shouldn't be lifting weights anyway. When did you watch him?"

"This morning, before breakfast. Aunt Vera said she'd watch us while he went into his room next to the pool so he could lift them. Miss Charity cooked everybody breakfast, but I said I wanted Toasted O's like Cliff. Then Cliff said he was going to go to his room to take a shower. Then he went to April.

"After I finished my cereal, I went up to find Cliff to show him my ribbon 'cause Aunt Vera pinned it on my chest. He was in the shower, so I sat down in the doorway and waited for him. You know what else is big, Daddy? His pee-pee. It's so big, Daddy. It's bigger than yours, way bigger."

Toby wiped the traces of shaving cream off his face and slowly turned around. "You went into his bathroom? While he was in the shower?"

"Uh huh."

"You shouldn't have done that, July."

"How come?"

"Because adults need privacy."

"But I used to take a shower and a bath with you and Mommy sometimes when I was littler."

"That was different. We're family."

"Cliff is family now. Isn't he?"

"Not really, July. What did Cliff say when you were watching him?"

"He didn't say anything. He was turned around.

Then he had soap in his eyes. That's when I saw his pee pee. Then he put his head under the water and started to wash his hair. He was taking a really long time so I went down to the playroom."

"Well, you won't do that again, right?"

"Okay, Daddy, if you say so."

"I do say so."

****

Tuesday, May 18, 2010, 10:15 AM

"Are you sure you can't come on my helicopter ride, Cliff?"

"No, May, I'm sorry. I can't. I don't like helicopters. I'll just wait here."

"I'll wait with you, Cliff."

"You don't have to do that, Aaron. I'll be fine by myself."

"No, it's all good. It's not like I haven't been up in Gypsy before."

"Thanks, Aaron. There's something I wanted to talk to you about anyway, if you have the time."

"Sure."

"Please, Cliff. Please."

"May." Toby took her hand. "If Cliff doesn't want to come, he doesn't have to. This is your day. Now let's…"

"But, Daddy, I want him to come."

"No, May, Cliff is an adult. If he wants to stay here, we're not going to tell him otherwise. He'll be here when you get back, and then you can tell him all about your ride."

May turned and started walking toward the helicopter, but then turned back and waved. "Bye, Cliff."

"Bye, May. Have a good time."

After Gypsy lifted off and the sound of her rotors faded into the distance, Aaron turned to Cliff. "So what did you want to talk to me about?"

"It's kind of difficult to talk about, Aaron, but I have to talk to somebody."

"Why not start wherever you want. I'll listen."

"Aaron, I think I'm gay."

"And?"

"Aaron … I'm gay. Well, I'm pretty sure I am."

"And how do you feel about that?"

"I don't know. I'm not ashamed of it. I've never been ashamed of myself for anything."

"And you shouldn't be. It's no big deal to me, but then I think you already know that."

"It just seems like it should be some big thing, but it's funny it doesn't feel that way. Not when I'm talking to you."

"Well, that's probably because I'm gay. I'm just a little confused though. You said it was difficult to talk about, but look at you. You just came out and said it."

"I know. Once I said it, it was okay, but I'm really not sure if that's what I am."

"Has it changed how you feel as far as sex?"

"Aaron, you know I'm a virgin."

"I know, but you're still a man. I would think you still have needs."

"I didn't. Not until recently that is."

"And that means…?"

Cliff blushed. "I've discovered … masturbation."

"You've discovered it? Like you never, and I mean ever, did it before?"

"No, never, but it … well it feels really good."

"I have wondered how you handled being secluded there with no outlet for sex."

"Aaron, I know you may not believe it, but let me be clear. I'm telling you the truth. I've never had sex with anyone, not ever. I only masturbated once and that was years ago. After Mom died, I didn't have time to think about anything else."

"Sorry, I know you told me, but it was just so hard to believe. The good thing is it sounds like that's all about to change. Just wait until you have a partner. There's nothing like it."

"I can't even imagine. Well, I guess I can."

"A lot of people fantasize when they masturbate. I know I did."

"Well, yeah, I think about things, but it's still strange to realize that that's what I think about."

"What's strange about it?"

"That I think … well I'd rather not say."

"That's okay. You could always try porn, but it's not realistic, and it's way over dramatized."

"I've never seen any."

"Why don't we just let that go for now? It's not important."

"It's why I think I am that's difficult."

"Uh huh."

"I mean it's what made me think it."

"Uh huh."

"Are you just going to say 'Uh huh' over and over again?"

"I'm supposed to be listening, remember? I shouldn't be asking you questions, and I've already done that. Sorry. I know it can be difficult to talk about, even if you don't realize it. Once you get started, stuff starts to pop into your head. I noticed you've hesitated a few times. It's best if I just let you tell me what you want to tell me."

"No, I'd feel better if you asked me questions, because I don't know how to talk about this."

"Okay, you said it's why you think you're gay that's difficult. Right?"

"Yes."

"Then I'll ask it. Why is the why difficult?"

"Because … oh man…"

"Take your time, Cliff, or don't say anything at all. You don't have to tell me. Like I said, all of a sudden it can become difficult."

"Aaron, it's who I think about. I'm … I'm attracted to Toby."

"What do you mean, attracted?"

"Aaron, there's just something about him. I've felt it for days. Then in the pool yesterday, before you all came out to watch July, there was this moment when July got excited after he made it across the pool the first time. He was jumping up and down and shouting. He gave me a hug and then told Toby to, so he did.

"Aaron, I couldn't let go of him. Then he sighed, Toby I mean. Then our groins were pressing together. I think I started it, Aaron. Something came over me. My body just reacted. Before I knew what I was doing, I was grinding my groin against his, and I started getting hard."

"I see. What did Toby do?"

"Aaron, he started getting hard too. I could feel it through our swim trunks. Then he suddenly pushed me away and told me to be cool about it for July's sake."

"How does that make you feel?"

"I don't know. It's was strange, but it was nice too. I don't know what to do. Toby's my boss."

"Have you acted on it?"

"What do you mean?"

"With Toby, have you done anything with him?"

"No, Aaron! Didn't you hear me? He's by boss, and he's straight. He was married, and he's got kids and anyway, I'm a virgin. I can't just force myself on him. That would be assault and besides, I've never been with anyone. I don't even know how to have sex."

"Hmm."

"What?"

"Nothing."

"What? You're thinking something. I can see it on your face. What aren't you saying?"

"I'm not sure."

"Not sure about what?"

"Just as it's not right for me to push you for answers, the same goes for me. Got it?"

"Okay, sure. Sorry."

"Right. So have you talked to him about it?"

"We started to, last night, after everyone went upstairs, but we really didn't say it out loud. He skirted around it, and I skirted around it."

"But you think you know that he knows that you know."

"Yeah. I'm sure. There's no doubt about it."

"Do you know what you're going to say to him?"

"No, but we're going to talk again. After everything settles down and everyone goes home. He's really stressed about his parents being here right now. It's best that I don't add to that."

Aaron exhaled a long breath.

"Aaron, what should I do?"

"Only the two of you can talk about these things, but remember, he's very vulnerable right now. He's just had a new baby, he just lost his wife, and today is the first birthday he's celebrating without her."

"I know. I was a psychology major. The first birthdays, holidays, and anniversaries of every special event for the first year are going to be extremely traumatic."

"Do you have any indication that this could be a phase, that he's just looking for comfort from anyone who can give it to him?"

"I didn't, but now I don't know. I didn't consider that."

"I'm surprised that I did."

"Yeah, but you're right."

"What about you for that matter?"

"What do you mean?"

"You've been very clear that you're a virgin. Suddenly, you've been thrust into a situation where a family has suffered a horrendous tragedy and is in need of sensitivity, kindness, and caring. Is it possible that you're sexual awakening has been imposed on your need to offer comfort and kindness?"

"I don't think so, Aaron. You're getting into some pretty deep stuff."

"You're not the only one who studied psychology, and besides, I've learned a lot from Jason since we've been together. Cliff, you're a kind and caring man. You always have been, as far back as I can remember.

"When you were on the field, you could be an animal, but you also picked up the guys from the other team you pummeled into the ground after a play. You'd brush them off and ask them if they were okay. You even helped them off the field if they got hurt. When the players on the other team made a good play, you congratulated them. It's just something that's in your blood.

"Cliff, only you can know what is right for you to do for him and how to help him, but you must never fail to consider how vulnerable he is right now. You don't want to do more harm than good."

"Last night, I told him I was going to resign over what happened, what we never said out loud. He got really, really upset. Aaron, he begged me. He literally begged me not to."

"Then don't. I can understand how desperate that could make him. He's floundering right now, Cliff. Think about the past week alone. I have no idea where this is all going to go, but if I have one word of advice for you, it's gentle. Be very gentle with him."

"I will, Aaron. I promise."

****

When Gypsy's door slid open, each adult, with the exception of Tobias, stepped down carrying a crying child. When they got to the hanger, Cliff and Aaron rushed up to them. All the adults had tears in their eyes.

Cliff went to Toby. "What's happened?"

"Later, Cliff, we've got to get them home."

"Mommy!"

"Mommy!"

"Mommy!"

"Mom … Mom … Mommy!"

Tobias walked up to Cliff and whispered, "It was May. While we were up there she said, 'Mommy's in heaven. Can we go up and see her?' That really got to Toby, but he held it together. He tried to explain that the helicopter couldn't fly that high. When she protested, he suggested we could all wave to her. Then he lost it. Then all the children lost it. We came right back down."

"I see," Cliff said. "It's a good thing you did. He's right. We should get them home immediately."

****

During the limousine ride back to the house, Cliff suggested to all the adults that they stay with the child they had carried off the helicopter until they'd calmed down. He also suggested to Toby that professional counseling might prove helpful for not only the children, but also himself. Toby asked Jason to contact the counselors that Penelope Whitley, the Administrative Director of Nathan's Promise had arranged for when

Sydney was in the hospital. A meeting was scheduled for the following day at the house.

Chapter Twenty-Two

Putting It All on the Table

Wednesday, May 19, 2010, 2:30 PM
"Hello, Mr. Jacobson. I'm Amanda Blum and this is Grady O'Callaghan. We were told you asked for our help with regard to yourself and your family. I specialize in child psychology while Grady's practice covers a broader range."

"How do you do? O'Callaghan's a strong Irish name. I don't know Blum."

"It's Jewish."

"Wonderful!" Toby waved his arm inside and stepped back from the front door. "Won't you please come in."

After he closed the door, Toby turned to face them. "I guess you're here to see me, Grady, and you, Amanda, are here for my children."

"Well yes, I'm sorry if that makes you uncomfortable."

"Not at all, Grady. I'm just a very direct person. I hope that doesn't put you off. I assure you, I didn't mean anything by it."

"No, it's fine."

"Why don't we go into my study and talk first so I know how this is all going to work with the children and me."

"Of course," Amanda said.

****

After Amanda and Grady were seated on the sofa, Toby took a seat in the chair next to it. "Is it okay that I use your first names?"

"If that makes you comfortable, Mr. Jacobson," Amanda said, "certainly."

"I don't stand on ceremony, Amanda. I prefer Toby."

Amanda and Grady nodded.

"I don't know how this all works. Do I begin or do you?"

"Why don't you tell us a little about your family, Toby," Amanda said, encouragingly.

"Sure. Have you been told anything?"

"Yes, a little, but we'd rather hear your perspective."

"Very well. I apologize if I hesitate now and then. This has been a very difficult time for me and my family."

"We understand," Grady said.

"I'll be putting it all on the table for you. Up until two weeks ago…"

There was a knock at the French doors.

"Come in," Toby called. "That's probably Cliff with coffee and tea."

"Sorry I'm late with this," Cliff said. "I had hoped to have it all put together before you got in here."

"That's all right, Cliff." Toby stood up. "Amanda, Grady, this is Cliff Turnbull, the children's nanny. He has something in common with you. He was a double major in college, child psychology and child development. He's been a tremendous asset and help since he got here last week."

"Hello," Cliff said. "There's an assortment of scones, muffins, and cranberry bread on the tray for you to try. Please help yourselves."

"Thanks, Cliff."

"My pleasure, Toby. Please let me know if you need anything else."

"Sure, Cliff, thanks."

After Cliff left, Grady began. "You were saying?"

"Yes. Sorry. Up until two weeks ago, I was a happily married man with a wife and five children. The youngest was born on April 10th. Then suddenly my life was ripped away from me when my wife, Sydney, died suddenly from what's called a cerebral hemorrhage."

"I'm sorry for your loss, Toby," Grady said, softly. "I truly am."

"Thank you. The past two weeks have been hell, and I've barely kept it together, but there have been a couple brief breaks in the clouds. Moments I never thought I'd see.

"My second son and middle daughter learned how to swim. I've seen my kids smile. I've seen them get excited. Those were the good moments, but I've also had a breakdown … twice … the second was the worst of them. My baby stopped feeding. My eldest son had the meltdown of all meltdowns. My second son was taken to the hospital for inhaling water while learning to swim. My middle daughter had a meltdown yesterday while we were taking a helicopter ride over the valley for her birthday. She wanted us to fly up to heaven to see her mother. Then all the children fell apart after I fell apart because I had to tell her that we couldn't fly that high. And finally, my house is now completely empty of family and friends who have been staying with us at different times over the past two weeks to help us through the loss of my wife.

"It's just me and Cliff here now." Toby took a deep breath. "I realize that to speak so directly sounds unfeeling, but it was the only way I could get through saying it without falling apart. I'm floundering here. I don't know what I'm supposed to do, or what I'm expected to do."

Amanda and Grady exchanged glances. Silence lingered for a moment. Then Amanda spoke. "Toby there is no easy or right way to tell someone about a loss you've suffered. You're doing fine."

"There's something else, but I don't know if I should mention it or not."

"The more information we have, the better we'll be able to help you and your family," Grady said.

"Okay. This is going to sound crazy to you, but my wife came to me as a vision above her hospital bed before she died to ask me to let her go. She's also visited me in my dreams a few times to tell me I need to move on and find someone who will love me. She insists I won't be able to take care of our children until I do."

"Toby, you've been through a horrendous loss," Amanda said. "The fact that you're speaking so freely with us is a testament to your resilience."

"I haven't been that resilient."

"What you've been through," Grady said, "is hell, Toby."

"So am I crazy? Is telling you that my wife came to me in the hospital and visits me in my dreams, crazy?"

"Not at all, Toby," Amanda said. "People process loss in many different ways."

"Do you think I was imagining all of it?"

"We're only just beginning to crack the surface of the way the mind works. We've learned that what we thought we knew with certainty in the past was more supposition than fact. There is nothing out of the ordinary here."

"I'm sorry, Amanda. I don't mean to push, but you didn't answer my question. Do you believe she came to me?"

"I don't know, Toby."

"Do you think it's possible?"

"I don't discount anything, Toby."

"I see. Well you can check with the hospital.

When Sydney appeared, the spotlight over her bed became brilliantly bright. The moment she disappeared, it burned out. No one else saw her. Only me. But I believe they weren't meant to. It was me she had to convince to let her die."

Toby lowered his head and silently sobbed, taking deep breaths in between. "I'm sorry. I really hoped I could keep it together for this meeting."

"Toby," Grady said, as he pulled a tissue from a box and handed it to him, "you're allowed to grieve. It isn't a switch you can turn off and on at will."

"I'm trying to keep it together for my kids. I have to stay strong for them."

"Toby," Amanda said, softly, "children need to know it's okay for them to cry. When they see a parent do it, it lets them know they can too."

"Well, that's a relief because I've let them know they're okay more than a few times. Jason said the same thing."

"Who's Jason?" Grady asked.

"He's my best friend. If it wasn't for him and his partner, Aaron, and the wonderful people they brought with them, we probably wouldn't be having this conversation. Jason saved my life."

"It sounds like he's a very good friend, Toby."

"He is, Grady."

"Moving forward is going to take time, and it's different for everyone. There is no plan to follow or normal" —Grady made air quotes— "pattern to it. You just go through it however you need to go through it."

"Thanks, Grady. Thanks for being so understanding."

"What are your concerns for the children, Toby?" Amanda asked.

"That they remain whole. That they'll become

happy again and stay healthy. That they grow up and lead happy, productive lives and find someone to love them."

"I think we all want that for our children," Amanda said.

"Do you think they'll be able to do that?"

"We can't predict the future, but we're going to do everything we can to help them."

"And you," Grady added.

"Thank you, both of you, for agreeing to do this. We really do need your help."

"Certainly, Toby," Grady said. "Amanda will meet with your children, together at first and then separately as she feels they need it. You and I will meet similarly if that's all right."

"I'd like that."

"You mentioned your nanny has been with you only a short time."

"Yes. He started on May 9th. He's been tremendous. It was Cliff who helped August with his major meltdown, and he was the one who taught May and July to swim. The baby has really taken to him too. He's so good with her, and the children just can't seem to get enough of him. They've already told me that they love him."

"How long will he be with you?"

"Forever, I hope. He moved right in and fit in immediately, and he can cook up a storm. We never needed any help before, but now, I need all the help I can get."

"Is there any constant female presence in the children's lives right now, or in the foreseeable future?" Amanda asked.

"There was. My Aunt Vera was here since two weeks before April was born, but she left this morning along with everyone else. She has her own life, and she had to get back to it. I simply couldn't ask her to stay any longer.

"My mother lives in town, and she's always popping in for a visit. She was just here for a few days. I'm sure she'll be visiting much more often now."

"May I ask why you chose a man for the children's nanny?" Amanda asked.

"I had no choice. None of the women the agency proposed could live in. The best they could do was someone from 7 AM to 5 PM. I was desperate, so I agreed to one of them, but it wasn't a satisfactory solution by any means. I needed someone here 24/7. As a matter of fact, if it wasn't for Aaron, my friend Jason's partner, we wouldn't have found Cliff. He and Aaron went to high-school together. Aaron was the one who recommended him."

"Oh, I see. Cliff wasn't with the agency."

"No, he was. They just didn't offer him."

"I'm sorry," Amanda said. "I'm a bit confused."

"So am I," Grady added. "Why not?"

"Because he's a man. They said they couldn't place him in a permanent position because none of their other clients wanted to trust a man with their children."

"That makes no sense to me. If he's qualified..."

"Oh, he's more than qualified. His resume is as long as your arm. When I learned all that, I grilled the hell out of the agency director. I ended up hiring him away from them. The director didn't like it very much, but it was made clear to her she'd have a discrimination law suit on her hands if she didn't let him go. She backed down right away."

"I don't know that it was discrimination based on what you've told us," Grady said. "There has to be more to the story."

"There is."

"Can you share that with us?" Amanda asked.

"It's none of your business and besides, it's not for me to say."

"Toby, we're only concerned with the welfare of your children and yourself. A female role model is important to the psychological development of children."

"Oh really? Says who, Amanda?" Toby began to raise his voice. "What do widowers do who have no help at all and don't have any female relatives? Are they unable to raise their children? I'll bet not!"

"There is almost always a female presence, even if it is in the form of a school teacher."

"All my children have female school teachers!"

"Granted, but there just isn't a lot of data right now pertaining to the raising of children under two unattached men in the same household, or even attached, gay couples for that matter."

Toby's voice grew ever louder. "What's that supposed to mean, Amanda? Are you telling me that my home isn't suitable to the raising of my children?"

There was a knock on the door. It slid open immediately. Cliff came right in and walked to the coffee table next to Toby. "I heard shouting. Is everything okay?"

Toby stood up. "I've a good mind to throw the two of you out of my house!"

"Toby?" Cliff placed his hand on Toby's shoulder. "Calm down. What's wrong?"

"They're saying my children shouldn't be raised by the two of us."

"We did not say that, Toby."

"It's Mr. Jacobson!"

"Why not?" Cliff asked.

Amanda looked at Grady. Her pupils were dilated.

"Go on. Tell him," Toby demanded. "If you don't I will."

"Mr. Turnbull," Grady said, "questions arose for us surrounding the circumstances under which you were hired as the children's nanny. We were trying to explain to Mr. Jacobson that children fare better when they have a female presence while they are growing up. Your presence here does not support that."

"I couldn't agree more," Cliff said with all sincerity. "We were fortunate to have my mother raise me and my brother and sister until I was eighteen. When she died, I had to find a way to raise my siblings or we would have been split up with them being put in foster homes because we didn't have any relatives who could take us in. I was able to convince a judge to give me custody of them.

"You don't have to tell me how hard it is, but we were lucky in that we were all older. It was hardest on my sister, though, because she was only thirteen when Mom died. Toby's children are still very young. It's going to be tough, much tougher, but with a supportive, loving environment, there is nothing that can't be accomplished. Now, what other questions do you have for me?"

Toby was fuming when Grady looked up at him.

"Are you sure, Mr. Turnbull?"

"Ask me anything."

"Why didn't the agency place you in any permanent positions?"

"Oh, that's simple. They thought that because I wasn't dating anyone and that I didn't list any female relationships on my application, that I was gay. What they failed to take into consideration was that I was completely and unequivocally committed to my brother and sister. I had no time for dating.

"When I learned the reason, I acquired the services of Mr. Joshua Bergmann. He's the attorney representing Aaron Jaeger and the other players who were terminated by the former coach and general manager of the Nevada Bighorns in their discrimination law suit. He was recommended to me by Jason Ackerman, the CEO of Jaron Enterprises."

"Oh, I see. The same Jason and Aaron you referred to, Mr. Jacobson? The ones who are building Nathan's Promise that's been in the news and will be affiliated with the medical center?"

"The very same," Toby said.

"I rarely use profanity, Grady," Cliff said, "and I apologize, Amanda, but it was none of their fucking business, and it's none of yours either. Now, is there anything else you need to know?"

"I think there's been a terrible misunderstanding," Grady said. "Your sexual orientation has no bearing on this matter, Mr. Turnbull. To be honest, my own brother is gay.

"What raised questions for us was that Mr. Jacobson was not forthcoming as to the reason that you were not placed in a permanent position, a matter which he himself raised. We would never have ventured down this path had he not led us to it. I am not trying to lay blame in any way, but once it was presented to us, we had no other option than to ensure that, how should I put this … that there was nothing nefarious involved. I truly apologize, but we are bound by the law in these matters."

"I understand," Cliff said, "but you must also know that anyone who is to be employed in a position where children are involved must have a criminal background check performed. The fact that I was employed by the agency should have been enough to determine that I had no criminal record."

"You are correct, Mr. Turnbull. Given the time, we would have come to that conclusion on our own, but things moved rather quickly. Again, I apologize."

"I need to apologize too," Toby said. He took a deep breath and exhaled, slowly. "I'm the one who brought it up. I think mistakes have been made all around."

"Then can we all move forward?" Cliff asked. "It's the children and you who need some help, Toby, not me."

"Yeah, but you're the one who's been raked across the coals here, Cliff. I'm sorry this was put on you."

"I've weathered worse, Toby, and I'm sure I'll weather it again. If you're finished with me, I have to get back to the children. They've been unsupervised for too long. Who knows what they've gotten themselves into by now."

"Thanks, Cliff," Toby said. "Call me if you need help."

"Not to worry. Whatever it is, I'll handle it."

After Cliff left, Amanda spoke. "That's one tremendous man you have there, Mr. Jacobson. I apologize for the misunderstanding. I want you to know that I have no concerns for your children whatsoever."

"Thank you, and I'm sorry for my temper earlier. Please call me Toby. Now how is this all going to work and how are we going to put my family back together again?"

"Toby," Amanda said, "it isn't a quick process. It will take months and months at best, if not years before things return to a new normal and that's what it will be, a new normal. What you knew as normal in the past is gone now. What we need to do is work toward building a new life for you and your children."

Chapter Twenty-Three

Confessions

6:00 PM

After dinner, and while the children were in the playroom, Toby called Cliff into his study. "Cliff, I think it's about time we finished that conversation we started the other night."

"I think you're right. I didn't bring it up before because of all that happened on May's birthday after we got back from the airport. Then, this morning, with the psychologists here, your plate was overflowing. When did you want to talk?"

"After the children are in bed, if that's okay with you?"

"Sure. Also, I've been thinking. You mentioned a few days ago that you wanted to start working out with me. I think the evenings would be best, after the children are asleep."

"Why don't we set that aside until after we've spoken? I don't know where our conversation is going to lead, so we probably shouldn't make any kind of plans until after then. Okay?"

"Oh, I see."

"What do you mean?"

"Do I need to be worried?"

"Absolutely not, worried about what?"

Cliff hesitated.

"Please, Cliff, you can say it."

"About whether I still have a job."

"Good God no! No! Nothing like that. Why would you even think that?"

"I don't know. Things have been so tumultuous. I

just wasn't sure."

"Cliff, I'm still under the belief, no the hope, that you'll stay with us forever, that is, if that's what you want."

"I'd love nothing more."

"Good. Then put your mind at ease. Your job is safe."

"Then we'll talk later?"

"I look forward to it."

"I better start rounding them up and get them in the tub, or they'll never be in bed on time."

Toby's eyes misted up.

"What is it, Toby? What did I say?"

"Rounding them up. That's what Sydney used to call it."

"I'm sorry."

"You never said that before. It just caught me off guard."

"I don't think I've ever said it before. It came into my head just now. Sorry."

"No, don't apologize. We'll talk later. Either I'll come find you or you can find me whenever you're free."

"Great, I'll see you then."

****

7:45 PM

When Cliff walked into Toby's bedroom, all the children were lying beside or over his lap on the bed.

"Okay, everybody, time for bed."

"Oh, can't we stay up a little longer?"

"Please, Cliff. Just a little longer?"

"I don't set the rules. Your father does."

"One more story, Daddy?"

"Please, Daddy? Can we?"

Toby shook his head. "Cliff's right. Besides, you're going back to school tomorrow, and I'm going back to work. We all need to get a good night's sleep."

"I'm not ready for bed," May said as she yawned.

"I think you are." Cliff lifted her and set her down on the floor. "Now come on the rest of you. Let's go. It's bedtime."

"Oh, all right," August moaned.

"Oh, all right," July said, copying his brother.

"Stop copying me, July."

"Why?"

"Because I said so."

"August, your brother looks up to you. That's why he does it."

"I don't care, Daddy. It's a ... it's a-noy-ying."

"That's a big word, August," Cliff said.

"I learned it from the TV."

"You know, my little brother used to imitate me too."

"And I'll bet it was a-noy-ying for you too."

"It was, for a little while, but I loved my brother. I still do. My Mom told me the same thing so I just let him do it." Cliff leaned down and whispered in August's ear, "He stopped doing it as soon as I stopped telling him not to."

"Oh." August smiled and put his hand on his brother's shoulder. "You can copy me all you want, July."

"Boys are dumb," June said as she marched out into the hall.

****

8:30 PM
Toby's study

"They're all out like a light," Cliff said after he slid the door closed behind him.

"Shouldn't we leave it open? In case one of them wakes up?"

"If you want, but I've got it covered." Cliff pulled three baby monitors out of various pockets in his pants. "One in the boys' room, one in the girls' room, and one in the nursery."

"Good idea. Come, have a seat here on the sofa. Can I get you something to drink?"

"No. Thanks, I'm good."

"Well, I need one." Toby got up from his chair and walked to the bar. As he poured himself a scotch, he began. "So…"

"So?"

Toby swallowed half of what he poured and then refilled his glass. "About the other night…"

"Right."

Toby walked back to his chair and sat down. "Have you talked to anyone about it? I only ask because you said you were going to."

"I talked to Aaron about it yesterday."

"Good. I don't need to know about it though."

"Toby, I don't mind telling you. I believed you when you told me the other night that I can trust you."

"Thanks, Cliff. I'll leave it to you then. Should I begin?"

"If you want, sure."

"Cliff, I was madly, deeply in love with my wife. I've never loved anyone more. We had the best life anyone could have, and I miss her terribly, but she wasn't the first person I fell in love with."

"I wish I had gotten the chance to know her, but it's strange. It's never happened to me before, but it's like I can feel something sometimes. Things pop into my head that I have no idea why they're there all of a sudden. Like earlier when I told you I was going to round up the children. I've never said that before about any of the kids I've been in charge of. I can tell by the way everyone has talked about her that they loved her very much. She must have been a wonderful person."

"She was, but unless it was by some bizarre stroke of fate, you probably would have never had the chance. You're only here because she isn't."

"Yeah, I guess you're right."

"Cliff, what I'm going to tell you is going to sound crazy, but I want you to know it's all true. She came to me the night she died. I had a vision of Sydney over her bed when they were about to start CPR on her, but her body was brain dead.

"She told me to let her go. She told me to be happy for her. I didn't want to listen, but she made me. She told me that I'd find someone to love and that that person would love our children. She told me to trust my heart, because it would tell me when I found the right person."

Oh, God, don't let him say it.

"Are you okay, Cliff? Sorry, I know this sounds crazy."

"No, sorry. Yes, I'm fine. Please go on."

"She told me that person would be a gift. I've had two gifts in my life, Cliff. Sydney was the second. The first was a year before I met her. I loved that person dearly, but it didn't work out. It couldn't for us, so I moved on."

"I'm sorry, Toby. That must have been tough."

"I really believe it was for the best, because look at what I have because of Sydney. I have five wonderful children, Cliff. I wouldn't give them up for the world."

"I can't imagine you could, Toby. You're right. They're wonderful."

"Cliff, I haven't talked to anyone yet about the other night, but I'm going to tomorrow."

"I thought you said you're going back to work

tomorrow?"

"I am. I'm going to talk to Jason."

"Oh, okay."

"Jason is my best friend. It's not because he's gay that I'm going to talk to him, it's because he's my best friend, but he's also something else. I told you I had two gifts, two people I loved. Jason was the first."

Cliff's jaw dropped. His body began to tremble. After a moment, he said, "I think I could use that drink, if you don't mind."

"Sure. Are you okay?"

"I will be."

"What would you like from the bar?"

"Whatever you're having is fine."

"Scotch it is then."

"Sorry, Toby. I'm just a little in shock. I would have never believed it If I hadn't heard you say it."

"It's true, Cliff. After I had my breakdown, I talked to him about our past. I asked him if he thought I was gay because when you guys were with me in the shower that first night, I had a flashback to my time with him."

Toby placed the tumbler in his hand. It trembled slightly. Cliff emptied the tumbler in one swallow.

"Another?"

"Yes. Please." Cliff handed it back.

As Toby returned to the bar, he continued. "I remembered loving him. It all came back to me when we were all standing naked so close together in the shower."

Cliff's voice trembled. "What did he say?"

"We talked a whole lot about a lot of things. He said he didn't know if I was gay, but what he did say was that he believed I look at people and see *them*, not what's between their legs. He said I fall in love with the person, not whether they have a penis or a vagina. When I thought about it, I realized he was right."

"Then you're a rare person, Toby. I think that's wonderful."

Toby handed the refilled tumbler to Cliff. It was three-quarters full. "So about what happened in the pool…"

"Yeah." Cliff took a big sip. "That was my fault. At the time, I didn't know what I was doing. It just happened."

"I believe you, but something did happen."

"I know, and I'm sorry."

"No, Cliff, please don't say that. It happened because … because I let it happen. When you hugged me, suddenly it seemed … well it seemed like it was natural. I wasn't embarrassed at all.

"I said what I said, using July as an excuse. I justified in my mind that it could be confusing for a young boy who just lost his mother to see his father embracing another man. But that's not the truth, Cliff. Can I be totally honest with you?"

The tumbler shook in Cliff's hand. "Of course." He took a mouthful of the scotch.

"Cliff, it felt good to me and that scared me."

"Oh my God!" Cliff downed the remainder of scotch from his glass.

"I'm sorry, Cliff. Please don't leave because of it. I promise it will never happen again."

"No. That's not what I meant and don't be sorry. It's how you felt. No one was hurt. Don't ever be ashamed of yourself for that. If I'm being honest, it felt good to me too."

"I think I need another drink. You?" Toby extended his hand for the glass. Their fingers touched.

"Definitely."

As Toby poured, Cliff continued. "I didn't want it

to stop. If you hadn't pushed me away, I don't know what would have happened. Some part of my brain took over and it was like I was just a bystander watching from the sideline.

"Toby, when I came here, when you hired me, everything I told you about me was true, except for one thing. You thought I was gay, or at least that I might be, and I didn't say anything to dissuade you otherwise. It means a lot to me that you didn't care. The truth of the matter is, I don't know if I am or not."

Toby returned from the bar to the back of the sofa and handed Cliff his drink over his shoulder. Again, the tumbler was three-quarters full. "I don't understand." Toby took a sip of scotch and remained standing behind Cliff.

"Toby, I'm … sorry, this is difficult. Um …" Cliff swallowed half the scotch, then put the glass on the coffee table. "Toby, I'm a virgin. I've never been with anyone. I've never had sex before." He lowered his head into his hands. His shoulders quivered, and he began to cry, softly.

Toby leaned forward and patted his shoulders, then he began to rub them. "It's okay, Cliff. There's nothing to be ashamed of."

"I'm not ashamed. I'm scared."

Toby leaned down farther and rubbed his back.

A moan rose from deep within Cliff's chest. "Toby, you better stop. That's making me … I've never been touched like that. It's confusing. It's making me feel things … things I don't understand, but whatever they are, I know they're wrong."

"I'm sorry. I didn't mean anything by it, but it's okay to have those feelings."

"I don't know about that, but it's okay. It's not your fault."

"Everyone does, eventually. So, you were saying?"

"Oh yeah, sex wasn't even on my radar. My only focus was on keeping my family together. Once I was here, and you made me that incredible offer, I didn't have to worry about my brother and sister anymore. I knew we'd be all right, but once that weight had been lifted, I lost my focus. I started to think about other things because I could, and I started to think about … well, sex."

Toby swallowed half his drink. "I'm sorry, Cliff, but I'm just a little shocked. I assumed…"

"A lot of people did. Anyway, when we were in the pool, and I felt your body against mine, well I … I just couldn't stop myself. I don't know what would have happened if we had been in the house alone. Not that I would have known what to do, but I'm sure I would have tried to kiss you."

"*What?*" Toby exclaimed.

"I'm sorry. I don't mean to offend you, not that it would have been a good kiss, coz I've never kissed anyone like that, but I would have tried. God, it could have gotten really ugly. I'm a lot bigger than you are and…"

"I don't believe you'd ever hurt me, Cliff. To tell you the truth, I've felt the same way. I don't know if it's just that my memories of having sex with Jason were reawakened or not, but I've thought about kissing you too. To be honest, I've thought about a whole lot more. I'm sorry if that makes you uncomfortable."

Cliff rocked back and forth. "I can't believe I'm having this conversation." He leaned forward, picked up his glass, and emptied it.

"Me either, Cliff, but I think it's good that we are. It's important that we clear the air between us."

"I guess you're right."

"So does it?"

"Does what, it?"

"Does what I said make you uncomfortable?"

"No. It doesn't, not really. Well yeah, I guess, a little, but I don't think I would be good for you, Toby. I have no experience at all."

"You'd be surprise just how much happens that you don't think about. Your body just takes over a lot of times."

"I can't believe I'm saying these things to you, Toby. It's surreal."

"For me too."

"Then there's the fact that I'm your employee. That really complicates things."

"It doesn't have to. I know what I'd like to do, Cliff, but what do you want? What would you like to happen?"

"I don't know."

"Do you want to know what it feels like to be with another man?"

"I do, but I'm scared too. Besides, it's not fair to you."

"Well, here's something to think about. We're both of legal age, and we're both attracted to each other for whatever reasons. If you want, and it's completely up to you, you could experiment with me, but only if you want to. You can take it as far as you want and you can go as slow as you want. There's no pressure and no expectations."

"You'd be willing to do that for me?"

"Yes, I would. I want to, and I need sex. It's been almost two months since … sorry." Toby paused for minute.

"Sorry. Sydney couldn't toward the end of her

pregnancy, and she just wasn't in the mood after April was born, but that has nothing to do with you. If it turns out that I'm not what you want or not who you need, it will be okay. I give you my word."

"So what would I do? What would we do? I don't even know how to start. I've read books about human sexuality, but not about having sex. Aaron said I might look at porn to get an idea."

"Most porn is unrealistic. It's titillating, and it'll help to get you off, but it's not real. It's more of a fantasy, so don't ever think that that's what it's like in real life."

"That's what Aaron said. Can I be honest with you, Toby?"

"Yes. Please do."

"I fantasized about you once."

"And how'd it go?"

"It worked."

Toby laughed out loud. "Sorry. Sorry, I'm not laughing at you. It just sounded funny how you said it. I'm flattered though, that you thought about me that way. The truth is, I did the same about you."

"And?"

"It worked."

Cliff laughed and Toby joined him.

"Would you like to try something?"

"Like what?"

High pitched wailing burst from one of the baby monitors.

"It's April," Cliff said. "She's probably wet and hungry. I better go to her."

"I know and besides, she'll wake all the others if you don't. Go. I'll be here when you get back."

"Sorry, Toby. I'll be back as soon as I can."

"I'll be waiting."

Chapter Twenty-Four

First Touch, First Man

9:45 PM
Toby's Study

"I've got her," Cliff said as he stood in the den's doorway with April in one arm. "I have to heat up a bottle for her."

"I understand," Toby said. "Thanks."

"It's my job. I'll heat it up and feed her, then I'll be back."

"Sure. Sure. I can go with you."

"No, that's okay. I'll be back as soon as I can."

****

10:30 PM
Cliff's Bedroom

When Cliff hadn't returned in a reasonable amount of time, Toby went looking for him. He looked in the nursery, but he wasn't there. Then he went to Cliff's bedroom where he found him, sitting on the edge of his bed. His head was lowered and his hands were folded in his lap.

"Cliff," he whispered as he walked through the door and closed it behind him. "I thought you were coming back downstairs." He approached the bed.

Cliff looked up. "I was, but then I got to thinking. I was watching April take her bottle. Toby, I'm so confused. This just isn't right, what we said to each other. Maybe it was the alcohol. I mean, what am I doing? You just lost your wife and here I am telling you I've fantasized about you. I'm supposed to be taking care of your children, not taking advantage of you."

Toby stood in front of Cliff. "Do you really believe it was the alcohol?"

Cliff looked into Toby's eyes. He slowly shook his head then looked away. "No."

"Who said anything about taking advantage of me? Cliff? I did the same thing."

"I know, and that's it. What would people say? What's wrong with us? You, a happily married man, telling another man he just met that he's been fantasizing about him, only two weeks after his wife has died."

"Crazy, isn't it?"

"Well, yeah."

"Cliff, I don't know what else to say other than I'm strongly attracted to you and it sounds like you feel the same way about me."

"It's the truth. I am, but it's wrong."

"I don't think it is, Cliff. I'm not looking for you to replace, Sydney. No one could ever do that."

"What are we doing then? What is this?"

"It's two adult men who have real human needs and who are attracted to each other, physically, and want to be with each other, or did I completely misunderstand what you said downstairs?"

"No, that completely covers it. You didn't misunderstand a darn thing."

"Then what's the problem?" Toby rested his hands on Cliff's shoulders.

Cliff's body trembled at his touch. "I'm feeling guilty, and I'm feeling confused about feeling guilty, and when you touch me…"

"When I touch you, like this?"

"Yes, it sends shivers through my body."

"I'm not telling you what to do, Cliff. Only you can make that decision." Toby stepped back. "Maybe you need to take some time to think about it. Maybe you need to wait because the time's not right. There's no rush. Only you know what you're feeling, but if your feelings are urging you to take this first step, maybe you need listen to your body. It sounded to me like you've been thinking about it for a few days, but now that it's right in front of you, maybe you're a little scared."

"I am, Toby."

"Cliff, I promise you, nothing will happen that you don't want to happen, but please consider that whatever you decide, it has to be right for you and you alone. I'm going to go back downstairs. You can meet me there if you want."

Toby turned around and left Cliff's room, closing the door behind him.

****

11:15 PM
Toby's Study

Many minutes went by. Toby finally gave up waiting and stood from his chair. As he headed for the door, Cliff came in.

"Sorry, Toby."

"Are you okay?"

"Yes, I'm fine. Sorry I took so long. I needed time to think. I thought about what you said while I took a shower, and...

"And?"

"And I'm here. I tried in the worst way, but no matter how hard I've tried, I can't make what I'm feeling go away. I can't explain it."

"Are you sure you want to be here? Maybe I led you in this direction because I thought you did. Maybe I pushed you to it. Maybe I misread you. Maybe I was wrong."

"No, Toby. I know I want this. I want it in the worst way. That's why I showered real good to make myself clean for you. I could have taken care of myself while I was in there, but I wanted it to be with you."

"I'm glad, Cliff." Toby stepped forward and rested his left hand on Cliff's shoulder. "You said you wanted to kiss me."

Cliff looked down at his shoes. "I did."

"We could start with that." Toby reached his hand to the back of Cliff's head and pulled it down farther. He brushed his lips across Cliff's and then kissed him at the corner of his mouth. "Is this okay?" He whispered as he brushed their cheeks together and then nibbled Cliff's earlobe.

"Yes." Cliff whimpered as fine tremors permeated his body.

Toby drew his cheek back and slowly brushed his lips past Cliff's again and kissed him gently on the other corner of his mouth.

Cliff followed his mouth and met his lips with his own. His mouth opened as he let out a moan.

Toby slid his tongue in and held Cliff's face in both hands as he pressed their lips together. As he moved away, he gently grasped Cliff's bottom lip with his teeth and pulled it with him.

****

"Oh! Oh! Toby!" Cliff pulled his head away and reached for his groin.

"What's wrong?"

"Toby when you did that, my body … I'm getting…" Cliff pressed his hand down against his growing erection. "Toby, I'm sorry. I can't stop it."

"Don't. Do you trust me, Cliff?"

"Yes," Cliff squeaked.

"May I touch you?"

Cliff nodded his head. "Mmm hmm."

"I'm not going to hurt you, Cliff. You can tell me

to stop at any time, and I will. I promise."

"Okay. What are you going to do?"

Toby reached down and traced the outline of Cliff's swelling penis. It extended well down his left thigh. When Toby squeezed, Cliff gasped. "Oh! Oh, my, G … G … God!"

Toby slid his hand along the growing member's length as he worked it up behind the pocket until it rested just below the belt, then squeezed the head.

Cliff's knees buckled, and he began to drop to the floor.

"Let's move you to the sofa," Toby said, as he grabbed ahold of him. He led Cliff by the hand and sat him down. "Unbuckle your belt and unbutton and unzip your pants."

"Okay. Toby, I'm so nervous." He fumbled with the buckle.

Toby moved in front of Cliff and pushed the coffee table back. Then he kneeled down. "It's okay, Cliff." He reached for the belt and undid it, then unzipped his fly.

"Now, lift your butt and pull your pants down to your knees."

Once he'd done it, Toby pulled them down to his ankles.

"Oh, Toby, it's getting bigger."

"I can see that. Now, pull your shirt up to your chest and raise your butt."

When Cliff lifted, Toby began pulling his boxers down, but the head of his penis got stuck in the elastic. Toby reached his hand in and freed it.

"Oh my God!"

"It's okay, Cliff. You're doing fine."

"Toby, the sensations… When you touched me… I can't believe how it feels. I … I…"

"Just let it happen, Cliff."

Toby pulled his boxers down to join the pants. He reached around and turned up the volume on the monitors for a moment. There was no sound from the children's rooms other than loud static, so he turned them back down.

"Now, pull off your shirt and slide your hips forward until your butt is at the edge of the sofa. Then put your hands behind your head and interlock your fingers."

"Okay," Cliff squeaked again. As he slid forward, he was forced to spread his legs apart, around Toby's body.

"Now lean your head back and close your eyes. I want you to focus on what you're feeling. You don't have to do anything."

Cliff did as he was told.

"I'm not going to hurt your, Cliff. I'm going to touch you in different places and in different ways. This can be intense the first time because the pleasure sensations can be overwhelming, so try not to cry out."

"Okay. Okay, I'll try."

Toby placed his hands against Cliff's groin, surrounding his penis and lifting his scrotum with his thumbs.

Cliff jumped. "Oh," he moaned.

Toby moved his fingers down to beneath Cliff's nearly lemon-sized balls. When he rhythmically raked the tips of his fingers beneath his sack, Cliff's shaft lurched upward. Toby watched the shaft pulsate as it filled with blood until it stood erect, hugging Cliff's abdomen.

Toby drew his fingertips up Cliff's thighs, up his hairy, rigid abdomen, until he reached his chest.

"Your six-pack, Cliff … it's so hard, like it's

made from cobblestones and your pecs are solid masses of muscle." He circled his fingers around Cliff's nipples and allowed them to linger there as he gently pinched them. One at a time he licked them, leaving a tendril of saliva to his mouth as he blew on them.

With each breath, Cliff's torso lunged forward.

When Toby drew his fingernails across his nipples, they swelled and hardened, forcing Cliff to grunt with pleasure.

Toby stood up and kicked off his shoes. Then he dropped his pants and briefs and kicked them away. He was semi-erect. He kneeled onto the sofa and then scooted up and slid his butt along Cliff's thighs. Ending in his lap, he thrust his groin up and down the rigid shaft as his own manhood continued to engorge with blood.

Cliff cried out. "Oh, God! Oh, God! Oh, God!" A bead or pre-cum emerged from the slit of his bulbous glans.

"It's okay, Cliff." Toby planted his mouth against Cliff's parted lips. "Just let it happen."

"Toby, it's … it's … I can't describe it. Oh, my God! Is that your penis … touching mine?"

Toby pressed a finger to Cliff's lips. "Hush."

When Toby drew his fingertips out to just beneath Cliff's armpits and down his flanks, Cliff moaned again. Then he slid the back of his right hand against Cliff's belly and drew it forward until his palm pressed against the massive, turgid rod. Focusing his contact along the shaft, he slid it up from the base while pulling it slightly toward him until it pressed against his own.

"Oh, God! Oh, my God! Oh, Toby. Oh, my God!"

By the time his hand reached the glans, it was well above Cliff's belly button just beneath his breast bone.

"It's quite large, Cliff." *Holy fuck it's a monster,* Toby screamed to himself inside his head. "There's a lot here to … how do I say it … to handle. Are you doing okay?"

"Toby. Oh, Toby. Oh, my God. Toby."

"I'll take that as a yes."

The bead of pre-cum rose up as more began to ooze beneath it. Toby lightly pressed his palm over the forming globule and moved it in circles, spreading Cliff's natural lubricant over, around, and under the bulbous head.

Again, Cliff's torso lurched forward. He reached for his cock, but Toby pushed his hands away and then blew a tight stream of air across the glistening slit. Once he had completely coated the head, he wrapped his hand around the glans and slowly slid it downward along both of their shafts.

Cliff's teeth closed over his upper lip. He grunted as his hips bucked up involuntarily, shoving his shaft through Toby's barely clenched fist and against Toby's erection.

As Toby slid farther down, his fingers began to splay apart. Their shafts were simply too thick to be encased by one hand alone.

"Are you okay, Cliff?" *Holy fuck!* Toby thought. *How am I going to get my mouth around him?*

"Yeah. Yeah. Don't stop. Oh, God. Please don't stop."

"Cliff have you ever had an HIV test?"

"Huh?" Cliff opened his eyes and sat forward. "No. I've never had sex."

"Just wanted to be sure. Now close your eyes again and lean back."

Once Cliff was in position, Toby slid his hand

back up their shafts and scooped up more of his natural lubricant. Precum began beading from Toby's slit. He mixed it with Cliff's and began sliding both of his hands down again, then he slid back to Cliff's knees and lifted his scrotum with is left hand and raked his fingers forward along the underside.

Cliff groaned. Then he began to moan, loudly.

When he lifted Cliff's scrotum and began massaging his balls, he hovered his mouth above the head and then lowered it until his lips made contact around the slit. He opened his mouth and darted his tongue along the frenum while he slid down over the head until it filled his mouth.

Cliff's hips lunged upward, driving the shaft to the back of Toby's throat, gagging him momentarily, but he began to suck and bob his head up and down, forcing the glans to glide between his lips and tonsils. When Cliff cried out, Toby slid his right hand up and down the shaft, while he gently squeezing Cliff's balls with his left.

Cliff opened his eyes. "I can't take it! I can't take it, Toby!

"Mmm," Toby murmured. He lifted his mouth. "You taste so good, Cliff. Lean back."

He slid back down to the floor and leaned his face in to tongue the hanging sack below the rigid shaft. He opened his mouth and sucked against Cliff's left ball until he was able to draw it in, but there was barely any room. It filled his mouth completely. He slid his tongue back and forth beneath it, massaged it against the ridges of his hard palate, then released it and drew the right one in, repeating the massage.

After releasing it, he blew a stream of air across the top of Cliff's scrotum, causing it to draw tightly up against the base of his shaft. He leaned in and licked and slurped and sucked around the underside and then made his way down over the perineum.

Toby raised his head. "Is this okay, Cliff?"

"Oh, my God, Toby. Please."

"Please?"

"Please, don't you dare stop."

"Then slide down a little farther and wrap your arms behind your knees."

The moment Cliff's ass was in the air, Toby slid his tongue farther down until he reached the puckered rose bud of Cliff's outer sphincter. As if licking a giant, spiral lollipop, Toby rested his chin on the sofa and slid his tongue upward in one, long stroke.

Cliff grunted as the outer sphincter immediately spasmed shut, but Toby dove right in and wiggled his tongue against it while his lips formed a ring around it, enabling him to apply suction. Slurping and sucking noises filled the room as Toby ate away and lapped like a hungry dog at his food bowl while he used his hands to gently ply the cheeks apart. The sounds of his slurping and licking were joined by soft, high-pitched squeals that escaped from Cliff's throat.

As Toby persisted, the outer sphincter finally relented and allowed him to penetrate farther in. The texture of tender membranes against his tongue brought back memories of when he performed the same ritual for Jason, and they spurred him on. Deeper and deeper he advanced until he reached the tighter barrier of Cliff's inner sphincter.

Cliff's entire body began to spasm and quake as he was driven to his first total body orgasm. A stream of precum shot from his shaft and sprayed across his face, into his chest, and then dripped down through the hair that covered his abdomen. Guttural, animal-like sounds filled the room as he bucked in orgasmic ecstasy.

"I can't … can't take … much more, Toby," Cliff grunted between breaths after the orgasm finally ended several minutes later. I feel like … I don't know what… I've never felt… Toby! Toby! It was … it was wonderful. What was it?"

"That was an orgasm, Cliff."

"But it wasn't like the ones I had before. This was different. Better."

"You don't have to shoot a load in order to have an orgasm, Cliff, but I'm glad it happened. I've only had a few over my lifetime."

"You're incredible, Toby, just incredible."

"We're not finished yet." Toby moved up and slid his mouth over Cliff's saturated shaft as he sucked in the residual pre-cum and drew more from the slit. "Like honey you are, Cliff. Like honey."

Toby sucked the head in again while he squeezed the shaft tightly and slid his hand down its length until he reached Cliff's balls. He worked the balls with his left hand as he pumped up and down on the shaft with his right. Then he came up for air.

"Sweet and salty and musky all at the same time."

He slid his mouth over the head and down the shaft again, as far as he could go, causing his jaw to ache at the expansion, while his left hand moved down to Cliff's anus and began to massage his fingers in. Then he came up for air once more.

"Your pre-cum is like ambrosia. I want more, Cliff. Give me more."

"Oh, God, Toby. It's going to happen! It's going to happen. It's…"

Toby felt Cliff's balls pull up tight against the base of his shaft. His hips trembled.

"It's going to happen, Toby! It's going to happen!"

Toby latched his mouth around Cliff's cock head and slid down as far as he could go while his fingers frantically penetrated and massaged the outer sphincter of his anus.

Cliff sat up and grabbed Toby's head with his meaty hands and forced it up and down his shaft, causing thick mucus to fill his mouth, making him gag.

"It's happening, Toby! It's happening!"

When it began, Cliff's body jerked, and his hips bucked. So overcome by the new sensations of ecstasy, he was forced to release Toby's head. When his body became wracked by uncontrollable spasms, his load erupted.

The first ejection was so large, it filled Toby's mouth and shot out past his lips, but he held on. He wrapped his right hand around the shaft and rapidly worked his mouth up and down past the corona while he swallowed wave after wave of Cliff's massive, musky spunk while two fingers of his other hand penetrated the inner sphincter and reached just far enough to graze against the rock-hard, plum-sized prostate.

Toby continued to suck, long after the final wave had been ejected, forcing Cliff's body to continue to spasm in erratic fits of pleasure while his fingers continued their assault on his sensitive, virginal prostate. With each breath he panted, deep, animalistic grunts rose from Cliff's throat.

Finally, Toby released the shrinking shaft and withdrew his fingers. He caressed the insides of Cliff's thighs for long minutes after he'd finished, and licked his balls and groin clean of cum while he softly hummed a seesaw of two, low tones. He returned several times to draw the shaft into his mouth, ensuring he'd pulled the last remnants of Cliff's first man to man encounter from deep within his core while he pressed his thumb against the perineum and drew it toward his balls and then again at the base, milking it up to the slit.

When there was no more to be had, Toby moved up and sat on Cliff's lap. He leaned into his chest and ran his hands through the thick fur that covered it and up and over his massive shoulders. Finally, he leaned forward and kissed and licked Cliff's face clean of precum, lingering over his lips several times as he whispered softly to him. "It was beautiful, Cliff. Thank you. Thank you for letting me be your first. I'll never forget it."

Cliff lifted his head. He was dazed, but awake enough to find Toby's face. He pulled it to his own and kissed him sloppily on the mouth. Then he hugged him tightly. A low, soft, hum-like growl rose from his chest. Finally, he spoke. "I'll never let you go, Toby. Never."

Chapter Twenty-Five

They're Going to Have to Love My Children First

Thursday, May 20, 2010, 6:25 AM
The Nursery

When Toby found Cliff, he was in the nursery, changing and dressing April.

"Good morning, stud," Toby whispered as he walked in, after closing the door behind him.

The back of Cliff's neck turned red as a subtle smile spread across his face.

Toby walked to him and wrapped his arms around his waist, pressing the side of his face against his back as he hugged him.

"What if the children come in?" Cliff whispered.

"Don't worry, we have a few minutes yet. They're still brushing their teeth."

"Toby, I…"

"I know, Cliff." Toby let go and stood beside him at the changing table. He reached up and caressed his back.

"Toby … last night … it was … it was like nothing I could have ever imagined. Is it always like that?"

"Better."

"God help me then. I barely slept. I kept reliving it over and over again. Your mouth … what you did to me with your mouth … I … I shot two more times after I turned in, once in the shower and another after I went to bed. I can't believe it. It's like it's been pent up in me for so long, and it just had to get out."

"And I thought I'd gotten rusty. It's been years since I had another man's cock in my mouth."

"Toby, the baby!" Cliff whispered, strongly.

"The baby has no idea what we're saying, but I'll bet you she can sense the emotions that are passing back and forth between us."

"Still, it feels wrong."

"Why?"

"I feel dirty, saying these things in front of her."

"Cliff." Toby pressed against his arm to turn him until he faced him. "Cliff, please don't think that. There was nothing … nothing dirty about what happened last night. It was one of the most beautiful experiences I've ever had."

"Me too, but…"

"But nothing. You're new at this. I promise it will get easier."

April began to gurgle and coo. "See, she knows. Look how happy she is."

Cliff turned back and finished applying her diaper. "How should we act around the children?"

"Like we always do, exactly like we always do. We shouldn't act any differently until we've got this thing figured out."

"Toby, I can't stop thinking about it." Cliff snapped closed the bottom two snaps of April's onesie and swaddled her in a receiving blanket. "It's like I'm consumed by it, and I want more, so much more."

"It was your first time, Cliff. It's like that. It'll get better. It'll become normal. I promise. Now, I better go check on the children."

Toby raised up on his toes and kissed Cliff on the cheek, then he headed toward the door. The door opened slowly.

"Oh, there you are, Daddy. I couldn't find you anywhere."

"I was just checking on your baby sister, June.

Cliff had to change her again."

"Oh. That's why he wasn't down in the kitchen."

"I'm headed there right now," Cliff said as he lifted April into his arms. "Are you hungry?"

"Famished."

"Famished? That's a big word."

"I learned it from Grand Mom." June began to imitate her grandmother. "'I'm just *famished*. I'm so *famished*. Miss Charity, the children are *famished*. When will lunch be ready?'" She giggled.

"Hey, young lady," Toby said, sternly, "it's disrespectful to imitate people, particularly your grandmother. I'll not have that in this house."

"I'm sorry, Daddy." June's bottom lip started to quiver as crocodile tears brimmed from her lower eyelids.

Toby picked her up and hugged her, then wiped her eyes with his thumb. "Okay then," he said as he kissed her cheek and put her down. "Now, dry those tears and go round up your brothers and sister. Then march yourselves downstairs."

"I'll get started on breakfast right away," Cliff said as she walked through the door. Then he said, "That was a close one," as he walked up to stand beside Toby.

"All she would have seen is me touching your arm. We're going to be touching each other now and then. There's nothing wrong with that."

"That's not what I was talking about. Ten seconds earlier and she would have seen you kissing me."

"Oh, that."

"Right."

"I'll try to remember."

****

11:15 AM
Office of the Vice-President, Jacobson

Construction

Toby stood up from his desk as he held the phone to his ear, waiting for it to be answered on the other end.

"Jaron Enterprises. Fiona speaking. How may I direct your call?"

"Hi, Fiona. It's Toby. Is Jason there?"

"Toby. It's wonderful to hear your voice," she said excitedly. Then her tone turned gentle. *"How are you doing?"*

"As well as can be expected, Fiona. Really, I'm doing fine. Thanks so much for asking."

"I'm so glad. We've all been thinking about you ... and the children."

"That's very kind of you, Fiona. Thank you."

"I'll get Jason for you right away."

For a moment, there was background music.

"Hey, Toby. What's up?"

"Jason, you got a few minutes?"

"Sure."

"This is a private call, Jason, just between you and me. If that's all right."

"Yes. Sure. Give me a moment."

There were muffled voices on the other end while Jason held the mouthpiece up to his chest. A moment later, he came back on the line.

"Okay, Toby. Aaron's left the room. Shoot."

"Jason, you remember what we talked about last week?"

"We talked about a lot of things, Toby. Can you give me an idea?"

"About me and Cliff?"

"You said a lot of things about Cliff."

"Well, it happened. Last night."

"It happened?" Jason emphasized *It*.

"Jason! We did it!"

"You mean you had sex." It was more of a statement.

"Yeah! Oral only, on him, but it was great!"

"To-by," he said slowly, emphasizing each syllable.

"It just happened, sort of, Jason, but it was consensual, I promise. We talked a lot. We had to stop coz of the baby. Long story short, he left to go to take care of her, didn't come back for a while. I found him in his room. We talked. I left him to think.

"After a half hour, I thought he changed his mind. I started to head up to bed, but then he came to me and said he wanted it. Jason, it was incredible! He's amazing, and that body. Oh, my God. He's an Adonis, but then I guess you know what I'm talking about, but he's even bigger than Aaron. It was so beautiful, being his first."

"I remember, but then, you were there."

"Exactly, just like you did for me. I'm so happy right now."

"Then I'm happy for you both, Toby. I'm sorry, but I have to ask. Do you think this could possibly be a rebound kind of thing?"

"We talked for a long time about that. I told him about us, you and me, I mean. I told him about Sydney being okay with it, with me being attracted to men, with everything really, and I told him about my vision of her and my dreams when she came to me.

"He's very smart, Jason, and very understanding. He asked all the right questions even before he admitted his feelings for me. He wanted to be sure there was no way he was taking advantage of me. He wanted me to be sure that I'd considered all the possibilities."

"His feelings? Did he say he loved you, Toby? Did you tell him you loved him?"

"No way, Jason. This isn't love. It's physical. It's

true that I like him a lot, but there's no way I'm ever going to love someone like I loved Sydney. I told him that. After all, she was the mother of my children.

"If I ever do fall in love again, whoever it is, they're going to have to love my children first. They're going to have to love them so much and so hard that they'd be willing to die for them. They're going to have to do all of that before I could ever let myself fall in love with them."

"Well it sounds like you've both given this a lot of thought, but I still have to caution you. Go slow. Be gentle with him. Yes, he's built like a brick shit house, but I really believe that emotionally, he's very young, very fragile.

"Remember what he's been through, Toby. Emotionally, he's a boy in a man's body. He was never allowed to grow up through those horrendous teenage years. He jumped from being a kid in high school to becoming a parent in a matter of a few days.

"Even though he acts and functions like a mature adult, he still hasn't gone through all that crap yet, like infatuation, falling in love for the first time, getting his heart broken a few times, and making some horrendous mistakes. I'm not saying he's immature. I'm saying he's green when it comes to youth's growing pains."

"I don't think you give him enough credit, Jason. We've had some deep conversations about his family, and he's been totally honest about how difficult it's been on him, but I'll follow your advice. I'll be very gentle with him.

"Good. Does Aaron know?"

"Not from me. I guess that's up to Cliff to decide whether to tell him. I have no idea if he will. Do you think he will?"

"I have no idea either, but you've requested

privacy in this matter, I give you my word. I won't say anything to him."

"Thanks, Jason. It's good to have someone to talk to about this."

"Of course, Toby. I understand."

"Well that's all I had. I'd planned to meet with you and Aaron about Nathan's Promise on Monday. Do you want me to meet you down in the valley at the site, or should I plan to fly up?"

"I'm not sure yet. I'll let you know."

"Okay, I'll wait to hear from you. I'll see you then."

"Thanks, Toby. Bye."

"Bye, Jason and thanks again."

"Any time."

****

4:45 PM
Jacobson Residence, Foyer

"Daddy's home!"

"Daddy's home!"

"Daddy!"

"Daddy!"

"Hello, everybody! How was school?"

"I'm so happy you're home, Daddy. School was weird."

"Weird? How?"

"Rosy Jean was nice to me."

"Isn't that a good thing, June?"

"Rosy Jean's never nice to me, Daddy. She said she had to be nice to me, but she wouldn't tell me why."

"Oh, I see." Toby closed his eyes. An image of Sydney appeared in his mind.

"Yeah, Daddy, me too. I got to be first in line for lunch and it wasn't even my turn."

"Well, August, it was still a nice thing for you,

wasn't it?"

"I guess. I think it's coz Mommy's gone. Everybody whispered when I got to my classroom. Even teachers in the hall were whispering, teachers who aren't even my teachers, and they smiled kinda weird at me too."

"I got to help Cliff feed April," May said as she jumped up and down with her hand in the air.

"That was nice, May."

"Yeah, and I got to burp her, too. Cliff showed me how."

"Then it sounds like you also had a good day."

"I did. I guess," May said, sucking her finger as she pointed the tip of her left shoe to the floor and twisted her foot back and forth.

"Daddy?" July tugged on Toby's pant leg.

"Yes, July?"

"I just had school. Nothin' special happened to me."

"Now, July," Cliff said as he walked up to them, carrying April. "Didn't you get extra time in the play corner today? That's what your teacher, Mrs. Finley, told me when I picked you up."

"Oh yeah! Daddy, I got to play in the play corner as long as I wanted."

"See, July, then you had a good day too!"

"Yeah. I forgot."

"Dinner will be ready at five," Cliff said as he rubbed his hand against the upper arm of Toby's suit jacket, "unless you want me to hold it for a little while. Would you like a drink in the meantime?"

"Yeah, I'd like that. Scotch would be great."

"Scotch it is. Now, for the rest of you. Your daddy's had a long day. How about we all give him a few minutes to relax."

Under mild protests, the children filed down the hall and went into the play room. Once they were out of sight, Cliff leaned in for a hug and then kissed Toby's cheek. "Welcome home. How was your day?"

Toby bristled ever so slightly. "It was good, Cliff," he said in a neutral tone.

"Is something wrong?"

"The children."

"But I thought … after this morning … you kissed me…" Cliff's shoulders sank.

"Cliff … Cliff, I'm sorry," Toby said as he reached to rub his arm. "I forgot. It's so weird. It's like we are … but it's like we aren't, too. This is so confusing."

"No, it's my fault. I was the one who warned you and here I am forgetting my own words. It's just that I'm so happy you're home."

"And I'm happy to be home, really. Sorry."

"It's okay. Today was surreal, being here alone with April and May and driving the children to school. I went in and introduced myself to the principal. Then she waked me around to the children's classrooms to meet their teachers.

"You should have seen the looks I got from some of the other children, bug-eyed and pointing at me and whispering while I was outside the door being introduced. I guess they're not used to seeing a man with a baby, papoose-strapped to his chest."

Toby smiled. "It's probably more like such a studdingly handsome, tall, young man."

"I guess. I did have to bend down a bit when I shook all the teachers' hands. …Oh, I get it. Studdingly handsome. You're too much."

"No, Cliff. You're too much."

Red began to rise up Cliff's neck. "Don't make

me blush." He fanned himself with one hand. "Good grief. I'm acting like a school girl."

"More like a school boy, and you're my school boy, all mine, mister. All mine." Toby smacked him on the butt. "I'm going to go get that drink."

"I did want to talk to you sometime this evening, about last night, and the nights to follow, if you know what I mean," Cliff said without a shred of innuendo.

"Then we're on the same page?" Toby asked, as he raised his eyebrows up and down.

"Oh no, no. I didn't mean it like that. I didn't mean to suggest that we … ah, that we … you know … would, um, should… Oh, God. More like whether and how, you know if it was possible … again … I mean … if we could?"

"Now I have no idea what you mean. Just spit it out."

"Well … that if we could do it again … sometime."

"Definitely. I'm looking forward to it. There's so much more, Cliff. We barely scratched the surface last night."

"I can't even imagine."

"Don't worry. I'm going to take good care of you. We'll go at your speed. Anything with you will be wonderful. Now, I'm going to pour myself a glass of scotch." Toby began walking to his study door off the foyer.

"Wait," Cliff said. "I also wanted to talk to you about the children. I caught myself several times today almost telling May how wonderful her Daddy is, but I did catch myself. Nothing was said."

"It's still new, Cliff … for both of us."

"So we can talk?"

"Yes, after the children are in bed."

Chapter Twenty-Six

Letters to Mommy

6:30 PM
The Family Room

Cliff and the children joined Toby for some television in the family room after they'd finished cleaning up after dinner and put the dishes away. After Cliff sat down, August and May climbed onto his lap. He wrapped his arms around them and then hugged them.

Toby did the same with June and July.

"Daddy, Cliff lifted me up so I could put the dishes in the cabinet. I never saw all the way up in there before, but now I was high enough."

"That's nice, June. I'm sure you did a great job."

"I like washing dishes, Daddy."

"Good for you, July. I know Cliff appreciated you helping him clean up."

"You didn't wash 'em, July," August said, "the dishwasher did."

"Stop bein' mean to me, August!" July shouted.

"Hey," Cliff whispered into August's ear as he tousled his hair and kissed the top of his head.

"Yeah, well I emptied it, August, and Cliff said I did a good job."

Cliff nodded. "Yes, you did, July."

"Yeah, well … well I stacked them."

"August," Toby said sternly. "This discussion is over."

August crossed his arms over his chest and stared straight ahead at the TV.

Cliff reached his hand to uncross them into his lap. Then he kissed his head again and jostled him as he hugged him.

"I put the forks and spoons and knives away, Daddy."

"And I bet you did a good job of it, May."

"I did. Cliff said so."

April began to fuss. "Right on time," Cliff said. I'll go heat up some formula."

"I'd like to feed her," Toby said. "I don't get to do it enough."

"Sure. I'll be right back with her bottle."

While Cliff was in the kitchen, Toby lifted July and June from his lap and then picked April up out of her swing. When he returned to the sofa, June and July snuggled close as he cradled April in his arms.

"She's so tiny, Daddy," July said. "Her hands are so tiny, and her feet too."

"Everything on a baby is tiny, July. You were this small once."

"I know. Mommy told me. I miss Mommy, Daddy."

"I miss her too, July."

When Cliff returned to the family room, all the children were crying softly. He looked at Toby, who also had tears in his eyes.

"They're missing their Mommy," Toby said.

Cliff handed the bottle to Toby and then lifted May and July up and sat down with them in his lap and then pulled June and August beside him. "When you cry for someone who's gone," he said, hugging them to him and kissing each of their heads, "it shows how much you still love them. I can tell you all love your Mommy very much.

"There's something I learned when I was a camp counselor that we did with some of the children. Do you want to hear about it?"

All the children sniffled and nodded their heads.

"I learned that even when the people you love aren't with you anymore, they're still watching over you, up in heaven. We would have the children who missed someone write them a letter or draw them a picture and then fold it up and put it in a special fire.

"No one was allowed to see the letters and pictures the children made because they were just between them and their loved ones. As they burned, the smoke carried them up to heaven for their loved ones to see. Would you like to do that for your Mommy?"

"Yes, I want to write to Mommy."

"Me too."

"Me too. I wanna draw Mommy a picture."

"And me. I wanna make a picture too."

"Then why don't all of you write your letters and draw your pictures while I go make the special fire out in the fire pit." He looked at Toby. "This will only take me a few minutes."

Toby mouthed, "Thank you."

****

6:55 PM
The Patio

Cliff took a hatchet from the storage shed and split tinder, thin slivers, and shaved kindling from several logs from the stack on the patio. Afterward, he laid them out into the shape of a log cabin, leaving a doorway for the children to insert their letters and pictures through. Then he arranged chairs around the fire pit. When the children and Toby came out, he was ready.

After Cliff showed them how to insert them, one by one the children leaned over the fire pit's brick wall and pushed their folded pieces of paper into the cabin. When they finished, Cliff pulled a folded piece of paper from his pocket.

"I have something to ask you all," he said as he squatted down to the children's level. "I know I didn't know your Mommy, but I feel very special and very lucky to have been given the chance to take care of her children, and I wanted to write her a letter too. I don't mind if you know what it says, if you want to."

"What do you want to tell my Mommy?" August asked.

"I want to tell her how wonderful and special her children are. I want to tell her how good and strong and wonderful your father is and how hard he's trying to take good care of all of you. And I want to tell her that I'm going to help him take good care of all of you—" Cliff's eyes welled up as he looked up to Toby— "for the rest of my life and that I love you all very much."

A sob burst from Cliff's chest. For a moment, he covered his mouth with the back of his forearm, then he exhaled hard, forcing it to be over. He wiped his eyes and looked back at the children.

"So, may I send my letter to your Mommy too?"

All four of them rushed toward him, plastering themselves against his chest, and hugged him.

"And we love you," August said as he buried his head into Cliff's neck.

"I love you, Cliff," July said. "You teached me how to swim."

"And you teached me too," May said.

"I love you, Cliff," June said as she started to cry.

Cliff pulled them all into a tight embrace. After a few moments, he let go and the children stood back. He waited for their answer. Suddenly, all together, they shouted, over and over. "Yes! Yes! Yes! Yes!"

"Thank you." He kneeled in front of the fire pit and added his letter to the cabin.

Toby cleared his throat. "I have a letter for

Mommy too." He walked to the pit and kneeled down next to Cliff. As he held April in his left arm, he pushed his letter through the cabin's doorway with his right hand and then moved his arm across Cliff's shoulders.

"Thank you for doing this, Cliff," Toby said as he rested his head against him. "You're a very special man."

After everyone had taken a seat around the pit, Cliff lit a long wooden match and inserted it into the middle of the cabin. In a moment, it caught and soon the fire spread to all of its four corners. As the smoke began to rise, July followed it as it traveled up into the sky.

"Hi, Mommy," he called. Then he started to cry. "I miss you, Mommy."

Soon everyone was crying as they watched the smoke rise skyward. As the intensity of the fire grew and consumed the walls and roof of the cabin, so too did the pain of everyone's grief begin to release.

August went to July and climbed into his chair with him. He put his arm around his brother and hugged him. "I'm sorry I was mean to you about the dishes, July."

"I know, August," July answered. "I miss my Mommy."

"I miss her too." August pulled July into his lap and wrapped his arms around him from behind.

When June ran to Cliff and sobbed in his arms, Toby scooped up May and together they cried until there were no more tears to shed. As the fire burned down, Cliff lifted his head skyward and said out loud, but softly, "I'll take good care of them, Sydney, I promise."

One by one each of the children and Toby looked up and silently or in whispers, mouthed words to follow the trails of smoke and they traveled upward. When the fire had reduced to embers, Cliff gathered up the children and then led them up for a second bath before bed because of the smoke in their pajamas from the fire.

While he did this, Toby carried April to the nursery to change her diaper.

When Cliff found him, he was snoring softly with April cradled in his arms. He lifted her from Toby's arms and moved her to her bassinet. Then he gently rocked Toby's shoulder until he woke up.

When Toby opened his eyes, he pulled Cliff to him and kissed him gently on the mouth. "You're such a beautiful man, Cliff. Thank you. Thank you for that. The children needed to cry, and so did I."

"I felt it was the right thing to do, but it's just the beginning. You all deserve whatever help you can get. I'm just a small part of it. Now, let's get you to bed."

Cliff followed Toby into his bedroom, but stopped midway between the doorway and the bed. "I'll leave you to sleep, Toby. You need it. We'll talk another time."

"Oh, Cliff, I completely forgot."

"Really, Toby, it's fine. Tonight was a very important moment for all of you. We'll talk later."

Cliff turned to leave.

"No," Toby called. "Please, Cliff, don't go. Come back. Stay here with me tonight."

"You need to sleep, Toby. You've been through a lot already."

"I don't want sex, Cliff. I want to hold you. Please don't leave me alone."

Cliff turned back and walked to him. He pulled Toby against him and caressed his lips with his own. "Okay, I'll stay. I won't leave you alone."

Toby leaned away and began removing his clothes.

Cliff took each article from him, folded it, and then draped it over the back of the closest reclining chair.

With just his boxer's remaining, Toby faced him to remove them and then stood naked in front of him. "This is me, Cliff, jelly roll and all. Did you mean what you said when you looked into the sky? Did you mean it for me too?"

Cliff lifted him off the ground and pulled him to him. "Yes, Toby, I'm going to take care of you. Jelly roll and all."

"Thank you, Cliff. I didn't want to be alone tonight and yes, I do need sleep, but I need to take a shower first. I won't be long."

****

As the water fell over his head and ran down Toby's body, Pachelbel's Cannon in D played over the speakers. He swayed with the music. He closed his eyes and thought of Sydney while he lathered shampoo into his hair.

Slowly, two strong arms wrapped around him from behind and pulled him backward into a wall of solid muscle. A bar of richly scented, masculine soap in a large meaty hand ran across his chest, down his abdomen, around his dick, and under his balls.

As his knees began to buckle, he was lifted into the water to rinse his face and then carried away and held in a powerful, yet soft embrace. When he regained control of his legs, he was gently set back down. The bar of soap was running over every inch of him while a second hand slathered the lather into every crevice, over every prominence, and into every recess of his body.

When the hands moved their focus to his cock and balls, they began to squeeze and caress and force them to slip between their fingers. As his shaft swelled, a hand moved behind him and caressed his anus, making slow circles while it probed inquisitively as more soap was added, until the lather was worked into a thick, slick lubricant.

When Toby began to thrust upward with his cock, a hand tightened around it. When he thrust his anus backward, fingers slid in and out as they massaged the tender, sensitive tissues, beckoning entrance.

When powerful words of love and longing entered his ears, his anus relented. "I love you, Toby," the voice coaxed. "I need you, Toby."

Images of passion and lust filled his mind while the fingers advanced.

"I want you, Toby, more than I've ever wanted anything before."

Sensations of arousal and enticement shouted from every nerve ending of his body, while fingers he did not yet know, danced over him and inside him, caressing his swelling pleasure orb. "Feel my love, Toby. Feel me inside you."

A pressure like he'd never encountered before grew between his legs. When he reached down to grasp it, it was withdrawn and pressed up against his back, then it moved between his legs again, and then again up his back, over and over again. Each time it slid past his anus, the sphincters spasmed tightly against the probing fingers.

"We will make love, Toby, but not tonight. Tonight is for sleep."

"No, please don't torture me, Cliff," Toby cried. "Please, I need this."

"Very well."

The fingers quickened their pace as their dance grew more frantic. As their pressure increased, Toby's body convulsed. His prostate tightened in on itself, and when the fingers sensed it, they pressed steadily upward and began to vibrate. The head of his cock swelled and grew crimson, and the veins along the shaft bulged to the point of rupture.

A wave of pleasure, like he hadn't felt in years, washed over him as grunts and groans rose from his chest. Involuntarily, his hips thrust forward as the first stream of cum flew from his slit and splashed against the shower wall. As the fingers pressed upward, wiggling and stroking inside him, wave after wave of cum was ejected from his core until his body collapsed.

The next thing he knew, he was bathed in the glow of the recessed infrared lamps in the ceiling. Warm towels caressed his body. A comb passed through his hair. Earthy scented lotion with traces of musk was applied to his skin and then he was lifted and carried to his bed.

As he drifted into sleep, he was cradled in a warm embrace that encompassed his entire being. The pressure grew again between his legs. As it pressed up beneath him and began to slide to and fro, his sphincters opened in invitation, and his cock swelled. In his last waking act, he pressed his body backward and then was lost to his dreams.

Chapter Twenty-Seven

Patsy's Coming

Friday, May 21, 2010, 6:45 AM
When Toby woke, he was alone in bed. *What a dream. Was that a dream last night? Oh, but what a dream it was.*

As his mind cleared, a scent he hadn't smelled in a long time hovered in the air around him. He sniffed his arms. Traces of the lotion that Sydney had bought for him the year before lingered on his skin. He drew his knees up and leaned into them. The same, earthy, musky scent was there as well. Even the sheets carried traces of it, but there was something else there, something that was too familiar to be present by chance.

Cliff. I didn't dream it. He climbed out of bed and reached for a pair of pajamas that were draped over a chair, yet he didn't remember placing them there. After finishing in the bathroom, he walked out into the hallway. The faint voices of his children rose up the staircase to meet him.

After descending the staircase, he walked down the center hall. There was laughter. His children were chanting something about French toast and sausage. He paused to listen to their unbridled joy, and his heart suddenly swelled when he heard *his* voice among them.

"Now who wants powdered sugar on their French toast?"

"Me!"

"Me! Me, Cliff!"

"I want it too!"

"Me too!"

"And who wants maple syrup and who wants

honey?"

"I want maple syrup!"

"I want maple syrup too!"

"And me!"

"I want whatever you're having, Cliff!"

"Well I'm having honey, July."

"Then I want honey too!"

"Me too. I don't want syrup. I want honey!"

"Me too!"

"Sounds like everyone wants honey," Toby said as he walked through the doorway. "That means I'll have honey on my French toast too."

Four freshly scrubbed, smiling faces turned to greet him.

"Daddy!"

"Daddy's up!"

"Good morning, Daddy."

"Daddy, Cliff made French toast again!"

Toby smiled as he walked to the table. "Good morning to you all as well."

"Good morning," Cliff said sheepishly as a huge smile spread across his face.

"Good morning, Cliff. Now, is there any room left at this table for me?"

"Come sit next to me, Daddy," May said.

"No, I want Daddy!" July shouted.

"You can both have me if you move apart. I'll sit between you."

"I guess that's settled." Cliff chuckled. "French toast, coming right up."

Cliff lifted a casserole dish out of the oven. The smell of cinnamon and egg mixed with the aroma of pork sausage, kept warm on another platter beside it, wafted through the kitchen. "August, would you please pour the orange juice for everyone?" Cliff asked.

"Sure thing!"

By the time August had finished filling glasses, Cliff had portioned out servings and began setting filled plates down in front of everyone. Then he took a seat next to August. "Okay, eat up!"

After the first several bites had been consumed, words were exchanged between the children in rapid succession.

"Mommy hugged me last night," July announced.

"Me too," May said, "and she hummed to me, too."

"I saw Mommy standing in my room, Daddy. She was smiling," June said.

When August didn't say anything, the other three children turned to look at him.

"Didn't Mommy talk to you too, August?" July asked.

August remained silent. Then a look of sadness spread across his face.

"What is it, August?" Toby asked. "What's the matter?"

"Mommy thanked me for my letter. She told me she knew I was thinking about her and that I missed her. That's what I wrote to her. She said everything would be all right now and she'd always be with me, but it's not the same, Daddy. It's not the same."

Cliff reached over to August and rested his hand on his shoulders.

"I know August," Toby said, gently. "We all miss Mommy, but I believe her when she says she'll always be with you, with all of us. No, it's not the same and no it isn't fair, but it's the best she can do. Shouldn't we be grateful for that?"

Tears spilled from August's eyes, then all the children began to cry, but their sorrow was softer than the night before. For several minutes, no one spoke.

"Well," July said as he wiped his eyes with the back of his shirt sleeve, "Mommy wants me to be happy, so I'm going to be happy for her." He picked up his fork and stabbed a piece of French toast and then sausage and with great ceremony, put them in his mouth. As he chewed, he hummed. The tune was Pachelbel's Cannon in D.

"That's Mommy's song," May said as she picked up her fork and started back in on her plate. "That's what Mommy hummed to me last night." A moment later, she joined July's humming.

Soon, August started eating and humming along with them and then May did too.

Cliff looked at Toby and Toby smiled. "That's her song," Toby said softly. "That's my Sydney's song, Pachelbel's Cannon in D."

****

No sooner had plates been cleaned, then the children carried them to the dishwasher. Cliff added the baking dish and then closed the door. "Should I pack you a lunch?" he said to Toby.

"That isn't necessary. I usually order out."

"Remember what you said to me last week? You were concerned about your weight, and I said I'd be happy to pack you a lunch. If it's not to your liking, don't eat it, but I want to help you reach your goal."

"Thanks, Cliff. I'd really enjoy that."

While the dishwasher ran, Cliff packed lunches and helped the children get ready for school while Toby went upstairs to shower and get dressed for work. He and the children were all ready at the same time and assembled in the foyer together.

"I'm going to try to cut out early today," Toby said at the front door. "Maybe, we can plan to do something with the children this weekend to help them focus on something fun."

"I'll try to come up with something," Cliff said. "Are there any restrictions? Should I try to keep it under a certain dollar amount?"

"Oh, I wasn't thinking along those lines so much as just doing something together as a family, and besides, I didn't mean to suggest that it was your responsibility. I'll give you a call before lunch. Maybe we can exchange ideas. I'm sure that whatever we come up with, it will be perfect."

****

9:55 AM
Office of the Vice-President, Jacobson Construction

Toby's desk phone buzzed. "Hello?"

"Toby, dear."

"Hello, Mom. What's up?"

"I've decided to come and spend the weekend with you and the children. I thought we might go to the lake tomorrow, make a day of it. We'll pick up a bucket of chicken on the way, and I'm sure with his culinary skills, Cliff can whip up some potato salad without too much trouble. That would be nice, wouldn't it? I'll arrive early this evening so we can get started bright and early in the morning. Cliff is still with you, isn't he?"

"Of course he is, Mom, but what's this about you coming for the weekend?"

"I want to see my grandchildren. They need me."

"Mom, last night was rough on them. We need some down time. We need some time to ourselves. They'll think they need to be on their best behavior if you come, and I don't want to add any more stress to their lives."

"Oh, fiddle-faddle, of course I'm coming. They're

my grandchildren. How could I possibly cause them stress?"

"Mom, you just left two days ago!"

"Toby, I promise I won't be any bother. Now what's this about last night? What happened? Tell me."

Toby put the phone on speaker and got up from his desk. He started to pace.

"Toby, are you there, dear?"

"Yes, mother!" he shouted toward the phone.

"Mother? You haven't called me mother in years. What's wrong? What happened?"

"The children had a bad night last night, but Cliff came up with a way to calm them down. Then this morning we had a minor meltdown at the breakfast table, but we got through it."

"Tell me what happened. I want to know everything."

****

10:20 AM
Jacobson Residence
"Jacobson residence, this is Cliff."
"Hey, Cliff."

"Hey, Toby. I'm glad you called I thought maybe we could make a picnic out in the yard tomorrow. I'll order some balloons and crape paper, make it like an early Memorial Day. I haven't made coleslaw in a while and you haven't had my potato salad yet. I thought I'd grill some hot dogs and hamburgers and barbecue up some chicken and pork ribs. Grill some corn on the cob and throw in a salad, and we'll be all set.

"That way we can eat off it all for a few days and spend all our time with the children. You know, not have to worry about cooking. If you'd like, maybe we could invite Aaron and Jason to come down for the day."

"Our weekend has already been planned for us,"

Toby said gruffly.

"Oh? Why do you say it like that?"

"My mother's coming for the entire weekend. She's arriving tonight, and she's already invited herself for dinner. I'm so sorry to put this on you at such short notice."

"It won't be a problem at all and besides, I think it would be nice to have her, don't you?"

"You don't know her like I know her, Cliff. She gets into everything."

"I don't understand. She seemed pleasant enough to me. What do you mean, 'She gets into everything?'"

"By the time she leaves on Sunday—God help us if she decides to stay longer—she's going to know everything there is to know about you and if you aren't careful, about us too. I'm warning you to be careful. She has this uncanny ability to weasel information out of people. She's a terrible snoop."

"Oh, it can't be all that bad."

"You haven't experienced Patsy at full strength yet. She's a force to be reckoned with, but you know what, I think I am going to go with your suggestion and invite Jason and Aaron to come down, and not just tomorrow but for the entire weekend. They'll provide a good buffer for us and a distraction for her. Maybe even Miss Charity could come. They're nearly the same age and Miss Charity has this way about her. She can cut through any bullshit and make it smell like roses. You know?"

"I'll just follow your lead, but if I'm being completely honest, I was hoping we could have another evening together."

"Cliff, we can't. I'm sorry. Not with her here. Not yet. With our luck, she'd walk in on us, all innocent like. Then there would be a scene, and I just can't risk that

right now. Darn! I was just starting to feel good about everything, and she has to go and throw a wrench in the works."

"Toby, it will be okay. I promise. We'll conduct ourselves with the greatest degree of decorum. She'll never suspect a thing."

"I hope you're right. Now, I have to go and call Jason. I'll let you know what's going to happen with them the moment I know."

"Then I'll wait to hear from you, and don't worry. I'll be ready, no matter who shows up at the door. Are you still planning on leaving early?"

"I'm going to head home as soon as I hang up with Jason. We have work to do."

"Could you do me a favor then?"

"Name it."

"Do you think you could pick the children up from school? I'm going to have to get cracking on dinner if your mother's coming. It's going to be tough topping my grilled salmon."

"I'll take care of it. I'll just take them out early on my way home."

"Okay, I'll see you then."

"Bye, Cliff, and thanks."

Chapter Twenty-Eight

Oh Her Broomstick

11:05 AM

When the doorbell rang, Cliff walked to the front door to answer it.

"Mrs. Jacobson, what a lovely surprise. Toby said you were coming, but I wasn't expecting you so soon. He's not home from the office yet."

"I'm sorry to arrive unannounced, but after I hung up the phone with him I realized what an imposition I've created for you. I've come to help."

"That's very kind of you, but I think I can manage. Why don't you make yourself comfortable in the family room? Can I offer you anything to drink?"

"Nonsense, I'm here to help."

Patsy turned around and called out to the car. "Veronica, put my bags in my room. Make a left at the top of the staircase. It's the last room on the left."

"Veronica?" Cliff asked.

"My girl. I'll need help if I'm going to look my best out in public at the lake tomorrow. Now what can I do to help?"

"Honestly, I don't know yet. I'm waiting to hear back from Toby. He's going to let me know if Jason and Aaron are coming and whether they're bringing Miss Charity with them. I've only just started to plan tonight's dinner menu."

"Toby must have failed to mention to me that they were also coming, but how wonderful. I can't wait to see what you and Charity come up with."

Cliff did not miss the suspicious expression on Patsy's face.

****

"I know exactly what Toby's doing," Patsy thought to herself, "but why?"

****

11:15 AM

"Hello, Jacobson residence. This is May."

"May, honey, why are you answering the phone? Where's Cliff."

"Hi, Daddy. He's upstairs with Grand Mom. She needed help with her bags."

"Your grandmother is there ... already?"

"Yes, Daddy. She and Veronica are unpacking."

"Jesus, Mary, and Joseph! She brought Veronica, too? Can you put Cliff on the phone, honey?"

"Okay, Daddy. I have to go upstairs. I have to put the phone down now, Daddy."

****

After several long minutes, Cliff picked up the phone. He was still in Patsy's room.

"Hi, Toby. Your mother arrived a little early to help me with dinner."

"Cliff, are you alone on the phone?"

"Yes, why?"

"Never mind, call me back on your cell phone. No, forget that. I'll be there in ten minutes."

"Toby, everything's fine. Don't worry."

"Everything's not fine, trust me! I'll be there a soon as I can."

"Are Aaron and Jason and Miss Charity coming?"

Toby didn't answer.

"Hello? There was no response.

"Hello? Toby?"

The phone was dead on the other end.

"Is that my son?" Patsy asked, walking up behind

him "Let me speak with him for a minute."

"I'm sorry, Mrs. Jacobson. It seems he's hung up already, but he'll be home soon."

****

11:25 AM

Toby's car raced up the driveway, nearly making a screeching stop when it reached the front entrance. As the children got out, they ran for the vestibule.

"Grand Mom!" they called out as they burst through the front door. "Grand Mom! Grand Mom!"

Posing like a runway model at the top of the staircase, Patsy called down to them. "Up here, my loves. Come see what Grand Mom has brought for you."

Just as Toby walked through the door, Patsy turned and disappeared down the hall, a trail of grandchildren in her wake.

"Well hello there, Toby," Cliff said as he walked in from the kitchen. "Welcome home."

"That woman," he said forcefully under his breath, "comes swooping in on her broomstick and…"

"Not to worry. Nothing's happened."

"Yet!"

"It's going to be fine. What's happening with Aaron and Jason and Miss Charity?"

"They're all coming, and Evelyn's coming too."

"Who's Evelyn?"

"Miss Charity's other daughter. You've spoken with Fiona. She works with Jason and Aaron. Evelyn works with Miss Charity."

"Well, that will certainly be helpful. I look forward to meeting her."

"Just don't let your guard down, Cliff, not for a moment. Please believe me on this."

"I won't. Now, when is everyone else arriving?"

"Within the hour. Miss Charity said she'll follow

your lead with dinner, but she also said not to worry about lunch for tomorrow at the lake. She's already planned it all out. She said she knows exactly what will impress my mother the most, and she'll talk you through it. At least that's one thing you won't have to worry about."

"Great! Well, I better get back to the kitchen. The groceries will be delivered within the hour. May's been upstairs with your mother since she got here. I have April in the kitchen with me. Maybe a good stiff drink will help to make things go smoother with your mother. Let me get it for you."

"Thanks, but first I have to go make an appearance. I'm sure she's already holding court. I'll be back down as soon as I can."

"Don't you want your scotch first?"

"No, I can't have liquor on my breath when I meet her. Otherwise, she could use that as a veil to begin her assault. She'll put me off guard by questioning me about driving with the children in the car after having had a drink. Then she'll go in for the kill."

"Really, Toby? But you didn't, drive the children after drinking, I mean. She doesn't seem at all like that to me."

"Cliff, she'd use it as an excuse. She's back just two days after having left. She's up to something. I just know it."

"Should I bring your scotch up to you?"

"No, you don't want to give her even the slightest opportunity to begin her interrogation. You've got to minimize your contact with her, even if I'm present. Do you understand me, Cliff?"

"Wow! You're really serious."

"Trust me, Cliff. I've known her my whole life."

"Okay, okay."

****

12:30 PM

The limousine followed a delivery truck up the long, winding driveway. As two men exited the truck and began unloading groceries, Charity and Evelyn got out and walked up to them. After putting down their suitcases, Charity asked, "May I?" Immediately, she began to look through the boxes they were pulling out of the back of the truck. She lifted a few things to inspect the contents.

"Perfect," she said to Evelyn, "It's going to be a formal dinner tonight. You're going to like Cliff, Evelyn. He's a master when it comes to food."

****

"Knock, knock," Charity said as she walked into the kitchen.

"Miss Charity! Thank you for coming. I can sure use your help. And you must be Evelyn. Hello."

"Hello, Mr. Cliff," Evelyn said meekly.

"Oh no, it's Cliff. I'm part of the help." Cliff laughed. "I'm the nanny and chief cook and bottle washer, literally the bottle washer."

"So where do you want us to get started?" Charity asked.

"Well, the groceries should be here any minute. We're having…"

"They arrived just ahead us. I looked through what you've ordered while they were unloading. They should be in here any minute now. Nice cut of meat, by the way. Is the beef tenderloin for tonight's dinner?"

"Yes, and twice baked potatoes, green beans, beets and beet greens with diced, smoked butt, and a balsamic vinegar reduction with a touch of sugar. We're serving pickled and fresh crudités with green goddess dressing as the appetizer, along with a tossed salad and my blue cheese dressing. Then orange chiffon cake for dessert."

"We'll get right on it, Cliff. Don't you worry about a thing. What do you want us to start on?"

"First, I'll go meet the delivery men to check over my order, then I'll get started prepping the tenderloin. I'm going to filet it open, stuff it with herbs and spices and then truss it up with twine. Can you handle the beets, greens, and twice baked potatoes?"

"Sure can," Charity said, "and Evelyn is a wonderful baker. Why don't you let her take care of the cake?"

"That would be great. We'll divvy up the rest as we go."

"We'll follow your lead."

"For the picnic I ordered five chickens, a whole rack of beef ribs, and four racks of baby back pork ribs. I figured we could cut up the chickens for frying or barbecuing, and I also ordered plenty of hotdogs, ground sirloin for hamburgers, and chili for the dogs. For the sides I've ordered two cabbages for slaw and twenty pounds of russets. There should also have been and a whole bunch of fresh produce for salads and other sides we'll serve with dinners."

"I saw it all. Now I won't have to place another order for the picnic tomorrow. We must have been thinking along the same lines."

"You'd be proud of me, Miss Charity. I knew Eugene wasn't coming to do the shopping, and I didn't have time to do it myself so when I talked with the grocer, I told him to select only the best, freshest cuts of meat, and I would accept only his prime produce."

"That's my boy!"

"Okay, stations everyone. We have four and a half hours to pull this off."

****

"Hey there, Cliff," Aaron said as he and Jason came in.

"Oh hey, Aaron. Hey, Jason. Thanks so much for coming."

"Don't worry. Toby's briefed us on everything," Jason said. "Need any help?"

"No, but thanks. Why don't you go up and unpack? Then you can find Toby. I'm sure he'd appreciate whatever support you can give him. He's stressed out to the max right now."

"We've already been up to our room," Aaron said. "Why don't we just pitch in to help out wherever we can?"

"I'd rather you go support Toby. We've got this all locked up right now. Miss Charity, Evelyn, and I can handle dinner."

"Very good, but call us if you need us."

"Will do."

****

"So how can I help?" Patsy said, as she posing like a fashion model in the doorway. I can handle a knife."

"Hi, Mrs. Jacobson," Cliff said. "I think we have it well under control right now."

"Nonsense. An extra pair of hands is always welcome."

Cliff hesitated for a moment.

"Can you cut up vegetables, Miss Patsy?" Charity interjected. "We're serving crudités as the appetizer. There's cauliflower, carrots, celery, broccoli, cucumber, and radishes that all need to be cut up."

"Yes, I can do that."

"Are you familiar with a mandolin, Miss Patsy? If you cut the carrots and cucumber on the bias with a

Julienne blade, it will create a very attractive presentation."

"I'm familiar with the concept," Patsy said with trepidation in her voice, "but I've never used one. If you show me how…" She cleared her throat. "I'm sure I can master it."

"Wonderful, Evelyn will show you. Evelyn, the mandolin is up in that cupboard," Charity said, pointing. "Take it down and show Miss Patsy how to use it and be sure to show her the metal glove and how to use the gripper. We don't want her losing any fingers along the way."

Patsy followed Evelyn to the cupboard and became busy focusing on Evelyn's instructions.

When Charity turned to look at Cliff, there was a twinkle in her eyes. "That should keep her busy for a while," she whispered, "and make her think twice about asking to help again. I don't know about you, but I don't like folks *helping* who don't know their way around a kitchen."

Cliff's body shook as he silently tried to suppress a laugh. Finally, he got control of himself. "I didn't even know we had a mandolin," he whispered back. "There hasn't been any time for me to go exploring yet."

"All in good time, Cliff. All in good time."

****

When Cliff found Toby, he was talking with his mother in the study. He couldn't help but notice the spot on the sofa where Patsy now sat. *I was right there just two night ago,* he thought as he stood in the doorway.

"Yes, Cliff," Patsy said, finally noticing him.

"Sorry to interrupt. I just wanted to say goodnight. I finally got the children all tucked away and asleep, but it was a challenge. They're very excited about your plans for a picnic by the lake tomorrow, Mrs.

Jacobson."

"I thought it would be good for them to get out of the house and do something fun. Why don't you join us, Cliff? Here, come sit down by me." Patsy patted the sofa next to her. "Take a load off."

"Oh, I wouldn't want to impose." *Oh, God, not there. I can't sit next to her there.* "I'm sure you both have a lot to talk about."

"Actually, we were talking about you, Cliff."

Toby pressed his hands along the sides of his head. "God help me," he mouthed.

"My son told me what you did for the children last night. I think it was wonderful how you put their minds at ease. What an ingenious idea you had, using the smoke from a fire as a metaphor for contacting their mother."

"I think you mean symbolism, ma'am."

For the briefest moment, Patsy's eyes turned cold as they burned straight through his chest. "I'm sure you're correct," she said, smiling like a fox apprising a chicken. "I always get those literary things mixed up. Now, come join us."

"I really appreciate the invitation, ma'am, but tomorrow starts early for me. I have to be up by five for my workout if I'm going to finish in time for April. She starts by six-thirty. If I'm not there, she'll wake the whole house up. That little one sure has a set of lungs on her. Then there's breakfast to get ready and then the children to help with their morning routines."

"Goodness, six-thirty?" Patsy shuddered. "That's ungodly! I've gone to bed at that hour, but never risen at it. You go and get your sleep, please. We'll have time tomorrow to talk by the lake. Plan on it, okay? I want to know all there is to know about you," she said, dripping syrup from her lips. Then her eyes squinted, and her face became serious. "After all, you're caring for my grandchildren."

"Certainly, ma'am, but you'll be bored to tears. I've led a simple life. There's not much to tell."

"I'm sure it will be fascinating."

"Well, anyway, goodnight, ma'am."

****

When Cliff's eyes met Toby's, his face softened. "Goodnight, Toby."

Patsy noticed the change in it immediately. As Toby answered, she was subtle, but she watched him just as closely.

"Goodnight, Cliff," he said.

Chapter Twenty-Nine

To Save a Life

Saturday, May 22, 2010, 11:40 AM

While May, June, July, and August kept their father busy in the water, and Jason and Aaron were diving off a board some twenty yards from the shore, Charity and Evelyn finished unpacking the luncheon they had prepared. Veronica pitched in by setting places at two picnic tables, setting close together near the tree line above the beach. Patsy saw her chance. She cornered Cliff the moment he set down the last box on the table after returning from the limo.

"Cliff, why don't we take advantage of this time to talk for a bit while my girl, Charity, and her girl finish with all of that. We just haven't seemed to find the time to get to know each other yet. I've picked out a spot right over there in the shade" —she pointed— "away from everyone, where we can sit."

Before Cliff could open his mouth to protest, she took him by the arm and led him away. Not waiting for an answer, she called over her shoulder, "You'll keep an eye on little April now, won't you, Miss Charity?"

August came up from the water and approached them from behind. "I have to go to the bathroom, Cliff."

Cliff gently disengaged himself from Patsy's grasp and placed his hand on August's shoulder as he began walking beside him. "You better let me go with you."

"I'm a big boy, Cliff. I can go by myself."

"I know you're a big boy, but I don't want you going in there alone. You never know who…"

August pulled away. "You don't have to baby me, Cliff!"

"Oh, let him go, Cliff. He's right. He is a big boy. Aren't you, August?" Patsy patted her grandson's cheek. "Besides, the bathrooms are right there. We can watch out for him while we talk."

Immediately, she retook Cliff's arm and began leading him toward the spot she'd selected, while August headed off on his own.

****

"*That woman,*" Charity said under her breath.

"Oh no," Veronica whispered.

Evelyn spoke slowly. "Mama, count to ten."

"That won't help, Evelyn. I've seen her kind, and I've seen the kind of trouble they can cause."

Veronica put a hand to her mouth to stifle a giggle.

"I don't know how you do it," Charity said to her.

"Oh, the missus doesn't mean to be like that. She just is. She really is a good person, deep down inside."

Charity shook her head. "Whether she means to or not, Missy, she's a pot just waiting to be stirred. I just know it."

"You're sure right there, Miss Charity, and sometimes when a pot isn't stirred, it boils over. I know. I've cleaned up a mess or two in the years I've been with her."

Charity planted her fists on her hips and made a sound of frustration.

****

Fifteen minutes had passed while Patsy skillfully made her small talk, completely distracting and disarming Cliff. Down at the shoreline, unaware she had begun to make her move and preoccupied with the three children in the water, Toby had forgotten about his mother. August still hadn't returned from the restroom. He was nowhere in sight.

Patsy went in for the kill. "So tell me, Cliff, what are your intentions toward my son?"

"I beg your pardon, ma'am?"

"You don't need to be coy with me, Cliff. We're both adults here. Don't forget, I've been around the block a few times."

"Ma'am, I…"

"I've seen the way you look at him, and … I've seen the way he looks at you, too. I know that look, Cliff. Now tell me" —her eyes narrowed— "what are your intentions toward my son?"

A shout came from above the tree line. "Cliff! Cliff, look at me!"

Cliff didn't hear it. He was too overwhelmed by Patsy's revelation. He began to stutter. M … M … Ma'am, I … I…"

August shouted even louder. "Cliff! Cliff, look at me, Look at me! Look how high I climbed! See I'm not a little boy!"

Cliff jerked his head around as he tried to locate the voice. The color drained from his face when his eyes focused high above Patsy's head at the tree line. He stood up and yelled. "August! August, stop! Stop bouncing on that tree! It's dead, August! It's dead!"

August had a hold of a limb above him while he continued to bounce up and down on another some twenty-five feet above the ground. "See, Cliff, I'm not a little boy! See how high I climbed, all by myself!"

Not looking, Patsy waved her hand behind her. "Leave him be. He's only a boy having a bit of fun. Now tell me, what are your intentions toward my…"

A loud crack shot out from the tree trunk at the joint of the limb where August stood. He slipped and lost his footing as the limb cracked downward. Standing on his tippy-toes, he could barely touch it. He screamed.

"Hold on, August!" Cliff yelled.

Charity cried out, "Lord, have mercy!"

Evelyn and Veronica shrieked as they watched August dangle by both hands.

Toby turned around from the children at the sound of the cries coming from up the beach and froze.

Aaron called out from the diving board down to Jason in the water and pointed toward the shore.

Suddenly, Patsy was sitting alone.

Cliff had disappeared from her sight. He planted his size thirteen sneaker just inches from her hands and bound onto the table, becoming airborne when he leapt to land ten feet away. The moment his feet touched down he began to run like he had never run before.

Patsy looked around to watch him disappear up the beach. Her hand flew to her mouth when she noticed movement, high up in the tree. She screamed.

"Hold on, August! Hold on!" Cliff cried.

In seconds, he'd covered the thirty yards to the tree line. In a single lunge, he flew above ten feet of bushes and brush to land at the base of the tree while yelling upward. "I'm coming August! I'm coming! Hold on, son! Hold on!"

August screamed. "Cliff, I can't hold it! I'm slipping, Cliff, I'm slipping!"

From all directions along the lakefront, people stopped what they were doing as they pointed and watched in horror at the boy dangling high in the air, twenty-five feet from the ground. Several people turned their video cameras toward the scene, capturing each second of the drama as it unfolded before them.

A thunderous, ear-shattering crack sounded from the ground beneath Cliff's feet and rumbled up through his body.

Cliff looked down at the ground. The trunk shifted toward him, ever so slightly. When he looked up, the entire seventy-feet height of the tree began swaying. Then it slowly moved in the direction of the limb August clung to. He would be beneath the tree and crushed when it hit the ground.

"August, let go! Let go, August! I'll catch you! I'll catch you, son!"

"No, Cliff, no!" August cried. "I can't! I'll fall!"

"August, I'll catch you. I promise"

"I'll fall!" August screamed. "I'll fall!"

"August, I promise I'll catch you, just like a football! Believe me, August! Believe me!"

****

"No!" August closed his eyes. "Mommy! Mommy!"

"Jump to him, August. He'll catch you." August heard his mother's voice. *"Trust him, August. You can trust him. Now jump, August. Jump for Mommy."*

As the tree began to fall, August screamed and let go of the branch. "Mommy!"

When his feet touched the snapped limb below, he pushed off and sailed away from the tree as the skeletal remains of the limb followed him down.

****

Like a wide receiver dancing beneath a ball as it sailed toward him, Cliff followed his descent through the brush as he prepared for the catch. The tree loomed closer and closer as it began picking up speed.

Cliff leapt into the air and caught August mid-flight and wrapped his arms around him. He braced for the moment his feet touched the ground, just into the sand, but his momentum carried him forward, forcing him to tuck into a ball and roll.

As the lowest branches of the tree loomed only ten feet above their heads, Cliff sprang from the spot after one summersault and ran while sand from their clothing spun into the air around them.

In two strides, he put another twelve feet between them and the trunk, but as he ran through the sand, the tree's lower limbs began crashing down, all around them, forcing him to zig and zag between them. The upper limbs, extending out more than twenty-five feet in all directions, followed behind.

When he felt a limb brush against his head, Cliff ducked and leapt sideways into the air, as he tried to move away from the tree while he wrapped his arms, legs, head, and back into a protective cocoon, surrounding August's body. He rolled through the sand like a pinball as limbs spiked the ground in every direction, acting as bumpers to block his way.

****

As the thunderous boom echoed up and down the beach and out across the water, the entire assembly of witnesses froze and held their collective breaths. For seconds, no one moved as they waited for signs of life from the balled-up human form that remained motionless, pinned beneath the tree's dead limbs.

It began with one, then another, then several more joined in until the entire mass of humanity moved as one and rushed toward them. Patsy was the first to arrive. She reached in, grabbing at branches and snapped them off in her bare hands, cutting them up in the process, as she pressed her way deeper and deeper into the bowels of the tree's brittle corpse.

When it became too dense, she was forced to bend down and then crawl on her hands and knees while she scooped and kicked out sand as she cried out her grandson's name.

"August! August! God, no! Please, God, no! August! August, answer me!"

When she got in close to their bodies, all she could see was Cliff's shoulders and neck, wrapped tightly around a blue shirt with a tuft of blond hair sticking out the top. Like bunches of knives that had been thrown by a circus performer from a distance into a giant target, branches and limbs were impaled into the sand all around them. She pushed and wiggled herself in farther and reached out her hand. It touched the hair. The head moved.

"August!" she cried.

"Grand mom."

All around her, limbs and branches began falling away as dozens of hands bent and snapped and pulled at them.

Toby pushed himself through the people and wiggled his way in until he knelt beside his mother.

"It's my fault, Toby!" Patsy cried. "It's all my fault."

Charity and two immense men, together, began heaving their bodies against larger limbs. Others joined in and, with their added weight, began to clear away a path. Someone dialed 911 and alerted the authorities that there had been a terrible accident.

"Mom, it's not your fault," Toby said as he reached in toward the two, still forms. "It's no one's fault."

"Yes, it is. If I hadn't distracted Cliff, August would never have gotten up into that damned tree. It's all my fault."

"Mom, no." Toby wrapped his arm around her. "It was an accident."

"Toby, you don't understand. It is my fault. Cliff is dead because of me. He sacrificed his life for August.

It's all my fault."

Tears began to fall from both of their eyes.

Toby wiggled in on his chest and reached out his hand. "August, are you okay? Cliff! Cliff, talk to me!"

"Daddy, I can't move. Cliff won't let go of me."

"It's all my fault," Patsy repeated. "It's all my fault he's dead!"

A shoulder moved, then the head. "No one's dead, Mrs. Jacobson," Cliff said slowly as he tried to shake sand from his hair, "but I can't get out. We're pinned under this limb."

Patsy shrieked in joy. "Oh, you beautiful man! You beautiful, wonderful man! You saved my grandson. You saved my August!"

"Cliff, baby," Toby said, "are you injured? Are you hurt?"

"I don't know, Toby. I can't move. I'm half buried in the sand. I saw an indentation so I dove for it. I think that's what saved us."

"We'll get you out, Cliff. We'll get you both out. Just hold on."

Toby forced himself in deeper as he dug away at the sand beneath himself and Patsy until he was able to touch them both. He kissed August on his forehead. Then he turned his head and kissed down as far as he could reach on Cliff's face, making contact with the bridge of his nose.

"You're my hero, Cliff. You saved my son's life."

"I just reacted, Toby. I saw August in trouble, and I just went for him."

****

The moment Jason and Aaron arrived. Jason organized the crowd, asking for shovels and buckets and anything that could be used to dig out the sand.

Aluminum pots that held simmering ears of corn and clams were dumped and used as shovels, frying pans and children's plastic buckets became spades, and serving spoons and ladles were turned into trowels. Behind Toby and Patsy, the brigade of troops that had amassed continued to break away at the tree and dig in toward them.

By the time the EMS and rescue crews arrived on the scene and headed across the beach toward the site, Cliff and August were nearly free. Patsy's once glamorous, silk neck scarf now adorned Cliff's head, applying pressure to bleeding from the top of it.

"Do you have pain anywhere, Cliff?" Jason asked as he kneeled down beside him.

"I don't think so, Jason, I'm just pinned. Nothing hurts, just my head."

Once his chest was cleared, Cliff was able to let go of August, who then immediately scurried into his father's arms and began to cry. With a little more digging, enough sand was removed beneath him so that with great care, Cliff unfolded his body and was pulled to freedom.

"God, that feels good," he said as his legs straightened out. "It was really cramped under there."

Aaron grasped Cliff's hand and pulled him up. As he stood, spontaneous cheering, applause, and whistling erupted from the crowd.

When the EMS crew got to them, they began checking both Cliff and August.

Cliff pushed them away and walked toward the lake, shaking sand from his head as he went.

Aaron followed behind.

When he reached the water, Cliff waded out to his waist and dropped forward into it, remaining submerged while he blinked and wiped at his eyes to remove the sand that clung there.

After climbing out, Aaron walked him to the EMT's who sat him down on a picnic bench to examine him, but they only found scratches, abrasions, and bruises.

Because the top of his head was only covered by a large area of ugly abrasions, it wasn't going to need stitches, but even with both his and August's tetanus shots up to date, the EMT's urged that they both be taken to the ER to be checked over.

Cliff balked at the suggestion, saying he wasn't going to be the reason for ruining the family's lakeside picnic.

Patsy rushed to him. She hugged him and kissed him all over his face, telling him how foolish and stupid he was to think such a thing when it was him who had saved her grandson, and all because of her own foolish meddling. His face was covered with imprints of her lips once she let him go.

After Charity told him that Evelyn and Veronica had already wrapped up and packed away the food, Cliff began to hem and haw.

Charity walked right up to him until their chests touched. "Now you listen to me, young man," she said, shaking her finger in his face. "You're too damned valuable to this family to take any chances. You're going to march yourself right into that hospital or I'm gonna drag you there myself."

A big smile spread across his face. Finally, he relented. "Yes, ma'am, but I'm not riding in an ambulance. Ambulances are for sick people."

Charity wrapped him in a bear hug. "Oh, you!"

****

Within minutes of their arrival at Hinnen Valley Medical Center, Charity and Evelyn acquired several ER gurneys, then Veronica covered them with sheets Jason and Aaron procured. After laying out all the food they'd prepared, the three women began filling plates. By the time they'd finished, the family, the entire ER staff, other visitors, and any patients who were permitted to eat from their picnic banquet had been fed.

When Cliff, August, and Patsy were released an-hour-and-a-half later, all the platters were empty, bowls and containers had been scraped clean, and everything was packed away, leaving no evidence that they had ever been there.

Chapter Thirty

An Ally in the Making

Sunday, May 23, 2010, 5:15 AM

Clean, preened, and immaculately dressed in a robin's-egg blue, lady's formal suit, Patsy found Cliff hard at work, exercising in his weight room. "I rationalized with myself that you'd probably take the day off from your workout after yesterday, Cliff," she said quietly from behind him, once he'd finished a set of sit-ups, "but then I remembered how strong your will is."

Cliff jumped up from the mat and turned around. "Mrs. Jacobson, how are you here? It's only quarter after five. I thought you said this hour of the morning…"

"I didn't want to interrupt your session, so I waited until you stopped. I'm sorry for coming in here like this, but I need to speak with you. It's important."

"I'm sorry. I didn't hear you come in. How are your hands?"

Patsy took in his muscular frame, the rippling muscles, his neatly-trimmed, fur covered, heaving chest and rigid, quivering, six-pack abdomen. Her eyes followed the clear-cut V that began at his flanks and ran downward to surround his generous bulge, barely constrained behind the two, thin articles of clothing he wore. The straps from his jock were clearly visible below the sweat-glistening muscular globes of his buttocks, now peeking below the skimpy, high-side-split pair of workout shorts that stopped just short of the tops of this thighs.

"My hands?" Patsy looking down at her upward turned palms. "My hands are of no importance" —she patted the bandages— "but thank you for asking. I guess they're better off than the top of your poor, sweet head."

"I'm glad to hear it, but my head is only scratched up. There's some on my back and a few on my legs and arms, but they're nothing serious. I think you suffered much worse."

"That's my own fault. If I hadn't…"

"It's not your fault, Mrs. Jacobson, and really, I'm grateful. You tried to save us, me and August. From what I've heard, you were like a Tasmanian Devil the way you went at that tree. Aaron said he could see branches flying everywhere as you disappeared into it." Cliff reached for a towel and wiped sweat from his face and chest. "Sorry, I must look a sight."

"A sight is putting it mildly, Cliff. I can't imagine the energy you must expend in order to maintain your, and pardon my directness, stunning, masculine physique. It's quite remarkable. I see why my son is attracted to you."

"Mrs. Jacobson, I beg your…"

"Patsy. Please, Cliff, call me Patsy. I can't stand formality, not where family is concerned."

"Family, ma'am?"

"If you call me ma'am one more time, I swear I'll…" She let the sentence drop.

"Mrs. Jacobson, I mean Patsy, I don't understand."

"I've observed, Cliff, that you're a man who speaks his mind. You're truthful and direct. I like that about you. I'm the same, but I'm not as gentle or considerate as you are in my delivery. I'll have to work on that."

"Yes, ma'am … um … Patsy."

"Now, please allow me to be direct with you. I know my son, Cliff. I've known him since he drew his first breath. He's a good man, a good father, a good son, and a good friend to all who know him. He doesn't have a mean or prejudiced bone in his body, and he's always treated people with respect and kindness. When my Toby falls in love, it's with a person's heart."

"I see that in him ... Mrs.—" Cliff hesitated. Patsy raised an eyebrow. "Sorry ... Patsy."

"I've witnessed the same kindness in you. You two were meant for each other. Though, for the life of me, I find it difficult to fathom how this could happen so soon after Sydney's passing. He loved her so very much.

"We had a long talk yesterday, Toby and I did. I guess I just have to accept what he told me about his dreams of her and what happened just before she died, as the God's honest truth. She was a very special one, that Sydney was. It brings me comfort to know that that isn't lost after we die."

"He told me as well."

"He also told me, Cliff, how close you've grown toward the children, and I can see how much they've come to rely on you ... and love you. That's not a small thing, and you have my admiration, respect, and gratitude for being that for them."

"Thank you. They're very easy to love."

"And my son? Him too?"

****

"Patsy ... I..." Cliff looked down at his hands, now folded in front of him. After a moment, he looked up and met her eyes. Suddenly, they were soft and kind. *Wow, she knows, but can I trust her? Yes. Yes, I think I can.*

After a moment, he spoke. "Yes ... Yes, I think I do."

"You think? Like it's the beginning of something?"

"Ma'am ... and yes, I know it's Patsy, but you're

older than me, and I was taught to show respect toward my…"

"Now don't you go and ruin what we've got going for us here, Cliff. Don't you dare call me the dreaded *E* word." Patsy's smile was genuine.

"Yes … Patsy. I've never been in love. There was never any time for a relationship."

"I know, Cliff. Toby told me about how you've sacrificed for your brother and sister."

Cliff couldn't hold it in any longer. Everything he'd kept locked down tight just poured out of him. "I don't know what it feels like to be in love, but I know I care deeply for Toby. I can't stop thinking about him. There's so much I want to do for him to help him. When he hurts, it crushes me inside. I've never felt this way about anyone before, except for Marshall and Whitney, but even with them, it's different. They don't take my breath away, but Toby…"

"Does? That's love, Cliff, pure and simple, whether you know it yet or not. So what are you going to do about it?"

"I'm not sure. I don't know what to do. It's so soon since he lost … Mrs. Jacobson, this is new ground for me."

"Then, if I may give you one small piece of advice?"

"Yes?" Cliff nodded his head. "Please do."

"Do exactly what you've been doing, because you're doing a world of good for all of them. I don't think you have it in your nature to hurt people so just be yourself."

"Yes, Patsy."

"I wanted to have this conversation with you first, to see where you stood. Now I know I can have the conversation I really wanted to have with Toby yesterday. I'll do that sometime this morning before I leave.

"I don't know whether he realizes he's in love with you yet, but after you saved August from that tree yesterday, and he was digging the two of you out from under it, it was obvious to me. It wasn't there a few days ago, but it's certainly there now.

"Patsy … we … we haven't…"

"No, I don't want to know what's happened or hasn't happened between the two of you. That's your business. I know Toby knows he really likes you, that's obvious. It's also obvious that he's attracted to you, physically, and no, he didn't tell me that, but I've seen the passion in his eyes these past two days when he looks at you.

"He may take a little while to come around, but eventually, he's going to realize that he not only loves you, but that he's in love with you. What I plan to do when I speak with him is let him know that I approve of you. That will be one obstacle he'll know he won't have to overcome."

"Thank you, Patsy."

"One last thing. I need to apologize to you for yesterday. I had my talons out, and I was ready to rip you to shreds if I learned that you were going to hurt my son or grandchildren or take advantage of them in any way. I've known more than a few gold-diggers in my time, so please know, it was nothing personal. I was just looking out for my own."

"Well, you certainly had me on the defensive."

"Put your mind at ease, Cliff. My talons are closed. You've made a friend here, but more importantly, you've made an ally.

"Whether this relationship develops further into commitment on both of your parts or not, and I'll be shocked if it doesn't, I'll always be on your side, that is, right behind my son and grandchildren."

"Thank you, Patsy."

She walked up to him and began to give him a hug.

"Patsy, I'm all sweaty, and I stink. Please..."

"Oh, hush and let me enjoy this brief moment. I haven't smelled the musk of a man in so long, I don't think I even remember what it's like." As she hugged him, she sighed. "Ah, now I remember."

****

7:20 AM
Toby's Bedroom

As Toby finished up from his shower, Patsy called in to him from his bedroom. "Toby, dear..."

"Mom? Mom, I just got out of the shower!"

"I know, dear. I've been waiting for you. Just be sure to put something on before you come out."

A moment later, Toby walked out in a robe with his hair still dripping. He found Patsy sitting on the edge of his bed. "Mom, why are you in my bedroom, and at this hour?"

"I want to talk with you."

"And it couldn't wait?"

"No, it can't. This is important, and I wanted to take advantage of not being interrupted. The children are having their breakfast right now so I know we have a few minutes."

"What could be so important?"

"Sit down, Toby. There's a few things I need to say to you."

"I thought you told me everything yesterday. I don't blame you for what happened to August. I thought I made that clear."

Patsy pointed to one of the two recliners. "Toby,

sit."

Okay, I'm sitting, I'm sitting."

"I apologized to Cliff this morning. I caught him while he was doing his exercises."

"Mom, Cliff's up at like … five."

"I've been up since four."

"Uh oh, this must really be serious." *Oh, shit. What's she gone and done now?*

"It is. As I said, I apologized to him for the way I acted toward him yesterday. I've come to realize that he's a very good man."

"Yes, Mom, he is. He wouldn't be here if he wasn't."

"He's a good man for the children, Toby, and I think he's going to be good for you too."

"What do you mean?" *She can't. No, she can't possibly mean…*

"You were so right when you told your father and me about how he cared for you after, … after you had your … your…"

"Breakdown?"

"Yes … that. I think he's going to be very good for you, Toby … in the long run. You need a friend, a close friend who you can count on through thick and thin. Cliff can be that kind of friend for you, as good a friend to you as … as Sydney was. He can be more for you than just someone who cares for your children.

"He's kind and caring and resourceful, and that shows in how he is with them … and with you. He'd make a wonderful father and a loving husband for the right person."

"I think you're right about that," Toby said. "He's practically raised his brother and sister, and with his degrees…"

"That's not what I mean. I'm saying to you, and

I'm only going to say this once, so listen carefully… I approve of him, Toby. In all ways, I approve of him."

"Mom … I … Mom, what are you really saying?"

Holy shit. She knows.

Patsy got up from the bed and walked to him. She leaned down and pressed her hand against his right cheek and kissed him on the left.

"Don't you dare let him go," she whispered. "Now think about what I said."

As she stood up, Toby looked into her eyes. There were tears welled in his.

She smiled, "I love you, Toby."

Toby's bottom lip quivered. When he blinked, the tears spilled over, and he nodded.

Patsy stopped at the door and turned around. "I'll be leaving now. I've meddled enough in your affairs. You need time to adjust to this new life that's opening in front of you, and you don't need me getting in the way. I'll say goodbye to the children, and then Veronica and I will be off. The car is waiting. I'll stay in touch."

Then she was gone.

For several minutes, Toby sat with his mouth agape, thinking. While he dressed, he watched out his window as his mother's luggage was loaded into the car. Then she and Veronica got in and they were gone.

He stood at the window in silence, hugging himself as he looked down at the spot where her car had been. Then he headed downstairs.

****

Toby was still sitting quietly in his study when Aaron and Jason walked in. The impact of his earlier conversation with his mother still hadn't sunk in.

"We've come to say our goodbyes," Jason said.

"So soon? I though you would at least stay for lunch if not for dinner, too."

"You and your family need some down time after yesterday, Toby," Aaron said. "You don't need us hanging around to keep entertained."

"It's not like that at all, Aaron. We love having you guys visit."

"That's nice of you to say, but we both think you need some time and space."

"You look preoccupied, Toby," Jason said. "Are you okay?"

"Yeah, I am. I had the strangest conversation with my mother this morning, or rather, she had with me."

"Is everything all right?"

"Yeah, I think so. It was just weird, like she was saying something without coming out and saying it."

"Well, you know your mother. She doesn't always say what she means. Sometimes you have to read between the lines to find the true meaning."

"Don't I know it." *No, I really do know what she was saying. I just can't believe it.* "Are you sure you don't want to stay until after dinner?" *Please stay. Once I'm alone with him there'll be no turning back.*

"No, we'll be going," Aaron said. "We've already told Miss Charity and Evelyn, and we're all packed. The car will be here in just a few minutes."

"Well, I'll miss you guys. You were both tremendous yesterday. Thank you again for all you did."

"Of course," Jason said. "What are friends for anyway?"

"The least I can do is walk you out."

****

After goodbyes were said and the limousine disappeared around the bend in the driveway, Toby, Cliff, and the children turned and walked back into the house.

Toby held Cliff back by the arm. "When you

have a few minutes, can you meet me in my study?"

"Sure, I wanted to talk to you too, but August has been a clinging vine since he got up this morning."

"I think he's grateful to you for saving him yesterday."

"Oh, I know, and it's okay, it's just that, well, because he's real clingy right now I don't think I could separate myself from him long enough for the two of us to be alone."

"You're probably right, and it isn't anything pressing. If we can't find the time before dinner, we'll talk after they all go to bed tonight.

"Also, I've decided to take the day off tomorrow, and I'm going to keep the children home from school to give them time to process everything after yesterday."

"I think that's a good idea, for all of you, but remember, the children see the child psychologist tomorrow and you have an appointment, too, with Grady."

"I completely forgot."

"August may even need a few extra days. You should ask Amanda about that and talk it over with Grady. Regardless of what they say, we should probably take this one day at a time."

"Sounds like a plan. Thanks for remembering. So if we can't make it happen before, I'll plan to talk tonight. Deal?"

"Deal. I look forward to it and there's a few things I need to tell you."

"Is everything okay? Can you give me a hint?"

"Yes to the first, and it's nothing that can't wait. It would be better anyway if it happened when we're sure we won't be disturbed."

Chapter Thirty-One

Saying the Words That Need to Be Said

5:45 PM

After the children had helped clear the dinner table and the dishwasher had been loaded, Cliff stopped Toby as soon as the four of them filed into the den to watch some television. "About tonight, after I've put them to bed, and I'm sure they're asleep, I thought I'd take a shower ... before we talked. Would you mind a slight delay?"

Toby's pupils dilated and the corners of mouth turned up, ever so slightly. "No, not at all. I was thinking along the same lines. A shower would make us more relaxed."

A smile, just as slight, appeared on Cliff's face. Toby's hand rested on the island not six inches from his. He slid his hand forward and touched the tip of his index finger over the tip of Toby's. "I'll see you then ... in your study?"

****

Toby shuddered slightly at the touch of Cliff's finger to his. "We could, or ... I have a better idea. Why don't we talk in the hot tub?"

"The hot tub? Really?"

Toby smiled. "Yes." Then his body suddenly stiffened.

Shit. What did I just say? My entire future could change, our entire future ... the kids. What am I suggesting by offering the hot tub? What if he doesn't want this? But he touched me. He touched me on his own.

But what if I'm wrong. I could be wrong. Maybe

he's just being kind ... a friend. Give him an out. Good God, give him an out!

"Is everything all right, Toby? The look on your face just now..."

"Yes, sorry, I just remembered something."

"Good, I really appreciate the invitation. I'd like to soak in the hot tub for a while with you. After yesterday, we both deserve some time to relax. I'll open a bottle of wine to let it breathe. If you like, I could make up a cheese and fruit platter along with some crackers, just like Vera did. How's that sound?"

Shit. Shit. Shit. You lost your chance.

"That sounds fine, Cliff. Sorry if I've seemed preoccupied all afternoon. I had a long conversation with my mother this morning. She said some things that gave me a lot to think about, things about the future. There's a lot we need to discuss, some very important things."

Cover yourself. Make it an excuse.

"And I'd like it to be as relaxed an atmosphere as possible. The more I think about it, the hot tub may well be the best place to do it."

Yeah, that sounds reasonable.

"You're right, the hot tub would be the best place. What could be more stress free? I'll meet you there once the children are asleep. And don't worry, I'll be sure to bring the baby monitors just in case they need me. Now, I have to go check on April. She's due for a bottle and if I don't get up there, we're all going to hear about it."

And then he was gone.

****

8:45 PM

The Solarium

Cliff looked up from the cheese plate as it sat on the edge of the hot tub when Toby entered the solarium. He'd been picking at it since five minutes after he'd set it down there.

"Sorry I'm late." Toby slipped off his robe, revealing his swim trunks. He slid into the warm, swirling water opposite Cliff. "I became lost in thought while I was in the shower."

"Is everything okay? I thought you might have changed your mind."

"Yes, Cliff. I'm sure it is. I…"

"Your mother came to talk to me this morning, while I was working out of all times."

"I know. She told me. She said she came to apologize to you."

"That's true, but she said a lot more than that."

"I'm sorry that happened, Cliff. She can be a real…"

"No, Toby, you don't understand." Cliff picked up the bottle of Merlot he'd opened to breathe and poured two glasses. "She was very kind, direct, but from what you've said about her, for her, kind."

"Really?"

"Yeah. I don't know whether you're ready to hear this, but…"

"Cliff, there's something I just have to say to you. Oh, sorry. You first."

Cliff handed Toby his wine. "No, please, go ahead."

"Oh, God, how do I say this so it comes out right?"

"Sometimes it's simplest to just say it."

"Please hear me out. I'll probably muddle this up a bit before I get to my point."

"Sure, go on."

"I don't know when I realized it, Cliff, but I've developed … well I've developed … I've developed feelings for you. All right, there, I've said it. After the other night, when you opened yourself up to me, and I…"

"Gave me my first blowjob?"

"God, two days ago I would have found those words arousing. Now they sound cheap. They cheapen the entire experience. It meant more to me than that, more than I realized at the time."

"And to me. Sorry, go on … please."

"Cliff, I'm sorry to say this, but you deserve to hear the truth. I lusted after you. I couldn't help myself. I wanted you for sex."

Cliff smiled. "Before two days ago I might have been offended by those words."

"I couldn't help myself. I mean, have you looked at yourself? My God, you're an Adonis and you're here, in my home. Every time you're close to me… Shit! Your musk… I mean, your musk … it drives me insane, and I've seen you naked. I've felt your naked body next to mine. I've felt your … I've felt your…"

"My cock?"

"Yes, damnit, your cock pressed against mine. I've made love to you with my mouth."

"I know, Toby, I feel the same way." Cliff moved across the hot tub and took Toby's hands in his as he turned and sat down next to him in the swirling water. "Your mother helped me to realize that. She told me some things I didn't think I was ready to hear, but I'm so grateful that she did. Otherwise…"

"Otherwise, without that opinionated, meddling, wonderful mother of mine, we might not be here right now."

"Exactly. Toby, I…"

"Cliff, I…"

They said the words together. "I think I love you."

When Cliff pulled Toby to him, Toby turned and swung up to straddled his lap. He wrapped his arms around him, pulling Cliff's face to his own. Their kiss was tender. Toby began to cry.

"Oh, you dear, sweet man," Cliff murmured. He pulled Toby in tighter and opened his mouth to him. Together their tongues sought out each other, swirling and twirling and probing as they sucked and nibbled and slurped each other in.

****

Toby reached down, to feel for Cliff's swim trunks, but what he found was a raging hard-on. When he pulled himself away, Cliff smiled as he held his trunks up above the water. They both began to laugh. Then Cliff threw them across to the other side.

Cliff pressed his mouth to Toby's again as he reached down and yanked at his trunks.

Toby wiggled out of them and then sat down, pressing and grinding his erect cock against Cliff's. He pulled his face away and burrowed it into the hair of Cliff's chest, drawing one nipple and then the other into his mouth while he encircled both their cocks with his hands and pumped them up and down.

When Cliff moaned, Toby took a breath and submerged. He slid Cliff's cock passed his lips and sucked on the massive, mushroomed head. It barely fit into his mouth.

Cliff hips bucked, driving his shaft to the back of Toby's throat, but Toby held on and wrapped his arms around Cliff's thighs. For another thirty seconds, Toby stayed under the water until he drew the first stream of precum from the depths of Cliff's loins.

****

Cliff cried out. He thrust so forcefully that it drove Toby to the surface. He pulled Toby off his cock and drew him to his mouth again, tasting his own essence as he sucked it from Toby's probing tongue. "Make love to me, Toby, please."

"Are you sure? Are you sure you're ready for this?"

"All I know is I want to feel you inside me. Please do it, please. I've dreamed of this. I can't go to bed one more night without it."

"I want it to be good for you, Cliff. You've never had a dick inside you before. Even as big of a man as you are, it can be painful your first time."

"I don't care. I want you to make love to me. I have to know what it's like to become a man. Fuck my brains out, Toby. God, I can't believe I just said that word, but I can't help it. I feel like there's a beast inside of me. It's taking over my mind. I want you. I want you so much."

"That won't make you a man, Cliff. You're already a man. You're the best man I've ever known."

"I'm a virgin, Toby. I can't become a man until I'm not one anymore."

"I understand what you mean. Do you trust me?"

"Yes, of course I do."

"I think I have some condoms upstairs. It will be easier for you."

"I don't want a condom. I want to feel you, not some piece of latex between us. Besides, I had them do an HIV test at the ER yesterday. It was negative so you don't have to worry."

"I wasn't worried about that. You gave me your word, and I believed you."

"Well, now we know for sure."

"The condom will help to reduce the friction you'll feel. Maybe let me begin with one on when I first enter you. Then I can take it off if you're feeling good about it."

"I'll follow your lead."

"There's some things that I'll have to do to prepare you. It shouldn't happen quickly. Please trust me on this."

"I don't care what it takes, I want it."

"Then let's go up to my room. Everything we'll need is there."

"Could we do it in one of the rooms in the guest wing? I'm afraid we'll wake the children if we're right across the hall from them."

"You don't have to worry about that. The walls are soundproofed. Sydney and I could get really loud and ram... Oh! God ... sorry, sorry about that."

Cliff smiled warmly. "It's okay. Sydney and you...?"

Toby hesitated. He smiled weakly. "As long as we close the door, they'll never hear us."

"Good, then let's go ... you stud."

"Hold on there. We've got to take this slow. First, you're going to drink at least three-quarters of that bottle of wine. It'll help to relax your smooth muscles."

Cliff grabbed his glass and downed it in three swallows. Then he picked up the bottle and emptied the remainder of its contents in less than thirty seconds. "Okay, I'm ready."

"If we're going to do this right, it's going to take hours. When is April due for her next bottle?"

"She's going about four hours between feedings at night now. She'll be ready by eleven."

"That should be just about right. I'm not trying to throw a wrench into your passion, but we should take care of feeding her after you're prepared and before we begin. After I've opened you up, I'll put a butt plug in to hold you open. Then I'll give her a bottle. We'll have hours and, believe me, the first time should not be rushed. I want to make sure this is a night you'll always remember, just like it was for me, my first time."

Cliff pulled Toby into a hug. "Thank you, Toby. Thank you for doing this for me. I have two bottles already mixed up in the fridge. All you'll need to do is warm one up for twenty-five seconds in the microwave.

"You know, I actually thought about finding someone to do it so you wouldn't have to. I wanted it to be you, but I didn't want to disappoint you because I'm a virgin."

"I'm glad you didn't. I'm so very glad. There's no wrong way to make love and it should mean a lot to any man to be asked to be someone's first. Meeting a stranger for a hookup can be dangerous. He could have had his own, ulterior motives. Now, let's get you upstairs."

Chapter Thirty-Two

The Massage of Your Life

9:30 PM
Toby's Bedroom

"I don't know, Toby. I'm a little leery about this."

"Cliff, if you're going to have anal sex, then you need to clean yourself out first. Otherwise, it can be a very … um … it could be very embarrassing for you. May I speak plainly?"

"Please do."

"It's much safer if there isn't poop inside you when something is being thrust in and out of your anus or that applies friction to the inside of your colon. Not only could some come out, but poop is full of bacteria and your colon is lined with mucus membranes. There's always a slim chance that a tear could be made in the membranes. You don't want that to happen. If bacteria gets through, it can enter your bloodstream. That only really happens if someone is using a foreign object that's very large or isn't designed for that purpose."

"How do you know all this?"

"Jason taught me all about it."

"Okay. Tell me again. How do I give myself an enema?"

****

When Cliff had finished and used the bidet, he got into the shower.

Toby joined him a few minutes later after doing the same. "You did just fine, Cliff. Now that you know what you have to do, I don't think you'll have any trouble in the future."

Cliff bounced back and forth from leg to leg. "I

don't care about any of that, Toby. I want you. Now!"

"Cliff, you said you trust me. Do you?"

"Yes. Of course." He reached for Toby's body.

Toby took a step back. "Then do that. I can see how horned up you are right now, but you've got to let me do this the right way."

"Okay. Okay. What do I do?"

"First, you have to make me a promise."

"I promise."

"No, you must promise me that you won't try to force me to do anything, and you won't try to make yourself come."

"Toby, I'd never hurt you."

"I believe you'd never want to do that, but you're probably going to get so aroused that you might try. Now promise me."

"I promise I won't force you to do anything."

"And you won't try to make yourself come. Say it, Cliff."

"I promise I won't try to make myself come."

"Thank you. We should start with you kneeling down in front of me. Then close your eyes and don't open them, and don't touch me, and don't speak."

Once Cliff was down, Toby gently grasped his head and leaned it back under the gentle flow of warm water. He watched it trickle down Cliff's face, through his hair, and down his chest to where the bottom of the V from his flanks met. He reached for the bottle of scented shampoo and lathered it in while at the same time massaging Cliff's scalp with his fingertips.

Cliff moaned softly.

After rinsing his hair, Toby saturated a thick, soft washcloth with lavender soap until lather spilled from it. He kneeled down in front of Cliff and kissed his eyes. Then he worked the cloth with his hands across Cliff's brow, down his nose, around his cheeks, and across his lips.

Toby leaned him back under the water again to rinse him. Then he brushed his lips across Cliff's while he began at his chest, working in circular motions around his sensitive, thickening nipples. "You trimmed your chest and belly hair, didn't you?"

"Yeah, it was getting a bit thick."

"It really highlights your pecs and six-pack. You can see every curve and ridge."

"Do you like it?"

Toby growled, then said, "I love it."

When he started down the ridges of Cliff's six pack, Toby squatted down and pressed his hips in close, rubbing his erection against the bulges. He leaned his face in and probed Cliff's mouth with his tongue.

A soft sound escaped Cliff's mouth.

As his body relaxed, Cliff lower himself until he was sitting on his ankles.

Toby followed him down until his buttocks was resting against Cliff's thighs while he continued to thrust his hips. When he felt the rise if Cliff's manhood pressing up between his legs, he changed direction and rocked his anus back and forth along the growing shaft, effectively preventing it from achieving its full state of arousal by pressing it down toward his thighs.

"Toby," Cliff whispered.

"It's okay, baby, no talking now."

"I can't help it," he whispered again.

"It's okay. Just feel me."

"Toby ... Toby, I..."

"I love you, Cliff."

Cliff's head fell forward. He leaned back and braced his hands on the shower floor behind him and moaned. "Oh... Oh... Oh, Toby."

Pre-cum dribbled from Cliff's slit, slicking Toby's ass crack as he slowed and quickened his pace. They stayed like that for minutes.

"Now stand up, for me, baby and turn around. Place your hands against the wall about a foot beyond each shoulder and spread your legs apart."

As Cliff complied, Toby continued. "I'm going wash the rest of your body from top to bottom and front to back. I'm going to do things to you that may drive you wild. I'm going to make you feel things that you've never felt before."

Cliff sighed. "Oh, Toby, when you talk like that…"

Toby squeezed a mild, musk-scented soap into a loofa and ran it across Cliff's shoulders and then down his back. "I'm going to stimulate you in ways you've never thought of, and you're going to want to come more than you've ever wanted to come before, but I'm not going to let you."

"Toby, I… Oh!" His toes curled as Toby ran the loofa around the meaty globes of his buttocks. His fingers clenched into fists.

"I'm going to take you to places you've never imagined."

Cliff thrust his hips forward as Toby ran the loofa along his butt crack and vibrated it against his anus. Then he slid it up and down the insides of his thighs and then under his balls.

"I'm going to hold you there, so close to the edge, Cliff, that it will drive you insane."

Toby squeezed lather into his hands, then soaped up his erect cock and slowly slid it up and down against Cliff's clenching hole while he pressed his body to his back and reached around to grasp Cliff's upright, swollen cock and cup his balls.

A groan escaped Cliff's lips. Then he began to whimper. "Toby, don't … don't make me … don't make me … I want to … I want to so much, but don't … Oh, God. I'm going to come. I'm going to come if you don't stop."

"You're going to beg me, Cliff. You're going to plead with me, but I won't relent. Not if you want this to be a night you'll never forget."

Cliff threw his head back as his body trembled. "Toby … Toby … please don't…"

Toby sat down on the tiles and slid his body between Cliff's legs as he turned around to bring his face in reach of his quivering, massive erection. "Oh, Cliff, it's glorious. It's the most beautiful thing I've ever seen."

"Don't touch it, Toby. Please don't touch it. I don't want to come. Not yet… Not yet!"

Toby kneeled in front of him. He grasped Cliff's hips and pressed them backward, allowing the stream of water to rinse away the soap, while beads of precum formed at the tip and were washed away with it.

"Trust me, baby." Toby pulled Cliff's hips forward toward him and leaned in, placing the tip of his tongue beneath the gaping slit at the tip of the head. When the next bead appeared, he surrounded the slit with his lips and sucked. He slowly opened his mouth until it slid over the entire head.

As pre-cum began to flow, he slid his tongue beneath the glans, barely grazing the length of frenum beyond the head until he reached the shaft. He opened his mouth and sucked in, sliding down the shaft, filling his mouth with the rigid meat. Then he slid back and pressed the tip of his curled tongue into the slit and began to scoop out the sweet nectar.

Cliff's hips suddenly lunged forward, forcing the glans past Toby's tonsils and down his throat as the first eight inches of shaft thrust through his mouth.

Toby gagged, and his jaw nearly dislocated.

"I can't help it. I can't help it," Cliff cried out as he thrust into Toby's face, driving his body against the tile wall.

Toby pressed his hands against Cliff's hips, finally dislodging himself from the soda-can-thick shaft. "Good God, Cliff, you're strong!"

"I couldn't stop myself, Toby. You were saying those things and then your mouth was on me, and it just … it just happened."

"It's okay, but man oh man. My ass is going to be mincemeat the first time you fuck me."

"I'm sorry. I'm so sorry."

When Cliff's eyes met Toby's, there was a look of horror on his face.

Toby began to laugh. Finally, he got control of himself. "No, Cliff, that's a good thing. I can't wait until I feel you inside me for the first time."

"But, Toby, I'm so big. I could tear you."

"Cliff, baby, it's not gonna happen. I've used dildos as big as you are. Not recently, but I have. It'll just take a little practice, but don't you worry. I can handle you, and besides, I have a surprise for you."

A smile spread across Cliff's face. "I can't wait then. You've made me so happy. I was afraid I'd never be able to do it with you, and I want to do it, so badly. I've dreamed about it, but I never really thought it could happen."

"It will. I promise. Now, back to you. Are you ready for the next step?"

"You mean there's more?

"You betcha."

"Then, yes … yes, I can't wait."

"How close were you to coming?"

"Really close, but it's like you said. You made me want it to happen, but I didn't get to that point."

"Good, you'll soon learn how much you can handle so you can take yourself just to the edge without going over it. You'll learn how to pace yourself and hold yourself there. That's what I want to teach you. The longer you can hold out without coming, the bigger your orgasms will be."

"Whatever it takes, Toby. Whatever you want to make me do, I'm in."

"Wonderful. Now, bend over the bench, lean on your forearms, and spread your legs. I'm going to start opening you up."

Once Cliff was in position, Toby knelt behind him and spread his buttocks apart. Starting behind his ball sack, Toby pressed his tongue firmly against the shaft of his cock and slid it upward, tracing the shaft as it ran along the floor of his pelvis, passed the P-spot, until he reached the outer anal sphincter. Making a wad of saliva, he slid it to the tip of his tongue and wiggled it against the puckered rose bud.

"Oh, Toby!"

Toby made a low, rumbling growl. "Good, isn't it?"

"Yes, it's incredible!"

"Now, get ready for the massage of your life."

Toby opened a jar of lube and slicked his fingers. Then he pressed inward with his tongue as he brought his fingers to the edges and began massaging the sensitive, spasming muscles. As he licked and drilled his tongue inward, the sphincter began to relax and open, allowing him to begin working the tips of both middle fingers in.

"Oh, my God! Oh, my God! Toby, oh, my God!"

Cliff's shaft bounced up and down. His scrotum tightened, drawing his balls up against the shaft while a steady stream of pre-cum oozed from the mushroomed head.

The more Toby licked and sucked, the more relaxed the sphincter became. He continued to advance, working in two more fingers. He rubbed them against the circular muscle beneath the sensitive pink flesh until the inner sphincter finally revealed itself.

Cliff's legs trembled. "Toby, my legs. They're going to give out on me. My body… It's getting so warm. It's spreading out."

Toby leaned back and remove his fingers. "Quick, Cliff, roll over onto your back on top the bench before they do and grab your legs behind the knees and pull them up."

The moment Cliff was in position, Toby spread his cheeks wide apart and drove his tongue inward, working it against the inner sphincter. He slid in two fingers from each hand and caressed it with the tips until it relaxed. When it opened, he scooped up a wad of lube and slid in the index and middle finger of his right hand. Then he pulled them back. He slid them in and out again and again, advancing a little farther each time.

Cliff's entire body began to shake. "Toby! Toby, what's happening to me? I feel … I feel so … so good."

"Just go with it, baby. Enjoy it for what it is."

With both his sphincters now completely relaxed, Toby added a third finger and slid them in to their hilt as he searched for the spongy, walnut-sized gland, but when he found it, it wasn't spongy anymore. It was firm and getting firmer.

"This is going to be so beautiful for you, baby." Toby gently caressed the gland, coaxing it along, further and further.

"What's happening to me?" Cliff cried out. "What are you doing?"

"Do you want me to stop, Cliff?"

"Are you kidding? God no!" Cliff's body shook as his prostate became harder and harder. "Oh, my God. Oh, my God, Toby! I … I…"

Toby felt the gland begin to rapidly harden. He pressed against it with more pressure until he felt the ridge that ran down its middle begin to form. He pushed his chest between Cliff's thighs and pulled the head of his cock into his mouth.

Cliff's body began to quake. Then it began to thrust back and forth against Toby's fingers, driving them deeper inside, rubbing them faster and faster against the spasming gland as the sphincters tightened. His feet curled so tightly they resembled fists. His hands gripped the wooden rails of the bench, turning his fingers white. Guttural grunts arose from deep within his chest and then suddenly silenced when his body locked in one gigantic spasm, turning his face beet red and stopping his breathing as his thighs clamped Toby's body between them.

His jaw clenched, his pupils dilated, and his eyes bulged. His majestic balls undulated in their sack as the shaft of his cock swelled further, turning purple as the veins threatened to burst, while his sphincters clamped down on Toby's fingers, locking them in place.

For nearly a minute, he remained suspended in a state of quasi-tetany as jets of clear, syrupy pre-cum were ejected from his core.

Toby slid his lips down the shaft as far as he could and swallowed load after load of Cliff's sweet, manly nectar, not allowing a single drop to spill from them.

When it was over, Cliff's body shuddered violently as he drew in his first breath. His legs became flaccid and fell outward, releasing their grip against

Toby's sides, and his sphincters went limp, releasing their grasp.

Toby inserted all four fingers of his hand and reached down with the other to pick up his largest butt plug.

"You're going to feel some pressure now, Cliff. I'm going to put something inside you to keep you good and open for when I make love to you." As he removed his fingers, Toby pressed the plug passed the gaping opening and slid it in.

As he drew in breath after breath, Cliff's color began to lighten. His cock, though still hard, lost its purple hue, and his pupils began to constrict back to normal. Still panting, he spoke. "What did you say?"

"I said I was putting something in you to keep you open for later."

"Is it in? I don't feel anything."

"Yeah, it's going to prevent the muscles from closing. You'll probably feel it in a minute or so."

"Okay. You know, I didn't really believe you. I didn't believe that what just happened to me could ever happen."

"Intense, wasn't it? Though I have to tell you, I've never seen one quite that powerful."

"What was it? What did you do to me? I've never experienced anything like it."

"It's called a total body orgasm."

"I still don't believe it. It seems impossible that something that intense could be real."

"Like I said, I've never seen one that strong before."

"Amazing, Toby. You're an amazing man."

"That was all you. I just led you there. It's a state of mind you put yourself into."

"It was my whole body, Toby, not just deep

inside my dick. It was my whole body."

"I know. That's why it's called a total body orgasm, and you know what?"

"What?"

"You can have a couple more."

"Really?"

"Yeah, after you've had one or more total body's where you've actually ejaculated, you're done for a day or even more. I was hoping you would be able to achieve one without coming, but you never know how people are wired. You're wired just right for them."

"What do you mean I didn't ejaculate? I came! I felt it."

"You had an orgasm, but you didn't actually ejaculate. You didn't eject any cum, any semen."

"Then what came out? I could feel fluid pumping."

"Your thick, sweet nectar—pre-cum, tons of it! And yours is delicious."

"Thanks, I guess."

"No, you don't understand. A lot of men only make a few drops at a time. You make it by the spoonful!"

"Have you ever had a total body … you know?"

"Yeah, more than a few times, but I had to achieve a deep state of meditation before it was possible. It takes me hours of focus in order get myself to that point. You did it in minutes."

"I didn't know what was happening to me. I had no control over it. It wasn't me. Toby, it was you."

"Maybe, but if you weren't receptive to it, it could never have happened. Hey, it's twenty 'til eleven. I'm going to wash up and then go give April her bottle. Let me help you to the bed first. I want you to lie down and try to stay relaxed until I return. The pressure from the butt plug might make you feel like you have to move your bowels, but it's just the pressure from the plug. Whatever you do, don't let yourself push it out."

Cliff reached down to his butt. "Oh, now I feel it. Yes, I can feel it inside me. Wow, how big is it?"

"It's as big as I am so I'll be able to slide right inside you. The moment I remove it, you'll begin to tighten down, but you'll still be tight enough to feel me."

****

Toby propped several pillows against the headboard and helped Cliff get settled. He walked to his dresser and lifted a napkin that covered a small bed tray. It held a bowl, dessert fork, and a glass filled with golden-yellow liquid. "Do you have any fruit allergies?"

"No, why? What's that?"

"I didn't think so. It's pineapple, baby. It'll sweeten your cum. Eat all the chunks and then chase them with the juice. Try not to get up to pee. It'll be better for you if you can hold a full bladder."

The corners of Cliff's lips curled upward. "You think of everything."

After carrying the tray to the bed and unfolding its legs, Toby placed it over Cliff's lap. He leaned down and kissed him tenderly on the lips then walked into the bathroom to quickly shower.

A few minutes later, he came out wearing a robe. "How are you feeling?"

"I'm good and thanks for the pineapple. It's delicious."

"Good. I'll be back in a little while."

Before closing the door behind him, Toby turned back. "Now remember, keep that plug in, or we'll have to start all over again." Then he left to take care of his daughter, closing it behind him.

Chapter Thirty-Three

You're Gonna Lose Your Mind

11:35 PM

Toby slipped into the room, being sure to latch the door behind him. The tray was on the floor. Cliff was waiting for him. "I'm back. She's all settled in and should be good for hours now. Are you ready?"

Cliff had scooted down in the bed and was now lying on his back. He looked toward the ceiling above Toby's head and blushed. The sheet was tented by his upraised knees.

"What's wrong?"

"I'm more than ready, but I'm a little embarrassed."

"Embarrassed, about what?"

Cliff pulled the sheet off and dropping his knees out to the sides. As he lowered his legs, his ten inch, soda-can-thick, rigid cock was revealed. A bead of clear, thick pre-cum oozed from the gaping slit and hung suspended by a thin, glistening thread as it slowly descended toward his abdomen.

Toby's cock lurched beneath his robe.

"I couldn't help myself. I masturbated a little. I had to. I couldn't stop myself. I hope I didn't mess things up."

Toby smiled as he walked toward the bed. "Of course not. Why would you think it would?"

"Coz I've never done this before. I don't know what to expect. I had to do it coz I felt a lot of pressure from the plug and then there were spasms, some of them sharp. I found that if I stroked myself, it helped to make them go away, and it made the pressure from the plug disappear. Then I couldn't stop. It felt so, so good, Toby, but I went real slow. You said not to let the plug come out and it was the only thing that worked. I just couldn't stop myself."

"That's my fault. I forgot to tell you about the spasms. They happen sometimes, especially in the beginning. Sorry." Toby caught the bead of precum on the tip of his index finger and followed it up to the tip of Cliff's glans.

"You mean it's okay? What I did, I mean."

Toby licked his lips. His voice was raspy. "Definitely."

"Good, I was afraid I was going to ruin the whole night. You've done so much to make this right for me."

"And you figured it out all by yourself. When you're just starting out, that's what you have to do a lot of the time." Toby rubbed the precum along Cliff's frenum then up and around the slit, spreading more of the fluid that oozed out over the glans with all his fingers.

Cliff's cock lurched. "Oh, God, that feels so good. Oh, my God ... I..."

He leaned down and examined the tip of Cliff's cock closely. "God, Cliff, I never noticed before, your piss-slit is immense. When you just contracted your PC muscle it flared open like a tiny mouth. You must hold a ton of cum inside you. If the slit is that big, it's coz it has to be."

Cliff blushed.

"You don't have to be embarrassed. You shouldn't be, not by your body. It's something to behold."

"I'm not used to this kind of talk. I don't know what's normal to say or not to say."

"Say anything you want, coz I'm gonna. Be proud of your body. I know I'd be."

"Toby, you're gorgeous, I'm just big."

"No, Cliff, you're a perfect a specimen. Sorry to use that word, but it's true. You're as perfect a specimen of the male form as I've ever seen in real life, in pictures, or in the movies."

Cliff blushed a deeper red.

"Did you know that about your slit?"

"I know my piss stream is wider than one of those fast-food straws. You know, the fat ones they give you so you drink the soda faster and have to fill up again? The guys in the locker room in high school used to tease me about how loud I pissed. Said I sounded like a horse or a garden hose."

"Yeah, I notice that."

"So what do I do? How do you want me to be?"

"We'll figure that out as we go along. As long as it's wonderful for you, that's the only thing that's important right now." Toby drew his fingers to his mouth and sucked them seductively. "Oh, God... Ambrosia! Sweet, so damned sweet. Pineapple juice does it every time." He sat down on the edge of the bed and ran his fingertips up Cliff's left flank. "Now lie back and enjoy."

Cliff closed his eyes.

Toby leaned down and flicked his tongue across Cliff's left nipple. "I can't believe I'm with a man as beautiful as you are. My God, your body is just so ... perfect." He pressed his mouth against the nipple and sucked it in.

Cliff moaned. "Mmm ... Toby."

Toby clasped the nipple between his teeth.

"Oh, my God!" Cliff's head twisted away, to the right. "Please ... do that again."

Toby dragged his chin through the hair the covered Cliff's pecs and sucked in his right nipple, tonguing it. Then he drew it between his teeth and pressed them together, gently nibbling it.

Oh… Oh… Oh, yes! It shoots right through my shaft, right up my urethra into the head. It's such a beautiful burn, Toby. My dick … it's vibrating on the inside. Again! Again!"

"Squeeze your anus tight for me and hold it for as long as you can." Toby leaned back and stood up. "Do you trust me, baby?"

"Yes … anything … anything!"

He bent down and opened the bedside table drawer, lifting out a large, black, bulbous, angled prostate massager. "We're going to do a switch."

After squirting lube over the bulb, Toby worked it along the length with his fingers. Then he climbed onto the bed and kneeled down between Cliff's thighs. "You're going to feel some pressure, but it's been in long enough that it shouldn't be too bad. Now try to relax your anus for me."

He grasped the external flange of the butt plug and slowly twisted it as he pulled back. As the massive bulb came into view, Cliff's anus flared out more and more until it was spread to the plug's widest diameter.

"Oh, Toby, the pressure, the sensation … it's incredible!"

"Good. Here goes."

With one gentle tug it popped out. Toby immediately inserted the butt plug and angled the flange forward to rest against Cliff's prostate.

Immediately, he straddled Cliff's legs and guided his thighs closed between his knees. "Tell me if there's anything I do that you don't like. This is all about you, Cliff … all about you." Toby slid his hips forward, then his pelvis downward, drawing his scrotum, followed by the shaft of his erect cock, along the length of Cliff's shaft from the head to his balls.

He licked the pads of this thumbs and spread his hands wide as he grasped Cliff's chest, rubbing his thumbs over both nipples. He splayed his fingers outward, resting their tips along the massive muscles' outer borders, then drew his thumbs across the sensitive, browned nipples, stimulating the erectile tissue deep within them. As they swelled, he drew his thumbs in circles around them. "Now, baby, squeeze your anus tight."

Cliff took a deep breath, held it, and squeezed. "Damn… Fuck! Oh, sorry, sorry for cursing. I don't do that. Oh, Toby the pressure… It's so intense."

"Cliff, it's okay. That's what we'll be doing. I'm gonna fuck you so hard you're gonna lose your mind."

"It's pushing that thing forward. The tighter I squeeze, the more I feel it. I feel it inside my … my dick now. It's inside my dick, Toby!"

"It's a cock, Cliff. Call it what it is. You've got one hell of a cock! Now squeeze again for a count of ten."

"One. Two."

Toby slid his hips forward, drawing the cleft between his butt cheeks along and around Cliff's shaft.

"Three… Oh, God! Four … Toby!"

Toby slid his hips backward, drawing Cliff's shaft deeper between the cleft.

Cliff's eyes clamped shut, his face drawn into a pain-like grimace, but it was pleasure, pure pleasure.

"Five… Fuck, oh, fuck! What's that thing, Toby? What's that inside you?

Toby bared his teeth. "Shut up and count!"

"Si … si … six … Toby! Toby, six!"

Toby slid forward, off Cliff's shaft. As the head of Cliff's cock popped up behind him, he pressed his pelvis downward, then slid back again, drawing the shaft up behind him.

"Seven."

"Mother-fucker... Eight! Eight, Toby, eight! My cock ... yes, my cock! Eight. Fucking ... glorious ... wonderful ... eight!"

Toby arched his back and lifted his hips upward, then slid back down again. The purpled glans atop Cliff's shaft flared outward as it was drawn between Toby's muscular, clenching gluteal folds once again. A stream of pre-cum shot out of the slit, reaching the nape of Toby's neck, as it landed in a column along his back, coating it before slowly sliding downward between the cleft, slicking the pathway as it entered. Cliff's shaft vibrated with the thrum of more blood rushing into it.

"Fuck! Nine! Nine! Yes, beautiful, magnificent nine!"

Toby reached back and in one flowing movement, removed his own, monstrous butt plug, then impaled himself with Cliff's vein engorged, ten inches of pure manhood, grimacing as each inch stretched him more and more.

"Te—" A high-pitched squeal escaped Cliff's throat. He never finished counting.

"God, the pain!" Toby moaned. "The sweet, beautiful, burning pain. Oh, Cliff, it feels like you're going to tear me apart."

Cliff shook his head and opened his eyes, a look of horror on his face. "Then got off me, Toby. Get off me before I hurt you. It's not worth it."

"Not on your life. It's worth every inch of you."

"I don't want to hurt you, Toby." Cliff moved to lift Toby off him.

"Don't you dare." Toby knocked his hands away. "It's incredible. Cliff, the pleasure pain is wonderful. Please understand, it's what I want."

Toby began to rise and fall along the length of Cliff's shaft, riding it in slow, steady, cycles. He looked deep into Cliff's eyes, nodding and smiling as he went. He drew the shaft out until the firm coronal ridge slid from him, leaving just the tip to hover within the opening of his sphincters. Then he fell back down, calculating his progress to ensure that he felt each and every ridge and bulging vein as it slid through his sensitive, stretched opening. For the next fifteen minutes, he watched Cliff watching him, as he slowly rode his shaft and drove his passion to a crescendo with whispered words of love and encouragement.

****

Toby smiled. He leaned down and planted his lips against Cliff's, then drove the length of his tongue as deep as he could into Cliff's mouth. Then he pulled away. "Squeeze yourself tight, baby. Squeeze for me now."

"Oh, Toby, it's so beautiful. I feel so … so … I don't have the words."

"I know, baby."

"I feel your love… Oh, Toby, you love me, you really love me."

"Yes, I do. Now let me make love to you."

When Toby lifted himself from Cliff, his anus hung open. The sheer girth of Cliff's manhood had stretched him farther than he had ever been stretched by a man, but it was good, it was so very good. After guiding Cliff's legs up in the air, Cliff grasped them behind the knees. Toby quickly climbed from the bed and ripped open up a condom.

Cliff shook his head. "No, I don't want it. I don't need it."

"But … we talked about this."

"No, I want you. I want to feel you, Toby. I want

nothing between us. I want nothing to ever come between us."

"If you're sure."

Cliff nodded, enthusiastically.

Toby climbed back onto the bed, reached for the prostate massager, and withdrew it. When he pressed the head of his cock against the outer sphincter, it parted without resistance, allowing him to slide his entire length right in. As his glans grazed Cliff's prostate, another stream of thick pre-cum was ejected from Cliff's slit. He gripped the back of Cliff's thighs and began to ride him, slowly increasing the pace and force of his thrusts.

Cliff's head rocked back and forth, his scrotum tightened, and his balls ascended. "Toby ... Toby ... yes. It's so beautiful. It's building inside me. It's building."

"Good. Control it, Cliff. Tell me what to do. Tell me to go faster or slower ... harder or softer. Guide me to what you want."

"Oh, Toby ... baby ... it's so ... so ... Oh, God! I don't know what... It's so good. Just keep doing what you're doing."

"Do you want to come? Are you ready?"

"No! No, not yet! Please, not yet. I want to stay here, right here."

Toby bent down and lifted Cliff's leaking cock to his mouth. As he placed his lips over the glans and sucked, he was rewarded with a fresh stream of pineapple-sweetened nectar. He rolled it across his tongue, around his mouth, then swallowed and sucked again.

Cliff groaned. "Fuck! Yes, yes, just like that! Just like that!"

Toby slowed the pace of his thrusts and opened his mouth as wide as he could. He slid down Cliff's shaft until the head hit the back of his throat. Then he relaxed the muscles and drove down farther, sliding the head deeper into the top of his esophagus where he lingered for a moment. He then bounced his head up and down along the rock-hard shaft. As he pulled back, he increased the thrust of his hips to a frenzied pace, jack-rabbiting Cliff's hole. The head of his cock, quick as machine gun fire, hammered against Cliff's prostate.

When Cliff raised up from the bed and braced his open hands down against the mattress behind him, Toby pressed outward against his knees, spreading them as far apart as they would go. With the top of his head now pressed tightly against Cliff's chest, Toby focused completely on his pelvic thrust assault.

Cliff arched his back as a high-pitched scream struggled to escape his lungs, but then his voice box began to spasm. As a rapid, raspy rush of air was forced out, he clenched the sheets into his balled fists. His body began to buck and quake. He fell backward.

Drenched in sweat, Toby pulled back and held himself in position with his glans barely breaching Cliff's sphincters and waited as he panted to catch his breath. A few moments later, Cliff shook his head and focused his eyes on Toby's face. "Again! Again! But this time, baby, kiss me and make me come!"

Toby lurched forward. As he pile drove his shaft inward, his hips struck against the meaty rounds of Cliff's buttocks. Cliff rolled his hips upward, pulling Toby along with them. He wrapped his arms around Toby's back and pulled his face to his own. With each concussive blow, the glans of Toby's shaft pounded against Cliff's prostate.

"It's going to happen, Toby."

"Me too, baby. I can't stop it. It's building so beautifully. I'm almost there. I'm nearly there. Oh, Cliff! Oh, Cliff!"

Cliff's prostate tightened until it could tighten no more.

"It's going to happen. Toby ... it's ..."

"Oh, Cliff!"

Cliff's balls pulled up against the base of his cock, and his vas deferens contracted. "It's going to happen. Toby, it's…"

"Oh, Cliff!"

"Yes, Toby! Yes!"

"Oh, Cliff!"

"Toby, it's happening!"

"Now, Cliff! Now!"

Stream after stream of fresh cum was expelled from Cliff's core. Toby broke away from Cliff's hold and planted his mouth over the streams of milky, spewing nectar as his own eruption began. As he emptied his load into Cliff's depths, he supped from Cliff's fountain, savoring every creamy, musky moment of their rapture.

****

While laying on top of Cliff, still planted deep inside him, Toby reached back and pulled the top sheet over the two of them, leaving just their heads and shoulders exposed. He leaned down as Cliff leaned up. Their mouths met as they wrapped their arms around each other.

****

After August made his way across the hall and two doors up, he quietly opened the door to his father's bedroom. As the door cracked open, he whispered his father's name. "Daddy, I can't find Cliff. I need…"

Neither Toby nor Cliff heard him.

****

After they broke apart, Cliff spoke. "Toby, I … I… Oh, Toby, it was so beautiful. I never knew, never dreamed it could be anything like that. I love you, Toby.

I love you so, so deeply. Thank you. Thank you for giving me that … for making it so beautiful and so special."

"Oh, Cliff, I love you, too, more than I can put into words. You saved me, Cliff. You saved all of us. The children … you love my children. What you did yesterday for August … the tender, gentle way you care for April… You've made such a difference for July. In just these few short weeks, you taught him and May how to swim. You're so good and careful with May and with June. I don't know how we could have ever managed if it wasn't for you. I can't imagine life without you … not now. Not ever…"

"I do love you, Toby. I really, really do, and yes, I love the children. They're such wonderful, complicated, beautiful little human beings, each special in their own little ways. How could I not? I know they're not my own, that they didn't come from me, but I love them as if they did."

****

August backed away from the door and close it, quietly. There was a smile on his face as he walked back to his room. After he crawled under the covers, he lifted a framed photograph from his night table and kissed it. "Good night, Mommy. I love you. And you were right, Mommy … Daddy's going to be just fine."

Chapter Thirty-Four

Dreaming of a Future Together

With the sun low in the sky and April in a papoose strapped to Cliff's chest, June, May, Toby, Cliff, July, and August held hands in a line, as they walked along the empty beach.

"I like honeymoons, Cliff." July looked up into his new father's eyes. "They're neat, and I love room service. I can eat anytime I want!"

"Yeah, honeymoons are cool," August said, "and we've got two dads now. Nobody's ever gonna mess with us!"

"Now, August, what did I tell you?"

"I'm sorry, Daddy. Just because Cliff can rip the head off a grizzly bear doesn't mean I can brag about him."

"Who said I could do that?" Cliff asked.

August kicked at the sand. "I said it, but Daddy said even if it was true, I shouldn't brag about it, coz bragging only gets you into trouble."

"Your daddy's right. Bragging can only get you into trouble."

June looked up, innocently. "Can you rip the head off a grizzly, Daddy-Cliff?"

"Oh, God." Toby groaned. "Here we go again."

"No, June, I can't."

"Eww, that's disgusting," May said. "All that blood!"

"That's a new word, May." Toby repeated it, emphasizing each syllable. "Dis ... gus ... ting!"

"I learned it from Cliff. He said eating peanut butter on bacon is disgusting, but I love it. You know what's really disgusting?"

"Eww, disgusting!" Cliff spoke in a high, squeaky voice. Then he giggled and flex his wrists while he waved his hands. "Eww, that's disgusting! Eww…"

"Is it ever going to stop?" Toby leaned his head against Cliff's shoulder and hugged one arm around his waist.

Cliff stopped and turned toward his new husband. As he looked down into his eyes, a smile spread across his face.

The children stopped with them and then formed a circle with their two fathers in the middle.

"Daddy?" May pulled on the pocket of his shorts. "Daddy? Daddy?"

Cliff leaned down and pulled Toby into a long, passionate kiss.

****

As August watched them, he got a warm feeling inside. *He's happy, Mommy … Daddy's happy again.*

He felt his mother's arms around him. *I know August … I know.*

****

When they broke apart, May was still tugging on Toby's shorts. "Ketchup on French toast, now that's disgusting!"

"Is not!" July shouted.

"Is too!" May shouted back.

"No, it's not, May." August spoke plainly. "I like ketchup on French toast, and peanut butter too."

"Eww," May shrieked. "Ketchup on peanut butter. You're disgusting!"

"No, silly, not ketchup on peanut butter, peanut butter on French toast."

July bent over, picked up a handful of wet sand, and threw it at May. "You're disgusting!"

335

June shrieked.

May picked up a handful of sand and threw it back.

"Daddy!" June shrieked again. "July got sand on my new dress."

April started crying. Toby looked up at Cliff, waiting for an answer.

Cliff smiled back. "Is this ever going to stop? God, I hope not."

****

Monday, May 24, 2010, 6:15 AM

When Cliff opened his eyes, he found Toby propped up on one elbow, watching him. "What are you looking at, my love?"

"The most beautiful man I've ever seen. You were smiling and sighing while you slept. You were so peaceful, so happy."

"Toby, I think Sydney came to me last night in my dreams."

"Really?"

"Yeah, it was so weird. You, me, and the children were all together on a beach, but it was through August that I heard her voice. I could hear him talking to her in his mind, and her answer. He told her you were happy again."

"And what did she say?"

"*I know*. She said, *I know*."

Toby's eyes glistened as a warm smile spread across his face. "She's right, and she'd want that for me, for all of us. I am happy, Cliff. I'm so, so happy."

"I know. Me too."

"I think she's watching out for us. I think she wants us to be together. She told me I'd find someone who loves me and the children as much as she did if I only opened my heart up to their gift. You're that gift,

Cliff, and I'm so happy that I did." Toby leaned over and kissed Cliff, tenderly. "Now, about what I was saying about the most beautiful man I've ever seen…"

"Oh? Go on."

"Let's start with your smile. Your smile lights up a room, and your eyes, they're soft and warm and comforting. Your body, well I could spend a day describing your body to you, and your cock … the things you can do with your cock…"

"Toby! Stop! The children might hear you."

"If you insist, but I could go on and on about it." Toby leaned over and brushed his lips across Cliff's, kissing him again.

Cliff sat up and leaned back against the headboard. "So, let me tell you about the rest of that dream I had last night."

"Go ahead." Toby crawled under the sheet and lifted Cliff's thick, flaccid penis into his hands. "Tell me about it."

"So we were all walking along a beach… Oh, that feels nice … and we were holding hands and the children… Oh, you wicked man … the children were talking about grizzly bears, and French toast … Toby, stop. I'm trying to tell you about my dream, and then I have to get up for the children. Now, where was I? Oh, yeah, peanut butter, and then ketchup of all things, and … Toby, if you don't stop, we're going to have a situation."

Toby mumbled something unintelligible.

"What did you say?" Cliff asked.

Toby slid Cliff's thickening penis from his mouth. Then he pulling his head out from under the sheet. "Sorry, your dick was in my mouth. I said, I hope so."

"You hope so … what?"

"I hope we have a situation. You're just too tasty to pass up. Now, I dare you." Toby smiled a wicked smile before sliding his head back under the sheet. "Try," he said from underneath, "just try to tell me about your dream."

Cliff's body jerked. "Oh, my God... Oh, baby ... baby... Oh baby, don't you dare stop!"

The end?
No, there's so much more to tell.
How about ...
Until we meet again.

The End

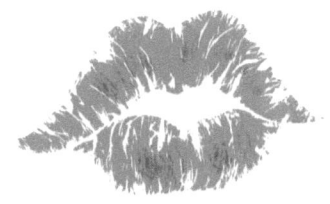

EVERNIGHT PUBLISHING ®

www.evernightpublishing.com

LOVE MY CHILDREN FIRST